Praise for *The Crimson Pact Series*

"Almost 30 years later *The Crimson Pact* supplants Clive Barker's *Books of Blood* series as the modern compendium of fantasy horror short stories. Though *The Crimson Pact* lacks the consistent voice the *Books of Blood* offer, there is something to be said for the variety of styles. Like the viewers of the classic *Twilight Zone* and *Outer Limits* television series, each reader is bound to have their own favorites. Whether you buy these for yourself or someone else, any horror, suspense, or dark fiction fan should enjoy the collection."—Lance Roth at Blog Critics.org about Volumes 1-4

"The demons are not your typical straight-from-Hell, pitchfork-tailed monstrosities, or (perhaps) even in any realistic sense of the term 'native' to Earth. No, the demons you will encounter in *The Crimson Pact* are rather more like H. P. Lovecraft's Great Old Ones—unknowable creatures from beyond the Void, waiting only their opportunity to invade helpless earths and rule them with devastation and despair." Highly Recommended —Author Michael Collings on Hell Notes.com about Volumes 1-4

"I applaud those who brainstormed this, and I can hardly wait to read the *Crimson Pact, Volume 2*. If you haven't partaken of this little jewel, I encourage you to do so, but beware, what lies beneath a mortal's skin could be something marvelously demonic."—MK Horror.com

---

"If you like demons and dark fantasy, if you love the constant struggle of good against evil (or at least human vs. something clawed and taloned), an endless eternal war between humanity and hellborn, then this is definitely the anthology for you." —Pippa Jay of Fantasy Book Review.co.uk

"If you like Dark Fantasy, you'll love this book." —Author Daniel Coleman, about *The Crimson Pact Volume 1*

"This is a volume for all those fans of demonology, but the mixture of genres, styles and authors means something should appeal to everyone. If you like some dystopian sci-fi with your demons, check out *Fight*. If you prefer some sweet yet gritty romance–with vampires too, no less– check out *Stumble and Fall* (one of my favourites, and with a favourite character from 1 and 2). *Singe, Smolder, Torch, Whither* left me squirming and looking for blue glowing eyes. For the conspiracy theorists, there's the voice inside the computer with *Whispers in the Code. The Recruit* is a modern play on the old contract with the devil. There's even a tale told from the enemy's perspective in *The Ronin's Mark*, an intriguing insight into the mind of one of the demon horde. There's a lot of swearing, guts and gore, but also triumph, tragedy and heart-warming moments. These stories can scare, disgust, or horrify you. They can also make you laugh and cry." —Pippa Jay of Fantasy Book Review.co.uk

THE CRIMSON PACT

VOL. 5

The Crimson Pact: Volume 5

Published by:
Iron Dragon Books

The Crimson Pact: Volume Five
ISBN 978-0-9850038-4-5
August 2013
10 9 8 7 6 5 4 3 2 1

For Karen Bovenmyer and Patrick M. Tracy.
Incredible writers and great friends.

Table of Contents

Foreword

This is the fifth and final volume in *The Crimson Pact* series. It all started with the origin tale, "The Failed Crusade" by Patrick M. Tracy in *The Crimson Pact Volume 1*, which is included in this book for reader convenience, though an older draft of the story is still available for free online at thecrimsonpact.com—please tell your friends and send them a link. The direct sequel to "The Failed Crusade" appears at the end of this book, which is also by Patrick M. Tracy. Several of the twenty-one stories presented here (and a few from other volumes) continue in "Sealed with Fire," which serves as the truly epic finale for the entire 106 stories set in this shared multiverse concept. Please do not skip to the end; read the other stories first, as your reading experience with "Sealed with Fire" will be much better having already read the other stories.

Charybdis

Dan Wells

"If everyone will please be seated, we can begin the demonstration." Dr. Chase waited while the room quieted down—thirty-two of America's most powerful politicians, military leaders, and intelligence workers. The metal doors locked behind them, part of the standard security protocols. The room was large and well-lit, an odd contrast to the doctor's growing sense of unease. He hadn't slept well in months, and in recent weeks his restless nights had been plagued with nightmares—no specific scenes or stories, at least not that he could remember, but merely impressions of terror, of revulsion, of an overriding *wrongness* he couldn't identify or explain. He'd been to the team's psychologists only two days ago and been assured that he was fine, that the project had not yet "touched" him, but he knew he'd been working on it too long. Longer than any of the others.

Longer, at least, than any of the others still free to walk around. He was team leader not because of his credentials but because the more senior members were now raving or drooling in small, padded cells not far from the room he was in now. Could he hear Dr. Cartwright screaming, or was it a memory? Even the ravings of his former mentors and bosses were a part of his research.

He suppressed a silent scream, holding perfectly still as he counted to ten and summoned all his strength to keep calm and silent. His next psych evaluation was only days away. *I don't know if I can pass it this time.*

"Thank you," he said as the room finally silenced. He recognized many in the small audience, but there were a fair number of new faces. He could tell by their nervous expressions that they had been told just enough about what was going on to make them very concerned. "This is the fourth annual report on the status of Project Charybdis; since our last report, BioNet has been wholly purchased by the US government, and I'd like to welcome the new members of the project. As always, the information presented in this meeting is considered top secret, requiring a level 0 security clearance. That's a short way of saying that you're not allowed to share this information with anyone at any level of clearance, including the people sitting next to you in this meeting."

"They've all been briefed on the restrictions," said a man in the front row. CIA by the look of him. "Get on with the report, but start with the origin, Doctor."

"Very well," said Dr. Chase. "Some of you already know that the oceanographic expedition *Orpheus-1* recovered an unknown substance from what appeared to be a sunken city in the southern reaches of the Pacific Ocean. I assume the exact location is not a part of anyone in this room's clearance package; I know they've never told me. Preliminary testing, much of it . . . accidental, on the part of the *Orpheus* crew, determined that the substance had a previously unencountered neurological effect, disrupting the transfer of serotonin, dopamine, and other chemicals in the brain, resulting in symptoms of mania, schizophrenia, hallucination, loss of inhibition, loss of memory, and in advanced cases a complete degeneration of higher brain function."

"Say that again in English," said one of the new politicians.

Dr. Chase swallowed, keeping his breathing even. "People exposed to the substance go insane," he said. "Over time, that insanity seems to inevitably manifest in uncontrolled violence, feral behavior, and cannibalism." He imagined himself tearing into the man's neck, a vivid, bloody vision, but he pushed it away. *One, two, three, four* . . . The counting helped him focus.

The politician shrugged. "This is hardly the only chemical that drives people crazy—I don't see how it warrants this level of security. We have drugs that mimic the effects of schizophrenia, for crying out loud; this isn't exactly new."

"That's true," said Dr. Chase, "and the neurological effect of the substance is not, by itself, the reason for the secrecy—though it is, I'll remind you, still *part* of the secrecy, and you're not allowed to tell anyone. No, what separates this substance from others are three things: first, BioNet's discovery that the substance's effect was incredibly fast, often showing results within seconds of physical contact; second, that the substance was capable of propagating itself in a controllable fashion." He swallowed, wondering briefly if the sudden surge of anger he felt was a side effect of the madness or his growing displeasure at the way the government was handling the project. It was getting hard to tell. "Finally," he said, "and perhaps most importantly, this project is secret because of the US government's decision to take advantage of these properties through weaponization."

"Hold it just a minute," said one of the political advisors. "You're saying this is a chemical weapon program?"

"Technically it's a biological weapon program," said Dr. Chase. "We're still not exactly certain what the substance is, but it follows just enough of our definitions for life—theoretical definitions, mind you, not biological ones—that we do classify it as a living thing."

"Biological weapons are strictly prohibited by international law," said one of the politicians. "If word got out that we were developing one, the entire nation could be sanctioned."

Dr. Chase nodded. "Now you understand the need for secrecy."

The room was silent, a silence punctuated by a couple of scattered curses. Dr. Chase studied the group, thinking for a moment—a single, fleeting nanosecond—that he could kill them all, right here, before any of them could react. He pushed the thought away as soon as it appeared, the habit so ingrained it had crossed the line into reflex. It was the reflex, though, that scared him the most: that a thought so terrible should be so common as to produce a thoughtless reaction. *Is this how it started for the others?*

Some of the people in this room had been involved with the project nearly as long as he had. How many of them had been touched in a similar way?

Dr. Chase switched on his projector. "We've prepared a brief movie clip to demonstrate the substance's effectiveness," he said, cuing up a video on his laptop. Someone turned off the lights, and Chase straightened up quickly, shaking his head. "Let's leave those on, please. You'll still be able to see the movie with the lights up, and frankly . . . you'll feel a lot more comfortable."

The lights came back on, and Dr. Chase started the movie. It was a live trial with a human subject, a death-row criminal who had volunteered for the program in return for certain monetary considerations paid to his family. Neither the subjects nor the families knew what the project was, of course, though a fabricated paper trail would show anyone who looked deep enough that the convicts were being trained for secret service in any number of heroic, patriotic, completely imaginary military operations. Real action-movie wish fulfillment. The reality was much more ignominious, and Dr. Chase didn't bother to watch the film; he'd seen it, and others like it, too many times already. He stared at the back wall while behind him the filmed subject first muttered then bantered nervously with the hazmat-suited technician administering the substance, then slowly began to whimper, then howl, then gibber loudly and fight his restraints, eventually chewing off his own tongue and shattering his own bones in a wild, heedless, sickening attempt to escape. The video cut off abruptly, but Dr. Chase knew what came next: a bullet to the brain, another end to a "successful" test. He closed his eyes, counting slowly while the stunned room processed the video. He turned off the projector.

"Those results are typical," he said softly. "We don't know what causes the reaction, but we do know through . . . extensive testing, that the results are both predictable and reproducible."

"What was he saying at the end?" asked one of the military leaders, a woman in a pressed green uniform. "It sounded like words, but I couldn't recognize the language."

"That's because it's not real," said Dr. Chase. "It's a common side effect of exposure to the substance, one which we initially assumed to be some form of triggered cryptomnesia—the sudden repetition of information the mind knows only subconsciously. People who recite poetry in their sleep that they don't actually know in real life, things like that. When we couldn't find any actual language even remotely connected to the things the subjects say, we eventually determined that it's just a random effect, some kind of interference between the mouth and the language centers in the brain. They think they're speaking normally, but the words just come out as gibberish."

"But it sounded so . . . linguistic," said the woman, "like it had a real structure to it."

Dr. Chase smiled thinly. "It's uncanny, isn't it?" He could hear the language, too, or he thought he could, and the more he heard it the more convinced he became that they were all speaking the *same* language. Some days he almost thought he understood them.

"I can definitely see the potential for weaponization," said a man in the back. "It reduces the enemy's physical effectiveness, it destroys their ability to communicate, and it makes them very self-destructive."

"Mostly just destructive," Dr. Chase corrected. "This subject destroyed himself because there wasn't anything else in reach, but if there had been, he would have started on that first."

"Still," said the man, "enemies who attack each other are the best kinds of enemies. I can see the potential, like I said. What I don't see is the means or method: how are we intending to apply this substance to an enemy target? Surely we're not just going to walk up and inject them, like we did with this guy?"

"Injection is quick, but hardly necessary," said Dr. Chase. "Any form of physical contact is effective given time, from breathing it in as a mist to just touching it with bare skin. The primary form is quite viscous, almost like a jelly, but it's amazingly durable and we can do just about anything we want to it short of rendering it completely gaseous. We can spray it as a pressurized mist from something like a crop duster or a smoke grenade. We can mount it to explosives, in a traditional grenade or a warhead, and it will survive the splatter. But I have to say that I strongly caution against all of those methods. We still don't know how long it 'lives,' and letting it loose like that is . . . highly inadvisable."

The CIA man in the front row spoke up again. "It seems to me like the ideal application is small scale, the kind of thing you'd use in an assassination. Killing a foreign leader has a whole host of dangerous political repercussions, but watching one go insane could in fact be very politically useful."

"That is, indeed, our primary avenue of research at this point."

"That *was* your primary avenue of research," said one of the project leads—a stern-looking senator who had spearheaded the government buyout. He was one of those who, like Dr. Chase, had been with the project almost since the beginning. He'd had very little contact with the substance, of course, especially compared to the doctors themselves, but even so . . . Dr. Chase couldn't help but wonder. There was an odd look to the man's eyes. The senator hefted a worn manila folder thick with paper. "We have a new direction we'd like you to pursue."

"Prevention?" asked Dr. Chase. He almost didn't dare to hope, as his constant requests had been invariably denied, but there was always a chance his superiors had seen the light. They should be working on a way to neutralize the substance, to destroy it utterly, not to weaponize it. Especially in light of their recent discoveries.

He thought of the main substance sample, sitting in a tank in a nearby lab—a motionless, meaningless ooze. In his mind it seemed to quiver, as if it could tell he was thinking of it. Chase felt violated and tried desperately to think of anything else, but the ooze was always there, impossible to escape.

The senator shook his head, a grim, almost wicked, smile playing across his face. "We're not reversing our position, Doctor, we're expanding it."

"This is not something we should be tampering with," said Dr. Chase, "in any sense—"

"Don't trot out the old ethical argument," said the senator. "This is a weapon, and weapons are used to hurt people, and you knew that when you signed on. None of that has changed in the last four years."

"Nothing but our understanding of the substance," said Dr. Chase. "I'm not complaining about the usage, I'm complaining about the thing itself. Part of our mission is to study the biology of it, to try to find how it lives, what it does, what it . . . wants. Everything we've learned points to a level of directed behavior we'd never suspected. I know it sounds ridiculous for what looks like a slime mold, but we've been able to detect not only instinctual behavior but actual choices. It is intelligent." He looked the man in the eyes. "It is aware."

"Are you serious?" asked the senator. "You think it's unethical to use this thing against its supposed will? You don't want us to enslave the innocent the little slime mold?"

"Exactly the opposite," said Dr. Chase, "and far, far worse. As near as we can tell, this substance loves what we're doing—it knows were using it as a weapon, as a means of killing and hurting and driving people mad, and it delights in it. That means it's not a weapon, it's an ally, and I refuse to ally with the kind of thing that gets off on that video we just watched. We think we're using it, but . . . I'm pretty sure it thinks it's using us."

"That's preposterous," said one of the CIA men. "It's not even biologically alive, you said so yourself."

"I know, but—"

"Project Charybdis will proceed as planned," said the senator coldly, "with a renewed focus on large scale deployment—your work to incorporate the substance into a sprayable mist could also be used to infiltrate a water supply. A single operative with the right access could take down an entire army with—"

"And infect an entire civilian population," said Dr. Chase harshly. "It's unconscionable!"

"War is unconscionable," said the senator. "With a weapon like this we could end any war before it started; we could lower combat casualties to zero; we could beat our swords into plowshares and live in a world without battle."

"A world ruled by fear and madness," said Dr. Chase. He stared at the senator, wondering how the man could even consider an idea like this, and then he saw it: the wild light behind his eyes, the perverse thrill twitching up at the corners of his mouth. He *had* been touched—the substance had gotten to him just like it had with the others. And to the rest of the room, too; some of them were protesting, but some of them were agreeing. How was that even possible? Dr. Chase watched the furor grow as each person shouted the others down, some in favor of the senator's plan, some arguing against it but only in favor of their own plans, all equally horrible. Any use of the substance, in any form, was too terrible to contemplate—

—unless.

The group was fired up; they were excited. Dr. Chase might be able to stop the senator, maybe, but he couldn't stop them all. One of these bloodthirsty maniacs would find a way to use the substance in the outside world, uncontained, and it would be the beginning of the end. The last gasp of civilization.

Unless I stop this, thought Dr. Chase. He had received a message a few days ago, one whose origin he couldn't determine, begging him to stop the project. It had arrived on the underside of his napkin at a restaurant, so unexpected and bizarre he still hadn't convinced himself it was real—it would hardly be the first time a Charybdis researcher had hallucinated. 'You must stop them,' it said. 'You're the only one who can.' Nothing else but the word 'Charybdis' and the picture of a quill in bright red ink. It hadn't made sense, and it still didn't, but the more his colleagues schemed over the ooze the more certain he became that the message was right, real or not. Perhaps it was only his subconscious urging him to act where no one else could. He had to stop this. Stopping the project now would be next to impossible—it had gone too far, pulled in too much money, piqued too much pride and greed and megalomania. The people in this room wouldn't let go of their superweapon unless he forced them, and forcing them would be . . . painful, to the say the least. He felt a surge of sickening glee and realized that in this one instance, his goals were aligned with that of the substance. *Death and madness. Giving this thing what it wanted is too horrible to contemplate, but just this once, destroying just this group . . . that would be okay. Wouldn't it? Then no one else could ever use it again. All I have to do is let it loose, just this once, and it's all over. In a beautiful orgy of teeth and nails and blood and guts and—*

No.

I have to do it. But I can't enjoy it.

"Ladies and gentlemen," he said, pulling a sealed metal box from beneath the podium. His hands were shaking with anticipation. "We've prepared another demonstration that I think you'll find very interesting." He entered his private passcode, and the seals unlocked, swiveling open with a hiss. He raised the lid and pulled out a small black tube. A sprayer. He suppressed a giggle.

The woman in the pressed uniform gave a small cry of alarm, and the sound filled Dr. Chase with a horrible thrill. He choked it back. In a few more seconds he'd be too far gone to care.

"This is the mist-based deployment prototype," he said, advancing forward as the group scrambled for the doors—all locked, according to standard security protocols. "I think you'll find that it's very effective."

The next few minutes were the last of his life. He'd told himself not to, but he enjoyed them very much.

About the Author

Dan Wells is the award-winning author of the John Cleaver series, the Partials sequence, and the many more books and stories in many different genres. He is a co-host of the Writing Excuses podcast, for which he's won two Parsecs and been nominated for three Hugos, and he also hosts the podcast Do I Dare To Eat A Peach with his brother, fellow author Rob Wells. He currently lives in Germany with his wife and five kids. He reads a lot of books, plays a lot of games, and eats a lot of food, which is pretty much the ideal life he imagined for himself as a child.

The Failed Crusade

Patrick M. Tracy

This is the origin story for the entire *Crimson Pact* series. "The Failed Crusade" first appeared in *The Crimson Pact Volume 1* in March 2011, and an older version of the full story is still available online for free. It is being re-published here as a convenience because some of these characters—and the premise set up at the end of "The Failed Crusade"—impact all of the *Crimson Pact* stories. The direct sequel to this story is presented at the end of this book, and features several characters from other stories within this volume. Please read this and all of the other stories in *The Crimson Pact Volume 5* before reading the finale story, "Sealed with Fire."

Part One: The Rusted Vale

News of our victory came not in the happy shouts of the freed multitudes, but in the groaning voices of the animate dead. Ours was a victory none would confuse with triumph. The best half of us lay broken within the Rusted Vale, the rear guard left to puzzle out the events that had been no more than far-off echoes within the smoke and crashing iron. We knew only that we had finally won, that the Crimson Pact was redeemed, that we could all go home. Tired as we were, no man lifted a fist to celebrate. No Blessed Woman smiled. No church Catechist recounted the litany of our good fortunes. The cost had been too high, the wager of battle too awful. In that moment, winning didn't seem to matter. It would not be long before we found that even the brief illusion of victory would tear away like fog before the wind.

We had to reanimate the dead to learn the terrible truth. When we could find corpses whole enough to take the enchantment, that is. Most of them lay in torn, unrecognizable chunks no bigger than a man's finger. Our front-line troops had been destroyed to a man. No living soldier remained to tell the tale. How had our enemies, at the moment of their apparent defeat, disappeared into a rolling, living explosion of acrid fire? What twisted plot had allowed them to lure us in, only to annihilate us and make good their escape? Only the dead knew.

The landscape, a blasted waste of flaming corrosion, would never again support life. Nothing wholesome remained. Trees were charred skeletons; grass had turned to ash; even the rocks were glazed with black, tarry soot that wouldn't wash away. The comrades we brought back had known torment no human mind could bear. Wrenching them back into their broken bodies was a crime we will spend our lives trying to forget. They screamed until we were forced to pulp their heads with the burial spades, providing us with nothing but fodder for night sweats and drinking binges.

You begin clean. You begin with fine intentions and a cause. The ending is always burnt black, broken promises strewn about with the dead and all you had hoped to do slipping through your hands like the steam of your breath in midwinter.

Some of us were learning these truths for the first time, most of us merely being reminded. The Spirit Coaxers, with their black candles and their guttural chants, summoned the ghosts back into the broken vessels of our fallen friends. For those who had the power over death's threshold, there was never so ill-favored a day. As bad as The Day of Burning was for all of us, it was worse for the Spirit Coaxers.

Nothing could be done. We needed to know what they'd seen at the front, what had happened, how things had gone so utterly wrong. A few of them had seen the last awful moments. From beyond death's veil, they remembered. Curse the gods, but they remembered it all.

It fell to me, General Cruek Ostor, to hear the gasped words of the dead. I carry every word verbatim, an entire army of nightmares within me, loose-ranked and mutinous, hollow-eyed as my own reflection after these many sleepless nights. Fragments of all the dead live inside me.

Often, but little could be understood amongst their anguished cries. "It burns! It burns!" they would scream. Or it would be the name of their mothers, perhaps their sweethearts they would never see again. Nothing useful. Sometimes, though, there would be a soldier who seemed to know. A soldier who, as we grew to understand the depth of our own futility, would prove to be a collaborator with the demon horde.

The most enlightening account came from a Catechist who had once been a scholar, historian, and poet. I have collected all of his written works, but none more important than this. His insistence on being with the front-line soldiers to record the events of what was to be our final victory led to his doom. It was a doom he chose for himself, I believe. He knew what was coming and welcomed his own destruction.

The mad proclamation from his tormented ghost will become his most enduring poem and must never be forgotten.

> *"From out of the dark, from whence no light could hope to escape, the demons yelled out, not in defeat, but mirth. All the assembled Kasu-Hurun demons, laughing at their cosmic joke, laughing because they had slipped free of their nooses and leaped outward into the unknowing worlds beyond. They laughed because some amongst us have always known their se-*

cret stratagem, always grasped the chains of dark iron and helped to pull them free. Every hemmed-in battle line merely sharpened the blade that would cut them free, every seeming victory a mere sham, a sacrificial gambit to bring them closer to their ultimate aim. It was they who encompassed victory on the day that was to be ours, and we were left holding only smoke and ashes. The Crimson Pact, a human endeavor, had bent like reeds toward the evil it hoped to fight. It suffered the imperfection of our very blood. We had always been doomed to failure."

Those words and others hang in the shredded tapestries of my mind. They were the best account we had. The nightmarish story from the Catechist is the closest to an explanation in the grim aftermath of our day of glory. Never has the taste of victory so quickly soured into defeat, and never have the square-cut holes into which the fallen heroes are lowered been more difficult to dig. The sky above us was a bruised, weeping purple, even at midday. It was a day in which you would search through the wreckage, following the sound of weeping, only to discover that those sounds came from your own lips. A day that all hope had ebbed away, replaced by a bitter tide of woe. I knew then that our long war had only escalated, spreading over the manifold worlds. I knew and couldn't imagine what could be done. Everything I thought I knew had been shattered, my soul a broken cup that would hold no wine.

I can no longer imagine I will see the conclusion of this war. It will devour me, just as it devoured the bravest front ranks of our army. Perhaps it is the nature of crusades to only leave wounds and burned-out places upon the ground, missing brothers and failed hopes. I hope it is not so, because our crusade, this Crimson Pact, must continue on if we are ever to mend all we have broken.

Who first swore the Crimson Pact? That was before my time, two lifespans of men before the season of my birth. I, General Cruek Ostor, am a military man, son of a family of stonecutters fortunate or unfortunate enough to have learned the craft of war alongside the sons and daughters of people of much higher stations. I have only my mind and my resolve, no gifts of magic or divine providence. I cannot see the events of the past or future, but only what confronts me at the distance an axe can clear. The War Masters taught me that the Crimson Pact was a blood oath to hunt the Kasu-Hurun demons to the end of the world, giving them no quarter and allowing them no sanctuary. That was enough. I replaced the hammer and chisel and the back-breaking stone saw with finer implements, replaced the rock quarry with the long, long road and the weight of armor upon my shoulders. It seemed like a fine bargain. I can't imagine ever having been so young.

People swear pacts out of need, self-interest, idealism. Ours was no different in this regard. Never mind the long-term costs, never mind the darkness that hides behind our own occluded vision. In a little while, all the goals and reasons will be lost, both fair and foul. Only the bloody inertia of the crusade is required.

Long before I cut my cheeks and touched my bloody thumbs to the page of the Pact Book, all but the grim need for victory had faded away. The longer we harried the demons, the stronger they became. They fed on misery, even their own. War suited them. Wound them and the scars turned their skin to iron and bone. Grow as merciless as they, and they only nodded in grim approval and fought harder. They never tired of it, though the same cannot be said for our own forces.

I have seen the finest men and women I know cut short or crushed in spirit as we walked our damned road. Whether lowered into the embrace of the soil or left to linger, hollow-eyed and spent but still alive, I count them as dead, casualties of an ambition crafted before our birth that will go on long after we are but dust. I wish I had the energy to rage against it, but I find that passion has deserted me. As well to be angry at the sunset as its fires fade down into their own darker ashes. As well to never try, in hopes of sparing yourself the chance at failure.

Here is what I know: What we cannot buy with blood, we will attempt to buy with magic. What we cannot buy with blood or magic, we will plead with the gods of the firmament to deliver for us. When the gods fail, we flail outward, grasping any dark tendril that will hold us from oblivion.

In our striving with the Kasu-Hurun, we made liberal use of every element at our disposal. I can't say which weapon was our undoing, or if it was all of them in combination, or if we ourselves lack the purity of purpose to accomplish any great goal without a corresponding tragedy. All I know is that we borrowed too greedily and too often, and this chilly failure is our notice that payment is due.

Two weeks had passed since the Day of Burning. The survivors had been occupied with the business of honoring those who had not survived. The Rusted Vale had become a land of graves, all the stones for miles around employed for sealing tombs against looters, human or otherwise. No one had the spirit for the usual ceremonies, the shouting and speeches about the fallen. There were no work songs, no crude jokes. The music of shovels cut the ruined earth. Theirs was the only distinct voice.

I sat on the ground, ash in my hair, blood dried on my face, knowing that I would never again be clean. My two captains, Bandarin and Kalamat, sat with me. Kalamat looked about like a man whose dinner disagrees with him but is afraid to speak to the cook. Bandarin evinced as much discomfort and sadness as his heroic features allowed. At last, the conversation we all dreaded came to pass.

"The soldiers want to go home, Sir. They've had a belly full. These last days, it's been undertaker's work, not soldiering. The demons are gone, and I don't see what more we can do. It's passed beyond what we can hope to change," Kalamat said.

"That is the way their thoughts run?" I asked.

"Some of 'em, yes. Some's of the notion that it ain't over, but that's the minority. You'll need to talk to 'em and give 'em some reasons to keep hoping."

"What do you think, Kal? Do you think such reasons exist?" Under that purple sky, the talk of courage and continuance seemed just a charade, made asinine by the foul breath we used to push it from our lips. I could barely hold myself up. The images of dead men screaming with the agony of reacquaintance with their own tattered souls, of putting them to silence with the rough end of a shovel—these things whirled behind my eyes like evil children who wouldn't stop their frolicking as the funeral procession passed upon the road.

Kal searched the cemetery plain with haunted eyes. "I think that sometimes we fail, and sometimes there's battles that can't be won, no matter how much gets sacrificed. I say we go home and send up wishes for forgiveness. That's just my feel of things, Sir, since you asked." He gazed down at his bandaged forearm. His armor hung in shredded ribbons, one of his eyes still swollen shut with a massive bruise that obscured his features and slurred his speech.

"I don't know if it's fair to ask them to go on," I said.

"Armies don't march on fairness," Bandarin pointed out. "They march on orders, and ideals, and hardened men who they trust to sell their lives only for the right reasons. They still trust you, Cruek. You're the man to keep them together, to see this through."

I scuffed at the lifeless dust near my leg, drawing a picture of an axe, as I always seemed to do. "They trust me?" I coughed, as close as I could come to a laugh. "How? Am I still a good man, after all this? Am I a man who could ask them to go on from here? I wonder. I don't feel like that man tonight."

Bandarin clapped me on the shoulder. "You're every bit that man. More so than ever, I think. It's good to have qualms after what we've seen, but the men need you to find a way to be sure again."

I nodded. Bandarin, face dirty and his leg held straight against a broken bone, was at ease with all of it, impervious to the frailties Kal and I fell prey to.

"With all the demons gone to . . . wherever they went, what can we do?" Kalamat asked me after some time had passed.

"Not all of them are gone," I said. "You know that as well as I do. Many passed through our lines on the march, and just as many remained hidden through their magic and their wiles. As to where they went, the dead Catechist said it plainly enough. They went out to the countless other worlds. We, through our own mixed efforts, gave them a leg up on this goal. I intend to find a way to pass to those other worlds. I intend to hunt down the remaining demons and press them for information until we find a way, and then we must prosecute the war wherever it takes us." I don't know if I really believed. Maybe saying it out loud began the process, hardened my resolve somehow. How could I even fathom the way to follow them into the beyond? Such things were the realm of Spirit Coaxers and Blessed Women, not soldiers whose feet were rooted in the mud. My words to Kalmat and Bandarin were like the grin of a man forced to kneel under the headsman's axe.

Kalamat sighed, seeming to fall into himself and become smaller with each hard word on my part. "I imagine some will agree. The rest can be made to. They swore the Pact, every man and woman among them." There was no pride or pleasure in what he said. Every noise of his lips and throat came out begrudgingly, clawing to stay unsaid.

"I'm not interested in making them stay if they can bear it no longer. If they feel called to stay . . . "

"If you stay, I stay," Bandarin swore, casual as ever with his fate.

"Kal?"

"Forgive me, Sir, but I don't think I can. My girls at home have grown up with nothing but stories about me. I've lost their faces in my mind. I don't think I've got even one sword swing left after what I seen."

"You've served well and done more than I could ever ask for, Kalamat. Go home. Enjoy what life remains to you. Just," I put my scarred fist against his heart, "stay for another few days, and I'll never call upon you again."

He lowered his head. "Thank you, General."

I rose and helped the hobbled Bandarin to his feet. We would have a long night of planning.

We gathered them together that next morning, such a legion as we still had at our disposal. I climbed atop a lectern made from the wreckage of wagons and addressed them.

"I know you warriors have been tested to the utmost of late. We have all come near to despair and had our moments when we thought we could go on no longer. What we have seen here in the Rusted Vale has been the cruelest trial yet. None of us stand here who have not lost those dearest to us and bits of our spirit with those passings. It appears that we have come to the end of a campaign, only to find that the march has only begun. The Kasu-Hurun have escaped us, yes, but we swore a vow that does not end with the disappearance of our quarry.

"There are yet demons abroad in our lands. In their damned brains, the secrets of our betrayal fester. I mean to chase every one of them to ground and know those secrets. We'll find a way to complete all we've sworn to do. I know you, and I know that you don't want to end things with the bitter taste of smoke in your mouths. I won't order you to continue. Each must search their heart for the will to keep going. It can't be enforced. If you have it within you to follow me, we'll march two days hence. Those who can't bear another day can report to Captain Kalamat and march for your homes. No less will be thought of you."

"So we can go?" a question flew up from the ranks.

"I would ask you to stay, but I wouldn't demand it from you. Examine your feelings about the Pact, and let that steer you," I answered. Despite my hope to refrain from holding the Pact above their heads, I'd done just that. Every day we find new ways to diminish ourselves from what we hoped to be as children.

"For me, there ain't nothing to go back to," another voice spoke. More than a few murmured in assent with this. "I'll keep on, if only to honor those we put down in the soil, my only friends."

I could only bow toward the sound of that voice. It had gone beyond any words of mine by then. Nothing I had said really made a difference, or said more than that soldier, whose identity I have never learned. As they chose, they stayed or left. Perhaps four in ten remained true to the cause. It seemed twice as many as I'd hoped for. With that, we broke into shards. I wonder if it was no less brave to give up on that day. For the rest, we went on, weighed down by the dross of our shame.

Part Two: Chainweight

We caught the demon Kaivahno at dusk by running him down into a hollow filled with saplings just beginning to regrow from a clear cut. It took every one of our crossbowmen to stop him, though he was no bigger than a boy in stature. Even when we saw him up close, writhing as our bolts pushed, hissing, out of his frail-looking body, he appeared as a human waif. He'd slain and eaten at least a hundred women—bone, gristle, and entrails. All he left untouched were the bones of the feet. With these, he created little sculptures he left for others to find. I had long since stopped trying to grasp our quarry's rationale. If they bothered with such logical things, would I be better for knowing it?

Bandarin, my most stalwart and closest comrade, dismounted and ran to the creature, pinning it to the ground with his spear. The demon released a multiple-voiced shriek that stung my ears and caused sparks like a grinding wheel to dance before my eyes. Bandarin never faltered. The best of us, the bravest, my own savior in countless battles, he was all that a fighter could be, unbowed even when the true folly of our quest had been revealed.

Bandarin somehow kept the demon pinned with his spear and drew his sword for a killing blow.

"Captain Bandarin, no!" I shouted. "We must have him alive."

"Not this time, General," Bandarin said. "Don't ask me to spare this one. His victims . . . they were naught but little girls, many of them." He looked back at me, pleading with dark rage in his eyes.

"We must have information before justice," I said, "but I promise you he won't survive the night."

Still, Bandarin wavered. His battle lust had gotten the better of him before. Was he going to disobey my order and dispatch the demon forthwith? No one who had seen its crimes would fault Bandarin.

Some of the wild light left my captain's eyes. Releasing his sword, he used both hands to pin the squirming demon to the ground. Thanks to Bandarin's discipline, this one would live to suffer our questions.

When the tendrils of hopelessness pierced me, Bandarin always stood true. His unwavering morale, his cheer when all about him lost theirs—these had been a rare comfort to me on the march. It had always puzzled me that the soldiers seemed ill at ease with him. I would have thought they would have thrown me aside and followed Bandarin alone, but they had not. Of course, I said nothing, the mute authority of my own command killing the words before they could hit the air. If I could have . . . but no, we do only what we do. Hopes and wishes don't come into it.

I turned to our Catechist, who sat his steed clumsily and tended to grasp the saddle horn with a white-fingered grip. In response to the demon's cries, he had clapped his palms against his ears. From the smell of his vestments, I thought that it was likely that he'd lost his water at least once on the ride. I ignored this. He was not a soldier, and, until we no longer needed his special skills, I would have to take who the Confederacy of Theologues sent, regardless of their shortcomings.

"What do you make his weight, Enlightened Rameau?"

"His . . . "

"Kaivahno, our quarry. Yonder demon. What does the evil little bastard weigh?" I half-shouted over the ongoing din of the cursed thing's pain.

The Catechist touched his fingers to his bald, tattooed head. "Nine stone. Perhaps a little more." The holy man shivered, vomited from his horse, and rode away. I could hear his placations to the gods, but I didn't think they'd listen. The fact that they worked through such a craven coward at all called their judgments into question in my mind. The ways of the gods grew more mysterious by the day.

Ullmer, the trapper, did his own calculation. "That's two hundred and fifty-one links of standard chain, General Cruek."

"Make it three hundred, Ullmer. Three hundred, at least. I don't want the demon to so much as wiggle beneath the burden."

With the human-shaped demons, chainweighting was the only thing that worked. Any locking mechanism would fall from them in a moment. They could escape even the sternest cell. Their own weight in iron, wrapped around them as tight as men could wind, seemed the only prison that would serve. Those who remained here after the Day of Burning were especially difficult to kill, the spies and trusted agents of the Kasu-Hurun. They had tasks to accomplish, fresh wickedness to perform. They also had information.

I had so far been unsuccessful in extracting anything but bragging, threats, and prolonged screaming from our demon prisoners, but they were our best hope of finding some secret, some tool to keep the war with their race from escaping us utterly.

"I hope that Catechist is fetching the Blessed Woman, General. The demon is growing rather stronger, and we'll need her here if we're to wrap him safely," Bandarin said, his voice ragged, sweat bursting from his brow despite the chill of the evening air.

Ullmer and his men swung free lengths of their chain against the demon's flanks hard enough to burst the gut and bone of any normal man. The demon continued its horrid screams, threatening with each muscular surge to escape from Bandarin's pin and run amok, killing horses and warriors alike. To keep the one tiny creature at bay, a whole team worked to their uttermost, steam rising from their faces, breath ragged, teeth bared in effort.

The Blessed Woman came down into the hollow a moment later, her presence causing the shouts and screams of the demon to increase twofold. With a gesture, the woman silenced the beast, forcing its body to convulse, then fall back in a swoon. She had been with us since just after the Day of Burning, nearly a year. She was tall and fragile of build, with but little feminine curve to her shape. I couldn't remember her ever saying more than three words together outside the formal proclamations required by her calling. Her eyes betrayed nothing, but some hint of pain lingered around her, some deep ache that had been etched into her deeper than any capacity to comfort could go. She wrapped herself in her shawl, which had once been crisp white but was now the same wash of gray that any light garment becomes when used too long upon the rough trails of war.

I acknowledged her, waving her forward to our prey.

She stopped, watching me for just a moment. "This one will

talk. Not the truth. Not at the beginning, but . . . " she looked at the ground now, "eventually, perhaps. Press him hard enough, and he'll talk." She touched my elbow, the first I'd ever seen her reach out in all that time. "Remember, though, that knowing doesn't always make it easier." That near her, I could feel her power thrumming in the air. Her touch was electric; my every nerve responded to her. My armor caused me some discomfort as my body flexed at her touch, but I kept it from my face.

"I need to know. Easy isn't a concern." My voice sounded disembodied, as if it came from someone else's throat.

Her eyes, just for a moment, opened up and allowed me a hint of what lay beneath her outward fortifications. "Of all the generals, I'm glad you were here to lead us."

I blew out air. "Why?"

"Because you know that things must go on far longer than our taste for them remains. You knew the agony of dawn to dusk work as a young man, and that familiarized you with the idea that our lives are leased stretches of time, made possible only by our capacity to withstand all the troubles of the day. You are not a romantic, to be heartbroken by some perceived failure or setback."

She turned away, leaving me to think about her words and wonder if they were true. She withdrew a short rod of maple, remnants of the bark still attached, and touched its end to the demon's forehead. It straightened, stiff as a fence post. Its eyes slammed open, the color of blood and grease, its mouth bristling with fangs, its hands turned to hawk talons, its skin colored ocher.

"In the touch of the natural world, you are revealed," the Blessed Woman said. "You are a stranger, an unwholesome vessel, a thing which does not belong and cannot fit. You can only destroy, corrupt, and sicken. In your passing, none will lament. I castigate you, demon of the Rusted Vale. You will accept your punishment with stoicism, and when next a wound threatens your life, your uncanny fortitude will not save you." Her words spent, she stepped back to my side.

Not needing to be told, Ullmer and his men finished chain-weighting the demon. Three hundred links, pulled taut and hard around the small body, nearly mummified the creature. A sheath of sackcloth stretched over the whole bundle, and four men hoisted the bound demon into a wagon.

"Thank you, Blessed Woman," I said. She stood near me, close enough for me to smell the tree sap scent that always seemed to linger near one of her calling.

"In confidence, you may call me Yasi." She gave me the smallest of all smiles, just a ghost within fog.

"I . . . yes, I will." My heart beat hard. I didn't quite know how I felt. It had been a long time since anything poked its head above the deep blanket of grim determination.

"Our newest Catechist is worth less than the horse that carries him. I'll help you with the interrogation, if you'll have me," Yasi said.

"Nothing we've tried yet has been successful. I'd welcome your help. It might chasten Kaivahno to know you're standing by."

"If they could be chastened, my dear general, they wouldn't be demons. I might be able to frighten him a little." Another smile, this one somewhat more fully formed.

I wanted to ask her why she was talking to me, and why now, and a helmet full of other unformed questions that I couldn't easily give voice. My tongue grew heavy and uncertain with those topics, though, and I remained quiet, watching her, really seeing her for the first time. There was an element of grace to all her movements. She wore a ring of silver on her finger and another on her thumb, that one larger, perhaps a man's ring. Those small clues made me think of all the tragic turns of fate that must dwell in her past. It was impossible for me to imagine anyone in my company not suffering the heavy toll of a dark road. Perhaps I'd become too good at guessing another's pain or had only imagined it.

Bandarin approached us then, and Yasi faded back into herself, leaving me to wonder why I'd been the one to bring her out in the first place, and what it might portend.

"They're setting up a tent on the cleared ground," Bandarin said, gesturing with his chin to where the cart had labored. "The men, as usual, will camp some distance away, just to be safe."

I nodded, saying nothing, gazing after Yasi as she floated upslope, neither slow nor hurried, perhaps more of a mystery than she'd been at dawn.

"You look tired, old friend. I could handle this one, if you wish," the captain offered.

I clapped him lightly on the arm. "No, I'll do it. You've had your measure of glory today, wrestling the creature to the earth like the Heavenwalkers from the old myths. Yasi and I will see to the ugly business of demon torturing."

Bandarin laughed. "Heavenwalker! You've clearly mistaken me for someone else, Cruek. I'm barely considered tolerable company in a noisy ale hall. I fall well short of the picture you'd paint around my head. It's easy work to follow when I'm lead by one such as you."

I shrugged. For a moment, all I wanted to do was tell him how much he was appreciated, but it was a clumsy thing to speak on, and the moment passed. "I'll tell you if we learn something useful."

"You'd better tell me first, old friend."

Bandarin walked away into the twilight and was gone. I led my horse back to where the tent was being erected, passing him off to a functionary who was no more than a dim outline against the trees. The sounds of hammers driving pegs, the talk of the men, the clatter of horses, booted feet, and wagons as the bulk of our forces moved away from the torture tent—all these things seemed to float slow on the air, every sound distinct and odd.

I saw two men move away when Bandarin came near and spoke to them. They moved with a purpose, and I wondered idly what it could be. I didn't know them, but it had been a long time since I'd cared to learn every face and name under my command. Too many had been lowered into the silence of a grave, too many lost friends to count.

The torture table seemed too large for the demon's small body. Even encumbered with heavy iron chain, his form sat in the middle of the stained, chipped wood like an afterthought. Some of them were so much larger, though size had little to do with how dangerous a demon might be. Uncanny things, they were rarely what they appeared.

Yasi, the Blessed Woman, held his ankles while I cut the rough sackcloth from him. The creature arched, every muscle contracting with manic intensity at her touch. He screamed. Though he was forsworn from making a sound, with only a whispered breath that silent scream filled up the tent.

When she took her hands away, Kaivahno slumped back to the table, sweating out vinegar and brimstone so pungent it assaulted the eyes. His grease and blood eyes rolled from one of us to the other, waiting for the next assault. I unrolled a kit of instruments. There was a mixture of tools within, any frightening-looking object I'd ever found. Many of them were a mystery, even to me. I kept them in the kit primarily for the purpose of fear and confusion. The needle-like rib bones from fish were useful, however.

We'd discovered that, for reasons unexplained, bones from fresh water fish were injurious to demons. This proved valuable when so many other methods of harming them were ineffective. Most wounds healed within minutes, seconds even. Not so with fish bones. Still, torture was not my trade, and I had no taste for it.

I found a device with sharp fish ribs protruding like a comb along one side of a hardwood shaft. I waved this over the top of Kaivahno's face for a moment, then gave him a meaningful look, but said nothing. Though still muted by Yasi's magic, I could hear his quick, indrawn breath. So much of pain is in the mind. Demons are superb examples of that. They can be torn and shredded, pierced by arrows and blades, and yet go on without the hint of concern for their injuries. Knowing that the wounds are transitory, that there will be no permanent scarring, they have the luxury of ignoring the pain. It is without meaning and import. With something that would cause them true harm, they are not so brave.

I pulled from my belt a small leather pouch and eased it open. I removed a pinch of its contents and sprinkled it over the demon's bare, clawed foot. His eyes flashed with the pain, his face contorting, his sharp, uneven teeth grinding at his lips until blood spilled out and ran down his cheek. It pooled, nearly black, on the table near his ears.

"Jewel dust. Amethyst, jade, and sapphire. I'm told it feels like unending wasp stings, or perhaps being flayed of your skin." I wiped the dust away, seeing the sudden, violent swelling of the skin, as if his foot had been plunged into boiling oil.

After several long moments, Kaivahno's body relaxed. The redness decreased but little. Yasi's castigation had made him far more vulnerable. I could dash his head loose from his shoulders, and he would know true death, whatever that held for a demon. The three of us in the tent knew well enough that he would not survive the night. The only question was how much agony he would suffer before the mercy of the end.

Yasi produced a small clay jar, sealed with wax and thin cloth. She swished around the liquid contents near Kaivahno's ear, her face masked in the veil of a thin, amused smile. "You know what this is, don't you?"

Slow horror grew in the demon's eyes. He turned his head away, looking at me, pleading with his eyes. The true features that the boy-like facade hid faded slightly, but he couldn't veil his true nature. Not in the presence of a Blessed Woman.

"If you want the mercy of a clean death, you'll answer my questions, and you'll answer them truly. I will give you a few minutes to make your choice."

Yasi and I walked out of the tent, standing together outside of even a demon's earshot. "What's in the jar?"

She turned her eyes to mine, only a few inches short of my own height. "The sweat of a good person doing honest labor. Nothing is more harmful to them, nothing makes them feel the pangs of all their sins so keenly."

I shook my head. "I'd never heard of this."

"It's secret knowledge, given only to the few. Most would miscarry the harvesting, or would use it to the wrong ends. It must be kept to the most trusted of allies."

"You told me," I pointed out.

"I did." She touched my cheek, then kissed me gently on the mouth, just a brush of soft skin against my wind-roughened face.

Blood raced in my temples. Vague bursts of light decorated the corners of my vision. Yasi turned back toward the torture tent, waving me to come with her. I did so, grasping her hand as I came even with her steps, my chest ringing with the shattered shards of abandoned hope, just now remembered.

Kaivahno's cheeks were wet with a coward's tears. "I'll talk," he swore. "I'll tell you everything. I . . . I don't owe them enough to withstand what you've got in store."

I turned to Yasi. "You believe him?"

She furrowed her brow, watching him for a long time. We both ignored the demon's imprecations, wheedling, and tears. "I do," she said at last.

"Very well, speak. When I'm satisfied, I'll see that you die easy."

The demon's tar and blood eyes bored into me. "You'll do it? Yourself?"

"If that's your request, yes. What would it matter?" I asked.

"They say," he paused, "my kind say that General Cruek Ostor is a man with iron nerves, a teller of truths. I trust you to strike quick and sure."

"Many things are said about me, it seems. My aim is keen and my hand unwavering when called upon to snuff out the life of a demon. I'll be the one who handles the killing implement, and I'll strike a merciful blow, though no such mercy was shown to my own absent friends."

The demon nodded, easing his head back against the table. It took a moment before he said anything. When he did, the sound of his voice was dry as two tinder twigs rubbing against one another.

"There are many worlds. No one knows their number. Some are so much alike to this one that you'd have to squint to see the differences. Others are . . . far stranger. Many of these worlds, up until recently, have been barred to us. We have been forced to congregate on a few worlds like this one. The ages of the universe change, though. Doors that have been shut are opening. It takes great magic, though, to move immortal creatures across the void, and there is no greater magic than the blood of suffering, sacrifice, and war.

"By your crusade and all those given up to the fanged mouth of oblivion, you helped us accumulate the power to leap free of this prison and make our way to worlds that are not yet inured to our presence."

I shook with the knowledge, unable to speak. Yasi gripped my hand hard, her eyes blinking against the tears that wouldn't be denied. This was the truth I'd chased so long. Hearing it, it was hard not to wish that I hadn't.

"All this time, all the killing was calculated, the fighting done at the Kasu-Hurun's pace? Didn't they fear being defeated before their goals were met?"

Kaivahno shook his head. "You don't understand. All the sacrifice was agreed upon in advance, carefully weighed and considered. Who did you think came up with the Crimson Pact? From the beginning, you have been . . . made to measure."

"And yet here you are, on the torture table and doomed, giving out all the secrets you bear to spare yourself from pain," I barked, rage and pain burning in my gut like coals from a forge.

"I am one of those sacrificed, one of the last. I always knew that this day would come. I'd hoped . . . hoped for longer, but I suppose that is the case with everyone. Because of my frailties, and because I can pass for human under the casual eye, I was to stay behind. Every group has those who possess whatever they wish, and those who duck low and must be satisfied with scraps." The demon's body and voice betrayed all the thwarted ambition and humiliation within him, emotions that I was well versed in.

"How do we follow them?" I asked. Out of the depths of my own sorrow, my own shame, the question swam up to the surface.

Kaivahno laughed. "Follow them? Why? Your whole crusade is a tool of our grand stratagem, the Pact simply a trick of the Kasu-Hurun. It's over. The prison door is open, and you can walk out!"

I shook my head. "I swore an oath. Not to demons, but to myself alone. The wording of my covenant is clear. Though the void should bar the way, I am still obliged to follow and destroy your ilk until death or victory comes to pass. I ask again, how do we follow?"

The demon was silent. Yasi put her hand upon his neck, wrenching a shrill scream from him, twisting him so hard that I could hear his joint locks and sinews creaking with the strain. "Answer the question," she whispered. Her tears fell upon his flesh and burned like acid, but her jaw was set.

Kaivahno fell back as she let him free. He swallowed, shivering, sallow with fear and with the unknowable pain of the damned at the touch of one who knows their weakness. "It . . . it could be done. With magic. The magic of the dead. There is a complication, however. One that the Kasu-Hurun didn't face."

"Speak," I commanded.

"A mortal can't pass the void intact. To walk that road, you'd have to leave your body behind. You'd have to pave that first step along the way with your own pain and death's blood. You'd have to be insane to try it."

"Then perhaps there is a chance," I growled. "A madman can do the impossible sometimes."

Both Yasi and the demon's eyes grew large and frightened. I am glad I never had to behold the expression that twisted at my face.

Part Three: Into Eternity

My axe fell. Kaivahno's head rolled from the table and thudded to the canvas floor. I opened the smoke hole at the top of the torture tent and took Yasi's hand. We stepped out into the clear night air before the demon's body began devolving into greasy smoke and vile tar. My legs shook with the burden of all the demon had said. I didn't doubt for an instant that his words were true. It was all too monstrous, too thunderous in its easy destruction of my last few illusions.

I let myself sag to the damp grass and look out over the sapling trees, just shadows in the starlight, whispering all my foolish hopes back to me. Yasi sat behind me, a leg to each side of my body. She pulled me back against her lap, her breast, putting her lips in my hair. Without the presence of the demon, her power hummed like the vibration of someone singing at full voice. "It's a lot to ask, even of the brave men you lead."

"It's too much to ask anyone, isn't it?"

"Perhaps." She stroked my cheeks and ran her fingers in my hair. "Will you tell them . . . all of it?"

"About the Pact? No. They're good soldiers. I won't make them carry that burden. We'll have to bear that part alone."

"You're going, aren't you? You'll go out into the unknown and face their wrath alone."

I didn't say anything, not wanting to, not wanting to think of it. I didn't know why Yasi had become mine, or how. She wasn't beautiful, nor was I an object of desire. We were broken people, hurt too much to be whole, but we had been fit together just in time for our kindling hopes to be crushed to dust.

"Cruek?"

"I'm going, yes. I have to," I told her.

She held me closer. "Then I'm going with you."

Gamlod the Spirit Coaxer was a huge man, fleshy and dark of countenance. He reluctantly discarded the joint of meat he'd been chewing. They called it beef, but I was fairly certain it was horsemeat. The men knew that as well as I and simply clung to the illusion of what they hadn't had for so long.

He rose, dusting his hands on his filthy trousers. "This doesn't sound like idle curiosity to me. Steering souls outward to the other worlds upon the moment of their deaths? Robbing them of whatever eternity they've got in store?" He shook his head, his jowls continuing to move for a moment after his bone and muscle halted. "A nasty bit of business, so far as I'm concerned. The soul grows exhausted here on the tangible world. It gets thin and worn as a kitchen knife too often sharpened."

"What I want to know is if it's within your power. Can you make it so a spirit could choose to travel across the void, rather than going to its rest?" I swallowed, looking around me for people I knew were not there. Spirit Coaxers were left to themselves.

The soldiers viewed them as inevitable elements of the struggle, but had no desire to share a fire with them. Though the hollow stare of a long-time fighter can be daunting, looking into the eyes of someone who can call back a dead soul and push it into the husk it recently vacated wasn't something any natural person would choose.

Gamlod looked up at the sky, which had clotted over with clouds now. Soundless flashes of lightening winked in the far off horizon. "I could do it. Compared to wrenching souls back from their reward, steering one just taking flight would be easy enough."

"Good. Think about how it would be done. Figure out the details and be ready to perform the spell by tomorrow," I said. The sound of it stunned the air around me. The knowledge that the flesh to be nullified was my own, the spirit to soldier on mine, surrounded me like rancid bog water. Yasi and I would face that doom because I'd been unable to dissuade her from accompanying me on the journey.

Gamlod held up his hands, palms out flat in a warding gesture. "Easy now, Cruek. If I weighed what we know about the other worlds against a palm full of spit, it would be the latter that would tilt the scales. Every world has its own rules. Maybe the traveler would remember everything from his previous life, maybe just vague feelings. Perhaps he would steal someone else's body, pushing that soul out of his skin in a flash. Then again, it's possible that he'd be born a babe and grow like anyone else. There's no way to tell."

"All journeys begin with uncertain destinations, Gamlod. This one is no different." I hoped to sound as off-handedly heroic as Bandarin, but failed.

The Spirit Coaxer looked between me and Yasi, setting his teeth. "Are you saying that you intend to send warriors across the void, so as to continue this war... somewhere out there?" he swept his hand across the vast mystery of the sky.

"I intend to go myself. Be ready by dusk. The Blessed Woman will go with me. Please make the preparations."

He bowed his head. From under the shadow of his hair, he asked a question. "What do you propose to tell the soldiers? You're responsible for them; they march at your behest. Something will have to be said. They've lost so much, and yet they remain true. What can we who remain possibly tell them?"

The last remaining vestige of my resolve threatened to collapse, but I held on. "Tell them that I have done something that I don't have the heart to ask of them. If they wish to follow, let them seek that path on their own. I will leave my journals. They hold any petty insights I may have made. Read them over, share what you feel would be most useful."

"You understand that some of them are crazy enough to follow you, right?" he asked.

"There are limits to what I can bear, Gamlod. Even if I'm tricking myself, I don't want to bear the burden of stealing eternity from them."

"You seem to be untroubled by the burden you've lain over my shoulders, Cruek."

"There is nothing about this that doesn't trouble me. Nothing is how I would have it, were there any real choices left."

"So you say. Know this, though. I won't be the one to free your blood and help you martyr yourself. You'll have to find a closer friend than I for that grim job." Gamlod turned away and walked to his tent with slow and tired steps. I turned back to Yasi, who touched my shoulder and steered me toward my own tent.

When we arrived, I held the flap open for her, offering my clumsy and wordless invitation. She took it, and we did not sleep, using up the last few hours like anyone who knew their life's cup had been drained to the dregs might do.

Bandarin squatted down and covered his face with his palm. "You've gone mad."

He held the final memoir I'd written as the day waxed and waned, as well as my journals stretching back as far as my ascension to general. I had just told him most of what I'd learned, all but the ugliest of truths. I'd shared my plans with him, my most trusted and cherished friend. The setting sun colored the horizon salmon, red, and gold. The air was crisp and clean, a wind having lifted the remnants of cooking fires away. "Perhaps I have gone mad, but I'm resolved. I have a hard thing to ask of you, Bandarin."

"You want me to be general? No. I'm not one to lead. I've got no head for it."

"Harder than that. I need someone to strike the telling blow. I trust no one else with the task."

Bandarin laughed, a coughing noise in his throat. "You are a hard man to know, Cruek Ostor. You're my best friend, and yet I have too many occasions to curse the day we met. It's a wicked thing you ask of me."

"Will you do it, and will you find a way to hold the men together afterward? I'm not asking you to lead them, but they trust you." Everything, even this conversation, had become distant, slightly unreal to me. I was already disengaging from the world, my eyes cast to strange destinations that even I could hardly guess at.

He stood up after a moment, meeting my gaze. "Of course I'll do it. Haven't I always been there to save you when things get rough?"

"You always have," I agreed.

With that settled, Yasi and I went to see the Spirit Coaxer. He looked at us with a sour expression and squinted into the brightness of the sunset. "Go into the tent and disrobe. I'll need access to every exit the spirit can use to escape the body."

We did as he said, no longer shy of each other after what had passed in the hours of the night. We were tired, only half present on the world, a foot already upon the uncertain road ahead of us.

Gamlod approached us with a wax pencil that smelled of smoke and pungent herbs. He marked our skin in seven locations, a few of them both private and uncomfortable. His heavy hands moved without sentiment or lingering care. He glared at us in between his guttural chanting and his rune-making, his dark face carrying an expression of infinite annoyance, as if he'd had a fine evening planned, and we'd spoiled it altogether with our foolish schemes.

"There. Die within a reasonable span, before the runes wear and the magic unmakes itself, and you'll be propelled along your way," he grumbled. "Damned fools."

"How long would the spell last?" Yasi asked.

Gamlod shrugged. "A few days. A week at most."

"Is there a method of . . . " I stumbled over the words now.

"Any violent death will suffice. I doubt that either of you will lie down and slip from life as an old farmer would, gazing at his bare toes as the light fades and the heart ceases."

I wanted to thank him, to talk about what might come after we made good our death, but his taciturnity stifled anything I might say. We dressed and left his tents without a word. Bandarin appeared, dressed in his finest remaining raiment, his face new-shaved and his hair brushed back.

"We should take a stroll out into the new growth and find a secluded spot for our—" he paused to shake his head, "—rather, your little adventure."

The three of us walked, unnoticed, out of the camp and into the scrub trees. It was a fine evening, a gentle twilight that made it possible, almost, to forget the Day of Burning. Almost. The sky still sometimes glowed with purple light, the wind still bore subtle hints of the Rusted Vale's taint. The healing would be a long time in coming yet.

"Tell them . . . tell them I found a way to rejoin the real fight. Don't tell them the details yet. Just say that I've gone to stalk the Kasu-Hurun in their new haunts," I told him, my voice quiet against the rustle of the limbs. The forest smelled like rotting leaves, rich soil, and hundreds of smaller scents I've never been a keen enough woodsman to learn. Crystalline elements of the sun shot through the upper branches, dappling the light on Bandarin's face. Yasi's arm wound through my own. I realized that I wasn't frightened. Whatever happened . . . I felt I was ready. A dangerous thing to imagine, dangerous as holding a razor to your neck.

Yasi stopped me. "You're smiling."

I shrugged. "Things have happened too fast for remorse."

"I wish . . . that I'd had the courage to . . . " She put her palm against my cheek. "It's hard not to wish for more. We had a moment, anyway."

Bandarin called to us from a short distance ahead. "Here's a spot, if you're ready."

We went to him. The three of us looked at each other for a time without knowing the easiest way to move forward.

"Well, how shall we approach it?" Bandarin asked at last. His good humor almost seemed at odds with the grim work I'd given him.

I looked to Yasi. "I don't like asking you to go first, but that seems the best way."

"By your hand, then," she whispered, the tears finally coming as we approached so near the end.

I nodded, bringing the long dagger out from my belt. I opened my mouth to offer her some consolation, some assurance. She put her finger against my lips, shaking her head. I put my off-hand around her shoulders and brought her near, almost an embrace. My dagger hand shook, but the killing stroke was so well ingrained that the arm knew its way, knew how to go between the ribs, through the lung, and into the great muscle of the heart.

Her eyes flashed, the strength going out of her legs. I put her down, the blood already wet and dark against her lips. On my knees, I watched her gasp against the inevitability of the void. The brightness faded from her, the body's vessel emptying. The chill feeling overcame me. I bowed my head, unable to think or move for a moment.

When I regained myself, I unslung my war axe and handed it to Bandarin. "I'm sorry to ask this of you, old friend, but with those muscles of yours, one stroke should suffice."

Bandarin, a strange light in his eyes, tossed the axe hard into the shadows of the wood. In a twinkling, his slim blade leaped into his palm. The sun was gone, darkness soaring upward from the rim of the world, yet doing all too little to hide the change upon my best friend's face.

"What?" I started, unable to even gain my feet. Bandarin loomed there, transformed, as if some long-held mask had fallen, revealing something terrible below. The blade flicked forward once, twice, three times, piercing me through the belly.

Ice and fire blasted through my system, my legs failing, blood coating me to the thighs as I fell. "Bandarin?" I gasped.

"One stroke? No, my old friend. I think I'll leave you with time to think about things. You'll need a few minutes of agony to make sense of it all, won't you?" His face twisted, almost as if the man I'd known all this time had never existed at all. I couldn't think, couldn't grasp the import of the betrayal.

"Why so confused, Cruek? Did you think that the hands of the Kasu-Hurun were so distant from you, so far from your breast all this time? We have been right here, at your shoulder all the way."

"You were a . . . "—I could barely say the word—"*traitor* all this time?" I must have appeared the grandest fool, so thoroughly had I believed his studied role of the stalwart right hand.

"Wasn't I too good to be true? Think on it, Cruek. I always worried that I overplayed the part, but with every eye squinting outward, I suppose that a bit of hyperbole was safe enough. Dark gods and demons of the Rusted Vale, but you were so easy to trick," he said, a cruel, silent laugh on the corners of his lips. He danced around me as the gut wound waxed so awful I could scarcely draw a breath.

"You were wrong about everything, my fine general. Every basic thing, every article of your faith . . . lies! Now, you're chasing silly hopes out onto other worlds, when you were too dim to do anything but help in the decimation of this one. Oh, Cruek Ostor, how can a hero die with such failure and shame. How?"

"You were what," I gasped, "what I needed."

"And you were what my masters needed, General. Until now. Those precious journals of yours? Your dying memoir? They'll all burn in my cooking fire tonight." Bandarin stopped for a moment, the rhyme and litany of his words interrupted. He looked down, seeing the sudden blood, the thick tip of an arrow protruding from his side, low above his hip and transecting the place where the kidney lay. A twang in the woods, and a second arrow grew from his neck, as if by magic.

Choking, Bandarin went down. He clawed at the ground and tried to scream through the gout of blood in his voice box. I rolled back, everything fading and becoming indistinct. I had been a fool. In every way possible, I had failed. I would die with shame, witness and cause of all the death surrounding me.

Above me, Gamlod's huge bulk loomed. "I always thought he was a traitor. Only now do we find out for sure. I apologize for the pain you're in. I had to let you have a lead, and I had to be sure."

"But what about . . . the Pact?" I asked. "How will they go on?"

"You're not so surrounded by enemies as the traitor would have you believe. The fact that you kept going when you could have so easily let go, that you've found a way . . . that makes up for everything else. I'll do what I can to hold the Pact together. Perhaps others will want to follow you across the void. Perhaps that can, in the long scales of time, make a difference."

I nodded, just a small dip of my chin. It cost me most of what I had left.

"I won't see you suffer further, General. Go now."

"No," I whispered. "There are things . . . not written. Knowledge. Might help."

The Spirit Coaxer nodded. He put his forehead against mine, and I could feel a path open between us, a road of spirits, as he accepted my thoughts and prayers yet unrecorded. "I have seen you, and I will remember," Gamlod said.

Ignoring all the pain, I grasped his shoulder. "This time, it will be different. It must be."

"I know, General."

Gamlod brought his heavy oak club high into the air and swung it against my skull with all the force of his huge body. I felt a jolt, and the pain was gone. Discomforts that I had lived with so long I'd become ignorant to them slipped away.

I stood up from the broken elements of my body. Gamlod saw me across the road of spirits. I rose up, the winds of a storm beyond all storms pushing me on my way.

Epilogue

Spirits tell their tales but rarely, and truth is hard to find, but all that I have spoken must be believed. I am Gamlod, and I have seen through the eyes of a brave man as he went beyond the veil. His words are spoken through me, his wisdom given with my voice. Our general has asked nothing in words, but his deeds and example are not to be ignored. He would not ask, but I will. Will you go beyond all that is sane? Will you brave death itself to regain your honor and redeem the Pact? The best of us are gone, and we who remain are broken creatures. We have done all that can be imagined. All that remains is the unimaginable, the unknown road that only the reckless and brave dare to walk. I intend to walk that road. Will you be at my shoulder?

About the Author

Patrick M. Tracy lives in Salt Lake City and works as a Network Support Administrator. He went to Northern Arizona University, graduating with a B.A. in English. He has been writing fiction and poetry for many years, and has numerous published works in both disciplines. Among his recent publications are the novellas "Darkness of the Sun" in *The Crimson Pact Volume 4*, and "Mungo the Undying" in *A Walk in the Abyss*. When not fixing computers or writing, he enjoys traditional archery and performing feats of strength. Find out more at pmtracy.com.

Eyes Only

George Strayton

New York City. 22 May 2018. 23:38

One hand held Finn on the steel railing of the Freedom Tower's rooftop, which was lit up with spring colors. The rest of him dangled thousands of feet above the ground. He saw his Sig 226 flipping as it fell at terminal velocity. Gusts of wind threatened to rip him off the Tower and send him flailing after it.

He looked up to see her standing over him just as her boot came down on his fingers and ground them against the edged steel of the railing's lowest crossbeam. Her extra-human strength would've instantly crushed a normal human's fingers into a messy pulp. But not Finn's. Though he felt the agony just as intensely, he did his best to retain his grip. His other hand was bleeding a river through the hole she had blasted in it, the same shot that had blown the pistol out of his grasp.

He locked eyes with her. Even her look of anger was somehow alluring. And he hated her for it. He hated everything about her. He wanted her dead.

But at the moment, she had the upper hand—*his* upper hand, to be precise. And clearly, she wanted him dead, too.

And yet he knew her twisted mind better than that.

"Let me up! You've had your fun!" he shouted up to her over the wind.

"Give it to me!" she responded. Then louder, more intense. "Now!" She was emotional, chaotic. Too much had happened in the past twenty-four hours for her to maintain any semblance of composure. She had lost all control. Which wasn't surprising. She lived her entire life halfway to irrationality to begin with.

With his free arm, he pressed the object inside his jacket closer to his chest. "Fuck you!"

In a blur, she brought her custom silver Varjag 9mm to bear, aimed at his forehead, and pulled the trigger—

The sanctified bullet struck home. He released the railing and dropped toward the earth far below, his body passing in and out of the light spilling out of the windows of the Freedom Tower as he fell, black suit rippling in the increasingly strong air currents...

Budapest, Hungary. 21 May 2018. 21:16

Finn sat in the passenger seat of the Volvo S80, feeling the motor thrumming as it idled. He kept his window cracked open an inch; quick gusts of frigid air blew in, flipping his black hair as he stared through the windshield. He eyed the Hungarian Parliament Building down the street. The gold, domed central rotunda featured a tall spire that drove into the night sky like a spear lit up by a dozen spotlights arrayed around it on the Capitol grounds. The entire, multicolored tableau reflected in the choppy water of the Danube.

Armed, uniformed guards, their breath blooming white in the cold air, marched patrol in pairs across the grounds at intermittent intervals, randomized so as to prevent anyone from determining and exploiting a routine.

"Can you shut the window? It's freezing in here." The request came from the young man in the driver's seat. McCormick, Jason. New to the agency, but not to the Cause.

Finn kept his eyes focused on a wide set of stairs on the left side of the Parliament Building that led up from a stone plaza along the river. He heard the question, but he didn't dare respond for fear of accidentally taking his eyes off those steps. In the single blink of an eye he could miss her.

"Okay, fine, whatever." Jason spun-clicked a knob on the dash, blasting the heat. The air came out hot and loud.

"Off." There was no particular intonation in Finn's one-word utterance, but it somehow conveyed the meaning "That's an order."

Jason shut it down, to the second-to-last click, anyway, so at least some heat trickled into the car. He pressed his hands against the vents to catch all the warmth he could.

"You know, it's hard to work an iPhone with frozen fingers." He continued as if Finn was about to interrupt, even though he wasn't. "And, no, I told you, those gloves you got me with the little finger pads don't work. You should get your money back."

To Finn, Jason was an odd "kid." He liked to call him that. He didn't know why. For some reason he was really calling himself an old man, rather than pointing out Jason's youth. The kid was in his late 20's—29, if he remembered right. Everyone figured Finn was in his early to mid-30's. Except his colleagues at the Agency, of course. Why was he thinking about this now? He hated when his mind started to wander off into some seemingly random direction. He had enough trouble without worrying about losing concentration—

"I still haven't gotten the mission specs." Out of the corner of his eye, Finn could see Jason fiddling with his mobile. "Are you sure this is legit?"

"How long have you been on field duty?"

He knew Jason knew where this was going. And it came across in his tone. "Yeah, yeah. Fine. There are rules and regs to this job, you know. But whatever, you're the boss. Apparently." That last word came out under his breath. Even though they both knew Finn would be able to hear it.

With a nearly imperceptible movement of his finger, Finn felt through his suit jacket to an interior pocket. It was still there.

Jason noticed. "What do you got in there?" he asked as if expecting Finn to reveal a juicy mission secret. Finn felt a split-moment of pride that Jason had even noticed.

"Above your—"

"—pay grade. Yeah, yeah." Jason shook his head. "You know, I'm gonna get promoted one day, and then you'll want to take back every time you ever said that to me, but it'll be too late."

All this time, Finn had never looked away from the stairs, hadn't even blinked. And it had just paid off. He tensed, though after millennia of practice, no one but would notice the incredibly slight spasm of muscles.

"She's acquired. Drive."

Jason was putting night-vision binoculars to his eyes—

Finn snatched them away. "Drive!"

"Okay, okay. Jeez. For a really old man, you're like . . . a really old man." He shifted into gear and peeled out.

"What're you doing?" He didn't let Jason answer. "I said 'drive,' not 'get everyone's attention.'"

As Jason wove through a narrow, single-lane, cobblestoned street, avoiding parked cars on both sides, he let go of the wheel, holding his hands up in surrender.

"Why don't you just drive, then?"

Finn flashed him a brutal look.

Jason laughed as he grasped the wheel. "Wow, dude, I was just kidding. I made a mistake. Don't kill me." Finn saw the nanosecond of fear appear in Jason's eyes as his grin dropped away. And now it was Finn's turn to chuckle inwardly

Seconds later, Jason pulled over about seventy-five meters from the eastern perimeter of the Parliament Building. Finn was already out the door. Through the open sliver of window he said, "Meet me at the rendezvous point."

"Wait," Jason called after him. "When? Hey! We didn't set a time—"

He pounded the wheel with his fist—causing it to honk once. Before Finn could come back to throttle him, Jason smashed the gear into reverse and backed the hell up.

At the same time, Finn shook his head and sighed at the sound of the car horn. But for the most part, he didn't give a shit. He was closing in on his prey, making sure not to run, but hurrying like anyone would on a cold night in Budapest. For appearances, he engaged the top button of his black pea coat, though he found the zero-degree temperature refreshing, even invigorating.

Or perhaps it was something else heightening his senses. The knowledge of what he was about to do. Of how much closer he was getting to doing it with every footfall. He almost smiled. Almost.

He reached the tall, black, intricately designed wrought-iron fence running the length of the Parliament's stone courtyard, grabbed onto a railing to being his ascent—

Just as a pair of guards came around a corner of the massive building and looked straight at him.

Or where he had been a split second ago.

Alarmed, the two guards shared a look, brought their AK-74 assault rifles—the updated replacement for the Soviet-era AK-47s—to bear, flicking off the safeties as they ran toward the fence, both scanning for signs of movement, one shouting into a shoulder-mounted walkie-talkie.

In the shadows at the top of the steps, Finn looked down on the guards as they sprinted away from him toward the fence and split up to run along it in both directions, searching for him. They'd spotted him, but he knew they hadn't seen her. She was too good. Far better than him. That was one of the things he liked about her... and yet it was also one of the only things in this world that scared the hell out of him. A shiver coursed through him, but not from the cold.

He reached up, felt the Sig 226 pistol in its shoulder holster through his jacket. An ounce of security. And yet what good would it do against a world of chaos? He was about to find out.

A half dozen more armed guards streamed into the courtyard from different directions, searching as they yelled to each other in Hungarian.

But it was too late. Their target was already inside . . .

. . . and on the hunt.

He'd already passed through at least a quarter of the building's six hundred and ninety-one rooms, avoiding elevators—he hated enclosed spaces; you never knew who might be awaiting on the other side of a door—but there were more than two dozen stairs throughout the sprawling place, so ascending through the dozens of opulent, labyrinthine chambers decorated in Gothic Revival style hadn't presented a problem.

He carried his jet-black Sig in his right hand, feeling the added weight of the silencer he'd attached, but, as usual, he hoped not to have to use it. Escaping attention was his primary method of accomplishing his missions, and there was no reason to change that tactic this time, especially given his continuing penetration into the heart of the building. It was as if he could feel all that brick, mortar, and concrete creating an increasingly difficult trap to escape.

He'd memorized the blueprints, so he reached the hallway to the target room within twelve minutes undetected, leaving no sign of his presence. The guards were still preoccupied with the "suspect" lurking around the perimeter.

He stopped at the corner and peered down, spotting two guards, the elite kind—after all these years he could tell simply from their bearing, but it also made logical sense given the identity of the man behind the door they flanked. They had Glocks in hand, eyes always on the move, ready for anything. But they kept sharing glances accompanied by stifled grins.

And now he knew for sure she was already inside. Shit. He had to move. No time for plans.

He slipped the pistol into the back of his pants.

Seconds later, the guards lay on the ground unconscious, their Glocks knocked halfway down the hall, their falls broken by Finn to prevent them from making any sound. He didn't take any pride in his own handiwork—it came with his heritage. He had just honed his skills over the centuries, the millennia.

He stood outside the elaborate wooden door outlined with gold filigree, ear pressed against it. He slipped the Sig out of his belt, cocked it.

That's when he felt his heart jumping, pumping so hard he heard it in his ears and felt it throughout his entire body. Which made listening at the door almost pointless.

The sound was muffled, but it was her voice. She couldn't be more than ten meters away, maybe seven. As soon as he went through the door he'd see her. And all hell would break loose.

He couldn't wait. *What's wrong with me? I shouldn't be doing this. I'm a fucking traitor. Fuck.*

But the feeling wouldn't go away. He needed to see her. And yet he had to stop her. At all costs. That was his objective.

But could he pull the trigger? He didn't like the answer that churned up from the chaos in his mind. At least, not on an intellectual level. In every other way, he was counting the seconds until he could see her face.

Either way, there was no time. He just wished the thumping chambers in his chest would calm down. But the pounding only grew stronger with each passing moment.

Stop. Just fucking do it.

He smashed through the door, aided by his extra-human strength. Fragments of wood frame flew as the door nearly tore off its hinges—

He had his Sig raised, and he used both hands to maintain a steady aim on his target.

She was waiting for him. She had sensed him. He should've known. He shouldn't have hesitated.

Across from him stood Arpad Vamosy, Hungarian Minister of State Security, eyes wide in fear despite the fact that he was clearly drunk. The muzzle of a silver pistol, a Russian MP-445 Varjag, pressed harder into his neck by a young woman, Andra Balanescu, who sat on a mahogany desk, her legs wrapped around his waist, black stockings visible up to their clips. Her other hand had Vamosy by the hair, keeping his head tilted slightly backward, as if she had just been whispering in his ear . . . which she probably had been.

Her black cocktail dress had come off her shoulders, revealing the top of a lacy black bra. A surge of jealousy ran through Finn, amping him up even more.

She locked eyes with him. "You're a bit late, don't you think?" Her English was perfect, but it was colored by her slight Romanian accent. Her straight black hair reached her jaw, the cut angled forward, longer at the front than the back, her brown eyes flecked with gold.

"I don't understand . . . " Vamosy said, his brain sending adrenaline coursing through his body to counteract the vodka he'd been downing all night—at Andra's behest, of course. Finn knew her routine.

"Shut up," was all she had to say. He complied instantly when she cocked the pistol, the hammer snapping back into place, ready to deliver the killing shot.

Finn just stood there, staring at her face—well, more than her face. It was everything about her that was fucking with his brain. Just his proximity to her was enough to throw off his killer instinct. When it came to him, she was a drug. And she knew it. And she liked it.

Finally, after what felt like minutes since bursting into the room (but in reality was only a few seconds), he spoke. "You know I could put you down before you could even pull the trigger."

"You could. But you won't." Her smile was infuriating and intoxicating at the same time. He should just send her back to Hell now.

Except she was right. If he did it, he wouldn't see her again in 666 years, if ever. And he didn't know if he could live with that.

He knew she could read every thought going through his head in that split second.

The standoff continued, neither flinching, despite their exchange and the thoughts and feelings racing within and between them.

The Minister, however, seemed about to lose it completely. "I told you, I can't tell you where it is—"

She yanked hard on his hair, eliciting a grunt, but kept her gaze fixed on Finn. "Do it." It was dare.

His finger brushed the trigger. He knew a single bullet would be enough to do the job. All he had to do was pull, just a few millimeters. . . .

But he didn't. He just kept staring into her eyes. He had so many things he wanted to say to her, but that wasn't his game.

She grinned, knew she was winning. Once again. "Okay, I propose the usual deal."

"Why do you always do this to me?" He wasn't whining. He was genuinely curious.

"We both know the answer to that."

From far off, he heard shouting in Hungarian. The staccato sounds of barked orders. Getting closer. Fast.

He shifted his aim from Andra to Vamosy, whose eyes now grew even wider.

"Tell her where the piece is," Finn ordered. "You've got three seconds. One . . . "

Three hours later, Finn and Andra lay next to each other in a king-size bed staring at the ceiling of a penthouse suite at the Budapest Gresham Palace hotel, naked, glistening with perspiration as they caught their breath. Both of them were . . . *aggressive* love-makers, to say the least. So it went with all of demonkind. Especially in this case. In this case because there was actually more to it than mere bio-chemical impulses; though they never discussed it, no matter how often Finn found himself wondering how he had become . . . compromised. He had no idea how Andra felt, though he had his suspicions.

Or, he could be completely wrong. If there was one thing he'd come to know about her, it was that she was totally unpredictable, like most of their kin.

"So," she said, glancing over at him. "How's the new handler?"

Straight from raunchy sex-talk to business. That was her modus operandi, all right.

"McCormick?" He had to think about it for a second. "He's a pain in the ass."

"You like him," she surmised.

"I can't stand him. I mean, maybe there's a *slight* chance he'll live long enough to make a good druid. Ask me again in twenty years and I'll give you the sitrep."

She couldn't suppress a chuckle.

"What?"

"Nothing." The single word conveyed mystery, superiority, and genuine mirth all at once. She was a complex woman . . . demon—succubus, if one wanted to be precise.

She gracefully rolled out of bed onto her feet and looked at him. Her body was perfect in that realistic way—not in the disgustingly thin "model/actress/whatever" skeleton-meets-botox way. His eyes flashed to the tiny mole on her hip, a mark he could never get out of his mind, no matter how hard he tried.

They shared a moment. For some reason he felt like she was giving him something. Something intangible, and yet real. He couldn't explain. Perhaps it was another one of those elements of the human body that evaded all understanding. Or perhaps he didn't want to know what it meant at all.

She grabbed a brown, intricately carved wooden box from the bureau. The motifs matched those of second-century B.C. Greece—alphabet to symbology. It told a complex story, but only to those who could translate the markings and then extract the metaphorical data from the literal translation.

"Thanks for your help in procuring this piece of the device," she said.

He hadn't moved from the bed.

"You used me." He said it in a way that conveyed playfulness rather than accusation.

Carrying the box, she walked toward a loveseat where some of her clothing had landed, including her bra. "We both got what we wanted."

As she gathered her things, he sat up on his elbow, watched her. "We can't go on like this. One of us is going to get caught. And that's not going to be good for anyone."

She placed the box on the couch as she slipped on her black panties. He noticed she never took her eye off the small wooden chest.

"Mostly you," she said.

"Maybe."

He paused as she continued to dress, then knew he had to just blurt this out: "What if we both quit our agencies?"

As her dress slipped over her head into place, she finally turned to him with a quizzical look. And then he realized the look wasn't surprise or confusion, it was anger.

"Don't start. We both know where everything stands. You turned your back on us. You betrayed us. I've had to make you out to be a better agent than you are to explain why I haven't killed you yet. Our people start out suspicious, so you can imagine what they're thinking now."

She snatched the box from the loveseat. This time it rattled as its contents—it sounded like a single metal object—slid around inside.

He was out of bed and closing on her. "You called me. You wanted me to 'catch' you."

"Because it served my purposes." She held up the box. "As you can see."

He slammed it out of her hands—clearly she wasn't expecting it. But something had flared up so quickly in him even he hadn't anticipated it. Which is why she couldn't have either.

The box hit the floor and tumbled, its gold locking mechanism preventing it from opening.

They were face-to-face, inches apart now. He felt a surge of emotion, which was only exacerbated by the rage he sensed exuding from her. Though sated only a few minutes ago, their primal urges had both been reignited. Which would mean another round in bed . . . or a fight to the death.

"Did you tell your headquarters about the 'informant's tip'?" she asked.

He eyed her, breathing hard.

"Did you?" she yelled. It was a sudden leap in intensity. "Because they could've sent someone else. In fact, they would have. Which means you *chose* this. You knew what this was and you did it anyway. If you regret it, you've got no one to blame but yourself."

"I could blame you."

It came out like a slap to the face. He felt her emotions overheat, about to explode. But she stopped herself.

She picked up the wooden box from the floor. As she passed him on her way to the door, she paused. "You should feel lucky today. I'm letting you live. . . . "

She crossed the rest of the way toward the door, grabbed one last item from the desk next to it: her silver Varjag. She slipped it through the long slit in her dress and into her thigh-holster.

"Bye, Finn." She opened the door and left. Let it close behind her on its own.

He could've said something, moved to stop her. But he hadn't. Part of him knew there was no talking to her when she was like this. The other part of him knew she was right.

What the fuck was he doing? What was wrong with him?

He backhanded a lamp off a table, sending it crashing to the ground.

In the surprisingly golden daylight of the usually gray Budapest, Finn headed over a rise on the sidewalk of a cobblestoned street, passing homes and businesses that had been there for centuries. A blink of an eye for him, but lifetimes of careful upkeep for humans.

Unfortunately for them, in the long run, it was all inconsequential. Wasted effort. The war continued and would only become increasingly more violent, lethal, and destructive on a worldwide scale. And it would happen more quickly the faster the Horde got its hands on the thousands of pieces of the Antikythera. They already had several hundred in their possession, as far as his own agency had been able to deduce through all the intel at its disposal.

But that was the thing about demonkind. They all had a sixth sense that enabled them to feel beyond the present. Or, put better, to feel the past and the future *through* the present moment, as if it were all happening at once. And Finn was no exception—

Shit. What was that? He had just felt something. It had happened within the hour, but the euphoria and emotional turmoil Andra had caused in him had served to scramble the focus of his extra-sensory perception (at least, that's what his druid handlers called the ability).

He ran. It all became clear. He knew what he was going to find.

He ran faster.

He came over the rise, saw the Volvo parked along the right-hand side of the downslope, humming as its motor ran—

Suddenly, he was at the driver's side door. Yanked it open. Saw it.

Blood and gore. Jason's neck torn out, veins and arteries severed by a jagged instrument and hanging out in various directions as if the attacks had come multiple times from multiple directions.

Jason still held his iPhone in his hand. It was three-quarters covered in and spattered with blood, leaving only the bottom of the screen and the home button exposed. The nerves to his hand had been cut first. It was a mess, total chaos—and yet completely calculated.

And that style belonged to only one person.

And Finn was going to fucking kill her—

His own phone rang. He answered. They wanted him to come in immediately. They knew what had happened. Via druidic seer, most likely.

"I'm going after her—"

The digitally warped voice on the other side of the line cut him off, its tone intense. "This was your fault, Finn. True, *she* did it. But it never would've happened if it weren't for you. *You* killed him."

He wanted to hurl the phone away, but something, some shred of what kept him on the side of the humans, stopped him as the voice continued.

"Did she get the piece?"

"She thinks she did." From his inside jacket pocket he slid out an engraved wooden box identical to the one she had been carrying earlier. "She has a copy riddled with flaws. It'll only set them back."

He wanted to point out that he had had a plan, that he had thought this through, that he hadn't caused Jason's death.

But to be honest . . . the voice was right.

"The usual pickup point. Wheels up in twenty-five minutes."

The call ended.

Finn stared at Jason's mauled throat. A flash of the agony he had suffered ran through him, but Finn instantly shoved it down. He looked into Jason's dead eyes. He couldn't say it out loud, but he was more sorry than he'd ever been, despite all the terrible things he'd done before joining the Agency.

But goddamn it, why had she done it? Why?

Because she's a fucking demon, you asshole. And so are you. You can't escape the chaos you bring to this world. Behold your handiwork. I hope she was a good lay.

Shut up! Shut up! Shut the fuck up!

He slammed his fist against the roof of the car to end the inner conversation and disperse the frenzied energy building up inside him. But it didn't work.

He was going to follow orders.

And then he was going to hunt her down and send her back to Hell, despite his conflicted feelings for her. He was sick of the twisted roller-coaster ride she kept him on. Love. Hate. Love. Hate. She enjoyed torturing him. And yet she couldn't keep away or kill him, either. It was as if hating her meant the same as loving her, so no matter what she did, she got what she wanted.

Well . . . fuck . . . her.

He put a hand on Jason's lifeless shoulder. *I promise, McCormick—Jason—I will kill her. No matter what.*

New York City. 22 May 2018. 22:54

He had tried to comply with orders. But he couldn't. He had no choice. At least, that's what he told himself. And it was probably true. Though he no longer trusted himself enough to know whether or not he was lying, even to himself. She'd either caught up with him, or he had let her find him. Either way, she continued to gain on him.

He sat in the back of a taxi as it raced through Battery Park. "Run the light!"

Without looking back, the cabbie yelled in his thick, Bangladeshi accent, "You know how much ticket cost? New York is rip off all taxi—"

"A thousand bucks should more than cover it." Finn shoved the cash through the hole in the Plexiglas.

The driver pinned the accelerator, racing through the red, causing cross-traffic to stop short and spin out with the screeching of tires and the typical New York sentiments regarding the cabbie's intellectual capacity.

Finn glanced through the rear window. The sleek, black Suzuki M90 motorcycle followed at incredible speed despite having to weave through the jammed-up intersection.

Andra didn't bother with a helmet. She stared at Finn, as if nothing around her even registered. It was clear she was fucking pissed.

Obviously, it hadn't taken the Horde long to realize she had a copy of the Antikythera device, a purposefully miscrafted piece. Which meant she knew he had the real one. And she wasn't going to stop until she got it back. The future of the war, of the world, of the entire goddamned multiverse, counted on it.

And, he knew, she hated that he had one-upped her for once.

More than anything else, that was the raging force that fueled her right now.

A part of him almost enjoyed it. Except he knew all too well he had turned a monster into an unstoppable beast. And he was her target, despite any other feelings she might harbor for him. At the moment, those were deeply buried. Or, more likely, their energies had been turned into their opposites and channeled into her blind obsession with her current mission. To get the piece and destroy him in the process.

She'd catch up any second.

Without warning, he opened his door and jumped out of the speeding taxi, twirling through the air, hitting the ground, rolling, coming up to his feet, his momentum causing him to slide a few feet to a stop.

Andra zoomed past him. But she was already swerving to swing back toward him. By the time he charged into the Freedom Tower, she'd spun the Suzuki around and gunned it—

He smashed through a plate-glass door and sprinted for the stairwell.

A moment behind, on her M90, Andra crashed through a massive plate-glass window, shattering it into a million shards. She hopped off the bike and ran, just as it slammed at top speed into a marble support column and exploded.

She tore the stairway door off its hinges and pounded up the stairs, gaining on her quarry.

He reached the top floor, bashed open the door to the rooftop. Rushed across, but found himself stopped by the metal railing that encircled the perimeter.

He heard the door burst open behind him, turned to see Andra coming out.

He already had his Sig in hand and was leveling it at her. "Stop—"

But she had her own pistol in hand and offered no warning. She simply fired, hitting his gun hand, the sanctified bullets nearly blowing it off. The pain caused him to jerk his arm back. The gushing blood made the Sig slick—it slipped out of his grip and dropped over the edge.

With his lightning reflexes, he reached over the railing to snatch it with his good hand—

But she kicked him over. He fell off the roof, but managed to catch the lowest rung.

A single hand held Finn to the steel railing of the Freedom Tower's rooftop, which was lit up with spring colors. The rest of him dangled thousands of feet above the ground. He saw his pistol flipping as it fell at terminal velocity. Gusts of wind threatened to rip him off the Tower and send him flailing after it.

He looked up to see her standing over him just as her boot came down on his fingers and ground them against the edged steel of the railing's lowest crossbeam. Her extra-human strength would've instantly crushed a normal human's fingers into a messy pulp. But not Finn's. Though he felt the agony just as intensely, did his best to retain his grip. His other hand was bleeding a river through the hole she had blasted in it, the same shot that he blown the Sig out of his grasp.

He locked eyes with her. Even her look of anger was somehow alluring. And he hated her for it. He hated everything about her. He wanted her dead.

But at the moment, she had the upper hand—his upper hand, to be precise. And clearly she wanted him dead, too.

And yet he knew her twisted mind better than that.

"Let me up! You've had your fun!" he shouted up to her over the wind.

"Give it to me!" she responded. Then louder, more intense. "Now!" She was emotional, chaotic. Too much had happened in the past twenty-four hours for her to maintain any semblance of composure. She had lost all control. Which wasn't surprising. She lived halfway to irrationality to begin with.

With his free arm, he pressed the object inside his jacket closer to his chest. "Fuck you!"

In a blur, she whipped her silver Varjag forward, aimed at his forehead, pulled the trigger—

The bullet struck home. He released the railing, dropped toward the earth far below, his body passing in and out of the light spilling out of the windows of the Freedom Tower as he fell, black suit rippling in the increasingly strong air currents. . . .

As he fell face-up, he saw an object gaining on him.

She tackled him mid-air, locking her legs around his. She reached into his jacket, pulled out the wooden box.

"You know we're both going back home," he shouted. Their true nature granted them incredible power, but the bodies they inhabited couldn't survive a fall like this.

"Do you love me?" she asked.

He couldn't even comprehend the question. He'd never even heard her utter that word. Over the course of millennia.

"Do you love me?"

No. He hated her. She'd killed them both for the Horde. And she'd killed Jason because she knew he would care. She did it to destroy his will. To control him. To dominate him.

And yet—fuck. He did. He did love her. He wished he didn't. He wished he'd never met her. He wished he never felt that elation every time he thought of her or when he found himself in her presence.

"Well?" she yelled. He could see in her eyes she really wanted to know. And she was really hoping for a particular answer. Like everything counted on it.

"You've only a few seconds!" she said.

"*We've* only got a few seconds!"

"So tell me!"

He didn't want to give her the satisfaction. But some part of him couldn't help it. "I . . . I hate what you do to me. I hate everything about you, everything you stand for." He felt sadness boiling up inside her. He had to tell her. "But . . . yeah, I do."

"Do what?"

"Love you."

A smile crossed her face. "That's all I needed to hear."

She yanked a ripcord and a paraglide bloomed out of her back, instantly arresting her fall.

It all happened too fast for him to try to hold on to her.

As he watched her sail around the Freedom Tower and out of sight, he hit the ground—

About the Author

George Strayton first played Dungeons & Dragons in 1979. He went on to design games for TSR, West End Games, Decipher, Goodman Games, Wizards of the Coast, and others. He has worked on more than three dozen game products, including *The Star Wars 2nd Edition Revised and Expanded RPG* and *The D6 System* customizable roleplaying game. He was nominated for an Origins® Best Roleplaying Game of the Year Award and an InQuest® Game of the Year Award for *The Men in Black Roleplaying Game*, and won the 2012 Innovative Game of the Year Award from I-CON for his original RPG *The Secret Fire*. (The roleplaying mechanics from *The Secret Fire* and its first supplement, *The Way of Tree, Shadow & Flame*, were used as a starting point to create the characters for "Eyes Only.")

In 1997, Strayton moved to Hollywood, figured out how to sneak onto the Universal Studios lot (through the Credit Union on Lankershim), and managed to get himself hired to write for the Sam Raimi television series *Xena: Warrior Princess* and *Hercules: The Legendary Journeys*. He went on to become a film writer/producer on movies including *Transformers*, *Dragonlance*, 2009's *Star Trek*, and the forthcoming feature *Xombie* for K/O Paper Products (producers of *Star Trek Into Darkness, Transformers, The Amazing Spider-Man 2, Fringe*, etc.). He's currently penning the screenplay *Escape from Quag Keep*, an adaptation of Andre Norton's *Quag Keep*, the first Dungeons & Dragons novel ever published.

He has written for the *Star Wars Expanded Universe*.

Kill the Child

Craig Nybo

Millions of sunflowers stared at me, each with its single eye—dark and accusing—as I pulled up to the ruined farmhouse at the edge of what must have been at least 100 acres of crop. I've never understood the appeal of sunflower seeds; too much work, all that cracking in your teeth and messy spitting.

I parked my car on the pea-stone gravel pullout of the dilapidated house and made my way to the front porch, screwing my fedora even tighter down on my head and checking the bulge under my left arm where I kept my gun.

The front door swung open even before I had a chance to knock. The woman standing behind it glanced up at me with a spent out stare. She looked me up and down then pushed a few wisps of hair back from her face with one hand while hitching a wayward strap on her filthy dress up onto her shoulder with the other. She must have either been baking berry pies or slaughtering an animal judging by the stains on the front of her dress. I kept my eyes up on the level, locked on her face.

"Suppose you came for her," the woman said. She couldn't have known whom I had come for, not really, but I couldn't help but believe that a part of her knew all along that I, or someone like me, would come eventually.

I opened my mouth to say something, but she turned and moved into the darkness of the house before I could get a word out. I followed her inside, letting the rotten screen door slam on its screaming hinges behind me.

As I followed her through the house, I felt relieved as I smelled the confectioner's scent of fresh baked pies—baking, not slaughtering. She'd kept the place clean. The whole leaning building would probably just fall down around her without warning someday, but at least she picked up after herself.

She led me through a dank kitchen and out onto the back patio, a tick-ridden turtle shell that threatened to cave in under my weight. In the back yard, sitting on a tire swing, dangling from an old length of hemp, I saw the child. With nobody to push her, she just sat there, motionless, facing away from me, hunched over the tire, her gunny dress draping around her like a forgotten towel. And there was that hair, just like in the case file I had found on my desk, corn silk white, flicking in the breeze, smoldering in the light of the dying sun, all innocent and free. Damn, I didn't want to stain that hair with blood. The thought of all that gore made me think of . . . berry pies.

"Been there all day," the woman said. "Just sits there most of the time, says ne'er a word."

I put my hand over the gun that sat like a steel heart under my bat-wing lapel.

"Your friend told me you was comin'," she said. "Said not to watch what you had planned for her." She flicked a horsefly away from her face. "Ward of the state, she is." The woman inclined her head toward the child. "But I have no stomach for the business the likes of you conduct. If it's just the same to you, I think I'll take your friend's advice and stay inside while you do what it is you've come to do."

"My friend?" I asked, feeling my blood take the fast lane.

"Yea," she said, flicking at another insect, this one imaginary. "The feller in the white car. One of those chop tops."

"Damn," I said and crossed the back yard to the child. I turned the tire swing around so I could see her face, cherubic except for the eyes; they glared back at me like chalk, no irises, no pupils. I knew the girl couldn't see, not the way we do at least. "Child? Can you hear me?"

She opened her mouth, a streamer of saliva rainbowed between her lips then popped apart. She uttered something guttural. It was all I was going to get from her.

A car crunched up along the pea stone in front of the house. I whipped around just in time to see the tail fins of a white, chop-topped '68 Cadillac pass out of view, obscured by the leaning wreck of a house.

"Damn," I said. I reached under my lapel and drew my gun.

I glanced back at the woman. She stared at the ground, possibly finding a grasshopper or an odd shaped stone, something uninteresting on which to focus her attention. "I guess I'd best be letting you and your friend get to your business. S'pose you can have a piece of pie when you're done." She let her shoulder sag. The wayward strap of her dress fell to her upper arm. She went back into the house.

I moved around the girl, putting her between me and the farmhouse, keeping my gun aimed at the ground, safety off.

I waited for him.

When he walked around the corner of the farmhouse, he wore a smile. He took off his hat and wiped his sweaty face with the sleeve of his expensive suit. "Whooeee, ain't it hot today?" he said.

"What are you doing here?"

"Sometimes I like to show up and watch. That's all. It ain't complicated." He spotted my gun, aimed at the ground and ready to roar. "Let's not get all stupid on this, son; what do you say?" he said.

A tracer of sweat broke free and crawled down my cheek. I felt the rebuking stare of a million sunflowers on me. I swallowed hard.

The man sniffed at the air and closed his eyes. His smile told me he found something sensuous there in the breeze. He opened his eyes and looked me up and down, keeping the smile; but I knew that his smile was loaded like a weapon. "Well, why don't you get it underway. I suddenly got a hankerin' for berry pie," the man said, mopping at his forehead with his sleeve again. "Damn, ain't it hot."

I raised my gun to the child's head. She turned her blank face up toward me.

"That a boy, now do your job."

"I d . . . don't know," I said, trying to sound strong, hating the stutter in my voice.

"What do you mean, you d . . . don't know? You turning into porky pig or something with all that d . . . don't . . . d . . . don't . . . that's all folks stuff?" He chuckled long and hard, slipping a hand under his lapel as he laughed.

I fired. I imagined the woman jumping, startled by the deafening report of my gun even from inside the house. Someday I would get a quieter weapon. The girl's head cocked to the side, toward the man, who had finished drawing his gun from beneath his jacket. The man leveled the gun at me, but something had gone wrong. He raised his empty hand up in a gesture that appeared to be supplication. Then he unloaded his revolver as quickly as his finger could pull the trigger.

I leapt at the girl, knocking her out of the tire swing. We both hit the ground hard beneath the oak tree. She felt almost skeletal underneath me. I craned my neck around and looked at the man. He fired wild, popping shots off at random into the sky, more concerned with the bleeding from where my bullet had entered his chest than in taking a proper aim.

I waited for him to empty his revolver.

I stood up. The child lay on the ground like a bundle of loose cordwood beneath me. I aimed at the fallen man and ran the six steps it took to reach him. He lay on the ground, fighting for each syrupy breath. I leveled my gun at his face and waited for him to speak. It didn't seem right for anyone to die, even the man in the white Cadillac, without uttering some kind of final eulogy. I didn't want to kill him. But I knew he couldn't walk away from this.

"You are selling us out, you know that," the man said.

"It's not right to kill the child."

"She's not a child. You know what she will become."

"Yes, but right now she's a child."

I pulled the trigger. A hole appeared in the man's head. Gore splattered on the grass beneath him. I don't think he died a painful death.

When I turned around, the woman stood on the dilapidated patio holding herself, perhaps against those damn staring sunflowers. "Not sure if you've done right," she said.

I moved over to the child. I bent down and hoisted her up into my arms. She weighed nothing, like her bones were hollow. I looked at the woman for a long moment, trying to find the right words to say. "Someone will be along for the body shortly." I flicked my eyes toward the man, crumpled on the crabgrass and clover. I thought I smelled vomit.

I carried the child to my car. I placed her on the black leather back seat, mildly concerned that the sun had heated the leather to the point of discomfort. She didn't seem to mind.

I fired up the V-8 and left the dilapidated house and sunflowers behind.

I held the child cradled like a baby in my arms when Ilene answered the door.

"Another one?" she asked.

"Do you have room?"

She sighed, a long, forlorn breath. "She'll need new clothes."

"I have a hundred dollars."

"Bring her into the living room."

I followed her into the house. She cleared away some clutter from a second-hand couch. A black and white television set spewed the cold dialog from *The Maltese Falcon* from its tinny speaker. I took a moment to watch Humphrey Bogart command the screen in the remarkable way that he always does. Bogart reminded me of the man that I had left bleeding back at the dilapidated house.

Someone would come for the man, if they hadn't already. And after they scraped him up from the woman's back yard, after they cleaned up the mess and finished off the woman, they would come for me.

"Put her here," Ilene said, tapping the couch with one hand.

I lowered the child to the couch. I put a throw pillow under her head.

Something rustled behind me. I turned and spotted two children, a boy and a girl, their eyes white from birth, sightless yet seeming to stare at me. The children stood on a grand staircase, fronted by a wrought iron banister.

"How are they?" I asked.

"Well." Ilene rubbed the child's hands, trying to bring warmth to them. "They hardly make a peep."

I bent down and kissed Ilene, a solitary peck.

She almost smiled. "What was that for?"

"I don't know." I shrugged. "They found me out."

Ilene sighed again, something she did well. She looked up at me. I had always thought her eyes looked like pennies, but I couldn't tell her that. "So you won't be back?"

I pursed my lips and tried to find the right words to say; they didn't come to me. "One way or the other, you won't see me again."

"I'll care for them," she said, glancing over her shoulder at the other children. "I'll care for them as long as I can."

Just like the man I had left on the lawn back at the dilapidated house, just like me, Ilene knew what the children would eventually become. But for now, they were just children.

I kissed her again. I couldn't help it. This time, she kissed me back.

After midnight I gave Ilene the hundred dollars and left her house. I knew I wouldn't see her again. I drove through the night, all the way to Denver. Somewhere between Wichita and Salina, I tossed my gun out the window. Somewhere between Salina and Hayes, I finally stopped weeping.

About the Author

Craig Nybo lives with his beautiful wife and kids in Kaysville, UT. He works as a creative director for mediaRif.com, a digital agency. Craig writes novels, short fiction, and screenplays.

As a musician, he has released several records with friends under the band names, Rustmonster and The Big Sky Country Boys. Craig also records solo work. He has released two records under his own name, Zombie Sing-a-long, and a sequel album, *Zombie Sing-a-long: Whistler and the Children (Part 1).*

As a filmmaker, Craig has written and directed many short films. His feature, entitled *Gabriella Sleeps*, is in post-production. He writes and directs many commercials and industrial videos as part of his profession.

Aside from writing, Craig enjoys playing in the Rocky Mountains, rock climbing, and canyoneering.

Club PK2

Justin Swapp

"Club PK2" is an indirect sequel to the "The Transition" in *The Crimson Pact Volume 1* and "The Merging" in *The Crimson Pact Volume 2,* both by Justin Swapp.

I can't say I was surprised by what I saw when I arrived at Spain's infamous Club PK2, or Pe-Ca-Dos, as the locals called it. Animated neon obscenities reflected off the sweaty, bald heads of a pair of Hispanic heavies barring the entrance. As I approached, they flashed their guns as if to say that this was the Latino district: their nightclub, their way, or you get the trunk monkey.

For an average guy, these two totem poles would make a formidable challenge, but I'd spent the last two years undercover earning the boss' trust—no small feat. A neatly organized row of men somewhere would tell you how hard that was to do, if they could still breathe.

Not just anyone gained admission to PK2. They scanned my wrist for the boss's signature implant. When I came up active in the system, they let me pass, but not without strange looks.

Clearly my non-designer jeans and brown leather jacket classified me as under-dressed. I didn't care. I wasn't there for the nightclub.

I had come for The Pit.

Ten floors under the noise, beneath all the bumping and grinding, the lighting was poor and the company stiff. But the air was still muggy and smelled of sweat and blood.

My kind of place.

My name's Tray; close friends call me Tres. I'm only the third life bound to my Codex, a cubed device my kind uses to store and protect our prior lives, pass on our former intelligences.

Before me, Zeffer had possessed the Codex, and Darius before him. They chronicled our kind's efforts and progress; protected it with their lives. I've often wondered why Zeffer chose me, but long suspected the reason.

I see things.

Things that zero-day tech implants can't even expose. It's not something I asked for, it's just always been there.

I stepped off the elevator into a large industrial space. Exposed ventilation ducts and piping hung overhead, and the brick walls gave way to various rooms shooting off the basement floor. I navigated my way past all the starched suits and docile dresses, gravitating from the caviar to the games. Cards or dice drew some, while the rest were attracted to the bloodier entertainment: animal fights and human death matches. For the private rooms, if you carried a fat wad of cash and a fistful of roofies, you were golden.

Someone had tampered with the boss' beloved sport, his moneymaker, and he'd assigned me to handle it. When the odds became predictable, the bets followed. The boss' little underground economy was pinched and the flow of money lopsided. The boss didn't let anything get in the way of his business.

João had won six matches in a row—unheard of. Several years ago, the prior record holder reached just three, before the champ ended up in a trash receptacle somewhere outside the city. The boss's handiwork, no doubt.

The win streak had broken the game. "You need circulation," the boss had said, "an ecosystem of up-and-comers, and . . . hope.

The crowd needs to root for an underdog. If you lose that, you lose the audience that gives its money away."

I was starting at zero. No suspects, no leads. My gut was to put the tampering on João. He stood the most to gain: the money, women, and fame. Maybe he used illegal weapons, cheated somehow. I'd corner him in the dressing room after the fight, if I found no other alternatives. Just me, him, and Mr. Knuckle Dusters.

I pushed my way through the hosts and waitresses working the floor and surveyed the room. Rich men and women, either drunk or almost there. No one stood out. I took a deep breath, not even sure what I was looking for.

I followed the flow of traffic to the other side of the facility until I reached the gathering for the fight. A beautiful woman dressed in a black business suit stood in the center of the death match ring and cleared her throat into a microphone.

"Good evening and welcome to this evening's main attraction. Tonight, our first contestant needs no introduction. Boasting the club's longest standing win streak at 6, local legend, João."

A fairly scrawny Brazilian stepped forward and mechanically raised a hand. *This was the killer?*

The crowd awakened with a few cheers and catcalls, but soon glazed over. The predictability of the fights had sapped its enthusiasm.

Next to me, I nudged a woman yelling louder than most.

"This'll be some fight, huh?"

"Won't last five minutes."

"Why's that?"

"Easiest bet in town. I've made thousands on João. Some claimed he was just good with a Taser or a Katana, but, even after they revoked the weapons, he still won."

Apparently, they'd changed the rules several times during João's reign. In The Pit, they secretly called it *Streak Management*. First, they'd banned the heavier weapons and took down the protective ring around the combatants. I guess the boss wanted the matches to be more intimate, draw the crowd in again. When the streak continued, they'd prohibited the tech too: stim packs, augmentations, and implants. He still won. Now, they reduced the fights to hand-to-hand combat. The fan feeling on this seemed mixed, but I saw a certain nobility in it.

"Seeking the PK2 title is accomplished mixed martial arts master, Ruby Marsh," the announcer continued, indicating a gorgeous but deadly looking redhead on the challenger's side. I recognized her from TV. She wore red compression shorts and a matching sports bra with the emblem of her own popular brand. The announcer paused to listen carefully to her earpiece. "For those of you who haven't placed your wagers yet, I've just been informed that bets against João are double the payout—tonight only."

The desperation was palpable, which only put more pressure on me. I examined the crowd again, beginning to doubt my instincts. Anyone could benefit from João's success. An accomplice? Perhaps someone weakened João's opponents. Maybe an undetectable poison of some type, or a paralyzing agent. Someone was trying to control the money and the odds. I had to figure this out. The boss didn't give second chances.

While the fighters warmed up, I managed a few more conversations. All I got was a bunch of drunk clichés and a few more gray hairs on my head. An old Asian man thought João was Bruce Lee reincarnate, one-inch punch and all. He swore João sent opponents flying across the room with his bare hands. A lady in an elegant mauve gown said he had mastered the kiss of death, and even went so far as to call him the Angel of Death. Yet another gushed about seeing João perform the five-point palm exploding heart technique, like he was some Kill Bill groupie.

Maybe it was kissing his victims that turned off the less enthusiastic crowd. I allowed myself a smirk. João was Brazilian after all.

As I drew closer to the ring, I encountered a powerful, pungent odor that stopped me cold. The Codex burned in my palm.

I tried, but couldn't place it. My mind flashed, and I could feel Zeffer's memory reaching out to my consciousness. A foreboding nostalgia overcame me, but nothing more. We had smelled it before . . . a very long time ago.

"Remember," the announcer addressed the combatants, "there are no rules. No one will save you. I'll call the fight once one of you can no longer continue. You're at the mercy of your opponent." She overdramatized, but it was truth. Someone would die here tonight, and I had to let it happen as I had many nights before. The thought sickened me.

"Begin!"

Both fighters nodded. Neither said a word. They just stared into each other's cold eyes and rotated around the ring. At first, they loosened up and then gradually circled closer, feinting and lunging at each other, each waiting for the other to make a mistake.

Ruby was the first to connect, bringing the surprised crowd to life. And it wasn't just any hit either. After a well-timed jab feint, Ruby launched a stiff kick down on João's right leg, which buckled like a cheap tent, and sent him crashing to the floor. João let out a terrible cry and cradled his injured leg.

Even if João overcame the pain of what was surely a fractured tibia, he would only be able to fight from the ground and poorly at best. The odds, fickle that they are, now turned against him. His streak would come to an embarrassing end, and my work would be done. Perhaps his winning streak was just that, after all.

An adrenaline-filled Ruby danced triumphantly around João, relishing the moment, raising her arms to rally the crowd.

Everyone was stunned.

"Wanna change your bets now, don'tcha?" Ruby yelled. "I'll make you all lose your precious money. I got your double payouts hanging." She grabbed herself and spit at the crowd.

Ruby turned back to the soon-to-be-former-champion whom she knelt behind, and grabbed his head with both arms. João winced in pain and clearly had no strength, no concentration to put up any real resistance.

João felt behind his fractured leg, and lifted his blood-stained hand, gaping at it in what would be one of the last moments of his life. Then he began mindlessly wiping the blood off onto his chest.

João's face reddened under the increased pressure of Ruby's hold.

Ruby shook her head and smiled. "Overpromise and under deliver, I guess." She looked down at João and took a deep breath, winding up for the fatal snap.

A dreadful crack silenced the room.

I considered Ruby and tried to reconcile João's neck with the sound we heard.

His leg, once bent unnaturally and hemorrhaging through his white pants, had snapped back into place, and, when it did, João smiled too, despite the obvious pressure Ruby added around his neck.

Judging by Ruby's face, she too realized something was wrong.

João's eyes opened wide, and strangely, his olive complexion returned to his face.

I blinked hard and searched for evidence of anyone else in the crowd witnessing the same thing I was.

Just smiles and blank stares. Their bets were still in play.

In a flash, João's pupils overflowed with dark red until the color bled over evenly into the whites of his eyes and then escaped as strands under his skin, streaking down his neck and toward his chest like dead veins, to where he had wiped the blood from his leg. Oddly, the smear now appeared to form something... a sigil?

My palm throbbed and began to burn. I made a fist as a strange sensation crawled up my arm and overpowered my mind. I blinked, and, for a moment, I was outside, in another city, in another time. I was panting... I had been running... from what? That smell... Suddenly, a sharp pain raked across my back and I fled again. I felt at my back and examined my blood-soaked hands, but they were not my pallid hands, but rather leathery, African hands, though the blood was just as red.

Zeffer, one of my former lives, and the second owner of this Codex, was communicating with me. He was being hunted. No... *we* were.

Unsettled, I blinked profusely, becoming mindful of the present again as João jerked his head violently, despite Ruby's hold on him. His neck clearly cracked this time, but his smile only grew wider as he turned to face Ruby.

The disbelief on Ruby's face gave way to sheer horror as João finished rotating, twisting his body back into alignment with his head again, snapping his neck into place.

"Holy—" Ruby released João and leapt back as if she had discovered a scorpion scuttling up her arm.

The audience gasped and opened up, distancing itself as João shot to his feet, no sign of duress or injury hobbling him.

I tried to move in, but the attendees were too enthralled and held their ground.

Without hesitation, João lunged at Ruby, throwing powerful blows with his fists and deadly strikes with his feet. Ruby blocked or dodged most of them initially, but the speed and power João employed lived up to its reputation this time. It was something special. No, it was unworldly.

"Stop!" Ruby collapsed under João's barrage of blows, shielding her face with her arm. Her voice cracked. "Don't kill me."

"But you won't draw them in while you're alive," João said, in a voice not entirely human. He laughed loudly and then, like a viper, thrust his hand through her guard and clasped her throat. In one fatal movement, he slammed her into the ground, squeezing incessantly. "You're nothing but bait."

Ruby coughed a throaty gurgle as blood began spilling over the corner of her mouth.

João kneeled over her, scowling condescendingly at Ruby as she writhed on the ground, repeatedly reaching weakly for something that was not there. He paused as she coughed blood over her chin, and then he gently kissed her cheek. His eyes flashed, and, in the same silent moment, Ruby's eyes began to roll into the back of her head.

The horde of people hailed the kiss, knowing it all too well. Hearing the mob, seemingly for the first time, João stood and ran a hand through his hair. He looked dazed, unsure of his whereabouts. The announcer lifted João's other wrist. "Give it up for João, still your champion, now extending his streak to 7! Is there no one who can beat him?"

I cursed something foul. This guy was dialing up the other side, and it clearly had gotten out of hand. My two jobs rarely clashed, but, when they did, this one took priority.

I rushed the ring, jostling through the oblivious people celebrating their winnings. Clearly they hadn't seen the same fight I had. I must have looked suspicious, because someone grabbed my arm and spun me around. In the same motion, I buried my elbow into the bridge of a bouncer's nose. He collapsed, cupping his face in his hands.

"I challenge João!" Breaking through the mob, I stepped into the bloodstained ring and over Ruby's lifeless body.

The bouncer started to rise up after me, but, when he heard me speak, he smirked, satisfied his problem would correct itself.

"Look, man, I'm finished for tonight," João said, giving me a once-over. He still looked a little cross-eyed, and I thought if I was quick, I could take him. "Work something out with my agent."

"We'll work it out now, you and I, one way or another." I might blow my cover, but so be it. I lowered my voice. "What did you summon?"

"What?"

"The sigil," I said, pointing at his bloody shirt.

"That?" João asked incredulously. "It's for luck, and so far it's worked every time."

"Where did you learn it?"

"From an old shop in a pueblo outside the city. What's it to you?"

"Come on. I just watched you put yourself through the spin cycle and come out on top of the wash. Now tell me where you really got that funky juju."

He shook his head, but I wasn't having it.

I dusted the rust off my right cross and caught him square between his cheekbone and his brain. He dropped straight to the floor.

I was in the wrong business.

"What's your problem?" João asked, taking a deep breath and pushing himself slowly on to one knee. He rested a moment and then rubbed his head. "Are you some kind of sick cult fan or what?"

"You wish. The fact that I'm here means you have much bigger problems than doped up, stalking groupies. Now, call your demon."

The crowd began to chant. *Fight, fight, fight.*

With the crowd behind him, João began to gather himself, and he looked pissed. He was poised to pounce on me and run my confidence through a cheese grater. When I thought he would lunge at me, a look of terror flashed over his face and he fell back down, retreating on all fours.

I spun around to a pale-faced Ruby, her head slightly off kilter and her deep eyes shrouded in a red, hateful shadow.

"Finally," she said, smiling, showing her new, incisor-like teeth, "after seven deaths." It took a deep breath with its nose, relishing the smell. "It's you. I've tracked you, hunted your former lives for so, so long. Seven lives are a small price to pay for but one of yours."

Instinctively, my searing palm opened and discharged my Codex; a small, organometallic cube which safeguarded the history of my people and our advancement against the demons. Each face of the cube bore tokens and symbols that, when activated, deployed anti-demon technologies. The markings began to glow, sensing something nearby that needed a cage.

The Codex grew wider, and the demon-Ruby's phantom eyes zeroed in. "And you've bought my prize."

She swiped at the Codex, but I rolled back on the ground and rebounded back on my feet. The crowd's cheers turned into wails as everyone scrambled for the elevator, trampling over one another. João too.

"Remember me?"

The demon-Ruby dipped her shoulders and then shook violently, jerking taller with each passing moment. A sinister, black goo wormed its way from behind her neck and squirmed into her mouth; it slapped around her arms and down her legs, finally eclipsing her body. Her hair sloughed off to the ground, and in an instant, her fingers dripped longer, like melting wax. Suction cups formed on their ends.

"Remember the taste of death? I took one of your former lives, but not before I could find that."

Her eyes dilated on the Codex.

"Well, here it is, you slimy leech," I said as I pressed a token on the Codex and opened a radiant beam of green light and directed it at the foul beast, blinding it temporarily.

It blared a nerve-shattering shriek. Dizziness overcame me, and my legs lost their strength.

Before I connected with the ground, darkness filled the room. The demon reached for me, latching onto my chest with its suckers, and jerked me its way.

I dug my heels in and tried to pull away as the demon reeled me in, but to no avail. My responsibility was to guard our secrets, and it was all I could do to hold onto the Codex. I could never allow it to slip from my possession, especially to a demon, no matter the cost.

"I will not be denied my bounty . . . my freedom again."

I fumbled the Codex for one of the unused symbols. "But you've just been freed."

"From the ties that bind me . . . " It slurped, and heaved harder. "Bind me to my master's domain, you fool. This world."

Finally, I gained a firm hold of the Codex and thumbed the first token I could reach, activating the device, then I rolled it onto the floor.

A pillar of green light burst through the symbol, then the panel I'd activated. Piercing the darkness, the Codex's radiance opened up until it made contact with the demon.

The suckers loosened and fell from my chest, and I gasped.

Fleeing into the corner of the room, the demon screeched. "You will be mine!"

The glow continued to fill the room, finally overtaking the beast. This time, upon contact, the light seized the monster and began to wrench the goo from Ruby's flesh. An invisible force, the light lurched the demon toward the hungry Codex, despite its attempts to resist.

"No!" It grabbed at the ground, its tentacles popping as its suckers lost effect. "I must sacrifice your life . . . " As the demon's shroud peeled away, Ruby's human remains fell to the ground. The spirit-like essence of the demon lifted up, captured in the beam of light. "End your bloodline . . . " The demon began to dissolve, unraveling into particles, merging with the light. "Destroy your Codex," it said as the last of the demon's hideous face faded into oblivion.

The steaming Codex rattled on the ground as the panel closed, sealing the green light again and veiling the imprisoned demon in a solemn darkness forever.

The boss won't return my calls, so, my information comes from the street. To my knowledge, João never did lose a match, but I heard he died anyway. Someone said they found him outside the city, in a trash receptacle.

About the Author

Justin was born with an active imagination on a U.S. naval base in Spain, but has spent most of his life in the shadows of the Rocky Mountains of Utah. He is bilingual and has lived all over the world. He has four children, two boys and two girls, and one wife. He doesn't have any pets that he's aware of, but his children have been known to hide things under his bed.

In his free time Justin loves to read, write, and play games. He enjoys his close friends and loves to make people laugh. To learn more about Justin, or his work, you can visit him at www.justinswapp.com.

Justin is the author of *The Magic Shop*. He has also been published in several anthologies, including *The Crimson Pact* (Volumes 1, 2, and 5), *The Memory Eater*, and *Short Sips: Coffee House Flash Fiction Collection 2*.

The Fourth Sign

Lawrence C. Connolly

The mansion occupied the top floors of an upscale high-rise a few blocks from the Indiana Convention Center, just west of Monument Circle. If it had had windows, I could have seen the State House from the foyer on the twenty-fourth floor. Instead, when the elevator doors opened, I found myself in a stone lobby with arched pillars and bas-relief walls.

She was there, waiting. High cheeks, strong eyes, short hair glowing like flame in the indirect light. She had the kind of build that seemed tailored for her pinstriped suit and sensible shoes. "I'm Devin Cloister," she said, offering her hand. No rings or bracelets, not even a watch, just smooth skin and a firm handshake. "Call me Dev."

I took her hand and introduced myself. Not that it was necessary. She had been expecting me, after all, and there was my nametag from the convention still hanging from a strap around my neck. I fumbled with it now, slipping it into my jacket pocket. Overly self-conscious? Perhaps, but I prefer keeping my name tucked away. I do a lot of ghost writing, work-for-hire under house names. You've probably read me without knowing. In any event, you're reading me now.

She slipped her arm into mine, led me from the elevator toward a vaulted corridor. "Were my directions clear?"

"Perfect."

"And the doorman? He didn't give you any trouble?"

"Not once I showed him your card."

Tapestries lined the hall. I glanced at one of them, took it for an antique, then looked again.

"You like it?" she said.

I slowed my pace. The woven pattern showed a band of warriors massed shoulder-to-shoulder, swords raised, breastplates flashing in a blood-red dawn (or was it evening?). There was nothing authentically medieval about the figures. Their hair, swords, and pectorals all suggested a modern aesthetic, the kind of buff-and-chrome imagery you might see on a RPG manual or epic fantasy paperback. If Frank Frazetta or Boris Vallejo had designed medieval wall hangings, this would have been the result.

"I took it for an antique."

"It is. Fifteenth century. From Drakenwall."

"Where's that?"

"Seahearn Province, north of Spar."

"I've never heard of those places."

"No." She picked up her pace. "I don't suppose you have."

We entered a large sitting room, vast and windowless, smelling of wood and wealth. A leather-topped table sat near a marble fireplace and a large medieval clock. Chairs stood at either end: one at a place set with three face-down cards, a manila envelope, and a thumb drive; the other with a single-serving bottle and a crystal tumbler, both on stone coasters. She gestured toward the place set with the bottle, inviting me to sit. "We'll get right to it, if you don't mind."

The bottle had just been opened, the cap placed on a linen square, bubbles rising behind an etched label reading: *Millennial Ice.*

"From east of Toba," she said. "Harvested from glaciers. Each sip is ten thousand years old, incredibly pure."

"Toba?"

"North of Vancouver."

At last, a place I knew.

"Help yourself. It must have been a hot walk from the convention. What is it out there? Ninety degrees?"

"At least." The bottle felt like it had come straight from the fridge—or maybe a short stay in the freezer. The tumbler misted as I poured.

"The best water in the world," she said.

I drank. It tasted cold. Nothing else. Like sipping a cloud.

"See what I mean?"

I drained the glass.

"Now to business." She opened the envelope, took out a contract and a check. "I want to commission a work for an anthology that goes to press first thing in the morning."

"Tight deadline."

"The editor has agreed to hold space for a 3,000 word-narrative written under the name specified in the contract. The title's also specified."

"'The Fourth Sign'?"

"You approve?"

"What if I come up with something better?"

"I'm sure you could if you had to. But it's the title I gave him. The contents page has been announced. The title's nonnegotiable."

I held the check to the light. "This is generous."

"Because I expect you to deliver."

"By tomorrow?"

"No later than 8:00 a.m. The editor's email is in the contract."

I recognized his name. He was also a writer, well regarded. I was pretty sure I'd seen his name on the list of convention authors. "So you're working as his contributions editor?"

"No. He's contracted all the other stories on his own. Yours is the only one I'm involved with. I've paid him to hold the space for us."

"And what's in this for you?"

"We'll get to that."

I flipped to the contract's second page. "What's this about imbedded JPGs?"

"Images. I need you to include them in the manuscript, exact positioning to be determined by the narrative."

"Illustrations?"

"Not exactly. Not illustrations, per se. We'll get to that too. Would you like to hear about the story?"

I set the check and contract back on the table. "That's what I'm here for."

"It's about an investor who starts her career dabbling in antiques. Medieval and Renaissance art. Tapestries, furniture, the interiors of old-world churches."

I considered the room we were sitting in: vaulted coffers, parquet floor, stone walls pitted with age—all of it looking as if it had been assembled from pieces of a medieval castle, carefully fitted to the steel and concrete of the building's interior.

"Get the picture?" she said.

"I think so. One good trade leads to another, and pretty soon she has money to burn. Private elevator, Gothic veneer, designer water."

"That's my story."

"But where's the conflict? Does she become overconfident, make ruinous purchases until she finds herself on the brink of foreclosure?"

"No. More interesting than that." She folded her hands near the three facedown cards. "The conflict begins the day they contact her."

"They?"

"This part is difficult to explain. I'll need to simplify it a bit, and you might have to streamline it still more for the story. But basically she has a series of dreams that seem to be messages from another sphere, dreams that make clear that her good fortune is being guided by forces beyond our world. They have made her wealthy beyond belief, and now they want her to pay them back by opening a portal, a means by which they might pass from their sphere to ours."

"And what are these forces exactly?"

"That's difficult to answer."

"Why?"

"Because we haven't got a name for them. Some might call them demons. Others might call them gods, but they're something else entirely, entities totally beyond our ken."

"And their reason for coming here?"

"That depends on point of view, doesn't it? I'm sure they would say it's to save us from the tyrannies that plague our world . . . set us free, in a way."

"So this woman . . . she's a lot like you?"

"You could say that."

"And the portal? What about that? Some kind of secret gate?" I looked around the room, considered the possibilities. "An antique door or cabinet? Something that opens into another realm. Step through it a certain way and—"

"No. Not like that."

"All right." That device had already been done, Philip Jose Farmer by way of Sinclair Lewis.

"Don't think of the portal as a physical thing." She opened her hands, fingers spayed against the facedown cards. "Think William Blake, Aldous Huxley, Jim Morrison—"

"The Doors of Perception?"

"Exactly. The mind as portal. But not just one mind. It needs to be a group of them. Not too many. Too many will distort the passageway, twist it, make it unnavigable. A coven of twelve might open such a door by holding a séance. But a crowd? A mob? That's a different kind of group mind. The scale for this sort of thing has got to be small, fewer than a hundred."

"So the woman in my story? She forms a coven, holds a séance?"

"Unfortunately, no. See, when the portal opens, it can't be confined to a small room."

"And the key that opens it?"

"Right." She picked up one of the cards. "That's where the signs come in. Each one contains a piece of the key. Together, they complete it and open the portal."

"So it's a quest story. The protagonist searches the world for the pieces of the key, finds them one by one."

"Perhaps." She kept the back of the card toward me. "The way you tell it is up to you. The important thing is that you include the images. Would you like to see the first?"

"I'm all eyes."

She turned the card over, and in that moment I wondered if her proposition might be an elaborate joke. I expected something profound, startling. What I got was:

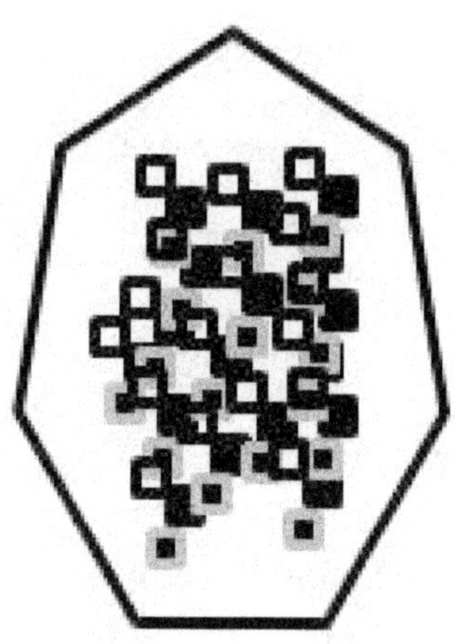

I leaned closer, thinking I must be missing something, hoping that maybe the odd little squares might realign into some recognizable shape, as in those Magic-Eye stereograms that were all the rage a decade ago. But there was no such revelation. "You're kidding, right?"

"Why?"

"What is it?"

"The first sign."

"I think I'm missing something."

"No." She returned the card to the table, facedown beside the others. "Remember, it's only a piece of the overall design."

"Where did you get it?"

"A graphics studio put it together, based on my notes and sketches. Took some time to get it right."

I imagined the studio rep sitting where I was now, torn between accepting the money and the prospect of working with a woman who was obviously as crazy as she was rich.

"And your notes and sketches? Where did they come from?"

"Dreams. Same place I learned about the source of my incredible luck."

"*Your* luck. So you *are* the woman in the story?"

"No. She needs to be a character. Based on me perhaps, but fictionalize, romanticized."

"An incognito warrior queen? Flaming hair and a pin-striped suit?"

"Whatever serves the story."

"Perhaps I could write what we're doing right now: about coming here, meeting you, looking at the cards. All fictionalized, of course. Names and addresses changed to protect the innocent."

"I'll trust your judgment in those areas. Shall I show you the second sign?"

"Bring it on."

She flipped the card, held it high.

Again, I leaned forward, partly to let her know I was playing along, but also hoping that this time the image might come alive, reveal its meaning.

Alas, it didn't happen. If anything, it seemed less inspired that the first:

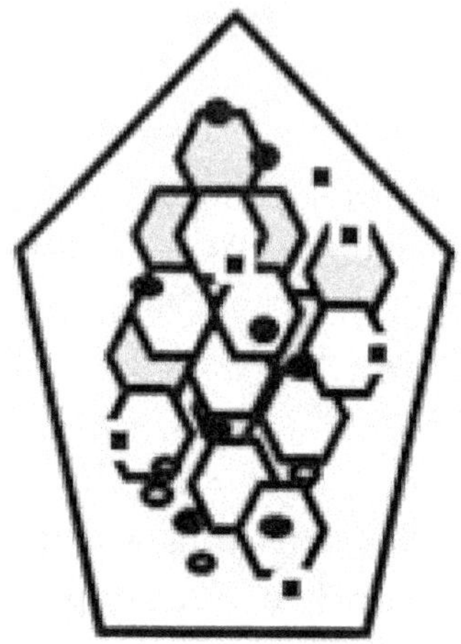

I glanced at her, caught her looking at the clock beside the fireplace.

"The card," she said. "Look at the card, not me."

I did as she said, realizing now that she was timing my exposure to the pattern. But to what end? The design remained as it had upon first impression: bland, random, meaningless. And yet, when I thought about the function such a pattern might serve in a work of fiction—

"All right. I think I've got it."

She put the card down.

"In the story, these patterns work like scan codes. Like those QR boxes or UPC bars that transfer data to handheld devices. You know, those little squares people zap with their smartphones."

"You think that analogy works?"

"Maybe. Think about it. Phones don't *consciously* process data. They simply scan patterns, receive the codes, store them in memory."

"That's pretty good, actually. I like that."

"But in this story, each image is only a piece of something bigger, like program bits that lie dormant until the entire code is in place."

"Sounds like a workable premise." She picked up the third card. "Ready for the last one?"

"Show me."

This time I knew what to expect. No instant revelation. No mind-altering epiphany. Just another random design:

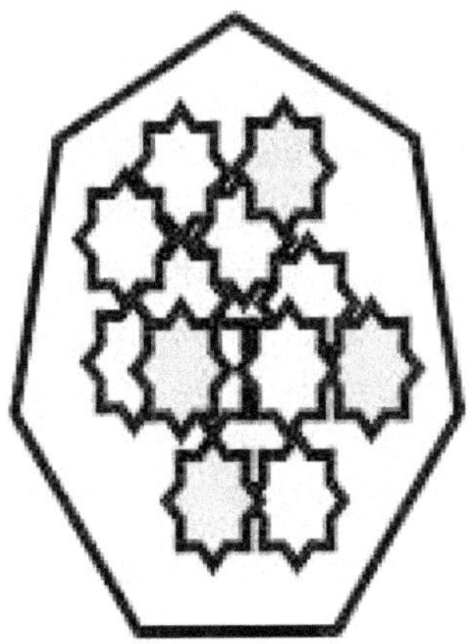

Again, she timed me, watching the clock. Then she put the card down. "Any questions?"

"Just the obvious. Where's the *fourth* one?"

"You tell me. You're writing the story. How're you going to spin it?"

I considered. "We've talked about covens, a small group of minds uniting for a common task. But the discovery of the fourth sign can't happen in a single room. You said that, right?"

"It can't happen in a *small* room. The host minds that engage it need to be dispersed, but preferably within a single, indoor space."

"A very big room for a very large portal?" I looked around at her widely spaced walls, cathedral ceilings. "A room like this, perhaps?"

"No. Bigger than this . . . and more populated. It needs to be a public space . . . say 500,000 square feet . . . with easy access to the city."

"Good luck finding—" It came to me then, the perfect location, less than three blocks away.

"Putting it together?"

"I think so. You said the book goes to press tomorrow? Print on demand?"

"Yes. It's an indie enterprise."

"If they pay the rush charges, waive the proof, they can have a hundred copies on hand by when? End of business Friday?"

"Just in time for an evening book launch."

"All right. So the book debuts at the convention. The editor is there, and some of the writers, and . . . say . . . twenty or thirty friends and fans."

"Twenty or thirty?"

"That's a decent number for a book party."

"There's over 40,000 people at the convention."

"But it's primarily a gaming convention. Literary fantasy is a small contingent within—"

"But the story's about cards," she said. "You talked about centering the story on our conversation, the two of us sitting in this room and pondering a set of mysterious cards. Gamers like cards, right? We could play that up. Do some flash promotion. Get maybe fifty people at the party."

"Or we could advertise free drinks. A bathtub of microbrews usually does the trick."

"I'll talk to the editor. Fifty people. It should be between fifty and a hundred people—to improve our odds."

"All right. So the books are there. A few of the authors read from their stories, say about five minutes each, little teasers to get people to pick up the books. Not everyone buys, of course, but most people take a look, flip through the pages, stop at the JPGs. But will they look at them long enough?"

"Some of them will."

"And the fourth sign?" I still hadn't answered that question, but it was coming together now. "The next day's Saturday. The biggest day of the convention. Most of the people from the book launch will be there, and that's when copies of the fourth sign start showing up, scattered on the freebie stands, food court tables, bathroom sinks—everywhere. Most people pass them off as some kind of scattershot advertising, but a few people—our coven of readers—they know what they are. They pick them up, look at them—"

"Bingo!"

"The gate opens."

She grinned. "They appear, beings from another sphere, and at first no one suspects a thing. It's just a show, right? But they keep coming, emerging from everywhere, spilling into the streets, invading the city! Or—something like that." She picked up the thumb drive. "The JPGs are here. Each is numbered." She passed it to me, then took a pen from her jacket pocket, clicked it, set it atop the contract. "Do we have a deal?"

About the Author

Lawrence C. Connolly's books include the novels *Veins* (2008) and *Vipers* (2010), which together form the first two books of the *Veins Cycle*. *Vortex*, the third book in the series, is due in 2013. His collections, which include *Visions* (2009), *This Way to Egress* (2010), and *Voices* (2011), collect all of his stories from *Amazing Stories*, *Cemetery Dance*, *The Magazine of Fantasy & Science Fiction*, *Twilight Zone*, and *Year's Best Horror*. *Voices* was nominated for the Bram Stoker Award, Superior Achievement in a Fiction Collection. He teaches writing at Sewickley Academy and serves twice a year as a residency writer at Seton Hill University's graduate program in Writing Popular Fiction.

A Simple Plan

Kelly Swails

"A Simple Plan" is the direct sequel to "Frankie's Girl" in *The Crimson Pact Volume 1*, "Hunters Incorporated" in *The Crimson Pact Volume 2*, "David in Disguise" in *The Crimson Pact Volume 3*, and "Family Reunion" in *The Crimson Pact Volume 4*, all by Kelly Swails.

Humans are stupid creatures. They are obstinate while being easily manipulated; selfish yet giving; observant but blind to what's around them. They're easy to control, which is why it's easy to create discord in this finite existence they call life.

And yet I'm writing this in case I fail.

I'm not planning to fail. I'm sure my brothers didn't either; death isn't something my kind thinks about. But they were defeated and so I can't afford arrogance. Underestimating the enemy is a mistake so many of my brethren have made.

One assumed his mistress would keep his true identity a secret and died in the ensuing altercation.

One failed to realize that employing a team of private detectives didn't exempt him from investigation.

Another failed to realize a woman with a camera can be much more than she appears.

A fourth thought that three women armed with nothing but knowledge and a curio full of relics was no match for him.

To further add insult to injury, all of these failures resulted from the same bloodline. A strong-willed woman who stared death in the face and won, begat another woman who did the same, and so on. Over the last sixty-plus years our paths have intertwined to the point of inevitability.

The last brother to fall used a woman to exact revenge on her family. He seduced her and took her virginity before he fell, leaving behind a small gift she doesn't yet realize she has. A baby. Half human. Half not.

A baby that, if everything goes well, will be fully under my control.

Unlike my brothers, I am taking a subtle approach. She will need to see a doctor to confirm her condition, and that doctor will be me. She will be vulnerable and scared and in need of a confidant; I will be that person. She will be distrustful of men; I will be a woman. I will outline her options while using my innate persuasive techniques to keep her from aborting her fetus. I will care for her during her pregnancy and deliver her baby. And at the crucial moment—after I cut the umbilical cord but before the baby takes her first breath—I will pass some of my lifeforce onto her. Just a little. Just enough to tip the balance.

She'll be *almost* half-human.

She will be the manipulator, not the manipulated. She will be so charmingly selfish people will think she's generous. Emotions or willful ignorance will not color her observations.

She will be my student.

And she will rule us all.

About the Author

Kelly Swails is an author and editor who lives in Illinois. Her work has appeared in several anthologies including *The Crimson Pact* series and *Boondocks Fantasy*. You can find her online at kellyswails.com. To her knowledge she's never crossed paths with a demon.

Someday

Donald J. Bingle

Someday they would come for him.

Someday, most likely in the pre-dawn darkness, with the planets still asserting their predominance over the night sky, the SWAT team's special personnel carrier would roll into the parking lot outside of his apartment, signaled only by the uncertain barking of a lone dog.

Someday, there would be a knock at the door . . . or perhaps no knock, just a crash as the wood of his double-dead-bolted door was kicked from its reinforced frame. In either case, a bevy of armored men in protective helmets would rush through to seize him or kill him, just as they always did from time immemorial when dealing with a perceived enemy of the state. History repeating itself, reflecting the same power structure, the same defenses, the same misunderstanding.

They would have no real information about him from the neighbors, but they would think they did. A "loner" the neighbors would say. "Quiet." "Keeps to himself." "Pays his rent on time." "Doesn't play loud music; doesn't cause any trouble." But the indicators would be there, the formulas fulfilled. "Never has any friends over." "Never seen him with a girl." "Wears the same plain clothes all the time." "Mutters to himself... averts his eyes... seems pre-occupied." And then there would be the clincher: "Gets a lot of deliveries . . . I think one was from a gun company."

He understood their concern, more than they could ever know. He knew the signs; he saw them everywhere. He understood the Beast; he battled with it every day, for more days than anyone could ever imagine.

And when that someday came and the men at arms flowed through the portal to his lonely life, to search for and seize his weapons of mass destruction, organized neatly within his bedroom closet . . . to search for and seize him, organized neatly within his mission parameters . . . he would have a choice to make.

Suicide by cop, an unloaded AK-47 in his hand—truly the weapon from hell—his angry mouth shouting words calculated to invite response, to confirm their fears, to justify their banishment of guilt in their own dark nights, later, alone. Or, to calmly raise his hands and lay down on the floor, compliant to their commands, ignoring the rough treatment when cuffed and frisked and wrenched to his feet and out the door to a locked van with wire windows and delivered to a locked room with bars on the door. There to sit alone with his thoughts 'til eternity or 'til death did he part, abandoning his quest in active form . . . left only to promote it through words, not deeds.

Either way, the evidence of his life's effort would come out. The mysterious background, or lack thereof. The many aliases. The moves from town to town to town. The outbursts at his various menial jobs, which had led, as he knew they would, to counseling and the vivid scenes of destruction and mayhem and retribution described in such sessions, not so confidential now, now that something had happened. Dark, violent talk flowed as easy as venom in the group sessions, where others of his kind, of his mindset, of his diagnosis, rambled their ravings, (whatever the current flavor of their disease: paranoid, schizophrenic, dissociative disorder, sociopath, psychotic personality, bi-polar with sadistic tendencies, angry loser, or all of the above).

And there would be sadly shaken heads and pity and tsk-tsking at the limited funding for mental health care, until the public read about the weapons, the frequent attendance at gun shows, the applications for carry and conceal permits, the subscriptions to magazines about guns and ammo, the militia pamphlets, and the survivalist literature. Then, there would be anger and dismissal and petitions for new laws to go with the old laws and he would be forgotten, dead or alive, though he knew most would prefer dead, even though he had never gone on a bullet-spewing spree, rampaging through a workplace or mall or theatre or . . . *shudder* . . . school.

Even though he had killed no one . . .

. . . as far as they knew.

He was on a mission, answering to no one in this world.

He knew. He knew the demons were powerful and insidious and dangerous . . . and most of all, evil. He knew they were clever, but miserly in using their power, and so liked to control the weak-minded and lonely. So he set it upon himself to appear weak-minded and lonely. Not to entrap a demon by himself becoming a target—not only do too few demons exist here for those odds to ever be in such favor, but he believed his strength of mind and purpose would overcome any such attempt. No, he pretended to become a misguided, violent soul to search for the many similarly-described others who were the demons' potential targets and hope to divide the sheep from the goats . . . individuals who were simply ill or poorly adjusted to the rigors of life versus those truly evil, truly possessed by the demons of the vale.

But the weak-minded and lonely, especially those demon-possessed, are difficult to find. The lonely do not, by definition, make friends easily. And those whose actions are controlled by sinister forces would never do so. Best to act like them, to seem to become one of them, to shun everyone and everything normal and beautiful, and to go to the dismal places where the weak-minded who demonstrate anger-control issues and dark thoughts are herded into the mental health care bureaucracy. In group sessions, he could meet and surreptitiously evaluate many, many loners and psychopaths with dark dementia, listen to their outbursts, and hear their fantasies . . . hear their plans.

Pride being a sin, demons are filled with it, and often boast of their dreams, so long as they believe no one of power is within hearing or caring.

And, of course, in addition to "knowing his enemy," he needed to know their capabilities, their access to weapons and tactics, their facilitators in the unknowing, unseeing world of normality. So he went to the gun shows and learned not only what and how much could be bought and how easy to buy it, but who else was buying, was boasting of the size and nature of their equipment, literally or figuratively. And he read the ramblings of the frightened and belligerent, where it is easy for evil to dwell hidden.

And every so often, his mission would bear fruit. He would find a man—they were almost always men, as demons prefer the power and strength and aggression arising from testosterone—with a gun or twenty and ample ammo and a plan. A sick, twisted, deadly plan. When he was sure, really sure, that the man couldn't be helped *because a demon was in control*, he would act. He would eliminate the threat by eliminating the source of the threat.

A mugging gone bad here, a faulty furnace there, a slip and fall in the tub. He tried not to repeat the methods too often. Although he killed serially, he wasn't a serial killer—he didn't get off on the killing or the method. He simply had a job to do, to rid the world of evil.

Suicides were the easiest to stage. When you were lonely and unliked, no one pressed to investigate your demise if the cause was obvious and easily understood by those not afflicted. Suffocation, car exhaust, and pills were all easier than a faked accident or even a staged hanging. All were less messy than slit wrists (parallel, not cross-ways, as all the serious wannabe suicides would know), even when done in a warm bath. Worse yet, a gun to the mouth (the suicide connoisseur's choice, as there is less chance of missing because of a sudden reflex at the last instant, than with a gun to the temple). But over time, he'd used them all.

Whatever the method of demise, parents, co-workers, and neighbors could go on with their lives, secretly relieved and no longer frightened that one day something worse . . . much, much worse—would happen. A rampage, a murder, a spree, mass fatalities. If such a terrible thing occurred, if innocent life was lost, they would have the guilt of not having done something else, something more, to prevent it—that is, if they lived to see the aftermath. The guilt of being secretly relieved at their son's or co-worker's or neighbor's death was far, far less with an accidental death . . . or even suicide.

And when the deed was done, when the quest notched up another sad victory, he would move on to another town, another apartment, another job, another group, another friendless existence.

And he would begin again.

Until that day, that someday, when he would be mistaken for the real enemy, for the mad dog loose in the school yard. When that someday came, he would be put down. Or, if not, caged for a lonely, miserable life . . . not really so different from the one he had now.

About the Author

Donald J. Bingle—Writer on Demand TM—is the author of three novels and about forty pieces of short fiction in the science fiction, fantasy, horror, thriller, steampunk, romance, and comedy genres. He is a member of the Horror Writers Association. Fans of this story may also like his other *Crimson Pact* tales, as well as "Gentlemanly Horrors of Mine Alone," and his collections: *Tales of Humorous Horror, Grim, Fair e-Tales,* and *Tales of an Altered Past Powered by Romance, Horror, and Steam.*

Hearts in Reverse

Usman T. Malik

The Diary of Sara Tilling, June 1st, '84 AA

It was Easter and the Easter bunny never came. I got mad, and then Daddy got mad at me when I said to go hunt the bunny down.

He looks at me all strange.

"What, Daddy?" I say.

He says nothing, just looks at me. There are circles under his eyes, deep as mud holes.

I start getting worried. "I'm sorry, Daddy. Mama said the same thing the other day. Said to shoot all fairy creatures down if they come live next door." I cross my arms. "What good is an Easter Bunny if he can't do what he supposed to do?"

"You'd kill a bunny cuz it didn't bring you gifts? Where's your heart, child?" His voice is deep and rumbly, like my belly is sometimes when I get hungry.

Is Daddy mad at me, or hungry?

Daddy looks at the sky. At the rug-shaped redness in the middle of it, where the boys whisper the demons came from. "Times. What times—" Daddy says and stops. He sighs and his eyelids go all pink and moist like he was biting onions or peppers.

"Believe it or not, Sara, there was a blue sky once," he says. "We messed it up."

"No, we didn't. Mommy says it's all God's fault. He did it."

"God had nothing to do with it. God didn't scorch the—" Daddy stops. His eyes are angry.

Already I'm regretting what I said. "Daddy, I'm sorry. Please don't be mad."

I want to run to him and hug his legs, but I'm afraid he'll shove me away.

I couldn't take my Daddy shoving me away.

"Once," Daddy says, "people believed in God. They believed in goodness and love and being neighborly—no matter who their neighbor was. Not like your Mama. . . . " He stops and looks at me. "I'm not mad," he says, quiet now so I can hear my heart beating in my ears. "I just love you too much to raise you wrong."

He reaches out and messes up my hair.

"Hey," I say, but I'm happy now that he's happy, and I let him.

"Just remember, baby," Daddy lifts a yellow pollen puff from my head and blows it away, "they're as scared as we are."

I wanna ask him how they got here, why they came if they're so scared, but Daddy's walking to his rocker and his pipe's coming out his pocket, so I say nothing.

The rug-like red hole in the sky seems to wink at me.

Johnny came to her in the middle of the night.

"Mama, my nose won't stop running."

Sara yawned and stretched her arms to wake herself up. The latest issue of the Journal of Herpetology had just arrived and she'd been reading it way past her bedtime. Now she got up, blew Johnny's nose, and checked his temperature.

Normal.

Probably picked up a daycare virus from one of the demon children, probably one of those little fucking werewolf creatures. She'd seen two of them at the daycare. God, she hated those filthy beasts with their matted hair and sharp teeth; she was always afraid they'd nick Johnny playfully and she'd have to get him tetanus shots or something.

Johnny coughed.

Sara poured a tablespoonful of anti-allergy and cough syrup, gave him the meds, and sent him back to bed.

By the next morning, his sinuses were dripping blood.

Two days later, after the terrifying, nightmarish ER visit, they were at his pediatrician's. Johnny's face was still splotched but at least he wasn't purple or gasping from the airway spasm anymore.

Johnny's pediatrician scratched his nose. "Isn't this the sixth time in the last few months he's had this happen?"

Yes, Dr. Useless, Sara wanted to scream. Instead she nodded, feeling a mother's ceaseless fear turn inside her.

Dr. Useless rubbed his nose again. A pimple on it popped and leaked pus. He wiped it with the back of his hand absently.

"We better get him to ENT," he said.

And that was how they discovered Johnny's disease.

The Diary of Sara Tilling, May 2nd, '89 AA

Father said he was going to Church, and Mother got mad. She called him a book-thumping asshole. She said, "What kind of God—"

Father went down the steps, his wide-brim hat secreting his eyes. I still remember that check-blue shirttail, all mussed up, curling in his butt crack, and how the fucking steps creaked with his fucking weight.

He never came back.

Johnny's ear and sinus canals are lined with dyssynchronous cilia, said the specialists.

What does that mean?

It means most of the hair in his airways doesn't do its job of repelling environmental toxins, chemicals, germs. It makes Johnny prone to getting infections of all sorts, and no medicines will fix this. Part of Kartagener syndrome . . .

They used strange names, but, really, words were useless attempts at control. Control, Sara knew, was impossible in such a situation. She was stunned. Her baby. Her only son . . .

How could they miss this, she screamed at the rapid succession of specialists that followed and explained to her all the things wrong with her son. In this day and age, how could they miss this when he was born?

They all shook their helpless heads. This sort of thing sometimes happened. Did the boy's father perhaps—

No! The boy's father was perfectly healthy when he fucked me and abandoned me. His cock was long and graceful, and it worked. It gave me Johnny, didn't it?

Their silent faces confirmed what the internet research had already told her: Johnny would never have a child. Johnny's seed would be barren.

Mrs . . . Mrs . . .

Ms. Tilling.

Of course, Ms. Tilling. But even more concerning than impotence is Johnny's heart. It's on the wrong side of his chest.

What?

This sort of problem comes up with other situs inversus issues, which of course means Johnny's bowels and bladder and other organs might also . . .

Their words were drifting; they came from some place far away. Sara couldn't understand anything beyond, *His heart is on the wrong side of his chest.*

Dextrocardia.

Johnny had dextrocardia. Sometimes mutant lizards had dextrocardia along with limb anomalies. Their hearts ended up on the right side of the chest during the embryologic stages.

Usually such creatures didn't last very long.

The last of her will broken, Sara broke down and sobbed. Johnny, her Johnny, was very sick. That was what they were all saying. Johnny would not get better.

Johnny was as good as dead.

She could see his death in their eyes, in the neutrality of their expressions. Unable to meet their wretched gaze, Sara took her son home.

Within three months, Johnny began to lose his hearing.

When she opened the door, one of the werewolf parents was standing there.

A seven-foot-tall hulking creature with forearms the size of spades, one wrist splashed with a Girls will be Girls tattoo and a pink Nine West bag slung over her shoulder. She—it—stepped back when Sara emerged from the doorway.

Sara didn't recognize it. She blocked the door with her body. "Yes?"

"Hi, my name is Genevieve." The werewolf nervously ran a violet fingernail the size of a butter knife down the guardrail. The screech made Sara grit her teeth. "Umm . . . Toby, my son, told me Johnny hasn't been coming to school?"

"Yes." Sara's grip tightened on the doorknob. "What do you guys care?"

"Toby does. Johnny and he are pretty good friends. Didn't you know?"

Sara didn't know. She guessed Johnny had deemed it wise not to tell her. Her sentiment on the matter was quite clear. "What do you want?"

The werewolf pulled back its snout; the pink of its nostrils reminded Sara of gutted snakes. The creature—Sara refused to call it Genevieve—sniffed. "I'm sorry for inconveniencing you, but… okay, look—" it withdrew a card from that awful, glitzy-pink bag, "here's a card for a specialist."

"What?"

The creature met Sara's eyes with its own rheumy ones. "We all heard of Johnny's ailment."

A migraine began to pulse at the base of Sara's neck. "Don't speak of my son," she said softly. "He will be fine."

"Sure." The werewolf tapped its claws on the handbag, its animal face a grotesque horror mask. "Sure." Gently, it tucked the card between the bars of the guardrail and turned to go.

"Hi," Johnny said.

He stood in the doorway with the miniature oxygen tank nudging his ankles. The nasal cannula snaked into his nostrils caked with blood from the rush of dry air.

Johnny smiled at the stranger. "Hi, Mrs. G."

"Hi, Love," the werewolf said, and Sara saw, to her horror, that a blood drop was welling up in the corner of its left eye. It bulged and broke surface and tracked down the werewolf's cheek. "How you holding up, little man?"

"Pretty good. How's Toby? He still carrying that dumb Dracula action figure around?"

Genevieve smiled, revealing sharp teeth. "Sure." Both its eyes were webbed with blood by now. It glanced at Sara and raised a hand. "Well, you take care now, little man. And take care of your mom too."

"Yup. Tell Toby hi."

The werewolf left, its paws clattering on the pavement all the way to the corner of the street. Sara turned to Johnny, to rebuke him, but his eyes stopped her. Old eyes, clouded with something that rained inward.

"Honey—" She didn't know what to say. His lips were trembling.

Johnny never cried, he never broke down; she was the one who did it for both of them.

"Baby, you okay?" She stepped close to him, tried to pull him to her, but he ducked and whirled.

Sara watched her son run inside the house, his oxygen tank bouncing after him like a dead puppy.

Listlessly, she turned and plucked the werewolf's card from the cold metallic grip of the guardrail.

The man who opened the door was not a man.

"Yes?" it said, and the horns in its neck bristled.

Sara wanted to turn away in disgust. These things—how they revolted her.

"Mr. Coldman," she managed to say.

"Is not seeing anyone these days." Behind the thick, telescoped lenses, the creature's eyes were yellow. Little black grains swirled inside them.

Filled with contempt. For me.

"Tell him I have something he needs." She tossed her head back defiantly. The darkness past the demon's feet heaved. Something crackled, and the tall demon tensed.

"If you so wish," it murmured. She knew it was not talking to her. Its sickly eyes found hers. "Flesh is flesh."

With that nonsensical statement, it turned and ducked into the darkness.

Sara followed.

The thing curled up in the hospital bed, surrounded by a filter mesh, was huge and ponderous. Its raw-red abdomen was bloated tumorously, the navel popped out. Its swollen, mottled tail lifted and fell with an audible *thunk*!

When Sara gasped, the dying demon stirred.

"Hello." Its voice was old and whispery. It made her think of winter wind soughing through gnarled branches. It made the hair on the back of her neck prickle.

"Hello," she said. There was a dead alligator in a corner, and the fly cloud above it buzzed angrily. "You must be—"

"Coldman. Agares Coldman." Its lips were covered with sores. When it turned on its side, the fluid shifted in its belly, blanching the flesh to a dusky gray. "You know who I am."

It wasn't a question. She nodded anyway.

"Why are you here?"

A raven the size of a tomcat flapped its wings behind the filter mesh, and the stench of its wings was a mix of death and rot, and this time. This damn, useless, miserable Anno Apocalypsi time.

She hated herself for doing this. For being here. All her life she'd hated them. All her life she'd despised their presence, their irreverent encroachment upon humanity.

"Encroachment?" the demon said, and Sara started and fell back a step. His jaundiced eyes were fixed upon hers. "Our presence. This encroachment upon your life. Are you for fucking real?"

It could read minds. How could've she forgotten? She stared at it, her heart hammering.

"Your life. Your sweet, wonderful life," it murmured. "Do you know who I really am?"

Her fingers fought each other. "Yes."

"No, you don't." When its lips parted, the raven cawed and pecked at its teeth. The bird cocked its head, and Sara saw a thick white worm struggling in its sharp beak. The raven jerked its head up, and the worm disappeared.

Bile rose in Sara's throat. She swallowed it back.

"You dumb, useless, meat-creatures," said the demon in its gurgling voice. "You fucked up and now you blame us. The hole that you ripped in the cosmic curtain with your quantum fuckery—we didn't do it. You did."

The room's temperature dropped. The flies rose and swarmed toward the bed. They hovered around the filter like airborne shadows.

"You brought us here. You metamorphosed us. You bound us with your physical laws. We're all mortal and dying because of *you*." Its eyes were filled with contempt. "And then you have the audacity to blame it on us."

"I never said—" began Sara.

"Silence, you wretch. You meat-bag. You father-fucked piece of shit!"

Sara recoiled. The raven screeched, a sound like a saw cutting through metal, and the fly swarm exploded against the ceiling, buzzing and thumping across the surface.

"Ooh, I know all about you. I can lick your brain," the creature said, and glee and something like longing crept into its voice. It tried to raise itself up, but failed and slumped back. A sore popped on its leg and splashed pinkish liquid against the filter. "Your dysfunctional human family—"

Sara clenched her fists. "Stop. I get it. I get the message."

"Daddy left you because he wanted to fuck you."

"Please," she whispered, feeling her vision throb with her pulse. Nauseous horror surged inside her. "Please don't. I'm sorry. I'm sorry I ever said anything. I—"

"Mommy screwed with your head," it crooned, "because she was terrified, and what's a little family terror shared between mommy and her princess?" It groaned and then giggled, the incongruous sounds grating across Sara's mind. "And your son—"

"Don't talk about him. Don't you dare—"

"Will be dead soon. Dead flesh. Meat suit to be hung in a deep, dark grave."

"Nooo!" Sara screamed. All the pent-up anger—the frustration and rage and those nights she'd spent waking up every five minutes, running to Johnny's room, pressing her tremulous palm against his chest to see if his betraying, awful heart was still beating, even if on the wrong side—bubbled inside her. The terrified hope that his traitorous body would give him enough time for her to find a cure.

The demon laughed.

She lunged at the filter mesh around him, trying to tear it down, but suddenly the raven was in her face, beating its frantic wings darkly, and the fly swarm was in her eyes, in her pores, her mouth, her nostrils, and the world was a hissing, buzzing, shifting black curtain through which movement was impossible.

Sara sobbed and fell to her knees. "Stop. Please. I'm sorry. Agares. Mr. Coldman. . . . "

The curtain peeled away from her, and the raven cawed and slid off. It fluttered its wings and perched on the creature's belly, its ebony eyes fixed on her, unblinking.

"Mr. Coldman, huh?" The demon hawked and gurgled spit in its mouth and spat it sideways into an aluminum basin crawling with maggots. "Not a filthy, encroaching creature anymore? Where's your gumption, girl? Where's the hatred?"

"I'm sorry," she said between sobs and lowered her head. "Oh, Johnny, I'm so sorry."

Silence. Sara's vision rippled with moisture. The world was dark in front of her, a filmy layer of filth made from death and disease and inevitable choices. Such a world, such a terrible, terrible world, where not even your thoughts were safe anymore.

When the demon spoke, his voice was soft. "Oh, shove your sorries where the fucking sun don't shine. You were here to make a deal. So say it."

"My soul," she said and wiped her eyes with the back of her hands. "I will sell my soul for my son's life."

"Lady, do I look like I deal in souls? I deal in tangible things and your soul is as useless to me as an angel's fart." He coughed and wiped his lips. "Demon magic is limited in this place. The rip in the curtain tore down our space-time too. It's your fucking physics. Won't let me do much." He lay a taloned hand on his belly and tapped it thoughtfully. "Although, I suppose there is something you could give me. . . . " His eyes glowed, and the tapping of his spoon-shaped talons sped up.

"What? What?" She got up and stared at him. "Anything. Anything for my son's life."

He cocked a fungoid talon at his face. "I'm dying here. Heart failure. Can you imagine?" He laughed. The sound throbbed in her head. "A demon who needs a heart. Angels wept." His eyes fixed on hers. "And you have a great, broken, full-of-anguish heart. I can see it beat full of life in your eyes."

She swept the mess of hair back from her eyes. It was wet with tears. "What are you talking about?"

"I will buy your heart in exchange for your son's life."

She looked at him, shocked and uneasy. "My heart?"

"I need your damn human heart, as much as it pains me to admit it." He leaned on his hands and forced himself so he could squat on the bed. He was smaller and older than she had first thought. White strands of hair spilled from behind his ear and nuzzled the sores on his cheeks. "Question is, are you willing to give it up?"

He was as stricken with age as anyone she knew. Everyone had heard they aged, but she'd never truly believed it until she met Mr. Coldman and saw his condition. The realization made something stir and turn inside her mind. These creatures got diseases and died too.

They needed too.

"Anything for my son," she said quietly. Her voice was warbled in her head. "But how do I know you will keep your promise? You said your magic was useless here."

"Yes, but not in the dimension where my kind was created." The demon winced and leaned forward. "In the darkness of human dreams lies the opening to the wonderland where I was made. Think of it as Hell. The act of transferring a human heart into a demon's body should create an unnatural bridge, which will gouge open that hole. Beyond that hole is my Other."

"Your Other?"

"The Other me. The Hell-me, if you will. My doppelganger." He licked his dry lips. "The source of demon magic."

"And I shall die once you have my heart." Her hands twisted inside each other. "How does it work?"

"A transplant of course. How else?"

"A transplant? An organ transplant."

"An organ transplant."

"Jesus Christ." Her eyes widened.

The demon winced and melodramatically clapped its hands over its ears.

"No surgeon will do it," she said.

"Yes, they will." The demon sighed. "Of course, they will. I may be a dying, spatially transplanted demon myself, but I still have that kind of pull." He winked at her. "In fact I'll do you one better. I'll have my doctor friends give you a new heart. Freshly grown, genetically."

She bit her lips. "If you could do that, why not get one for yourself?"

"Again, it's a matter of physics and physiognomy. Demon DNA doesn't work well with human machinery and chemicals. The process was tried and was an utter failure."

"What then if your body rejects my heart?" She knew a few things after speaking to specialists about the process, but Johnny wasn't a transplant candidate. "Human medicines might not work."

"Who said anything about human medicine?"

She fell silent. The raven—that had been until now quietly hopping back and forth on the bed—rose and landed atop the dead alligator. It began to nibble at the gator's eyes.

The demon's eyes never left hers. "My doctors will get you a fresh heart, but understand that it will die too. They don't know why, but genetically grown hearts fail after a few years."

She smiled bitterly. "A few years. Dead after a few years." She closed her own eyes and rubbed them. Red spots danced in the black behind her eyelids.

"Better than none," he said. "Better than a dead son, don't you agree?"

She had nothing to say to that. Instead she said, "Your word. That my son will be cured."

"My word. Once that bridge between the worlds is formed, the doppleganger's magic will work. It will fix your son." His eyes were clear and frosty, but they didn't lie. "My word."

Sara nodded. Suddenly, she was tired and weak and sleepy. The world was a wreck, but who cared? Her son, her Johnny, was all that mattered.

In the Year of the Apocalypse '97, Sara Tilling gave her heart to a demon.

So there they lay side by side on the twin operating room table, his sulfurous eyes emitting an oxidative mist from the Propofol the doctors administered. Sara lay there and watched his skin change color rapidly as the drugs hit the inhuman receptors in his tissues, triggering biochemical reactions unprecedented in the annals of medicine.

Xenotransplant is the term, Sara thought. Inter-species transplant.

It made her close her eyes and giggle even before they shot her full of anesthetic.

In her ether dream, she was a microbe drifting through the darkness of herself. Surrounded by a living capsule lined with arms like rockets, she blasted through alien corridors that quivered gelatinously at her passage.

Johnny. She was looking for Johnny.

Instead she found the demon's magic.

The doppleganger was a tall, gangly man with reptilian eyes. The skin above his spotless black suit was pebbled in pink and palomino unlike the hellish-red all the outdated demonology books described, and, when the light in the grotto changed, a third eye flickered in the center of his forehead.

Parietal eye, Sara's herpetology-filled brain whispered. A light-sensitive parietal eye.

The better to pin you with, my dear.

"Hello," she said to the demon-double, and the capsule around her bubbled and melted away.

"Hi." His slitted pupils expanded and something dark passed behind them.

Sara perched on a rock outcropping in the middle of the pulsating grotto.

The demon in black sat on his haunches and stared at her. She noticed how his ankles became mottled and turned dusky when he crouched.

Lack of oxygen. A failing heart. Just like her son. Her head spun from the strangeness of it.

"You found me," Mr. Coldman's Other said.

Sara lowered her head and gripped the edge of the rock. It squirmed in her hands. "I came to help my son."

The Other grinned. His gums were studded with razors. "I know what you want." He watched her through slitted pupils.

Sara smiled. On her face the smile felt like a wound. "Save my son."

She had fancied death to be a black-and-white film, surreal with a chiaroscuric beauty that would delineate the soulful absence of life.

Instead, death was boring. And slow.

The doctors swam around her, their limbs elongated and seeming to float. The ET tube rippled in her mouth as an OR technician ambled to the Harvest Cube and drew out the shelf with the freshly grown heart.

The pulseless heart was deep red, nearly purplish.

Lack of Oxygen, Sara thought in death.

They placed it inside her carefully cultivated chest and sewed her back up.

"Good as new," said one of the doctors. She remembered his voice. He was the one who had ordered the junior resident to start cracking her ribs.

Sara felt the new heart beat in her chest for the first time; and at once death sped up. Loud voices, a phantom surf (my pulse!), the rising mounds on her skin as blood rushed through her pores. She tried to wake up, but the drugs wouldn't let her.

The last thing she saw before a second, more vibrant, darkness took her was the rapidly hitching vertical slits of the demon's eyes, as it gazed at her.

This world. We are all hearts in reverse here, someone said.

Then she was out.

The Diary of Sara Tilling, August 5th, '97 AA.

About a month ago, I gave my heart to a dying demon.

The xenotransplant was a success. The doctors are still marveling at the wonder of it. The World Now Development Reconstitution (WONDER) Project is furiously writing it up. Interspecies dialogue teams are exuberant.

Most of all—and perhaps oddly—I'm happy and at peace in a long, long time. I don't know why.

Maybe it has to do with Johnny.

Two days after the transplant, Johnny woke up with up another nosebleed.

I freaked out and rushed him to his pediatrician, and Dr. Useless scratched his pimply nose again and murmured that something was different this time. Something didn't quite make sense. He ran a series of tests and X-rays, and told me in a dazed voice that the original diagnosis must have been wrong.

Johnny's heart is in the center of his chest and a little to the left.

Exactly where it is supposed to be.

The doctor also did an audiogram on Johnny and said his hearing had improved miraculously. He cannot explain it. But I can.

Seems like Agares kept his promise.

Maybe demon magic can cross over sometimes.

Maybe, my peace has to do with knowing that I will be dead soon. Some of us do better once we know death is certain and our time is short.

I had a dream last night about my mother. It was about the day she secretly went to Church and I followed her.

In my dream, Mama's dress was black and rippled in the night wind. She was lighting candles on the altar, as I watched from the shadows of the vestibule across the neverending pews. The candle flames blazed as tears ran down her cheeks, and even though I couldn't hear her murmurs from afar, I remember dream-thinking she was saying, I come, O Lord, I come.

I remember turning and running madly down the steps of the church that hunched in the darkness like a beast. Such a hypocrite, my mother. All her life, she hated God and this curse He's unleashed on the world.

But then a realization hit me in the dream, and I staggered and stopped.

Maybe she didn't hate God. Maybe she just hated Father.

I don't know if that's true, why it would be. But if it is, it makes me sad.

I'm sad for these people, my people. I'm sad for these strangers that have been forced into our midst. They never asked for it. Did they? Something snapped in the universe, and plop! Here they are.

Giving my heart up has changed me, I guess.

Sometimes I wish I had grace in my heart before I gave it up. If I did, maybe some of it would have passed into the demon's soul.

A demon graced?

Maybe that's exactly how it should be.

She took Johnny to the park.

It was a new spring day and the blossoms were furrowed. Dandelion heads floated drunkenly around them as they settled under an old elm and watched the squirrels chatter. Beautiful day. Beautiful world.

Sara's heart skipped a beat as if in reminder. She glanced down. Already, she could see the absence of skin dimples in her ankles from fluid retention.

Death in waiting.

"Beautiful day, isn't it?" She smiled at her son, who would grow tall and handsome and healthy and live a long, long life. "Such a bright, beautiful day."

Johnny kicked the elm trunk hard and ran around it. "Ring-around a rosie, a pocket full of posies," sang Johnny softly, his face full of tree shadow. "Ashes! Ashes! We all fall down."

Sara's smile faltered, but for only a moment. Perhaps, that was what it was.

Ashes. Ashes. We all fall down.

But she had no cause to complain. Not now when Johnny was with her, alive and healthy. Not when he wasn't a mutant lizard anymore.

About the Author

Usman T. Malik is a Pakistani writer who lives in Florida with his family. He is a member of the Codex Writers Group, Florida Writers Association, and the Horror Writers Association.

To date, he has sold speculative works to *Daily Science Fiction, Crimson Pact Volume 4, Space and Time, Papercuts, Deep Magic,* and *Eye to the Telescope*. He was accepted to the 2012 Clarion West Speculative Fiction Writing Workshop, where he was under the tutelage of *New York Times*' bestselling authors and editors, including Neil Gaiman and Ellen Datlow.

In his spare time, he dreams. Of ghazals, chai, and a better world for all. You can find him at www.usmantm.blogspot.com, or follow him on twitter@usmantm.

White Dog, Black Demon

Danielle DeLisle

The massive white dog, once called Angel by a loving family, watched the demon's saliva drip onto the teenager's shoulder. The creature clung to the alley wall several inches above the boy's head. Long wormy tendrils fanned out and waved mere centimeters from pockmarked skin. Gluttonous folds formed a mouth at the larger end of the slug-shaped body.

Angel's nose prickled with the odor of anger, sharp like tin cans, coming from the teenager. Satisfaction, bitter like dandelions, oozed from the demon in steady, slow waves.

"I'm not coming back," the teenager said into the phone. "I don't give a shit what he says. I'm changing my name, too. You can call me Nobody, because that's all I've ever been to you."

A tendril dipped into the boy's ear.

"Fuck off," Nobody shouted. "You can't protect me. You won't even help yourself."

The demon retracted the tendril and shivered in pleasure. Tears leaked from Nobody's eyes as he leaned near the entrance to the alley. Three steps and he would be on the bright, busy street beyond, but he kept his arms tucked against his body and curled into himself.

One baseball-sized paw followed another and Angel limped further into the alley from the other side. The years gripped hard on his stocky frame when he moved. In his younger days, he once fought two demons, alone. Other dogs like him, blessed by the light, cowered at such odds, and the pain was the price he paid for such acts. He wove his way around a beat up couch and broken microwave. His nose caught the scents of urine and feces. Thick, white fur and bushy curled tail picked up small sticks and other debris as he continued forward.

Three of the demon's tendrils broke off from feeding and reached out for Angel. Bone spikes protruded from the ends, dripping black liquid, the deadliest weapon it possessed, but only used for the last strike. Angel stopped several feet from Nobody. He'd never seen such a large demon. It was as large as Angel himself.

His paw twitched and hit a can, which rolled across the cracked asphalt and clanked out into the street. Nobody saw Angel and pressed his back against the wall. The phone hit the pavement and cracked. The nauseating, rotten smell of fear hit Angel's nose. Nobody reminded him of his family, the one he had lost long ago. The memory of his boy picking him up and nuzzling his puppy fur comforted him before sleep, which often came in moldy boxes or dirty doorways. So young then, he hadn't known how to fight, and he couldn't protect his family when the demon came for the father.

Nobody wore clothes the same style as his boy used to wear, and underneath the emotional scents a familiar youngness and boyness that tripped all the instincts in Angel's old bones filled his muzzle. Nobody smelled like he hadn't been helped in a long time. Angel couldn't save his family that night, but maybe he could save this boy. The humans didn't know the danger. They couldn't see. He tipped his head and a paw came up slowly to bat the air between them.

help you please

Nobody backed away from him. He tripped over a box and fell to the ground. Angel took two more steps and put his paw in the air again.

help you please

The fear scent diminished. Nobody distanced himself from

the wall slightly. Sometimes, if the demon was small, cutting off the fear and anger was enough to make it go away. Angel could track it down and kill it once Nobody was safe. His ears remained perked, however—because of the very largeness of it he couldn't be sure. A whine of worry escaped him.

The demon, for its part, decided not to take the interruption lying down. Its body stretched until it loomed and curled over Nobody like a large black wave. Death closed in. Once a woman had pulled out her own intestines with a fork. Another woman had pulled out her fingernails and then swallowed bleach. It took four dogs, one of whom died, to put that demon down, and this one was much bigger than that. Angel still bore the scars underneath his fur.

danger danger

He barked the warning, and the sound bounced off the walls of the alley. The wave of black continued to swell. Angel growled and leaped for the closest tendril. He felt the squishy sensation of the demon in his mouth. He shook his head and bit deeper. Black liquid seeped into his mouth from the wound. Tendrils whipped his back, trying to get him to release.

The boy shouted, and the sounds of running reached his ears. The demon formed so fast Angel lost his hold. He yelped as he fell to the ground. It was, quick for something so large. His large brown eyes glimpsed the last bit of the tail that disappeared around the corner after Nobody. He'd underestimated how long the boy had been under its influence. Once upon a time he would have known. He would have realized. The demon had to kill the Nobody now. Their relationship was so intertwined one or the other had to die.

Angel chose Nobody, and he pushed himself on arthritic legs around the corner.

come help demon help

He called to the dogs in the area. The barking and the biting hadn't worked. He could usually immobilize the stronger demons when he bit into them, at least enough so he could take them out permanently. This one was strong.

People crowded the street, but they gave him a wide berth when he passed. Angel smelled meat, bone, gas, flowers, anxiety, and fear. His legs protested the activity pressed upon them with throbbing pain. Ahead of him Nobody wove through the crowd shouting. The demon followed, braiding in and out between people's feet, trailing its tendrils along the ground. It was nipping at Nobody's heels.

Nobody tried to go into the shops, but the few dogs in barking distance blocked his way. They needed someplace open, and free of most humans. It would be easier to take it down. The three dogs worked together to help Angel funnel Nobody and the demon down the street until they were torn away from their duty by their humans. Only three other dogs managed to help in the street, and they wouldn't be able to help in the fight ahead. They guarded families—some dogs chose that life—but after his family died he had chosen a different life.

sorry sorry, they cried to him.

His body wanted to rest. His head longed to slip between his paws and dream, but the cries of the boy in front of him spurred him on. He took to a run with long strides, and his fur flowed back in the wind. His ears streaming out behind him while the pain in his legs grew and his tongue lolled out of his mouth in effort.

In front of them a park came into view. Pine trees lined the entrance like sentinels throwing their strong scent into the air. Nobody ran through the gate, and the demon followed. Angel barked. Returning barks reached his ears, eager, but too few.

ready we are ready

Nobody, the demon, and Angel raced down the dirt path surrounded by grass. A cobblestone circle surrounded by grass and a large statue of a woman provided the best place for a last stand he could hope for under the circumstances.

The boy reached the statue and leaned on the base for support. Sweat matted his hair to his head and his shirt clung to his skin. The demon, just behind him, reached out a large vine-like tendril for the human's leg—the rotten smell from it masking everything else. Angel focused on it and growled, trying to divert attention. The whip marks from the alley burned on his fur.

Nobody shuddered, and the fear emanating off him reeked of fish. He tried to gain purchase on the base of the statue. He reached as high as he could to pull himself up, making loud gasping sounds while he did so.

Angel pushed off with his long legs to launch himself toward the demon. He heard the cries from Nobody, who had managed to climb on top of the statue's base. His focus on the enemy in front of him, he barely looked up to note Nobody's position. Images of his boy being ripped apart by kitchen knives spurred him on—the two-pound puppy he'd once been whimpering in the corner.

The demon lashed into him with its tentacles. They burned and stung, but he kept his bite on it. He hit the ground after one whip across the muzzle, but he recovered quickly, teeth bared, pain momentarily forgotten.

Down the path two dogs came from two different directions, running toward him—a small terrier and a bulky bulldog. They joined Angel and lunged at the Demon with their teeth and paws without hesitation. They tore into it. Their noses buried deep in its viscous skin.

The leashes they'd torn from their owner's hands flew behind them like kite tails. Their paws and muzzles came back covered in black.

The demon spread out like jam and whipped tendrils out, hitting the terrier, who yelped and then went back on the attack.

Angel didn't stop despite the blood clotting on his fur from its tendrils. He used his weight to pin the demon. It rolled and threw the dogs off. The dogs took turns, hoping to weaken it. The bulldog stepped back, panted, and went for more.

His bites came slower and slower and the demon, discounting a few bad bites, did not show signs of stopping. Three dogs would usually slow one down by now. Not only did it not appear badly injured, but its mass had attached itself to the base of the statue where Nobody screamed for help.

Tendrils reached out from the slug-body. The spines protruding and ready to strike the death move.

He got his feet under himself and clambered toward the demon. He shoved his body between the demon and Nobody.

The spine struck home in his side.

He landed on the pavement hard—the poison already taking his body. Angel rose and opened his jaws as wide as he could. He bit down into the black mass as hard as his ebbing body would allow. His blood and bite had hurt the demon, true, but now he used it all. The spike continued to puncture his side. Good. He got stung again and again. Angel's blood and saliva co-mingling with the demon's in ever increasing amounts. Weakening, killing both.

Angel held on.

He watched his last attack make it succumb to death. It flattened out and was no more.

One paw rested across his nose, and his liquid brown eyes stared straight ahead at the dead creature. His fur rustled in the light wind. He heard the sounds of sneakers coming up behind him. He smelled boyness, and then felt a hand on his fur.

The two dogs who'd helped him brave the beast paused a moment in respect and turned to leave, back to their humans.

rest hunter, their goodbye, passed on as they disappeared over the hill.

"I don't know what. . . . " Nobody said "You saved me somehow from something, didn't you? I saw. . . . "

A small sound of movement and Nobody knelt in front of him. Angel watched tears leak out of his eyes for the second time in so short a meeting. Nobody's other hand stroked Angel's large head. He whined in pleasure, even as the pain continued to slip through his body like wires. His breath coming harder. He vaguely remembered this . . . petting.

"Thank you," Nobody whispered.

He let his tongue search out Nobody's hand and licked it gently.

welcome

Then he was being lifted clumsily in what, somewhere in the back of his brain, he knew as a loving embrace. He sighed. Now, he could rest. He could rest. Rest.

About the Author

Danielle DeLisle is a writer of fantasy, science fiction, and horror currently living in Texas. Originally from Vermont, she has lived in many places around the United States seeking out the stories she wants to write. She also considers herself a teacher and actress, both of which help her in her writing life in surprising ways. She is a graduate of the Odyssey Writing Workshop, Franklin Pierce University, and Southeastern Louisiana University. She once spent a summer as an autopsy assistant, which helped her to decide she should follow her dreams. This story is dedicated to Jack, who will always be Angel.

The Last Reprise

Patrick M. Tracy and Dale McClenning

The street fair was filled with colors, with people sitting on the sunlit grass. A small child ran by Kasim with a purple and yellow streamer trailing in his wake, shouting for his companion, an older brother by their similar looks, to chase him. The brother complied, soon catching the boy and pulling him, giggling, into his arms. College students with the day free to idle played Frisbee near the small lake at the park's center.

It presented an idyllic scene, like an outwardly-perfect apple with a worm twisting at its core. Kasim looked down at his hands, wondering if they'd be able to do what was needed. After the breaking, his fingers had been held together with surgical pins and immobilized for months. He had to swallow hard as the images came back to him, the sounds of his own screams as Modo-Hesh brought a bar of bronze down on every finger echoed in his head.

"I enjoy these things," Modo-Hesh had rasped, his voice all rusted nails and sharp rock. "For you, this is the fate worse than death. What is more cruel than to live broken, to live as a shadow, having once had power? Now, it will ache you in spirit, like the pain of a deposed king in exile. I take away what makes you." And the bronze bar descended again and again. Perhaps, inside Kasim's mind, the bar would always be falling, destroying what he was.

He would never be the violinist he'd once been. Even after almost two years of painful recovery, the damage Moto-Hesh had done to him still caused his hand to ache and burn whenever he tried to play. He was not destroyed, not quite. His neck would not bow that easily. He would try, at least once more.

Tanya and Julien had been with him for a time, for the worst of the healing. Alone, he would have succumbed, and all the demon had whispered into him would have come true. His friends had done what they could to rebuild his shattered spirit while the doctors tended to his hands. They'd done what they could, taken care of him when there was nothing but pain pills between the screaming. But things grew worse, and they'd been needed elsewhere. The nature of the world was changing, regardless of how they struggled against it. The Artists had a measure of power, but they were being overwhelmed. The evil in the world proliferated far faster than the beauty they were able to create.

"What we are must suffice, for we can be little else," he told himself.

A passing young woman with curly brown hair overheard and veered toward him as a ship might with no one at the helm. "Yeah, man. I've been trying to tell myself that, but, like, the words wouldn't cooperate. What's that from?"

Kasim made himself smile. He didn't remember the last time he'd done so. The expression felt foreign, though it had once come as naturally as breathing. "An old book. You would not know it."

The woman stood close to him as he unpacked his violin. He took the soft cotton wrapping from around it, lifted it slowly to his shoulder and plucked the strings to check for his tuning. The woman smelled like marijuana and sex. She breathed avidly, watching him as he tuned up. Her mouth was just slightly open. He could see a stud in her tongue. Celine had worn one like that. Kasim banished the thought, looking away, squeezing his eyes shut for a moment.

"Violins are wicked," the woman said.

Kasim imagined her usage of the word meant something on the order of "very interesting," but he chose to take her literally, if only out of some sense of spite. Thinking about Celine, about all the others who were no longer present on the world, enriching it with their songs, stories, music, and art, brought a cruel edge to the surface of his soul. His mouth quirked, and he answered.

"They can be, yes. This one, however, has been consecrated with the blood of the unavenged. It is a talisman and a relic. In the right hands, it has more power than any sword, any gun. I pray to the brave forebears that I prove equal to the task I face today. I hope to honor this blessed instrument one last time."

The young woman, who wore a T-shirt manufactured to appear older than it was and artfully ripped blue jeans, took a step back. "That's intense."

Kasim didn't bother to answer, instead bringing the bow across the strings to create a strange and haunting chord. Using wide vibrato, he let the tone bleed on between sharp and flat. A small child nearby began to fuss and cry at the tone. Kasim continued into the piece, which was filled with challenging atonal segments, alternate time signatures, and diminished ninth chords. Tricky elements of the piece that sounded like mistakes to the uninitiated soon drove the crowd further from him, banishing the stoned woman with them. Just as well. The closer they were at the pivotal moment, the more they would be forever seared by what he hoped to accomplish.

Kasim finished that piece, one his teacher had called "Oerovasa," and continued on with a loud, grating piece filled with blunt-string rhythmic passages and long, quavering single notes that died away like the suffering of an animal with a killing wound. He played it well, hitting the notes, holding the difficult rubato despite the pain. His quarry was close, somewhere here in the park. Inside one of the shoppers at the art stalls and shaved ice vendors, Uchasa the Soulstraddler occupied a host.

There was a chance . . . just a chance that he could be driven out. The pain in his fingers and hands, up the carpals and into his wrists, had started. Kasim gritted his teeth and played on, drawing glares from those nearby now, and the occasional look of pity from those who didn't grasp the complex symmetries within the notes he played. The piece was not for them. Their ears were not attuned to such things. Every note in his song of pain and woe would bring a demon closer to him, drawing it like the scent of blood on the wind.

And there he was, the quarry Kasim had traveled all this way to find. Uchasa had chosen a young man with dark blond hair and freckles on his shoulders. He drifted closer, drawn by the harmonies carefully written backward, turning inward on themselves and biting at their own themes before they were fully articulated.

The boy Uchasa rode gripped his girlfriend's arm tightly, the hard white of the clenched fist visible at his knuckles, the pain around her eyes perfectly clear. She did not look up or around, only at the ground several paces in front of her own feet. A fading bruise marred her neck. Those closest to an occupied host suffered the worst fate. The proximate, the loved few who would doubt the change in their friend or paramour even up until the killing stroke—these were the first to fall, and the last to know. For these unlucky few, Kasim had to act, had to continue playing despite the raw, red pain that nearly equaled the breaking itself.

The boy lingered close now, and with each harsh draw of the bow across the violin's strings, Uchasa boiled closer to the surface. The boyish face wore the feral, wicked grin of the monster who had been chewing at his soul and bending him to the will of the Great Enemy. The notes, pitched for a demon's taste, lashed against the captive, cowed girlfriend like a riding crop. She struggled. The afflicted host twisted and shook at her arm, grinning absently.

"Joey! Let me go, please," she whispered, pulling hard against the adamant grip on her wrist. "I don't like this music."

"I do," he told her, voice full of menace. "I like it almost as much as when you cry."

"Just let me go over and sit by the lake, okay? Just right there," she pleaded, pointing out the lakeside, well away from the harshest transients of the music.

"I want to see you, Shelly. Every minute. If you book out on me, you know what'll happen."

Kasim invented a sudden cadenza of wild notes that sounded like a seized bearing in a large machine, distracting Uchasa and allowing the girl to get away. She walked fast, head down, until she got to the lake. She sat at the water's edge, hugging her knees, rocking slightly. Kasim knew she cried. He'd been trained to know these things. Better that she cried now, while she was still able to do so.

Uchasa stood close, his eyes glazed, his head nodding to the deviously complex triple rhythm of the piece.

Just one more step. One more.

Kasim continued on, his hands in agony, his spirit and flesh scourged by the undertones of the demon's music as it was empowered, amplified by his consecrated instrument. Dogs strained on their leashes and broke away from alarmed park patrons. Little children became red-faced and belligerent. Kasim played on, at the edge of human endurance.

At last, Uchasa was within reach, close enough to touch.

I can do it. I must.

Kasim muted the strings suddenly. Uchasa's host quivered, the fog of delirium lifting. Kasim forced his hands, willed them to do what the Great Enemy never imagined he'd be able to do again. He began to play Hallasaar's twenty-second arpeggio, the second most beautiful piece of music conceived by the mind of man.

Uchasa's host collapsed, holding his palms against his ears, mouth agape in a silent scream. Kasim was doing it. He was playing it once again. The pain, for just one brilliant moment, was as nothing. Gravity was nothing. Time did not exist. There was purpose and perfection in the universe, a place where demons could not go and could not corrupt. The spirit of the great master infused him, stiffening his ruined bones, making him more than he was. The notes surrounded him, waxing with all the power of the dawn over still water. Memories of his happiest days flashed against the back of his eyes, things he had not dared to consider, things he had forgotten, things he had lost forever.

The respite was short lived. Fire crawled across him, agony like molten lead flowed through his ravaged fingers. Kasim burst into a sweat so hard that the neck of his violin was slick with it. He hoped it was sweat and did not look. It didn't matter now. There was only this one thing. Life had narrowed to this. Whatever the pain, he could take it.

The piece concluded, note for note, and some bystanders had burst into tears, while others stood in rapt wonder, but it was not enough. Uchasa still lingered in the host, blindly trying to crawl away from its nemesis, this absolute majesty of sound.

Kasim let himself breathe two breaths and wipe the perspiration from his brow, then placed bow to string once more. The fret board felt sticky now, strange. His fingers weren't stiff anymore. They were almost pliable, like they had once been.

The twenty-third, then.

A tear stood in his eye, for he knew what it meant. For himself, for everyone.

He began to play. There was no pain now. There was only a strange uncertainty, a sense that his body was not his own, that it had become vague and ill-defined at the edges. Ten bars into Hallasaar's twenty-third arpeggio, there was only music such as could only be understood by those who had attempted to stare down the sun and failed. Music so grand that a man might put out his eyes to hear it again, to take it unto his soul for all time. Eyes shut tight, there was no line between Kasim and the music. He existed only as a transmission point for the sound, and the sound exploded out of him, unhindered by the limitations of the flesh.

The piece ended, and the violin fell from Kasim's hands. On the ground, the host had been wrenched asunder as if by a thousand fish hooks being pulled from every part of him, leaving only a bloody and unrecognizable mass of tissue. Uchasa was gone, but it had been too late for the host. The great burden of chastising the unclean settled heavier upon his shoulders. One was so often too late, mortal skills insufficient to do anything more than avert greater disaster.

Kasim looked at his hands and knew that he would never have to consider the burden of his skill again. Each finger on his left hand had broken once more, shards of bone sticking through the twisted wreckage that had once been an instrument without equal. His right wrist hung, useless as a toy with broken springs, already swollen to double its normal thickness. The pain settled upon him. Nothing could blunt it now, nothing could mend what had been sundered.

The bystanders began to scream. The mixture of pure tones, flats, and sharps was untidy, like the noise of an orchestra tuning up. Running footsteps provided inconstant percussion behind the din. Kasim walked down to the lake, to the girlfriend, who would forever bear the wounds Uchasa had marked upon her soul. She would bear the scars he had put there, too. The savior who arrives too late, who possesses insufficient power, finds himself doomed to be a despised apologist.

"I am sorry. I did all that I could, but it was not enough."

She looked up at him and did not speak. Her eyes were barren, empty places that couldn't be crossed, wastelands she would be doomed to wander. Kasim turned from her and waded into the water. There were swans at the far side of the lake, gliding easily, so graceful. The struggles of humans and demons seemed far away, watching the silent birds on the water. All that he had done or failed to do felt distant to him.

He waded further in. Kasim had never learned to swim, and he didn't attempt to do so now. It was enough. It was more than he'd dreamed he could do. The Great Enemy's schemes had been thwarted, at least for a moment. He would not call it a victory.

"Celine," he whispered, just before the darkness of the water enveloped him and gave him silence at last.

About the Authors

Dale E. McClenning was born in Springvalley, Illinois, and has lived his whole life in the Midwest. While dreaming of writing since junior high, he took the long road of first getting a bachelors and masters degree in mechanical engineering, marrying his high school sweetheart, Daphne, and raising two boys before getting serious about writing. This is his first story to his credit.

Living in Indianapolis and working for Rolls-Royce (not the car company, the turbine engine company, so don't ask about a discount), Dale spends most of his free time with family including the other girl in his life, his two year old granddaughter, Illyria, who is already convinced that the computer exists to play her games instead of letting grandpa write his stories.

Patrick M. Tracy lives in Salt Lake City and works as a Network Support Administrator. He went to Northern Arizona University, graduating with a B.A. in English. He has been writing fiction and poetry for many years and has numerous published works in both disciplines. Among his recent publications are the novellas "Darkness of the Sun" in *The Crimson Pact Volume 4*, and "Mungo the Undying" in *A Walk in the Abyss*. When not fixing computers or writing, he enjoys traditional archery and performing feats of strength. Find out more at pmtracy.com.

Just Desserts

Michaele Jordan

"Just Desserts" is the direct sequel to "Arrival" and "Digging In," both featured in *The Crimson Pact Volume 4,* and both by Michaele Jordan.

The ground was shaking. Not just the ground—the earth, the sky, the entire cosmos was quaking and shivering. But Blossom did not fall. Mostly because she had already fallen, collapsed suddenly onto a park bench she'd had the good fortune to be near. There she half-lay, clinging to the arm rail and gasping and heaving, as cramps rippled violently through her swollen abdomen. The pain was so fierce she scarcely noticed the apparent upheaval of reality.

Her agony and the trembling of the world faded almost simultaneously. She continued to clutch at the side of the bench for several minutes, still retching slightly, such attention as she could muster concentrated mostly on trying to spit the vile taste out of her mouth. Which didn't mean she failed to recognize the other sensation. Something similar had happened before. She raised her head a trifle. The park was still spread out around her, fresh and green and dappled with flowers. There was a bed of daffodils just up ahead, and the air smelled of lilac. No sign of the end of the world. Everything looked normal. Not even a change in the weather. She let her head fall back down.

Nobody else had noticed anything last time either, she recalled. But there had been a moment when it seemed that the world had gone away. It had been caused by . . . by a hole in reality, a temporary non-place where the world really had gone away. Some kind of . . . gate. And, last time, someone—something—dangerous had come through. She'd had to kill it. She shook her head. She probably wouldn't be able to do it again. She was still weak and sick from last time.

"Miss? Are you all right?"

She went rigid from shock at the unexpected voice. But it didn't sound threatening. Very slowly she lifted her head. There was a man behind her, leaning on the back of the bench. Something in the way he held onto the rail looked off balance, as if he, too, had felt a tremor in the ground and nearly fallen. And the expression on his face was dazed. Had he come through the open gate? His eyes were so very strange. Alien. He seemed to be looking at her with concern. But surely, if he had come through the gate, he would be more concerned about himself.

He was still looking down at her. She should answer. "Yes, I think so. Thank you." He went on looking at her. Such strange eyes. They almost glowed. "And you? Are you all right. You look . . . Did you fall?"

"Yes. No. I mean. . . . " He smiled, a little nervously. "May I join you?" He didn't really wait for her nod, but came around—still holding very hard onto the bench—to sit beside her.

She pulled herself upright to make room for him.

"Yes, I did fall, and I am a little dizzy. But I don't think I'm hurt." He drew a very deep breath. "There, you see? I'm fine."

"Did you feel it, then? The earthquake?" She cocked her head, waiting for his answer. If he had felt something, that would prove he had come through the gate.

"Earthquake? Is that what it was?" He smiled again, more confidently. "I certainly felt something. But I did not expect you to have felt it, too." He paused, and his smile grew broader. "Now I understand why I have come to this place. You are one of us."

It took her much too long to answer. "I don't know what you mean." She shook her head. "Are you hungry?" She knew he must be. "You must be hungry." Just thinking how hungry he must be made her hungry.

But he went on looking at her as if she had not spoken. "You are not from here—I know it. There is a shimmer about you and I know my kind. You are not of this world."

Of course he recognized her. Just as she recognized him. But she did not intend to discuss it. "There's a café near here, by the gate. Or an inn down the road, if you would like something more substantial." He would be in need of something very substantial. She rose. "Let me show you the way."

He rose also, a little unsteadily, and then stood looking down at himself—his feet sticking out of his trousers, the swinging hem of his long, skirted coat, his long-fingered hands—with a bewildered expression, as if he had never seen any of them before. She knew the feeling. Eventually his hands found his pockets and explored them. Then he looked up and said, "I'm afraid I don't have any money for a café."

She thought for a moment that she had misheard him. When she had first arrived, she had certainly not worried about paying for food. Although she often paid for food now. People did that here. But still. "Not to worry," she told him. "We will work something out."

She took him to the inn and ordered a roast. They knew her there. They knew she liked her roasts very rare. When the food came, he stared at it. His eyes grew huge. His nostrils flared as he inhaled. His hands clenched. Clearly he was nearly overcome by the intensity of his desire.

But he picked up the utensils and, glancing around to see how other people ate, carved a small bite off the roast and put it in his mouth. Then he closed his eyes. He did not merely smile. His face grew blissful. It took him a long time to finish chewing and take another bite. She could eat a whole dinner in less time than he took to eat one bite. "Things are very different here, are they not?" he murmured.

Because the food tasted good? "Different from what?"

He cocked his head and gazed at her with a bewildered expression. "Why do you keep pretending like that?"

Quite suddenly she found herself standing and pounding a fist on the table. "I am not pretending!" Even as she turned and ran, she shook her head in astonishment at herself. She did not recall ever having raised her voice before. She was not behaving normally. People were turning to stare. It was important to behave normally.

Outside, she leaned against a wall to catch her breath. It must have been because she was so very hungry. A terrible waste of food, this being sick every morning. And now she had walked away from lunch. She had best get home and eat—heartily—before she made more mistakes. She was scarcely out of sight of the inn when she heard music. Beautiful, beautiful music.

The town center was almost deserted, with all the little shops and businesses closed for lunch. But at the corner of an alley, a lone street musician played, apparently for his own enjoyment since he had no audience. He had a monkey dancing by his side. He was only playing a pennywhistle, but he played with great skill, and Blossom was drawn to him as if mesmerized, trembling and hungry. The little monkey was quite tame, not even on a leash, and dressed in a red coat and cap. It stopped dancing as she approached and whipped off its little cap, holding it out for alms.

She did not pay the monkey. The young man looked up when she drew so close that her shadow fell across the stop-holes in his instrument. Seeing the desperate look in her eyes, he lowered his whistle and asked, "Are you all right, Miss?" Twice now, that a man had said those words to her today.

She collapsed into his arms so that he fell back into the little cul-de-sac behind him, out of sight of the street, even if there had been anyone on the street to see. "I am now," she whispered. Behind them, the monkey jumped up and down shrieking, but there was no one to hear. She gave it a little kick as she came out of the alley afterwards, and it fled, still chittering and sobbing.

Then she wandered for a long time—hours or even days, she didn't know—walking up this street and down that one, without watching where she went, reflecting on her recklessness. She reminded herself sternly that she was a stranger in this place. She needed to be careful. She could not afford to attract attention, shouting in restaurants and luring musicians into alleys right in the center of town, in broad daylight. If there were trouble she would have no recourse.

Eventually she grew tired and went home. She had never used to get tired. Just the opposite, she'd often had to pretend to be tired, because her strength was so very abnormal. But ever since that last time . . . Whatever it was that had come through the gate, it had hurt her badly, leaving her body bloated and increasingly misshapen. Now she was always getting sick or tired. It made her angry. And reckless. And hungry. She would have to be more careful.

She put her key to the lock, only to find that the door was not locked. She knew she had locked it. She had been caught out by carelessness last time, and had since taken great pains to remember to lock the door. She stared at the unlocked door growing angrier and angrier. And so, hungrier and hungrier. And since she was hungry—and not really all that tired, not by normal standards—she walked into the hallway to confront the intruder.

It was the 'man' from the park. He was perched on the divan in the sitting room, cradling a bundle in one arm. It was wrapped in a blanket and, although she could not see what was in it, it looked about the size and shape of a baby. He smiled and rose when she came in and, shuffling his burden to the other arm, offered her his hand. She did not take the hand. She did not enter the room. Instead she backed up a couple of steps.

His face fell. "Oh, please," he said. "Don't be angry. I'm here to make peace."

"By breaking into my home?" she inquired.

He shrugged and looked around. "I didn't really mean this as a break-in. I haven't stolen or damaged anything. I just wanted to wait for you, and it was . . . cold outside." He smiled and laid his bundle on a chair, the soft tufted one with padded sides that would protect the bundle from rolling. Then he dropped down into a formal bow with elaborate hand flourishes, just like the gentlemen of the city. "I am Captain Djhoourackh of the Ninth Regiment, and I give you my word—" For whatever that's worth, she reflected. "—that I will neither harm you nor constrain you, and will depart on your command." He raised his head just barely enough to glance up at her. "Won't you hear me out, pretty Blossom?"

"Djhoourackh? Nobody here will be able to pronounce that. You had better make it Jules." She pulled a little chair out from the corridor wall and sat. It was spindly and uncomfortable, but she did not intend to go into the sitting room with him where he might cut her off from the exit. "How do you know my name, Jules? Or where I live?"

"The server at the inn knew you, and said I could get your address from the butcher," he replied, sitting back down on the divan. An embarrassed look crossed his face. "I'm afraid I finished off the lunch without you. Every bite." He shook his head. "I was so hungry I couldn't resist. But you won't be billed for it." He grinned, ruefully. "The way you ran, they didn't believe I was your friend. They made me wash the dishes, and I indulged them, as is proper in this strange place."

She almost laughed out loud. "So, you've been busy."

He nodded solemnly. "I have, very. When I was done with the dishes, I went to the library." He pulled a thick stack of newspaper out of his coat and sighed. "They warned us that the portal would probably not send us all to the same place, but nobody said anything about our not arriving at the same time—we thought the transition would be instantaneous." He laid out some of the newspapers beside him. "There's a story here about an incident six months ago. Two inexplicable murders, in a church. The priest disappeared right afterwards, and it is suspected that he, too, came to an evil end. These killings were not ordinary murders. The victims were not merely made dead—they were carved like meat. So there was another one of us already here, and hungry, six months ago."

He looked up at her as if he expected a comment, but she said nothing, so he laid another newspaper on the divan. "And you were here when it happened, because you had arrived even earlier. You were associated with the church. Here's an announcement of last year's spring concert. With profuse thanks to you for all your hard work in organizing it." She still said nothing. He folded up his newspaper and met her eyes. "This other one was just a foot soldier, a brute too stupid to consider his situation or control his most bestial impulses. He must have found you and ill-used you."

She did not answer him, but he took her silence as approval of his assumption.

"You didn't want to acknowledge me because you supposed that I would be the same." He rose and came toward her.

She rose also and backed away. He stopped and extended a hand. After a long moment of thinking it over, she permitted him to take, not her whole hand, but her fingers.

"You must have fought him—and fought bravely—for here you are, still alive. Even if he escaped you, you must at least have forced him to flee."

She almost started. He had not escaped. But Jules continued unaware. "I am an officer. Not like that one. It is obvious to me that here, hugely out-numbered in this very odd place, we need to stand together. I am appalled that you were ill-used by one of our own, and I offer myself to you as an ally. And surely, in your condition, you need an ally."

On hearing that, she did start. "My condition? What do you mean?" But the answer was ridiculously obvious now he brought it to her attention. She sank back into her chair as the import of his words struck her, sank so suddenly and heavily that it might almost be said that she fell.

He put an arm around her—which, strangely, she permitted—and raised her back up to lead her to a more comfortable chair, plucking up the bundle so she could sit in a soft sheltered place. "Surely you knew? Or at least suspected?"

She shook her head. "It never crossed my mind. I just thought I was sick, or wounded inside." She reflected for an instant. "I suppose I didn't think it was possible." She looked up at him, considering. "You say he is not dead?"

He shook his head. "Did you think he was?"

She shrugged. "I hoped."

"He must have lain low to recover from his wounds, or left the city. But now he has returned and struck again." He sighed and sat back down on the divan, next to all the papers. "When I came out of the library, I was accosted—jumped, even—by a hysterical little monkey. It clung to my leg and pulled at me, crying and begging, until I followed it. It led me to a pool of blood. Nothing left but the clothes and some bones. Not even all the bones, but they were fresh. And this." Juggling his bundle into the crook of one arm, he reached into a pocket and pulled out a pennywhistle. "So we will have to track him down. He is not rational enough to be any assistance to us. And our position here is too tenuous for us to permit him to jeopardize it."

She chose to ignore the suggestion. Instead she asked, "What's in your package?"

He smiled hugely and proffered it to her, turning back a corner of the blanket so she could look. "An orphan." The monkey stirred—disturbed, perhaps by the draft on its face—and stretched a little red-coated arm, before nestling more closely against Jules. Then it sniffed and jerked its head up to stare at Blossom. It screamed—a shrill, piercing noise that inspired Blossom to cover her ears—and, bursting free from the blanket, leapt at Blossom, with its mouth open wide and its teeth bared.

Jules moved quickly, catching the creature before it could bite her. It struggled weakly against him, turning its head to hiss at him.

"Isn't it adorable?" he asked. "So hideous. So primal. Like the voice of the creation."

She froze. "Get that thing out of here."

"Oh, dear." He chuckled. "It does seem to have taken a special dislike to you, doesn't it? And it was so friendly before." He started to wrap the blanket back around it, but it writhed in his grasp and bit him. He yelped and let it go.

Or rather he tried to let it go. But it had closed and locked its jaws so that although he tried to pull free, it still hung from his hand. Even after he jumped to his feet and shook his hand it hung on, swaying. It occurred to Blossom that if he swung his arm hard so that the monkey struck the wall, it would probably be knocked off. But apparently Jules did not think of that. He just barked, "Let go!" as if he thought it would follow orders.

Blossom rolled her eyes, and reached for the stack of newspapers. Rolling them up into a tube, she swatted the animal hard. It was only newspaper, of course, but she was a strong woman, and the blow knocked the monkey to the ground, unconscious. She looked down at the limp creature. It was not dead. She wished she had had a crowbar.

Jules paused long enough to suck at the bite—which was not bleeding as much as she would have expected, just two nasty, oozing punctures—and knelt down by the monkey, winding the blanket tightly around it so that even if it woke it was already restrained. Blossom only barely waited for him to stand up again. "Get out."

"But. . . . "

"No 'buts.' I said, 'get out.'" She heard her voice rising to a shrill note and took a deep breath. But not quite so deep that she allowed him a word in edgewise. "I have heard you out, as you asked. And now it seems you want more. You want me to give care and shelter to a bad-smelling beast that bites. You want me to go out with you hunting for a dangerous monster that has already nearly killed me once, presumably because you also want me to assist you with fighting it. I decline the invitation. You said you would leave if I told you to go. You gave your word. I am telling you to go."

He stood very still, clutching the monkey-filled blanket in front of him, staring at her with his mouth half open, revealing gritted teeth. There was anger in his eyes, but he straightened his back and closed his mouth—pressed his lips tightly together, in fact. He nodded curtly—almost a small bow, except the bundle was in the way—turned, and walked out. She watched him go, locked the door behind him, and fastened the chain. She turned around, but did not go back to the sitting room.

Instead she leaned back against the door and cradled her arms around her belly. How had she failed to notice its unmistakable rounded shape? But now that she knew, it explained much. Conversations that had broken off suddenly when she came into a room. Long calculating looks. Even, once or twice, a snicker behind her back. Worst of all, she had not been invited to help organize a spring concert this year, and there was always a spring concert.

Tears welled up in her eyes. She could not live without music. But an unattached woman carrying a child . . . She shook her head. They did not approve of such things here.

And now there was this . . . this person. He had left when she ordered him out, but could she trust him to stay away? She sighed. She would have to leave town. Go somewhere else and say she was a widow. Maybe even change her name. A pity. She'd grown quite used to Blossom.

First she packed a small case, just a few clean under-things and toiletries. Then she took the larger carpetbag to the larder. There was too much meat to take it all, but she did pack a couple of hams, a leg of lamb, and a half-dozen briskets, with steaks and sausages wedged into all the corners and cracks. There was just too much left to waste, so she sat down and ate it, smiling. She didn't often permit herself a real feast.

She left a letter for the lawyer, instructing him to sell the house and hold the money until she called for it. Speaking of which . . . She crossed to the fireplace and, reaching an arm out to each side, she hooked her fingers around the great hearthstone and lifted. Underneath was a hole with a metal box in it. Not the most secret hiding place in the world, but she didn't know anybody else who could lift the hearthstone, so it was safe enough.

The box wouldn't quite fit into her small case, so she just poured in its contents—mostly jewelry and gold coins, along with a few rolls of bills—on top of her clothes. She'd get a new box later. Perhaps she would also come back in a year and collect the money from the lawyer. Money was often useful—the people here would do almost anything for it.

Ready to go. On the way to the door she was careful, as usual, to avoid looking at the mirror, lest she be mesmerized by it and stand gazing pointlessly into it for an hour or more. She was reminded that Jules had passed by that mirror, too. Twice, both on his way in and then on his way out. Yet he had not been troubled by it. But he was a man, and she had noticed that men did not pay much attention to mirrors. He probably hadn't even looked.

The train station was busy. There was no need to stand in line for a ticket. She could always buy a ticket from the conductor en route. So she boarded the newest looking train—it was northward bound—and settled into an empty first class cabin. Leaning back, she glanced casually out the window.

And there was Jules, just up ahead, with one hand holding

the rail as he boarded the train. In the other hand he carried a large birdcage, with the monkey curled up inside. She immediately dropped the window blinds, then jumped to her feet and reached for her bags. She would get off the train right away and find another going the opposite direction.

Too late. The train jerked to a start, throwing her off balance. She landed heavily in the opposite seat, nearly pulling the bag of meat down on top of herself. But the train was not going very fast yet—perhaps she could still jump off. Spreading her feet in a most unladylike stance to steady her balance, she resumed tugging at the carpetbag. Just as she got it over the edge of the luggage rack a voice intruded.

"Oh, Miss, let me get that for you! It's surely much too heavy for you." Two arms intervened between her and the bag. Blossom stared at Jules with gritted teeth as he chivalrously raised her bag back up to the rack. Was he following her? Clearly, he had come straight to her carriage. Or was he somehow drawn to her? Perhaps that was the nature of the portals and the auras of those that passed through them?

Having safely stashed her luggage, he turned toward her. "Miss Blossom!" he exclaimed, quite as if he'd had no idea who she was. Which didn't really prove he wasn't following her. "You've changed your mind, then? I am delighted!" Unable to think of any possible response, she sank back into her seat. He sat beside her. "You saw the news, I presume?" He pulled a folded up paper from his pocket and brandished it.

It reported a dramatic murder in a small town in the north. "You think this is . . . his work?" she asked.

"Definitely. I admit, I don't know how he could have covered so much distance so quickly. But the details are unmistakable. See here—" His voice broke off. For a moment she supposed he was simply rereading the text, as he was plainly pointing at the second paragraph. But the silence dragged on and she looked up.

He had raised his head to look at her. But just before his eyes came to rest on her face, his glance had fallen on something else. Now he sat frozen and staring. Very carefully, she peeked out of the corner of her eye to see what was behind her. Despite her caution, she was almost caught. The window had turned into a mirror. She didn't know quite how, and dared not look closely to find out. Presumably just some trick of the light striking the burnished slats of the blinds.

He was helpless. If only she had a knife! But she was out of the habit of carrying a weapon. And he would be strong. If he woke—which he would—she wouldn't be able to take him without a weapon. Instead, she extracted herself gingerly from the seat without touching him, lest she wake him. A pity about the meat—she would have to leave it. She probably didn't have more than a few minutes—the light shifted with every movement of the train. Even reaching around him for her small case without jostling him was difficult, and while she was doing that, her foot brushed an obstruction.

The bird cage. He had set it down by the door. And inside it, the monkey was stretching and lifting his head. It would see her and scream. Ah, well. She supposed there was time for a quick snack.

Her hand was in the cage and around the monkey's neck before it had finished opening its mouth to scream. She pulled it out of the cage and opened her mouth. Blossom had been very surprised to discover that the people here could not unhinge their jaws enough to open their mouths very far. She therefore took pains not to let it be known that she could—and, indeed, there were none living who had seen her do it. There was a sharp, satisfying crunch as her teeth closed around the mouthful, severing the tail.

The train was not going very fast yet. Within two minutes, she was jumping from it onto a grassy field, clutching her case under one arm. She was still congratulating herself on her escape as her feet touched the ground and a wave of pain enveloped her. The agony swelled up voraciously until blackness took her.

She woke. She was lying on something soft in a place that was dark. For one dreadful moment, it was the same as when she had first arrived—a total absence of memory, her past as unknowable as her future, her identity erased by a total absence of information. She tried to turn her head and a wave of pain swept through her. Which reminded her that she had known worse pain. She'd known it recently, in fact. Her name was Blossom and she had jumped from a train. Good to know. How she had gotten from there to here was still a mystery.

Her eyes—and mind—were out of focus and the light was very dim, but there seemed to be a figure seated in a chair beside her. She squinted and her eyes remembered how to see. There, not so dim after all. The man in the chair was Jules. She definitely remembered Jules. He was holding a small bundle wrapped in a blanket, but she also remembered that he could not possibly be holding the monkey. She considered asking him where she was, but decided against it. "Jules?"

"Blossom!" He leaned forward eagerly. "You're alive. I was beginning to doubt you would make it."

She suppressed a smile. "Yes, I believe I am." Mentally she examined herself. The last bits of pain were fading. "In fact, I'm fine."

"That's good. Because you'll need to be." He sighed. "I don't know how much you remember, but it seems we are not alone here. And apparently our colleagues do not share my enlightened views on cooperation." He shook his head in a gesture of annoyance. "We were attacked. I am ashamed to say it, but it took me entirely off guard. It must have struck me from behind, so suddenly that I knew nothing of it. One moment I was talking to you and the next... You were gone, I was alone. Even the monkey was gone. Except.... " His face hardened. "There was the poor creature's tail on the floor. And then I saw you, outside on the ground, unconscious. Our attacker must have flung you from the train. So I jumped off after you."

Blossom stared up at him. Could he actually hear what he was saying? She nodded at his bundle. "Then that is not the monkey."

He laughed. "Of course not!" He rose from the chair, sat down beside her on the bed, and laid the bundle inside her arm. "I thought you would know somehow. But, of course, you were unconscious. This is your baby. He's early, but he's strong and healthy." Jules opened the blanket enough to reveal the little face. The creature looked a lot like the monkey to Blossom. Apparently Jules did not agree. He stroked the baby's cheek and smiled. "The first of a new generation. He looks completely human, don't you think? Not even a shimmer about him."

She took the baby in her arms, since Jules seemed to expect that, and it nuzzled up against her, looking for a nipple. "He was born here," she pointed out. "He never had to pass through a portal." As Jules leaned over to admire the baby, his coat swung open. Blossom was extremely interested to see a flash of steel. "Why, Jules," she murmured. "Or should I use your proper title? Is that a short sword in your coat?"

He glanced down at the makeshift sling in his coat and laughed. "I'm afraid I don't have anyplace else to put it. I lost the scabbard some time ago." He gazed tenderly down at Blossom and the baby. "Perhaps I should get a new one, now that I have the future of a new colony to protect."

She laid the baby down and reached up to him. "Dear, sweet Jules," she whispered. "You were right that I need an ally. And it is so wonderful how you always find me." He cocked an eyebrow at her beckoning tone and moved smiling into her arms. Which brought him close enough for her to grasp the sword. "I am so lucky to have you nearby," she sighed as she slit his throat. She went for a quick kill, so he wouldn't have time to fight. He lived just long enough to give her an angry look of betrayal, before his expression was washed away in a gushing fountain of delicious blood.

She laughed and let the blood spill into her mouth. A lot of it would be wasted, but she was too intoxicated with the taste of it to care. When the flow had subsided, she tore off an arm. So much better than the local meat! It tasted of home—wherever home was.

While she dined, the baby rolled over and squirmed forward. She looked down at him in curiosity. Very precocious. A normal newborn wouldn't be able to do that yet. After nuzzling at the bedding, the baby got a bit of the blood-soaked sheet in his mouth and started to suck. And suck. Blossom chuckled. The baby looked up at her and smiled.

She recognized that smile. And knew better than to turn her back on it. So she smiled back and reached out as tenderly as she had toward Jules. Not until she had a hand on her child did she unhinge her jaw and open her mouth.

About the Author

Michaele Jordan was born in Los Angeles, bred in the Midwest, educated in Liberal Arts at Bard College and in computers at Southern Ohio College. She has worked at a kennel, a Hebrew School, and AT&T. She's a bit odd. She lives now in Cincinnati with a foolish cat, a long-suffering husband, and many invisible playmates. Her first novel, *Blade Light,* was serialized in Jim Baen's *Universe*, followed by *Mirror Maze* from Pyr Books. Her shorter works have appeared in *Buzzy Magazine, Redstone Magazine,* and the *Magazine of Fantasy and Science Fiction* (not to mention *The Crimson Pact, Volume 4*). You can visit her website, michaelejordan.com while waiting for her upcoming steampunk adventure, *Jocasta and the Indians.*

Red Snow

Zachary Hill

January 21, 1944. Fifty miles west of Novgorod, Russia

Svetlana Drugov's frozen breath came out like thick fog and circled around her like clouds clinging to the mountains. Old snow crunched beneath her boots as she trudged onward, refusing to let cold feet bother her. She squinted at the blinding white landscape broken only by the trunks of trees that broke up the monotony. She imagined the black trees in the distance were letters, forming incomprehensible words on perfect white paper. So long ago, her life had been about reading and writing papers at the University of Moscow. She missed printed words and their beautiful clarity.

Books made sense. They had been the only things she understood until she picked up the Mosin to the fight for the Motherland. The rifle made sense. It was simple, pure, and logical. Now she didn't have time for books. She only had time for orders and her rifle. When she looked through the scope and saw a fascist invader, she knew exactly what to do. She never hesitated. Not after three long winters fighting the enemy.

The dusty libraries and stuffy classrooms had become a distant memory as the war went on endlessly, though she dared hope victory was coming, as the Germans were on the run. Their lines were breaking apart across the whole Eastern Front, and she found herself marching in a nearly abandoned sector to meet up with partisans who had some vital information about how to take a town on an unimportant road.

She turned back to look at Katya, her spotter. Instead of the long, bolt action Mosin, Katya carried the stocky PPSH with its fat drum. Wisps of Katya's blonde hair fell down from under her fur hat. A white scarf covered her face, and all that showed were her icy blue eyes. She was whistling "The Sacred War," something she did when she was bored or annoyed.

"This is your fault," Katya said.

"Yes, it's my fault my mother decided to give birth to me in this general area," Svetlana said.

Colonel Sharpov had chosen her because she knew the terrain. She had been born and raised in the small town of Plyussa, about fifteen kilometers away, and her father and grandfather had taken her on many goose hunts in the region. They never took her on the wolf hunts, the hunts she wanted to go on the most.

So, instead of joining the rest of their comrades in the offensive against the retreating fascists, she was stuck looking for a farmhouse where she was supposed to meet the partisans.

What a waste of her time and talent. After all she had done, all she had proved, they sent her and Katya to do this? How many Nazi officers would she have killed if she were part of her unit chasing the fleeing fascist columns? Five? Ten?

There was a time when all she wanted was to finish her history degree at University. She had been in the middle of writing a paper on the exploitation of the working classes by the French aristocracy during the Middle Ages when everything changed. One minute she had been in her literature class and the next someone was shouting that they were at war with Germany.

"This farm house would be easier to find if there were actually any landmarks. Yes, yes, it's easy to find! It's the second house past the snow," Katya said.

As long as they followed their compass and went west, they couldn't miss it. But Katya was irrational when she was in a bad mood, which was often. She'd be much harder to tolerate if she weren't such a good spotter.

Svetlana remained silent and kept her eyes open.

"You have any idea how close we are?" Katya asked.

"No."

"You sure we didn't pass the road?"

"Yes."

"Would we even know?"

Svetlana shrugged, which probably wasn't noticeable through her many thick layers of clothing, the outer layer of which was dirty white, like the snow.

An hour later they came to a rotten fence that stretched to infinity in each direction. There were a few tracks of passing carts. No evidence of mechanized vehicles or boot prints.

"The road," Svetlana said.

Katya stomped up beside her and looked to her left and right. Svetlana pointed left. They were to take the road south until they came to a farmhouse with a stone wall.

"How far?" Katya asked.

"Three kilometers."

Katya nodded and walked into the ditch alongside the road. She was bothersome, but she knew her job. They would stay down low in the ditch, as the snow wasn't too deep, and remain out of sight. One of them would peer over the lip every so often, as they wouldn't be able to see anyone coming while walking in the bottom of the ditch. She found it always better to see the other side before being seen. It made things much simpler.

Life was simple. Serve the Motherland and Stalin. Serve by killing the enemy. Her father had been a soldier and had raised her to know what one's duty was. Never back away. Always confront the problem without hesitation.

She had attacked her studies in the University with the same zeal. It was her purpose to get an education for the betterment of the Motherland. That had changed the day she picked up the Mosin rifle for the first time. Religion was a tool to keep the workers in their place, but that had been the closest thing to a religious experience she had ever had. It was almost as if she were made for that rifle.

As they came closer to where the farmhouse was supposed to be, Svetlana covered her mouth with her scarf to keep the clouds of her breath from being seen and lay down and took out her binoculars. Even magnified, all she saw was white. The wind picked up the loose flakes on the snow's surface and filled the air with a thick curtain of white.

"You think these partisans actually have anything useful?" Katya asked.

"Maybe."

She didn't like to have her time wasted.

As they walked on she gave the hand signal for Katya to go silent. There would be no more speaking from this point on.

A little while later a black shape emerged from the darkening wasteland. The sun sank lower in the purple sky, and that left her very little time.

She glanced back to make sure Katya saw the shape that was possibly the house. Katya looked through her binos.

From there on they crawled in the ditch until a stone wall became visible. This was the correct place.

A faint yellow light glowed on one side, probably a lantern through a window.

The briefing said that they were expected.

Still, she wasn't going to just walk in there without scouting the place out first.

They crawled their way along the ditch until they were directly in front of the house. One man in overalls stood by the front door. The ember of a cigarette made him stand out in the growing darkness.

Then the two of them crept to the back of the house, which had two boarded-up windows. One had light coming from a few gaps in the boards.

She gave the gestures telling Katya to wait here and cover her as she snuck to the window. Katya nodded and readied her PPSH, eyes open for any sign of movement.

There was no one Svetlana would rather have than Katya watching her back. For a city girl who hadn't ever touched a gun until the war, she was a damned good soldier.

Svetlana held her rifle out in front of her as she quietly crawled to the window. Once she reached the house, she got up to her knees and peeked in through the gap in the boards. The window was filthy, and all she could make out were several dark shapes of people inside, at least six. No one was talking, and it was impossible to tell anything more, except they smoked Russian cigarettes. They were the cheap kind like her father smoked.

She frowned and made her way back to Katya.

"Six or more inside," Svetlana whispered, "but I can't tell any more than that."

"I'm not going in there blind."

"No choice."

"Very well, blind maybe, but not defenseless."

Katya patted the grenade hooked to her belt. It was a German "potato masher" she'd looted from one of her kills.

Svetlana nodded her approval. Katya hid the bulky grenade up her sleeve and kept her other hand on the cord, ready to set it off.

Her Mosin was too long for fighting in such a cramped space, so she undid the clasp of the holster of her Nagant pistol.

Once ready, they stood up and walked around to the front of the house, trying not to startle the guard too much. He almost dropped his cigarette and fumbled with his rifle when he saw them.

"Stop right there!" He called out.

They stopped.

"You asked to see us," Svetlana said.

The man took a moment to look them over, and she noticed his posture loosen. "They said they were sending their best sniper."

"She is," Katya said.

"But you're a woman." He stared at them, mouth agape.

"Comrade," Katya said with a tone as sharp as broken glass, "don't be afraid. We're not here to shoot deserters. We're here on orders."

"Yeah, sorry, just wasn't expecting you so soon." He lowered his rifle, but never took his eyes off them.

"Who's in there?" Katya asked.

"Hold on," he said.

The man knocked on the door and said, "Uncle Belochkin, they're here." A few seconds later it opened and two men in Russian winter clothing stepped out. The men looked the two of them over. The one in front was older and had a long beard and baggy pants tucked into black boots. He was dressed as a peasant, but he carried himself with authority and his eyes showed a burning intelligence.

"I am Belochkin. Didn't know if your colonel would send anyone. Good. Before you come in, do not be alarmed at what you see. Let me explain. Please."

He then stepped aside and motioned for them to enter.

The man told them not to be alarmed, but now she was alarmed at what she wasn't supposed to be alarmed about.

Svetlana looked at the faces and postures of the three men and didn't see any signs of aggression or deceit. She turned to Katya, who gave an almost imperceptible nod.

They didn't have much choice at all. This is what they'd come here for.

She stepped into the house but kept her hand near her pistol.

Even before her eyes could adjust to the gloom inside, she snapped her pistol out of its holster and pointed it at the man in the German officer's uniform.

"Put it down! He's with us!" The bearded man said from behind her.

The smoky room was filled with six men and one woman. Most were dressed like Russian peasants, but there were two Germans. One was an officer, a Captain. He wore western-style winter clothes with a large fur-lined hood. The big soldier beside him wore a white coat and had hard, dark eyes. His hand moved toward the Luger pistol at his side.

She didn't lower her gun. From the corner of her eye she could see the barrel of Katya's PPSH leveled at the people.

"What's going on here?" Svetlana asked.

"They're on our side," Belochkin said. "They only wear the uniforms. They're with us, not the enemy."

The man in the officer's uniform smiled and said in Russian with a thick German accent to the partisans, "Hot temper."

That was almost enough to make her shoot him. But the man could be an agent of some kind. A spy.

Belochkin stepped out in front of her with his hands spread out. "Please, lower your weapons and let us explain."

She looked to Katya and nodded. None of these people had gone for their guns. If this was a trap, it wasn't a very effective one. They both lowered their guns.

"Thank you," Belochkin said.

"Explain," Svetlana said.

"You must trust us, please. These Germans brought us something we needed. They are friends, from before the war."

"I don't trust traitors," Katya said.

"Neither do we," Belochkin said, "but we trust these men. They are our brothers."

"What help do you need from us?" Svetlana asked, still angry her countrymen were associating with their enemy.

"The village of Gorodiche, do you know it?"

"I know it," Svetlana said.

"There is a sniper there who is slaughtering both sides. He has three hundred kills that we know of."

"Nikolay Yakovlevich Illyin has almost four hundred," Katya said.

"This man started two weeks ago." Belochkin did not appear to be joking despite the dark laughter coming from Katya.

"You must be mistaken," Svetlana said.

"I swear that I'm not."

She looked around the room at the grim faces and nodding heads.

"How?" she asked. "This is not possible in such a short time."

The partisan leader looked down at his feet. "My men and I have tried to kill him several times, but we do not have the skill. We've lost half our group."

"This sniper is Russian?" Svetlana asked.

"He was Russian," Belochkin said. "He's a lunatic now."

"What makes him so special that he can kill so many?" Katya asked.

"We don't know," Belochkin said.

This was the first time she felt he wasn't being honest with her.

"Tell me," she said.

The woman stepped forward. She was deep in grief and tears had left channels on the dirt coating her cheeks. "It doesn't matter how he does it. All that matters is that in another two weeks he'll have killed even more. Mostly our countrymen. What more do you need to know?"

This madman was murdering her fellow soldiers. Yes, he was killing Germans as well, but the thought of her countrymen being slaughtered by one of their own sickened her. Svetlana's one desire was to protect the Motherland, and if this story was true, not even orders from Colonel Sharpov would stop her from going after this mad sniper.

She turned to Belochkin. "Where was he seen last?"

"In Gorodiche," Belochkin said.

"How far away is that?" Katya asked.

"Seven kilometers southwest of here," Belochkin said. "He ambushed a retreating German column three days ago."

"How do you know he's still there?" Svetlana asked.

There was a noticeable pause before Belochkin answered.

"We were there this morning. He's displaying his trophies. I don't think he'll leave them."

"What trophies?" Katya asked.

"The bodies," the woman said.

"He is mad," Katya said.

"In a way," the woman said.

"We will go now," Svetlana said, edging toward the door.

"And put down this rabid dog," Katya said.

"Wait, that's not all," Belochkin said.

"We know our job," Svetlana said.

"This man is different," the German officer said. He slowly lifted a small antique wooden box off the floor. He handed it to Belochkin.

The partisan leader showed the box to Svetlana. It had a quill engraving painted the color of old blood on the lid. "Take these. These are . . . high precision bullets, custom made for accuracy and lethality."

Svetlana took the box and opened it. Inside were 7.62x54r rounds in velvet-lined slots. They were silver and the jackets looked brass. But what caught her eye were the tiny markings all over the bullet heads. She picked one up and held it close. It was some form of writing that she didn't recognize at all. Persian, maybe?

"What is this?" Katya asked.

Svetlana looked to Belochkin and waited for an answer. He sighed and shook his head before answering. "This man . . . he does impossible things."

"Enough. Let's go," Katya said.

"What's he using?" Svetlana asked.

"A British Enfield."

She looked at the bullet again before putting it back in the box.

"You're not telling us everything," Svetlana said.

"No, I'm not," Belochkin said, "but you wouldn't believe me."

Svetlana bit back her words. Perhaps she wouldn't.

"Don't underestimate him," Belochkin said. "He's far more dangerous than any soldier you've met. Use those bullets against him. That's all I should tell you."

Svetlana took a moment to take in his face and the faces of a few others.

"If this is a trick or some kind of trap, I promise I'll return for you," she said.

"It's not," he said.

With that she tucked the wooden box under her arm and they left the farmhouse. They went to the road and began walking as the sun barely poked above the cloudy horizon. Katya walked backwards, watching to see if they were followed and keeping her gun aimed at the house.

"You believe this?" Katya asked.

"I don't know."

They slipped into the ditch and moved as fast as they could until the darkness slowed them. Only the faint light of the moon allowed them to see. After about five kilometers, Svetlana guided them away from the road and they made their way through the sparse trees. The plan was to insert themselves into the village before sunrise. That way the enemy sniper wouldn't be able to observe their approach.

Around midnight they came to the first set of houses that marked the beginning of Gorodiche. A part of the house was burnt down and the barn doors were smashed off their hinges.

They kept to the shadows near the walls of the buildings and hurried from cover to cover. One would stay on over watch as the other moved. The smiling moon gave them just enough light to keep them from crashing into everything.

Then she saw the skyline of the town. The onion-domed church steeple jutted up to impale the moon. The cross on top was missing.

"We need a place," Svetlana said.

Katya nodded.

They both knew what kind of place. It needed to offer concealment, a quick escape, and most importantly, visibility.

Down the street was an intersection. Most of the buildings were one-story houses and, unlike the city, the houses here were spread apart, sometimes with a good fifty meters between each house. Changing positions during the day without being seen was going to be problematic. Most houses had fenced-in yards for gardens and animals. Rows of thick pine trees blocked her sight.

She had forgotten how much she disliked the country.

One of the houses at the intersection had a second story with small windows jutting out from the attic, one on each side.

Svetlana pointed to that house. Katya took a moment to look it over and then nodded.

Now they only had to get across a block and a street that had fences, trees, and lots of open space with nothing to cover them but the half-darkness.

They observed their route and took a long time to look for any hidden sniper who might try a shot at them in the moonlight. They didn't see anyone. That didn't mean the enemy wasn't there, just that they didn't see him.

"I go first," Katya said.

"Wait." Svetlana kept her eyes open for the enemy, and another on the sky. A few moments later, as she had anticipated, clouds covered the moon and the village darkened. "Go."

Katya dashed across the yard and threw herself over the fence. Grace wasn't possible in a bulky snowsuit, but she did manage to be fast.

She made it to the doorway of the house facing the intersection without being shot. Svetlana scanned the town again before making her dash across the yard, sticking to the same frozen ground Katya had used to avoid leaving tracks. When she got to the fence she grabbed it with both hands and used her momentum to fly over it.

After clumsily landing on her side, she scrambled up and ran across the yard and into the open doorway. Katya was behind a couch but looking through a window across the room. She was only a dark shape in the black room.

No shots, no signs of movement. They must have made it without being seen.

They repeated the maneuver to cross the street, but this time Svetlana went first. Once inside they scouted the ground floor thoroughly before going up to the attic. From the center of the room, Svetlana could see in four directions. They were higher than the surrounding houses and could see all four streets, though not very far in the darkness.

The attic was bare, flimsy wooden walls that stopped most of the wind and had a crib and a cot on one side. A chest and broken mirror were in a corner. An antique blanket with bright red traditional peasant decorations covered the cot.

There were no signs of the owners and there were no lights in the village.

Katya had the first watch and Svetlana slept. A few hours before sunrise, Katya woke her for her turn by kicking her foot.

She was sitting in a wooden chair well away from the windows when the sun finally came up. Being close to a window was a great way to give away one's position.

As the street in her view became illuminated, the depth of the problem became apparent. Lining the street were the crucified bodies of town's people, old men, old women, small children, and dozens of German soldiers. Their bellies had been cut open, and their frozen entrails were spilled out onto the street. She also spotted a lot of dead German infantrymen lying in the snow beside abandoned vehicles. A handful of dead Russian soldiers were scattered among them as well.

She had seen what cruelty the fascist invaders were capable of, but this was something altogether more horrifying. This was inhuman.

She kicked Katya awake and pointed to the window. Katya took a moment to glare at her for the rude awakening before looking out at the terrible scene. Her scowl froze in place.

"Lunatic," Katya finally muttered.

"He's an animal," Svetlana said.

"Time to hunt our wolf."

As the sun rose higher Svetlana was able to make out more of the village. The onion-domed church steeple was the most obvious place to hide. Since she knew that, so did their target. He wouldn't be there. She would like to have seen the town from there though.

Katya took two windows and Svetlana took the other two. With luck the enemy wouldn't know they were there and they could catch him off guard.

She was used to this, the waiting. The papers the commissars handed out always made the stories of the heroic snipers into exciting adventure tales. The reality was that being a sniper involved a great deal of waiting around for many hours, sometimes for days. She sat on the trunk with the blanket over her shoulders to cover her white snowsuit. Katya had found another blanket and had done the same.

Noon passed by with no sign of the target or any other living thing. Even the birds, dogs, chickens, and goats were gone.

The first real sound she heard that day was when Katya unscrewed the lid of her canteen to take a drink.

Katya went back and forth from scanning precise areas through her scope to scanning the larger view with her eyes. She avoided eyestrain that way.

The sun sank lower and lower in the sky, and more shadows appeared to cover any sign of their target.

As the sky was growing purple she saw something. She made a faint 'hiss' sound through her teeth to alert Katya and then looked through her scope.

Two hundred meters away a figure emerged from an alleyway. The man dragged a corpse of a fat woman by the ankles, and he had a rifle slung across his back.

She didn't hear her, but she felt Katya move slowly behind her. Svetlana knew without looking that Katya was looking through her binos.

"Man in Russian clothing. Enfield on his back," Katya whispered.

"I'm taking the shot."

She put the pointed post of her scope's sight onto the center of the man's back. She took a slow breath in and then released it in an even exhale. In the pause between breaths she was left with a small moment of stillness. In that moment she squeezed the trigger as gently as if she were caressing the cheek of a newborn baby.

The gun went off. The blast and recoil were like the voice of an old friend, comforting and always welcome, but sharp and echoing in the enclosed attic.

Her training allowed her to see through the distraction of the firing gun and to where her shot landed. The bullet struck the man right between the shoulder blades. There was a spray of blood and he fell into the snow.

She felt the hot breath from Katya as she silently chuckled.

"That was easy," Katya said.

"Wait."

Svetlana watched the man. He was still moving.

As she watched, the man stumbled to his feet and then, as gracefully as a ballerina, he unslung his rifle and aimed it right at them.

The window exploded and they threw themselves to the floor.

A second later another bullet tore through the wall and hit the cradle behind them.

"Go!" Svetlana shouted.

The rotting wooden walls offered them no protection. For the briefest of moments, Svetlana wished she were back in the concrete Hell of Stalingrad where most walls could stop anything less than a mortar round.

They made it downstairs as more bullets ripped into the attic. Katya paused in the middle of the house. They couldn't run back across the street or they'd be in sight of the enemy.

Svetlana motioned for her to go out the back. They ran out the rear door and passed two houses before going into the busted door of the third. It was one story, but had four windows and a clear view all around it. Not ideal, but they shouldn't stay outside any longer.

They went in and took up positions in the shadows while looking out at the direction the madman might come from.

"What happened?" Katya asked.

"Don't know."

"You hit him."

"I know."

None of it made sense. What she'd seen was impossible. Yes, she had seen people survive direct hits. It was rare, but it did happen. But this man didn't appear affected at all. Not only did he fire back, but he knew right where they were. No one was that good, especially after taking a fatal shot from a large caliber bullet.

The sky was now a dark purple, and once it was night they'd move to find a new position and start the hunt all over.

"His spine should have been shattered," Katya said after a long silence.

Then she remembered what Belochkin had said.

She reached into the pouch at the small of her back and pulled out the wooden box with the special rounds. She opened it and pulled out one of the bullets to examine it.

"Superstition," Svetlana said.

"That man should be dead. That isn't superstition."

"It's impossible."

"Agreed, but we both saw it."

She wanted to argue and quote Lenin and Marx, but she knew what she had seen. This man was not human.

Her mind raced through possibilities from a secret scientific experiment to the dark tales her grandmother used to tell, but each one seemed more improbable than the other.

She worked the bolt of her Mosin slowly to make it as quiet as possible as she unloaded the four rounds left in the magazine. Then she loaded five of the fifteen rounds the partisans had given her.

They stayed in the abandoned house for a little while longer and ate some of their canned rations. She wasn't sure what it was supposed to be, but she guessed it was some kind of meat. Katya guessed beans.

Suddenly the window exploded and the can was blasted out of her hand. The food in the tin can flew in all directions, and a split-second later the report of the shot came. It was all almost instantaneous, but judging by when the sound arrived, the bullet had come from at least five hundred meters away.

It was impossible. It was too dark to see anything, let alone into a dark house through a dirty window.

Her mind went over just how impossible it was as she and Katya scrambled for cover out of sight of the now broken windowpane. At night she couldn't even see through her scope let alone see a target so far away.

What was this man?

Katya's eyes were wide and her mouth was still filled with food. She was clutching her gun to her chest and breathing hard. Svetlana had never seen Katya afraid of anything.

"We need a plan," Svetlana said.

"Yes, run."

"He might see us leave and shoot us."

Katya threw her left hand in the air. "Then what do we do?"

If they stayed there, he'd get closer and might be able to pin them down. They had to move.

Svetlana pulled out her only RGD1 smoke grenade.

"Maybe he can't see through this."

Katya nodded.

Svetlana pulled the pin and threw the grenade out the window. As soon as the smoke began poring through the window, they ran for a window on the opposite side of the house.

Another shot tore through the wall behind them. He knew they were trying to escape. She ignored the other shots that ripped through the smoke and climbed out the window and kept running.

They made it to the next house and used it for cover just long enough to go out a window and crawl on their bellies to another house. Once inside they stayed clear of any windows. Katya rigged her stick grenade as a trap on the front door, so if someone opened it, they would pull the string and set it off. Except for the windows, the door was the only way in or out.

That night they stayed up in the narrow attic of the house. Neither of them slept. Every sound was potentially the unstoppable lunatic. This man couldn't be hurt by bullets and could see in the dark. There was no telling what else he could do.

The sun was a welcome sight, and with the morning also came their ability to shoot back.

Katya had dark circles around her strained eyes as she sat deep in thought. "I know that look," Svetlana said.

"I might have an idea."

"Tell."

Katya looked up at her with a furrowed brow.

"You don't like your own idea?"

"I don't."

"Do you have another one?"

"No."

"Then tell."

"I draw his attention, force him to come inside. He sets off the grenade. If it doesn't kill him, it will distract him."

That was a bad plan. It put Katya in too much danger. They both risked their lives with every mission and battle, but this was unacceptable. She couldn't lose her only friend.

"No, no, no. Stupid plan."

"You have a better one?"

"No, but we don't use that plan. Understand?"

"Understood."

They waited. The sun rose higher in the sky but still no sign of this lunatic. She knew he was more than a crazy man. He wasn't human. She knew it, but her mind kept grappling for a rational explanation.

"He's out there," Katya whispered.

Svetlana nodded. The man knew roughly where they were and was probably just waiting for them to make a mistake. She had a bad feeling he could wait a lot longer than they could.

She lay with her back against the wall and took out her pocket mirror with a long handle. She raised it to the open window and took a look. The sun was behind them so she wasn't worried about the mirror flashing and giving their position away.

She saw nothing. The village with its bare wood houses with pointed roofs was still and silent.

Then the mirror exploded. The remains flew across the room, and she felt a sharp pain in her hand, probably from flying glass. A spot of blood was forming through her glove near her index knuckle.

"I'll draw him out," Katya said.

"Don't be an idiot."

"He knows where we are."

"He's faster than me."

"Then I hope you're wrong about that."

Katya went to the door facing away from the window the enemy had shot through. She looked back at Svetlana and smiled. "For the Motherland."

Then Katya ran out the door and dashed across an open yard. There was a house in between her and the enemy, but he had to have seen her. Svetlana peeked one eye over the side of the window. She knew his general location: a block away on the other side of an open field. There were several houses there and he was in one of them. The line of crucifixions hadn't reached this edge of town, and the view of the doorways and ground floor windows was clear.

Something moved. In the doorway a figure emerged. He had a dark tarp over himself and the barrel of his rifle stuck out. He maneuvered to get a shot at Katya, walking quickly without taking his eye from his scope.

Svetlana stepped back from the window and brought her long rifle up.

The man's head turned. As she acquired him through her scope she saw his pale face look right at her. He looked like a corpse, but with inhuman speed he brought his rifle toward her like a snake striking.

As the barrel of his gun shrunk and only became the dark bore that carried her death, she lined the sight post of her scope onto his chest. She didn't have time for one of her long, carefully aimed shots. She had to shoot now or he would shoot her.

All the possibilities that could happen if she missed rushed through her mind. She had to block them out and focus. She had to remember her training. The muscle memory took over and her body knew what to do.

Her breath froze in her chest and she squeezed the trigger. The metal plate of the stock shoved her shoulder and the barrel kicked up. Smoke and the bitter smell of burnt powder filled her senses.

Through her scope she saw blood erupt from the enemy's chest. He staggered back and tripped over his own feet.

She yanked the bolt back and slammed it forward, loading another of the special rounds into the chamber.

He flailed around, but he did not get back up. She watched him through the scope, as he struggled to reach the sling of his rifle, but apparently he couldn't move.

Svetlana met Katya outside and they made their way around the open field, staying close to the fence and bushes. Together they approached the bleeding monster. She kept the rifle trained on him in case it was some kind of trick.

The man laughed as they came within a few steps of him and stopped when their eyes met his. He touched the hole in his chest. "This was not one of your bullets, was it, comrade?"

The man spoke with a perfect Muscovite accent, but she had the feeling he wasn't actually speaking Russian.

"If I had known you had those," he said, "I would have been more cautious."

"Shoot him!" Katya shouted.

His eyes narrowed as he looked Svetlana in the eyes. "Don't rejoice too much. There are more like me, and I'll come back and take another body. This will all happen again, sooner than you think. You cannot stop—"

Svetlana fired and blew the top of the lunatic's skull off in a black mess of bone and brain matter.

She stood there, looking down at the bloody body of the monster that had killed hundreds. Katya was breathing heavily and kept her gun pointed at the corpse.

"What was he?" Katya finally asked.

"Don't know."

"I need some vodka," Katya said.

"We should speak to the partisans, if we can find them."

"Thank them for those bullets."

They walked to the plaza of the corpse-filled town. All the death was proof enough that there was no god, but after seeing what she had seen, she wondered if perhaps the devil himself, or one of his demons, had come to Gorodiche.

The world was a much more dangerous and evil place than she had ever imagined. If there were more like this man, she would find them and put a bullet in their heads.

No matter what it took.

No matter how long it took.

Going back to University did not seem so important now.

Katya stopped walking. She made a choking sound and coughed, bending at the waist as if she were going to vomit before falling to her knees.

There was no wind, but the air became colder around them. Katya stopped coughing, and her whole body shook as if she were having seizure.

"Katya? What's . . . ?"

Katya turned her eyes toward Svetlana with the slowness of an approaching winter. They weren't Katya's eyes. Or at least, whatever was behind them wasn't Katya. They showed a wild-eyed derangement that Katya would never have.

"Comrade, I told you I'd be back." The perfect Muscovite accent so unlike Katya's.

This was impossible. The old priest in her village used to tell stories from the Bible about such things, but that was all just made-up superstitious nonsense. Still, she remembered the name for this: demonic possession.

"Even now, you refuse to believe. Your friend here believed. Left her door wide open for me."

"Get out of her." Svetlana raised her rifle and pointed it at Katya's chest.

"I don't want to."

"Get out!"

"Or what?" The demon smiled and looked down at the PPSH in its hands, then glanced back up. "I could do a lot of harm with this toy."

"No, you won't."

Svetlana's finger rested on her trigger, but she didn't want to shoot. She couldn't kill Katya. "What will it take to get you out of her?"

The demon cocked its head to the side and considered her for a moment. "If you let me go, I'll take this body for six days and seven nights. After that, you can have her back, good as new."

And during that week he'd kill hundreds more. He'd kill her countrymen. He'd kill innocent people, like the women and children in the town.

The demon slung the PPSH over its shoulder and looked back at Gorodiche. "I'm going back for my Enfield. Or maybe I'll find a better toy, like one of those German MG-42's. Now I could kill a lot of weaklings with one of those."

"You're lying. You won't give Katya back."

"I don't have to lie. I can cause the most pain by telling the truth. Yes, I'll give your friend back, but she'll carry the memories of everything I did with her body, and everything I let happen to her. She will live with the pain, and you'll live with the knowledge that each one of those many deaths could have been stopped if you had a shred of courage." The demon smiled. "Or, shoot your friend now, and save hundreds. Either way, I win. Choose."

Svetlana thought the crucified people in the town were staring at her, begging her to pull the trigger. She wondered how many had been alive when they were nailed up and then disemboweled. They were her countrymen, her people, and they had to be avenged.

But if she let the demon go, she'd get Katya back, and then maybe they could hunt the monster down and kill him for good. Someone had to know how to do such a thing.

But how many more would die if she did nothing right now?

"I see you're too indecisive. I'll take my leave then. You'll know where I am if you listen to the reports from the front."

The demon turned and walked away while whistling Katya's favorite patriotic song, "The Sacred War."

Svetlana raised her rifle and looked down the iron sights at Katya's back. She imagined her friend's smile, and then she imagined another town, torn apart as if a pack of wolves had fallen upon it.

Her people had suffered enough. She had to do this for the Motherland.

She pulled the trigger.

About the Author

Artist and author Zachary Hill has drawn pictures and written stories for as long as he can remember. In high school he filled up notebooks with stories and illustrations. In army basic training—after lights out—he wrote using a flashlight. During his two deployments to Iraq he wrote stories during his down time. He was always thinking about a creative project he wanted to work on, or about something he wanted to learn. He pursued his studies and graduated from Southern Virginia University with degrees in History and Art. He taught English in Italy and fell in love with the majesty of Rome and the elegant decay of Venice. He's written several books, including *Gorgon* and *Uprising Italia* (a zombie apocalypse novel set in Italy). He illustrated *New York Times'* bestselling author Larry Correia's *Grimnoir Chronicles* from Baen books. He loves pizza and Mountain Dew. You can find him at his fiction and art blog, Broken World, or his history blog, Minimum Wage Historian.

Upon the Point of a Knife

Bradley P. Beaulieu

I

As the sun set over Providence, Jonah Bloom lay at the end of Dorrance Street where the street gave over to the railroad tracks. His hands were cupped over his head while the five boys who'd caught him there surrounded him and kicked at him mercilessly. How long the beating lasted Jonah couldn't say, but eventually they stopped and watched as he writhed on the cold ground. Jonah hugged his ribs. He sucked air through clenched teeth. Each inhalation was pure white pain. A simple shift of his leg brought torture to his ankle. Luther, the tallest and the leader of the vicious boys, had stomped on it, and when he had, Jonah had heard something snap like a twig in the dry heat of summer.

Jonah had asked for it, he supposed. He'd run when they'd found him again. It was the fourth time, and he knew what was coming. The other three times they'd held him down and cut him, once to each hand and once to his right foot. They'd waited weeks between each assault—why, he had no idea—but he was sure this time they'd come to finish what they'd started. They'd cut his left foot, and he wasn't about to let them have their way. Not without a fight.

Some fight. Young Caleb had tackled him from behind before he'd gone a hundred strides.

As he lay there, they stripped him of his worn-through shoe and held his leg tight. They stuffed the sock down his mouth and clamped their sweaty hands over his mouth while Luther pressed the tip of the knife deep into the sole of his foot.

As it kissed his flesh, Jonah thought he heard laughing. He wasn't sure if it came from the boys or himself. Or maybe it was some long-forgotten memory dredged up by the pain. Just as they had the other times the knife had pierced his skin, visions came to him: golden-white light smothered by darkness. Like a storm cloud blotting out the sun, the light was soon gone. The light had been wonderful, a thing to make the soul sing, and now it was gone, utterly consumed by the darkness surrounding it, and it made Jonah wonder what he might have just lost. Much, certainly, but like a blind man standing before the stark beauty of nature, he had no idea *how* much.

Luther leaned down over Jonah. "It won't be long now." The rusted sky and the setting sun outlined his angry face, and for a moment Jonah swore his eyes were aglow like flames in the pits of hell. His features grew and distorted. His nostrils flared, black pits completely out of proportion with the rest of his face. His teeth unsheathed like snake fangs.

A trick, Jonah thought. A trick of the pain and his bottled rage and the darkness of the coming night.

Jonah blinked, and the visage was gone.

From the nervous glances the other boys were sending in Luther's direction, Jonah had the impression that Luther's warning wasn't something he should have shared. But soon after, Luther had pointed with the knife down the alley and they'd all left Jonah there on the street to bleed on his own.

While gripping his foot to slow the flow of blood, Jonah laid his head down—he hadn't meant to; it had just happened—and when he woke, it was to the sound of clopping hooves. He was unsure how much time had passed, but the sky was dark now, the moon a sliver of fresh, curled wood. The rattle of steel-rimmed wheels against cobbles filled the streets of Providence. A wagon, Jonah thought, near the chapel, perhaps, or the mayor's house.

By the time he realized it was going to come very near, it was too late to run. He'd managed only to lever himself to a standing position before the carriage turned up the lane. The driver's bench was empty, but the four horses clopped on until the coach came abreast of Jonah, then it sighed to a stop like a raft against the shallow banks of a river. Jonah backed away and leaned against the bricks of the old warehouse. He stared into the dark depths of the carriage but could discern nothing. He could smell plenty, though; not merely the horses, but the smell of loam and burnt cedar. It irritated his nose and throat. Made his eyes water.

"Years ago, in the woods, not three miles from this place, I saw a wolf." The voice came from somewhere deep inside the carriage, but to Jonah it felt as though a hand were reaching for his throat.

"Did you?" Jonah replied, his voice like the shrill call of a frightened wren.

"It was wounded, and the other wolves had come for it."

Silence followed, and it made Jonah realize just how still the city had become. There was no sound whatsoever. No calls of mothers nor fathers nor children. No rustle of branch nor leaf. No dogs barking nor the flapping of bats as they flitted through the night. It was unnatural.

"Wolves don't bother with their dead," Jonah said. "They leave them to rot." He'd seen one once. In winter, half decomposed with a stag's horn sticking from its gut. It hadn't been bitten by other wolves. They'd left it alone to die.

A deep chuckle came from the coach, a sound like breaking stone. "You're new here."

"I came from Crick Hollow last spring."

"Boys don't take to you much, do they?"

"Take to me too much, as I see it."

Again that dark chuckle. It set Jonah's skin to crawling, especially in the night's cool, clammy air.

"Maybe you should listen to them."

Jonah paused. "Would you?"

And now a full laugh. It made Jonah want to double up and retch.

"The wolf. It was small. Smaller than the others. Wounded in one leg. The others were closing in, nipping at its heels when it turned to face another. Eventually it began to tire. You could see it in the way its tongue lolled, the way its tail hung low. What do you think happened then, Jonah?"

Jonah blinked. He hadn't told the man his name. "It ran?"

"It waited until the largest came near. And then it shot forward and clamped its teeth around the other's throat. The pack moved in, trying to pull the wounded wolf away, but with three violent shakes their leader's neck was snapped."

Something spun out of the carriage—a sharp gleam catching the moonlight, then a clang as it fell against the cobbles.

"From that day forward, those wolves followed the smaller one."

Without another word, the horses began clopping away. Soon the coach was gone, into the night toward the great mansion on the hill north of the city.

Jonah limped forward, grimacing against the pain, and found the very knife Luther had used to cut him four times now. He took it up, noticing for the first time how fine the craftsmanship was—the gleaming hilt and pommel, the tooled leather grip, its keen edge. It was worth more than Jonah had ever seen in his life. But that wasn't what he was thinking about. It was the power the mere holding of it granted him.

Suddenly he could think of nothing but Luther and his cruel, smiling face, and the pain he'd caused Jonah. As he stood there, holding the knife, the darkness he'd glimpsed when the knife had sunk into his flesh returned. The laughter returned as well, but this time he was all too sure it was his own laughter, no one else's.

In the wake of the carriage, he shuffled down the alley toward his hovel while wicked thoughts of Luther played within his mind.

Wounded wolf, indeed.

The rain drove down over Providence. Clouds the color of sodden ash draped the city, but far to the west the sky was clear, the sun a glowing ember just above the horizon.

Jonah came to a skidding stop along Chalkstone Street, just before a stone wall with baroque iron fence-work running atop it. His breath came in great gasps as he looked beyond the wall to the mansion that stared down at him dispassionately. He would need to go to that place and speak with the man who lived there, but not yet. Not yet.

He turned instead and headed for the alley that ran north toward the cemetery. Someone was squatted down behind a rain barrel. Jonah held the knife tight in his hand as he treaded carefully forward. The rain slicked the blood away from the blade, making it come alive as crimson gave way to clean, bright steel.

"He won't save you."

Luther's voice. Weak and tremulous as a newborn calf's, but there was defiance as well, as if he thought he'd have the last laugh on Jonah after all.

Jonah paused, unsure of himself for the first time since leaving to hunt for Luther in the southern streets of Providence. But the knife gave him strength—it refused to let the hatred that had bloomed within him wither—and soon he was taking steps toward the rain barrel and the dark form behind it once more.

"He'll give you to them," Luther said, "as he did me."

Jonah didn't know what he was talking about, and he didn't care.

Luther tried to fight him off, but Jonah had stabbed him

once already, and he was weak. Jonah kneeled down next to him, slapped away Luther's pitiful attempts to stop him, placed the tip of the blade against Luther's chest, pommel pointed to the rain-dark sky. And then he leaned slowly down and over Luther's body, a lever prying the boy's soul from an imperfect, ephemeral frame.

A whine escaped Luther. A child's whine, a whine that said he'd never wished his life to go this way. There was a part of Jonah that was repulsed by what he was doing, that was sickened by it, but that part was soon smothered by the will that had dominated him since he'd picked up the knife.

At last Luther fell silent. Providence came alive as lightning galloped across the sky. There were eyes in those dark clouds—eyes and a wicked smile—and as the thunder played over the city, Jonah heard only dark laughter.

As the thunder faded he heard footsteps, and then the explosive clap of a whip just next to his ear. Bright pain blossomed across his cheek and he cowered, but the laughter he'd heard in the clouds now resounded within him. He was afraid, but there was something that forced him to stand taller, and he was glad for it. He'd never been able to defend himself. Not until he'd taken up the knife.

Jonah turned. Six paces away stood Quinn, a constable who'd been chasing Jonah for months for petty theft. He wore a long, oiled overcoat and a tricorn hat that dripped rain from its brim. He held a whip at the ready, the length of it trailing behind him on the rain-pattered stones. "Quietly now, Jonah. You've done enough this night, you have." He tipped his head up and looked to the rain, the clouds. "We've had darkness enough." He flicked his wrist, the whip slithering momentarily. "So, quietly now."

Other men moved in behind Quinn and spread out quietly and effectively, two with cavalry sabers and one with a musket—though what good that would do in the rain Jonah didn't know.

Quinn glanced to his men for effect then regarded Jonah once more. "Drop the knife, Jonah."

Jonah looked down. Regarded the bloody knife held in his right hand. "I won't," he said. "He deserved it."

Quinn shook his head. "Not for you or me to decide, though, is it? Let Judge Hollis be the one, Jonah. If what you say is true, he might set you free after you make reparations to the woman you stole from. So drop the knife."

"I won't."

Quinn seemed saddened by this, but his arm still swung forward, and the whip still arced out.

Lightning struck nearby, the entire scene going blinding white. Jonah heard the whip crack as the thunder shook like cannon-fire, except Jonah was no longer standing in front of Quinn and his men. He was now ten paces behind them, staring at their backs.

They looked around, confused. Jonah backed away, sending one quick glance over his shoulder toward the mansion.

Now, he thought. Now it was time to see the old man.

By the time Quinn gave chase, Jonah was up and over the fence.

Neither Quinn nor his men followed.

Jonah reached for the door handle. His fingers had barely touched the cold metal when it swung wide before him. As the light fell upon his hand he realized how much blood was there—Luther's blood and his own blood from the stinging wound Quinn's whip had given him mingling together. He rubbed it away on his trousers and stepped inside as lightning crashed nearby. He found himself in a large foyer. The cavernous interior was lit by a small candle on a table. No, he realized, not a candle. A bright flickering light floating above a brass censer.

Stairs with marble banisters led up and up and up, the top of them lost to the darkness. The floor was covered with inlaid marble tiles Jonah daren't walk upon for fear of marring their perfect whiteness. Oil paintings twice as tall as Jonah and wide as an oxcart hung from the wall, one of them showing mountains of men fighting with muskets and bandoliers, except they all seemed mad, eyes crazed, mouths pitched in misery. Each fought their brother, leaving untouched the dark enemy standing atop the hill in the distance.

"Are you going to wait all night?" The voice from the carriage beckoned from an open doorway further down the hall.

Jonah treaded carefully and stepped into a grand sitting room. An ancient man waited in a cushioned chair with a tartan blanket across his lap. A fire sat raging in the fireplace nearby, making the room feel as though it had been cast into the pits of hell. It smelled of burnt cedar and strange spices. It made Jonah's nose itch, made his eyes water.

As he stepped forward, the old man leaned deeper into his chair, the light from the fire casting the deep canyons of his face in bas relief. His skin was trapped in deep wrinkles but also scars that looked as if they held meaning.

Meaning or power, Jonah thought.

The man's smile revealed a ruin of teeth. After glancing at the knife still in Jonah's hand, he released that laugh, the one like a stone slab crumbling to pieces.

"Why did you want him dead?" Jonah asked.

"I wasn't the one dreaming of his death, Jonah."

For the first time, Jonah felt truly afraid. He was in much deeper than he'd realized. "Then why did you want me to kill him?"

"Do you care?"

"I do."

Firelight played against the caverns of his cheeks, his eyes glimmering from within the hollows of his face.

He was measuring Jonah, weighing his mettle, and in that moment Jonah didn't know what he would choose, but he felt the wicked weight of the knife in his hand and decided that in fact he *didn't* care.

"There are paths one might learn, Jonah. Paths that would bring you sway you've never dreamed of. I heard you those many nights, whispering thoughts of revenge. I heard the hatred, the desire never to be caught like a fish on a line again." He leaned forward and peered into Jonah's eyes. "Was I wrong?"

Jonah swallowed. He knew his answer would decide much. He might still leave this place—strike out from Providence and find another city in which to live—but that choice had been open to him ever since Luther had found him, ever since he and the others had tortured him. He hadn't left because deep down he'd wanted revenge, and this old man had delivered it to him.

"You weren't wrong," Jonah finally said.

The old man leaned back into his chair, his smile widening.

"Very well, Jonah. Very well."

II

Jonah walked openly down the center of the city. The moon had risen, staring down half-lidded as if it approved of Jonah's purpose. He came to Williams Hall but stopped as a boy came skidding to a halt practically at Jonah's feet. A nearby gas lamp lit the boy's surprised face. He was skinny and wore a woolen cap and fingerless gloves and shoes with the soles ready to fall off into the slushy snow. He had the same build that Jonah had had at that age—how long ago that seemed now—he had the same dark brown hair, the same freckles on his cheeks. This wasn't what gave Jonah pause, though—the city was full of such boys; what was one more?—no, it was the degree to which he reminded Jonah of himself those many years ago after he'd first arrived in Providence, before he'd taken up with Gideon. He'd come to the city after his parents' death in Crick Hollow. He'd had no one else to turn to, no*where* else, so he'd come to the city in search of a job and shelter, anything that would keep him alive.

When the stiff winter wind blew Jonah's long coat wide, the boy saw the knife in its ornate sheath hanging from Jonah's belt. The surprise on his face twisted to fear and then outright terror. He knew Jonah, or at least what the stories told. He stood there, petrified. There was a time that Jonah might have taken him to do his dark business just to see his reaction, but the truth was there was much to do this night, and he could afford no distractions.

The years with Gideon had given him the sight. He could see how pure this boy was, how good despite the confidence games he played for his aunt. Had Gideon needed a disciple now instead of ten years ago—by the damned, had it been ten years already?—he might have chosen this very boy. *You're all too replaceable*, Jonah thought, but then again, so was Gideon. Jonah knew that now. The old man was beginning to show more and more signs of age, and soon enough he would pass and leave his legacy to Jonah.

"Go on," Jonah said, and the boy was off, skidding along the snow-covered streets.

Jonah continued to the back of the hall where Caleb stood smoking a rolled cigarette. The end lit umber as he drew breath, shading his face ruddy, and then it was gone. After a nod, Caleb flicked his cigarette away and they both took the nearby stairs down into the low cellar of the opera hall—a crawl space that held a dozen old padded chairs, now ruined, and several empty casks that had once held whiskey. In the center of the space was a man twice Jonah's age, his wrists and ankles tied by thick leather cords to iron spikes that had been driven deep into the concrete floor. Fat beeswax candles were lit and placed at his hands and feet and above his head. He was gagged, but his eyes were free, and they pleaded with Jonah.

And Jonah actually paused. He'd performed the reaping many times. He'd taken what Gideon needed and brought it back to him. This man like all the rest was a criminal, bought from the warden of the state prison for little more than one might pay for an old horse. So why was this man affecting him so?

It must be the boy, he decided. A momentary lapse in will.

Jonah crouched forward, pulled his coat wide, and in one smooth motion drew his knife. He hovered over the man, who was sweating fiercely and breathing like he'd been running a race.

Jonah untied the gag and threw it to one side.

"Stop! Please! I ain't got nothing you want."

"I've untied you"—Jonah twisted the knife leisurely until the point was facing down toward the man's chest—"so you can say your final words."

"I ain't done nothing to you or yours!"

"Not true."

Gripping the knife tightly now, Jonah could hear the truth in those words. He could feel the wicked things just beyond the pale, watching and waiting. Jonah knew the truth of things now. Gideon had showed them to him. The demons were hungry to cross, but they were kept at bay by a thin but effective veil erected eons ago by long-forgotten souls. Or perhaps it had always been there—who knew the nature of such things? There were ways for the demons to cross, however. Through death. Through death they could come and they could live in the world for a time. And in this way, Gideon could use them.

Jonah lowered the tip of the knife.

"Please, I'll do anything!"

"There's only one thing left for you to do," Jonah replied softly, and with that he thrust the knife deep into the man's chest.

He screamed, only for a moment, but his eyes held Jonah's with a look of accusation and pain and confusion. And then, as always, all faded until there was a strange peace upon him. He'd gone, his soul going wherever souls went, and in its place one of *them*—a demon—had come. As Jonah withdrew the knife, the demon was drawn up and into the blood-slicked steel.

There were days Jonah didn't much care about the demons hidden inside the knife he brought back to Gideon, but today he dearly wished he could drink from the same cup. The place at the center of his breast tickled, ached for it. But there was no way he could do such a thing. Gideon hadn't yet shared those secrets.

But he would. One day he'd come to trust Jonah fully and reveal the last of the mansion's hidden mysteries.

The knife was now utterly clean. Not a drop of blood was upon it. Jonah sheathed it and slouched toward the exit, nodding to Caleb.

Caleb nodded back, a look of revulsion on his face.

Not so different from the dead man only moments before his death.

Jonah kneeled before Gideon. Nearby, the fire raged. Jonah was now all but numb to the pungent smell it gave off. Gideon's dark robes were pulled wide, revealing pasty white skin and exposed ribs and a smattering of age-whitened hair around his nipples and the center of his chest. Just over his sternum was a scar roughly the width of a knife. *This knife*. Except it wasn't merely one scar. It was composed of *many* scars, one on top of the other, many only partially healed so that it looked like a tragic landscape, a travesty mocking the way the body should be.

"I'm dying," Gideon said as Jonah brought the knife up and held it in both hands.

Jonah paused. "You're not dying."

"I am."

"You've years left."

"Days, Jonah. Days. You'll feel the same when the time comes. The sight"—Gideon stared at the knife, then at the nearby fire—"the sight reaches beyond these walls, beyond these minutes of our lives and into the days and weeks ahead." Gideon's face hardened, the grit returned to his eyes, and he nodded for Jonah to continue. As Jonah shifted forward and held the knife before Gideon's chest, the point resting just above the mass of scars, Gideon took one deep breath. "I can no longer see such things. And so with this"—he touched his finger to the very tip of the blade—"I shall pass."

Jonah drew the knife away, but Gideon, pale hands quivering like a babe's, drew it back into place.

"Worry not, Jonah. I knew this day would come when I selected you. Among all the children in the streets of Providence, in all the decades of my searching, you were the one I needed."

"You've been sick is all. Soon your health will return—"

Gideon gripped Jonah's wrists tighter and eyed the fire. "We're not far now, Jonah. We're close to setting them free. I knew from the moment I took up that knife that I would not be the one. But you! You may be different, do you hear me? And if it isn't you, certainly the one you *choose*, so choose with care." He released Jonah's wrists and pulled his robe wider. "Now come . . . "

Years ago, when they'd first performed this ritual, Jonah had been unable to comply with Gideon's demands. To stab someone—no matter the rage he'd unleashed on Luther—was not something Jonah had brought himself to easily, but when Gideon closed his eyes, the feelings of rote ceremony returned, and Jonah thrust the knife deep into Gideon's chest.

He held the knife firmly in place, yet something had changed. This was vastly different than every other time they'd done this. He didn't feel the trapped demon filling Gideon's frame. He felt the opposite, Gideon's soul slipping into the blade. In his panic, he withdrew the knife before Gideon's final breath had passed. God's breath, the knife had claimed Gideon's soul such that both—demon and Jonah's master—were contained within it.

Jonah had known he would have to take the knife himself one

day, but he wasn't prepared to do so so soon. There was nothing for it, though. What needed to be done needed to be done. The slick blood upon the knife was beginning to vanish. Before it was fully gone, Jonah turned the knife and held it against his own chest. He felt the tip pressing through his cotton shirt, felt it pierce his skin, and with that he felt Gideon's screaming soul, a torment given him gladly by the demon.

Without another thought he pulled mightily upon the knife, the blade slipping deep into his own chest.

The pain of it was like a hammer blow. Gideon and the demon were both infinitely more clear than before—it was the difference between lidded eyes on a lazy afternoon and staring wide-eyed at the sun. Jonah screamed, but he heard little, only the rush of his own blood, the laughing of the demon and its brethren who watched from within the fire. He was surprised by the level of power the demon yet wielded, but Jonah was not a man unprepared. Gideon had trained him well, for this was not so different from culling the souls from the condemned men in the cellar of the opera hall, except now the demon tried desperately to control him. It flayed at Jonah's mind, trying to bend him to its will.

But Jonah was ready for this as well. The same hatred that had been unleashed when he'd murdered Luther those many years ago blossomed once more. He unleashed it against the demon, and soon the twisted creature and Gideon both passed beyond the veil, leaving much behind, a power Jonah had never felt before.

It was too much too handle at once, though, and Jonah soon fell into darkness.

Jonah watched as Caleb, Henry, Gilland, and Gideon's other lieutenants carried the ornate casket slowly into the crypt. Many from Providence had come to witness these final rites. Most were simply curious what had happened to the man everyone whispered of—whispers only, for they dared not speak too loudly about a man who could draw the breath from them as they slept. Others had come to pay respects to Gideon's successor, Jonah. And a few had come to watch as their mortal enemy was at last laid to rest. Edward Quinn was one such. The old constable had risen in the world. He was the mayor now, and he'd been arraying his policemen and constables for years to try to catch Gideon in his foul arts, but he'd managed little more than catching a few of Jonah's crew. He'd also broken up the ring in the state prison that had supplied Gideon with bodies, but that had merely forced Jonah to make arrangements with an asylum on the outskirts of Boston.

When the ceremony was done—a fire and brimstone affair given by a Protestant priest who vanished the moment he'd finished delivering the sermon—the crowd began to disperse. Some came to shake Jonah's hand, one man even bending down to kiss the onyx gemstone set into his burly gold ring. Last was Mayor Quinn. He stopped short of Jonah as the wind soughed through the winter-bare branches above them. "Had I known what would happen"—he sent a look over his shoulder where, beyond the crypts and graves, beyond the stone cemetery wall, the three peaked towers of Gideon's estate could just be seen—"I would've gutted you instead of given you that scar."

The urge to touch the scar left by Quinn's whip was nearly overwhelming, but Jonah resisted and stared placidly into Quinn's eyes. "Why didn't you follow me if you were so worried?"

Quinn didn't answer at first. A sound came from the crypt—Caleb and the others performing their own rituals before the crypt was sealed. "I ask myself the same question." Quinn's right hand twitched at his side. "Nearly every day I ask it, and the simple truth is I was a coward then."

"And you're a coward no longer?"

Quinn's nostrils flared. His twitching hand touched the pocket of his long woolen coat. It was an awkward and tentative motion, as if he wanted to go further but couldn't. Jonah could sense the steel hidden there—a loaded six-gun with a mother-of-pearl handle. He'd come here to kill Jonah, and he might have if Jonah hadn't been prepared so well. Gideon had been able to see men, see into their souls, from the demons he'd consumed over the years. Gideon, when he'd passed through Jonah and beyond the veil, had given much of this knowledge to Jonah.

Quinn's fear radiated from him like heat. He struggled to throw off Jonah's will and put his hand on the butt of the pistol. He wanted dearly to gun Jonah down in front of everyone, and he knew he had to do it here, where Jonah was weakest, and he had to do it now, when Jonah was still immature in his dark crafts.

Just then Caleb exited the crypt and stood suddenly taller, watching the two of them and making himself ready to move. After a glance from Jonah, however, he relaxed.

Quinn's hand made it as far as the split in his coat, then it returned to his side and his eyes relaxed. He had a defeated look to him as he spoke the words, "Good day to you, Jonah. I'm saddened by your loss."

III

Jonah sat in the chair by the fire, staring into its wavering depths, wondering, not for the first time, just how old this gateway might be. Gideon had been right those many years ago. Jonah could see more than just the minutes around him. He could see into the days ahead, even weeks sometimes, but what Gideon hadn't said was how it also opened up the days of the distant past. As he looked into the fire now, he could see a barren hill, the very one upon which this mansion had been built. It showed a pristine land, well before man—red-skinned or white—had tread upon it, and he could feel the power that rested there. It was a place that had been waiting through the ages until there were those it could ensorcel into opening the paths to the demons beyond.

Gideon had been right about another thing. The gateway had

been close to crumbling when Gideon had passed. It remained close now, and Jonah wondered how much it would take. How many more times his failing body would need to take the knife from Caleb.

He was growing old, a man well beyond his prime, a condition made worse by the draining rituals he performed at the behest of the demons. He knew he would soon need to choose a successor of his own. Caleb had been asking him to do so for years, and he'd recently grown more bold, disobeying Jonah and arranging on his own for the condemned to be brought and put under the knife.

For years Jonah had continued to do the deed himself, but as time had worn on he'd become weaker, in body if not in mind, and he'd been forced to remain at the mansion as Caleb culled the souls and brought the knife home. There were days when Jonah felt ancient, days when he didn't know if he could take another, but he was now well and truly trapped. The demons controlled him as much as he controlled them. He had power over man, but very little over himself, and almost none over the inevitable tearing of the veil between this world and the next.

Rain pattered against the roof of the mansion. Flowed noisily down the gutters as lightning crashed. Caleb had been gone a long time, much longer than he should have, and that worried Jonah, for in recent days the vision gifted him by Gideon, once so clear, had become as unreliable as Jonah's failing heart.

The front door rattled open, the sound of the rain like meat thrown into a freshly hot skillet, and soon Caleb's old, limping form led a young boy into the sitting room. He must have been nine, perhaps ten years old. "Since you won't go see for yourself," Caleb said as he scrubbed his stubbled chin and neck, waiting for Jonah to draw his own conclusions.

Jonah stared at the boy, and his heart faltered. He coughed, his body folding forward. The boy was pure and bright, like the first clear rays of sunshine after the heavy rain of spring. He was exactly what Jonah needed, of course, someone pure who might be turned. It was this boy's purity of heart that drew the demons forward. It was his corruption that would weaken the veil, as Jonah's had, and Gideon's before him. There was little doubt that this boy would break down those walls once and for all, but it only served to remind Jonah of what Gideon had done. He'd robbed Jonah—taken his childhood and his future and given it to the demons. Jonah had once been pure and full of hope as this child was, but that had been stolen as well, currency in this foul bargain.

"His name is Lucas," Caleb said.

For some reason the fire raged hotter than Jonah could ever remember it. They knew, Jonah realized, and Caleb did as well. Caleb looked into the flames and smiled—at long last he'd found the one who would tear down the walls—and when he turned his eyes on Jonah once more, Jonah knew that Caleb would not allow him to ignore this boy, to say it was not yet time.

"Come here, Lucas," Jonah said, his voice scratchy from disuse.

The boy didn't move. His eyes were red, and there was an exhaustion about him that ran deeper than his fear, but there was more, something strange but oh-so-familiar. Jonah just needed to dig deeper to find it.

Lucas hadn't moved, so Jonah willed him forward, forced him to take one tentative step, then two, until he was standing directly before Jonah. Jonah took the boy's hand in his own. He looked deeper into his soul than anyone else before him, and he remembered with crystal clarity standing like this before Gideon, before Luther had cut him for the first time. It was a memory hidden for decades by Gideon's power, but he remembered now how exposed he'd felt then, and he knew that Gideon had seen in Jonah what Jonah was now seeing in this boy.

Jonah's hands shook. His mouth went dry and a strange lump formed in his throat. He wanted desperately to drop Lucas's hand, to send him away if only to protect him, but he couldn't let Caleb see how much it was affecting him.

This boy was a conduit to another world—not the world of demons, but a world of brightness, of good. Be they angels or saints or divine beings—who knew the truth of it?—what was clear was that they were creatures of preservation and peace, not damnation and death. Lucas and others like him protected this world from demons, but they couldn't do so if they were taken by the likes of Jonah and turned to a darker path.

"Take him away," Jonah said to Caleb. "He's not ready."

Caleb considered Jonah's words, then took Lucas by the shoulders and guided him toward the door. "Wait in the coach." When Lucas had gone, and the front door had rattled home, Caleb returned and stood before Jonah, the fire playing over his face like armies on a battlefield. "You saw what I saw. He's ready."

"Not yet," Jonah said carefully. "But he will be. He needs hate in his heart, as I had hate. He cannot be turned like this."

Caleb chewed on these words for a good long while. "I'll turn the boys on him, then."

Jonah smiled. "Of course. And in a few months, he'll be ours."

Jonah stood before a marble hearth, teeth gritted against the pain running through his entire body. Unlike the fire in his own mansion, this one was utterly mundane, and it left Jonah chilled to the bone. Over the years the need to touch the demons had grown at least as large as his need to eat, and his distance from it now left an empty gnawing inside him.

A pain that would only grow worse, Jonah knew.

As the rich walnut pocket door slid open behind him, Jonah felt the bones in his shoulders pop. Another side effect of the changes he'd set into motion last night after sending Caleb away to Norwich. The pain in his shoulders—in fact, the pain everywhere in his body—flared for a moment before returning to its ever-present ache. Part of him wanted to abandon this foolish plan, to return to his seat by his fire to wait for the inevitable, but the glimpse he'd seen through that boy, that bright white light . . . . The same was hidden within him. Somewhere. It had been obscured by the layer upon layer of misery he'd inflicted on the world, but it was still there. All he needed to do was uncover it. Or enough of it to save that boy.

"I never thought to see one of Jonah Bloom's men within these walls." As his manservant slid the doors closed behind him, Quinn sidled toward the fire, his eyes never leaving Jonah's. When he came to a rest only paces away, Jonah thought surely *then* Quinn would recognize him. But he didn't. He merely stared and snapped, "Well, what does he want?"

"All these years," Jonah replied easily. "Fifty, nearly, and you don't recognize me?"

Quinn started at the sound of his voice. Jonah's voice hadn't changed. Not yet.

"Jonah?"

"I've come to offer you a proposition. One I imagine you'll find agreeable."

"What sort of joke is this?"

"It isn't a joke. At least, not on you. I need your help, and if all goes well, you'll get your wish. You'll be rid of me once and for all."

"What's happened to you?"

Jonah's knee popped audibly. It was the worst one yet, causing his leg to buckle, but he remained standing as pain like an ice pick jabbed through his kneecap. "Let's leave that aside for the moment," Jonah said unsteadily. "Let's talk instead about what I've left behind. I've left behind my mansion, in which a terrible secret lies. I've left behind my men, who will even now be searching for me. I've left behind my knife, the one you saw me with so many years ago. I've left behind much, so that you might have a future."

"I?"

"You. The sons and daughters of Providence. Indeed, the world."

Quinn looked as though he were about to smile, but he seemed to sense the seriousness in Jonah's voice. "I won't be tricked, Jonah."

"No, you won't be. Not any longer. There's an asylum near Boston. Did you know? It's where I've been getting souls for nigh on twenty years."

"Why tell me this? Why now?"

Jonah took a deep breath as his ribs cracked and snapped, making themselves wider at Jonah's command. And then his skull made a sound like a walnut being crunched underfoot, and it brought on the worst pain yet. Jonah collapsed to the floor. He cradled his head with his arms, as if by doing so he could keep himself together and ward off the pain at the same time, but it did nothing to help. He writhed there for long moments, but then slowly, the pain subsided and he pulled himself up, inch by inch, until he was standing and facing Quinn once more.

"I am telling you this," he said after one faltering breath, "so that you'll know where Caleb gets his men should I fail. But more importantly, I'm telling you so that you can arrange for me to be brought to our man there."

"Who?"

"Why, the one who runs the asylum, of course."

Jonah stared at the ceiling of the cellar as men arranged candles near his hands and feet. The changes to his body had finally, mercifully, stopped. But the pain had not. His bones, his muscles, his tendons, even his skin hadn't been ready for such a rapid change. The simple act of breathing was misery.

The days after his transfer into the asylum had passed like decades, Jonah waiting second by second for his cell to open, for men to take him and place him in the wagon they'd had made especially for transfers such as these. He thought Caleb had made other arrangements, or that Quinn had thought better of their arrangement and betrayed him. He thought surely he'd be left here to rot.

But at last men did come, and Jonah was placed into chains and wrapped in darkness and transported back to Providence and down at last to this cellar.

Jonah moaned, and Henry struck him soundly across the cheek. He pulled a short knife from his belt and hunkered over Jonah, no longer recognizing the man who lay before him. "Quiet, now, or it'll go bad for you." He brandished the knife before putting it away and returning to his chalk.

He worried that Caleb might not come, that he might not bring Lucas, but eventually the door to the cellar opened and footsteps scraped down toward him. And there, standing over him, was Caleb. Jonah had not felt the traitor up until that moment. He'd spent decades with Caleb, and he'd abandoned the cause they'd both set for themselves. But Caleb had never truly been his own. Nor had Henry or Luther, or even Gideon for that matter. Neither had Jonah himself, not once the knife had touched him.

Jonah looked up into Lucas's nervous eyes, watched as he stepped forward holding the knife Caleb had already given him.

"Stand over him," Caleb said.

And the boy complied, but only because he was scared beyond comprehension. Jonah could see now that Lucas wasn't ready. Caleb had rushed things in Jonah's absence. Jonah nearly wanted to laugh. This might foul everything. Lucas *had* to stab Jonah. There was no other way.

When Gideon had died—the moment Jonah had stabbed him—his power had transferred to the blade, but it had done so only because of the demon trapped there by Jonah. Jonah's use of the blade to gather that demon had prepared Jonah to become Gideon's successor. Or, more accurately, it had prepared the blade. Now, though neither Caleb nor Lucas knew it, the ritual was being performed incorrectly. With the blade empty, there was no demon to shepherd Jonah's soul to Lucas. Lucas would not be imprinted upon the blade. It helped Jonah to know that Lucas's bright soul would not be sullied much in this process, but the most important thing was that the knife would not transfer Jonah's power. It would instead kill him. His soul would at last be mercifully, blessedly beyond this plane, untouchable. And it would undo what Gideon and so many before him had built.

But it all depended on the thrust of this knife by Lucas's hand.

As Lucas bent over Jonah in the stillness of this cramped space, Caleb backed away. Lucas had been told what he had to do. He held the knife ready, the point facing down toward Jonah's bared chest, but it was quivering so badly Jonah thought he might drop it.

"It's all right," Jonah whispered to him. "This is but a small payment for the sins I've carried out."

"Quiet!" Caleb snapped from the darkness.

Lucas's nostrils flared. His eyes stared deeply into Jonah's as his fingers flexed over knife's worn leather grip. The blade's edge reflected the candlelight with a wicked gleam, but to Jonah it looked like the light that was still hidden deep within him, and it only served to remind him how dark his life had been. Jonah shared this with Lucas now—the demons scrabbling inside him, the veil between worlds, the fact that Jonah acted as the conduit, the medium between the two—and he prayed the boy would understand.

"Do it now," Jonah whispered.

"Quiet!"

Lucas's fingers adjusted their grip.

"Do it!" Jonah pleaded.

Caleb stalked forward, ready to silence Jonah by force if need be, no matter what the ritual called for.

"Do it, please!" Jonah shouted at Lucas. "Release me!"

"No!" Caleb yelled, understanding finally coming to him. He lumbered forward, reaching for Lucas.

Lucas's expression, almost crazed with worry before, went soft. He'd seen. He'd seen at last the torment within Jonah, but more importantly, he'd seen what might happen were Jonah not taken now. Just as Caleb reached for his collar, he brought the knife down, sharp and hard, into Jonah's chest.

Jonah felt his body twist away from the pain. He heard Caleb screaming at Lucas as he pulled the boy violently away and sent him skidding across the dusty floor. He saw the worry in Caleb's face, and Henry's and Gilland's as they came to stand over Jonah, who had begun to return to his natural form.

The pain of it was like distant thunder. What Jonah felt was not his physical pain, nor the worry he'd had only moments ago, but the sense of deep satisfaction as the gateway—embodied in him since Gideon's death—began to unravel. The demons were torn away, sent back across the void to the dark beyond. And the gate itself began to close. It would take months, perhaps years, to close fully, but eventually it would, and that in turn would remove one of the pathways for the demons to enter the world.

Caleb, enraged beyond reason, snatched the knife from Jonah's chest. "Why?" he screamed.

Jonah didn't answer. He merely smiled as Lucas scrabbled away and fled the cellar. As the wooden door slammed open in his wake and the cold wind howled down and over Jonah, he heard not the laughter of the demons, nor the sharp questions of Caleb, but the keen ringing of a bright and beautiful bell somewhere in the distance.

About the Author

Bradley P. Beaulieu began writing his first fantasy novel in college, but in the way of these things, it was set aside as life intervened. As time went on, though, Brad realized that his love of writing and telling tales wasn't going to slink quietly into the night. The drive to write came back full force in the early 2000s, at which point Brad dedicated himself to the craft, writing several novels and learning under the guidance of writers like Nancy Kress, Joe Haldeman, Tim Powers, Holly Black, Michael Swanwick, Kij Johnson, and many more.

Brad and his novels have garnered many accolades and most anticipated lists, including two Hotties—the Debut of the Year and Best New Voice—on Pat's Fantasy Hotlist, a Gemmell Morningstar Award nomination for *The Winds of Khalakovo*, and more.

Brad continues to work on his next projects, including an Arabian Nights epic fantasy that will be published by DAW Books in 2014 and a Norse-inspired middle grade series. He also runs the highly successful science fiction and fantasy podcast, Speculate, which can be found at speculatesf.com.

For more, please visit www.quillings.com.

The Search for Crystallized Ginger

Chanté McCoy

The man brushed aside yet another cobweb, no longer flinching at the silken touch. In the black, forgotten spaces of the master's cellars, the webs hung abandoned, the spiders long gone, starved to death.

Hungry and weary, he yearned to turn back, but Kûru dared not. The cook threatened to flay him with one of his shiny knives and then cast him to the narrow streets of Karim Shar to beg for his bread if he returned again without any crystallized ginger. Kûru believed him; he'd witnessed the pock-faced chef chop off a serving girl's finger for stealing a fig.

In yet another room, Kûru looked around. In these dark corners, everything looked the same. Even the man himself was beginning to resemble the contents. His dust-filled loose curls, face, tunic, and baggy *shalvar* pants were just as gray, their details eroded as if centuries old. Only the set of old bronze keys, which he tried on the locks until he found the right one, retained their original coloring.

Kûru had never been so far in the labyrinthine depths and doubted anyone had in generations. Any ginger in these recesses would long be turned to the same dust that layered the forgotten urns, chests, and broken statuary. He placed his flickering torch into a metal ring embedded in the wall and reached for a small wooden box, his fingers sinking almost to the second knuckles in the fine dirt, which rose in a puff. Coughing, he pried it open only to find fragments of crumbling cloth. Disappointment mingled with relief washed over him. At least it wasn't another of the many desiccated rats, or worse, human bones. Earlier, he'd discovered a collapsed skeleton crammed into an urn and topped by a clearly cracked skull. Only slightly less disturbing were the thin bones of a severed hand displayed in a cloth-lined box, as if a gift of finely crafted jewelry.

Kûru wondered if the master knew the depths of his holdings, let alone was responsible for some of the morbid contents. The rich man's deeply lined face and graying hair spoke of a long life, enough time for those bones to have lost their flesh. And the whisperings among the servants suggested a temperament capable of cruelty. Kûru shuddered at the possibilities growing large in his head, not only for the victims or for himself should the master ever notice him, but for the master's young wife glimpsed in the dining hall.

Kûru exhaled a deep breath. He had long since given up on finding the candied delicacy for the evening's feast, a meal likely sitting heavy in the guests' bellies already. Still, he pushed aside his loathing of bones and cobwebs, opening more boxes and tipping more urns. He would exhaust every possibility to plead pardon if he ever found his way out again.

Hours passed until he finally reached the last room. Tired and disheartened, Kûru used the only key that had not worked on any other door. He forced the resistant lock to open and began to slog through the dusty contents, glad he was almost done, but suspecting the chef might still beat him despite his efforts.

It was in the farthest corner of the chamber that he found an indistinct, dust-buried oil lamp forgotten by time. The lamp obviously contained no ginger, but he picked up the oddity to inspect it closer. The long nozzle appeared clogged, and the lid covering the pouring hole was also plugged. An initial swipe along its side revealed a bronze surface engraved with strange markings. Kûru assumed the etchings made words, although they looked unlike the markings on the master's parchments and skins. He peered closer at a larger image stamped on the side: oval shaped, pinched on the ends, with a circle in its center. *An evil eye?* he wondered, wiping it again to clarify the design.

He never knew for certain. The lamp exploded in a flash of brilliant light, and dust blew around the room in a vortex of frenzied energy like a dust devil in the dry desert. Kûru cowered on the floor, coughing and covering his eyes . . . until all was still, but he was no longer alone occupied the room.

A gaunt creature with narrow features perched on a shelf, looking about itself. No cloth covered its smooth yellowish skin, for here was no human bound by such concerns.

Fear gripped Kûru but for a moment, replaced by joy at the good luck befallen him. A grin creased his dust-crusted cheeks. He'd heard the stories, the tales of others rewarded, so why not he? Emboldened, he stood up to face his good fortune.

"Djinni, having freed thee, I ask for my three wishes."

The creature stared down at him, hissing in apparent rage. Kûru hesitated, expecting more gratitude.

"I wish for enough gold to fill this room."

Only silence filled it in response.

"Gold?" it echoed after a while, its eyes tapering as it peered down at the man. "By what enterprise will you earn this precious metal you covet?"

"Earn?" Kûru blinked in incomprehension.

"I see," the creature said. "Your wish is for me to provide this gold."

Kûru nodded eagerly, relieved this exchange now proceeded according to script. He already entertained visions of all that his newfound money would buy. Like the master, he too would enjoy the plumpest figs, dripping honeycomb, and the finest wines of Assyria. Dressed in the silks of the Orient and fragrant oils in his beard, he would command respect among men and attention from lovely women. Why, he could even afford a wife and know the touch of a woman.

But, he desired the love of but one woman, the most beautiful he'd ever seen, though much of her beauty was left to his imagination for all the veils she hid behind. He'd only seen her eyes, the color of almonds, and dreamed of peeling back those embroidered cloths to discover more. Now, those almond eyes would see him as a man on par with the master, not just a servant warranting little more than a glance.

"You have another wish?" the creature prompted.

"Yes, I wish the wife of my master to be my own."

The creature's mouth seemed to soften into a smile. "You lust after this man's wife, envious that he beds her in the night?"

Confusion again washed across Kûru's face. "I . . . I love her."

The creature's head tilted. "Does she return this love?"

"No. When I have the gold, she will."

Yes, she will love me, he thought, certain that only his impoverished state stood between him and the love of the young woman. Thinking more, though, Kûru quickly spied a flaw in the plan. The almond-eyed wife could not simply leave the master for another man, even for one as noble and great when no longer dressed in rags. They'd be scorned by all, for the master might rid himself of his wife but not the other way around. Anger filled Kûru, desperate for a solution.

"Djinni, I know my third wish."

The creature leaned toward him. "Yes?"

"I want the master dead."

"Ah," the creature said. Its long tongue extended as if catching flies. "Giving death is something I do."

Kûru clapped delightedly at the prospect of all his wishes coming true.

The creature hissed and pointed a clawed finger at him. "I shall give this death, but not at the bidding of such as you."

Kûru stammered. "And the gold. . . . "

In the flash it had taken to escape the lamp, the creature vaporized again, this time seeking out the servant.

Kûru screamed in shock and agony but lost the battle within seconds, relegated to a corner of his own mind. The new Kûru spread out his hands before him as if testing their control. A plan had already formed.

"Tell me," it said to the amorphous fragment of what had been the man. "How rich is this master?"

"One of the richest in town," came the whisper. "Are you not djinn?"

The demon laughed aloud, its time-leached humor restored. It granted that the man had the right of it, whatever his wishful thinking: moneyed men were powerful men, capable of so much more.

The demon weaved its way out of the cellar. It wouldn't need this vessel for long.

About the Author

At any given time, Chanté McCoy is reading a handful of novels, taking a continuing education class to dabble in her latest interest (NOTE: she has no future in belly dancing), or hiking the mountains of Utah with Elvis, her 110-lb Doberman Pinscher. Visit chantemccoy.com to follow her blog.

Guardian of the Headwaters

Brad R. Torgersen

Brother Ersu was out of breath when he reached the crest of the hill. Cool, wildflower-scented air cut sharply in his heaving lungs as he eased himself into a prone position behind the trunk of a fallen tree. Before him, a vast alpine basin lay half full of water. The kind of clean, utterly frigid water only the Five Sisters could yield. Nearest the shore, the tops of living trees projected from the lapping surface, their branches still green with needles—evidence of the rapid rise in the level of the natural reservoir.

On any other day, the wilderness-loving and aesthetically-minded monk would have been delighted by such a tranquil scene.

But today he frowned, having eyes only for the cause of the water's rise.

A tremendous bulwark of jumbled ice stretched across the mouth of the valley, several tens of man-heights tall and perhaps a fifth of a league in width. Runoff that ordinarily would have trickled into the birth channel of the River Ornax now built behind that glacier—and thousands of farmers on the plains, who each depended on the Ornax for irrigation at planting time, heard whispers of famine in the late spring wind.

Brother Ersu quietly turned and put his back to the log, letting the warmth of the sun bathe his face while he considered what he had just seen. In his left hand he clutched a sigil-carved wooden staff: the symbol of his station. His right hand—the

Marked hand—lay curled against his side, shrunken on its twisted arm since the day he had been born.

The monk did not begrudge his deformity. Not anymore. During his years of study with the Order he had learned that such was the price of power, and amongst the Brotherhood, all men bore such Marks. It was said in scripture that the Maker did not give Gifts without exacting a price, and for those with the power that *was* Power, this price could sometimes be high. The elders of the Order were rich with power, and yet their bodies lay inert, misshapen, cradled in wheeled chairs, their mouths barely able to speak and their legs barely able to walk, much less run.

Which was why Ersu, a natural runner, had been selected.

Three weeks earlier, Ersu had been returning from the market when he'd been stopped by the blind beggar who took up residence at the side of the great western road. A foolish man, the beggar ordinarily told wild and often ribald tales in exchange for coins or a meal. On that particular day the beggar was shouting at the top of his lungs before a small throng of travelers.

"Did you see it?" The beggar whooped, standing on his little wooden stool. "It came out of the sky, red as blood!"

The crowd was murmuring quietly: had the beggar finally gone mad?

"Red as blood!" he shouted again, shaking his fist at them.

"What are you talking about?" Ersu said from the back of the group.

"Shooting star. Across the dark of the moons!"

Ersu gently nudged his way forward until he was face to face with the beggar. Whereas the beggar's beard was long, tangled, and matted, Ersu's was properly short, trimmed, and clean. Ersu's robe also clearly identified him for what he was: a scholar of the Power. The crowd quieted down in order to hear the exchange between the beggar and the monk—who surely knew more about celestial signs and portents than anyone among them.

"It's difficult to understand how you could have seen what we did not," Ersu said, smiling slightly. "If events had transpired as you describe, the Order would be aware of them. And taking steps to understand what they mean."

"You think you are wise," the beggar said bitterly. "Monks who sit in their library all day, never showing their faces to the world."

"I'm here aren't I?" Ersu said, an eyebrow raised. "Clearly, not all of us are hesitant to let the sun shine on our faces. We study what we know to be true about the universe. Which is why I am quite sure we would have known about this 'shooting star' long before even you knew of it. Who told you this happened?"

"Nobody told me," the beggar said, his chin thrust outward and his clouded eyes blinking furiously.

"Yet you described a red—"

"I know what color I said it was. And I *saw* it."

"How?"

"In *here,*" the beggar said, pointing to his head.

The crowd groaned and began to move away, shaking their heads and muttering: yes, the sometimes-entertaining beggar had clearly lost his faculties. They had better things to do than heed the ravings of a crazy man.

Ersu considered.

It was said that the beggar had not been blind his whole life. The milk that covered his eyes had come upon him when he'd been an older boy. At which time his father—a harsh and unforgiving merchant traveling the great western road—had abandoned the lad. Thus his blindness was not a Gift in the same way Ersu's malformed arm was a Gift: Marked from birth.

Thus the beggar had no Power.

"You swear this is the truth?" Ersu said sternly. "Spreading false fear is punishable by the constabulary."

"I swear it," the beggar said stoutly.

"Tell me everything you remember from that night."

"I laid down to sleep like I always do, just me and my blankets, and little Kiki."

The small mongrel dog that lay at the side of the beggar's stool poked its head up, giving a gentle tail wag.

"Some time during the night, the dog started barking like the world was going to end. Jumping about and yapping and howling that sharp little *oooooooo* howl that he sometimes does when the moons are full. But I knew from hearsay on the road that the moons were at wane that night, so I couldn't imagine what got Kiki so riled up. I rolled out of my blankets and called to Kiki to quiet down, but she wouldn't stop. Then—"

Suddenly the beggar's chin trembled.

"Go on," Ersu said.

"It came to me. Like a dream, but solid and sharp. I *saw* the black circles of the moons against the white stars, and this red streak like a coal from a camp fire went across the moons. It moved slowly at first, then suddenly picked up speed and flashed down towards the earth."

Ersu was motionless.

His logical mind wanted to dismiss the account as a fantasy. Something this momentous would have been seen by others. The Brotherhood had several astrologers on hand to watch the skies every clear night. And during the last waning of the moons, it had been very clear. Yet the monks making observations had not reported anything. Nor had any news reached the order from the constabulary, who took watch over the market, the road, and all else in the surround.

Yet . . .

The beggar was stiff in his conviction.

And try as he might, Ersu could detect no falseness in the beggar's words.

"Did anything else happen that night?" Ersu asked.

"No. Though I didn't get any more sleep, I can tell you that much. It took the rest of the night to calm Kiki down, and when the warmth of the sun touched my face the next morning, I had to get back to work. A man's got to feed himself, you know?"

Ersu noticed the small, battered kettle that sat opposite the dog, on the other side of the beggar's stool. Only a few, low-denomination coins lay at the bottom. The beggar wouldn't be buying much food today. And the crowd—who might have been willing to contribute, if the outlandishness of the beggar's tale had not put them off—had moved on.

Ersu fished in the thick belt of his robe, finding his tiny coin purse.

He dropped a substantial donation into the kettle.

The beggar smiled broadly, hearing the satisfying clink and rattle of the large coin as it hit, rebounded, and settled to the bottom.

"The generosity of the Brotherhood is appreciated," the beggar said. "Forgive my poor manners earlier. I am afraid I spoke with proud anger."

"As do we all at times," Ersu said. "Thank you for giving me this information."

"You believe me?"

"I don't disbelieve you, let's put it that way."

The beggar's smile faltered.

"Fear not," Ersu said, putting his good hand on the beggar's shoulder. "If this thing you have experienced is an ill omen, the Order will take steps to combat it. As we always have. May the fortune of the Five Sisters bless you this day."

Ersu pulled his hand away and made the customary, habitual signs in the air—which the beggar could not see, yet seemed to sense.

The beggar swallowed a lump in his throat.

"Thank you," he said.

And with that, Ersu was on his way.

He'd no sooner returned to the portico of the monastery when one of the young acolytes rushed up to him, breathless with the news brought by the constabulary: the river was running dry.

The plains council needed accurate information if it was to combat whatever evil had dammed the headwaters of the Ornax.

The party of riders which preceded Ersu had never returned.

Whatever ill had stopped the river and consumed the mounted company was obviously beyond blade and arrow.

It was thus decided that a holy man—one who knew the power that *is* Power—should be sent.

Alone, armed with silence and his Gift, such a man might make a successful reconnaissance of the river and return in time for a proper response to be marshaled.

So, where the riders had gone in thunderous authority, Ersu went with the softness of a fox. He took only his staff, his customary calf-strapped sandals, a small pack with provisions, and a canvas mat with blanket, and he'd donned a deer-skin tunic with wool undershirt—to defend against both cold and rain.

For weaponry, Brother Ersu carried nothing greater than a small cooking knife.

The monk ran for almost five days, picking his course carefully in parallel with the bed of the Ornax, and yet distant enough that anyone—or anything—watching the course would not see him. If his right arm was useless, his legs were made of iron, and his heart and lungs pumped with the efficiency of a windmill. Occasionally he reached out with his Power to find a spring for refilling his waterskins. This he did only by necessity, as extensive Power use would almost certainly signal his presence to whomever or whatever lurked in the shoulderland of the Five Sisters.

At night Ersu made tiny fires, for warmth against the chill and to cook any game he happened to take during the day. Here also he was cautious, for the killing of any large beast would not only be wasteful—Ersu had no means of preserving or carrying large amounts of meat—it would reverberate through the ether to any soul receptive enough to sense such bloodshed.

At last, the monk arrived at the lake, but not straightaway. Still wishing to avoid the eyes of any who might be watching, he left the birth path of the river and journeyed far around, climbing a substantial wall of rock until he came out on the lip of the basin, in a place greatly distant from the head of the Ornax.

Looking to the lee of the ice dam, Ersu could see a path—almost like the trail of a snail—leading his eyes further up into the tree-lined hills. There the greenery gave way to the white-cloaked flanks of the nearest Sister. On that distant slope, Ersu could make out a huge wound in the permanent ice pack. The swath from the wound—filled with snow, crushed rocks, and broken trees—led directly down to the far side of the dam.

Ersu was immediately struck by the artificiality of the glacier's fall. Not only had the ice made far more progress in a single season than could be accounted for naturally, a barely-perceptible flavor of *consciousness* lingered on the dam. As if the calving from the permanent pack had been purposely steered to its current location, against alternate paths which might have met with less resistance.

Ersu felt a chill touch his heart.

Even the entire Brotherhood, with all their minds focused on the task, could not have hoped to dislodge such a massive quantity of ice from the nearer Sister, nor drive it so deftly that it exactly and completely blocked the Ornax at its source.

Whatever evil had occupied this place, its potency surely dwarfed the monk.

He sighed, realizing his heart had begun to beat with fear.

An ordinary man would have turned and fled.

But Ersu had been commissioned—he had to know more before he could report back on what he'd seen.

Ersu loosed a waterskin from his belt and gargled its contents before spitting, then swallowing, spitting a second time, and finally swallowing several welcome gulps. For food, he gnawed a quick meal of hardened bread, voided his bowels into a hole he scraped in the hillside, then he gathered his pack and staff and began picking his way cautiously back down to a point where he could slip into the tree line.

From there he made his way around the dammed reservoir towards the glacier itself.

By the time Ersu peered out at the jumbled wall of ice from a copse of trees that lay almost directly at the dam's nearer end, the sun was greatly lowered in the afternoon sky. The massive boulders of frozen water in front of the monk were gorgeously arrayed in a kaleidoscope of milky blues and grays that made even the cerulean of the lake pale in comparison. Their faces bled rivulets of purity in the afternoon sun.

The monk temporarily tensed, eager to walk out and touch the ice—to use his Gift.

But Ersu waited, for fear of disclosing himself to his as-yet unseen enemy.

Patience would reward where haste brought sorrow.

So, like any good Brother, Ersu sat in the grass at the tree line and meditated.

Afternoon turned to evening, and the evening turned to night, and Brother Ersu kept his thoughts and mind open to the world around him, passively letting the ethereal flavors of the earth and the water and the air seep into his bones. Whatever wrong lay here, if it still lingered, he hoped to sense it. Eventually the moon came out and the deep chill of the mountain night was upon him, so he unrolled his canvas mat, lay down on it, covered himself with the wool blanket, and let himself fall into dreamless, concentrated slumber.

At midnight, clouds rolled in. A storm began to drop its load to the ground.

Awakened by the first fat drops, the monk rode out the storm as best he could. Hypothermia would not touch him so long as he kept an internal mantra going: a simple but effective chant which translated a small part of his Power into body heat.

Ersu chanted slow and long and used just enough energy to keep from going into the death of cold. Too much effort and he risked exposing himself to anyone else able to sense the Power.

The rain pummeled the surface of the reservoir like a million little hammers.

Lightning flashed and thunder rolled.

Once, during a particularly violent lightning strike—which arced across the face of the lake and split a tree on the far slope—the monk jumped to his feet as he thought he witnessed a lone, pale figure on the crown of the glacial dam.

Frozen with fascination, Ersu looked in astonishment at what for all intents and purposes seemed to be a tall, remarkably beautiful woman.

She was naked and her skin was pale—as white as the ice upon which she stood. Long, soaking-wet hair hung down her back past her knees, and large, round breasts shadowed a slim waist on top of enticingly wide hips.

Ersu would have been instinctively lustful if not for the fact that every bare inch of the woman exuded Power.

The monk gasped and collapsed to his knees, ignoring the rain that continued to fling down upon him.

The sight of the albino apparition pressed the air from his lungs and made his Marked arm spasm in agony. Never before in his whole life had he felt the presence of so much raw Power, not even in the quorums of the elders of the Order, which pooled the greatest amount of Power in all the western plains.

This terrified Ersu.

He crouched lower to the ground and wrapped his arms around his chest.

Would she see him? And if so, what would happen next?

The woman's arms were raised high and her head was facing into the belly of the storm, as if she communed with it.

The monk watched in fascinated, petrified silence.

Darkness flooded the scene briefly, before another close pass of lightning again lit the dam, showing the woman in the same position and at the same place. Ersu could see no Marking of any kind upon her, and when the darkness came again, to be split by a third explosion of electricity arcing in the low clouds, she was suddenly gone from the crest of the dam, as if she'd never existed at all.

Ersu *felt* her vanish before his eyes could clearly register the fact.

For an instant, her titanic Power surged.

Then, there was no Power at all.

Ersu suddenly gasped and doubled over, gulping in air with his heaving lungs.

For the rest of the miserable night, he watched. And waited. And yet the woman did not return.

Until the rain finally stopped and the clouds began to dissipate and the monk recovered his sodden wool blanket and resumed his internal ritual invocation of warmth, generating just enough heat to let him lay back and sleep.

This time, he could not help but dream—restless and disturbing nightmares derived from the Order's oldest legends of the ancient gods and goddesses who were said to have once walked the Earth. In his somnolent torment, Ersu approached one such deity, pleading for mercy, and was struck down like an insect.

In the morning, Brother Ersu woke late.

His body was stiff and cold from the damp night, and he tasted rawness at the back of his throat. He greatly desired a fire with which to heat some water and brew a tincture that might ward against sickness.

But Ersu dared not. Especially if he'd actually seen what he thought he saw. The smoke would act as a beacon.

Next, Ersu considered the apparition he'd seen on the dam. In all the lore of the Order, it was told, only the divine bore Power without Marks.

Looking apprehensively out from his hiding place among the pines, Ersu again observed the crown of the ice dam and thought he could see some subtle difference at the spot where he believed he had seen the woman standing in the torrent the night before. He also noticed that the water level behind the ice had risen substantially—more vital water that would not reach the plains.

He scanned the dam, sensing as far as he dared for anyone else in the vicinity. Then—satisfied that he was alone—Ersu secured his pack and draped his soggy blanket across a tree limb, grasped his staff, and set forth.

As Ersu approached the glacier dam he was hit again with the raw size of the glacier's boulders: their impossible weight, and the terrible exertion of will it must have taken to move them. The low popping and shifting of their massive bulk within the guts of the glacier could be felt as reverberations in both earth and air.

When the monk reached the nearest boulder, he cupped his staff with his Marked arm and gently reached out his good hand, placing it on a thigh of the ice. The sharp cold shot up through his palm. Amazingly brilliant trickles of melt water bathed him to the wrist. Reaching with his mind and murmuring softly to himself, Ersu could sense that the ice itself was not ill: no force could utterly defile such a vast amount of virgin material. Not this close to its source, the Five Sisters.

"So they sent a Brother," said a voice.

Ersu jumped back, startled to the bone.

An old woman stood about two-dozen paces away. She was wrapped in a shawl of rough, thickly-woven cloth. Her face was drawn and shot through with lines and wrinkles, and only a few wisps of white hair poked out at odd places from under the hood of the shawl. She held on to a small tree limb like a staff, using it to support her stooped weight.

"Who are you?" Ersu asked, his heart beating rapidly in his chest.

"I walk the shoulderlands of the Five Sisters," she said. "It's been a long time since a monk of the Order showed his face up here."

Ersu took a couple of steps toward her and searched his memory.

Ah, suddenly he had it.

"Tebbat," Ersu said.

The old woman's mouth curled into a sour smile with few teeth.

"That's one of my names," she said.

"Do you know what happened?" Ersu asked, pointing to the dam with his staff.

"The glacier cut loose and stopped here."

Ersu wrinkled his brow in annoyance. The old woman was being coy.

"The elders speak of you, Tebbat. You are Marked. You have the Power. You know as well as I do that this was no natural act."

The old woman spat a cackle.

"What does it matter?" she said. "Gonna be a dry year on the plains. Followed by a big flood. Wouldn't want to be living down on the great western road. It'll be disaster upon disaster."

Tebbat seemed to take pleasure in saying the word *disaster.*

"Did you cause this?" Ersu asked, sweeping his good arm in the direction of the ice.

Again a spitting cackle.

"Boy, even if I had the Power to do it, why would I?"

"Indeed," Ersu asked, "why would you? The elders speak of your having been expelled from the Sisterhood. Before my birth. It was a rather dramatic break, I am told. You would not heed the admonishments of your superiors."

"Fools," Tebbat said. "Stuck in their ways. I gladly came here, to explore my Power without restrictions or rules. To be free."

"And has this *freedom* come with a price?"

"You know not of which you speak," she said, her mouth forming a bitter frown. "Go back to the plains council, little monk, and tell them to get ready for a hard year. Maybe the worst in living memory."

Ersu waited, watching the old woman. Her sudden appearance couldn't be a coincidence. Was there a connection to the apparition he had seen during the storm?

"I can't leave until I have more information," Ersu said.

"The plains council can do nothing about this," Tebbat said, pointing her walking stick in the direction of the dam. "It'll be here as long as it takes for the ice to melt, or for the water to begin running over the top, then there will be a killer wave crashing down the Ornax and into the plains, fierce and deadly."

"Yes, that seems self-evident."

"So what more can you hope to learn?"

"I am seeking information pertaining to three things," Ersu said. "They may or may not be connected."

"Yes?" she said.

"At the last waning of the moons, a strange report surfaced: of a shooting star, red and baleful, crossing over the darkened faces of the moons and settling to the earth."

"Didn't see it," she said. Though something about the look in her eye told Ersu that Tebbat wasn't being entirely truthful.

"What else?" she asked.

"Last night, during the thunderstorm, I am sure I witnessed... a personage. A *being*. Up there—"

Ersu's arm pointed to the top-most center portion of the dam.

"The goddess!" Tebbat said gleefully.

"Yes," Ersu said. "Or so she seemed to be."

"I know of her."

"Did *she* cause the glacier to fall?"

"I don't know."

"Then, was she responsible for the disappearance of the riders who were sent here previously? To reconnoiter the riverhead?"

Tebbat hesitated.

"It's never wise to upset a divine one."

"How would you know?" Ersu pressed. "The old deities exist mostly in fable. None of the elders have seen such a being, and there are some who speculate that they may not have even existed at all, outside of legend."

"Like I told you," Tebbat said, "the Brotherhood and the Sisterhood are stuck in their ways. For many a year I have lived in the shadow of the Five Sisters. There is Power up here, independent of any Gift. Wild Power. Perhaps what you saw was merely the personification of that wild Power. Wouldn't surprise me if the Five Sisters have gotten tired of the people of the plains. Maybe it's time the people of the plains were taught a lesson?"

Ersu stiffened. Tebbat spoke of the pending famine and flood as if they were cruel jokes—which she seemed to find particularly amusing.

He opened his mouth to retort, but she turned on a heel and was marching back into the tree line—far faster than a woman of her age had any right to be moving.

Ersu trotted after her, but as he pushed his way into the pines, he realized she'd disappeared as deftly as she'd appeared.

Angry and befuddled, he considered what next to do.

If he left now he could at least warn the plains council and the elders among the Brotherhood of the danger. Perhaps people could abandon the plains over the summer? But to where?

Ersu walked back to the glacier dam.

He put his good hand back on the ice, which practically burned his skin it was so frigid.

Probing a little further with the Power, Ersu recognized that the ice was largely stable—the shear weight and breadth of the glacier prevented it from crumbling. For now. Time enough to do more study.

For the rest of the morning and part of the early afternoon, Ersu circumnavigated the dam and the lake it had created, looking for the old woman. When he could not find her—not even the Power gave any hint as to where she'd gone—he returned to the place where he'd started and began climbing up the dam itself.

The monk gripped his staff in his good hand and began awkwardly picking his way up the ice until he was walking unsteadily along the crest of the dam proper: slowly making his way arm-length after arm-length towards the spot where he believed he had seen the visage of the alabaster-white woman in the rain.

It took over an hour to get there.

Ersu's path was obstacle-laden and treacherous. On one side lay the imperceptibly rising blue water. On the other, a jumbled slope dropping many, many man-heights down to the bottom of the canyon—where the Ornax traditionally began its long journey out of the mountains.

The monk took great care.

Upon reaching his target, Brother Ersu got down on hands and knees and began examining the ice.

The spot was no different from any other. Not to the unaided eye.

But Brother Ersu was not unaided. He saw with the power that *was* Power. Something in the ice nagged at him, irritated his unconscious. Risking a little more force, he delicately lifted his staff and placed its heel on the spot, and began to whisper softly. The sigil-carved wood responded immediately to the will of its master, and quickly Ersu began to see the memory of the ice, back through the minutes and hours of the morning, back to the break of day, back to the night, until he felt his Marked arm quiver.

In humble acknowledgement of the great forces of the Earth, he asked his question: *who and what are you, oh beautiful and terrible wraith of the storm?*

There was a sudden groan from within the dam. The ice complained at having to divulge its secrets.

Ersu gritted his teeth and increased the volume of his asking, risking his life on the belief that if he could identify what he had seen in the storm, he would then know enough to flee the dam, return to the plains, and lay the burden of this knowledge on the brows of men more capable of bearing it.

But luck was not with him.

An unseen force suddenly sucked the air from his lungs.

He did not need to look up to know who had returned.

Ersu pitched away from the spot he was examining and almost slid down the ice toward the rear of the dam. His staff held him balanced on the precipice until he regained his feet in time to see his enemy approach.

She stood fifty paces away from the monk, on a patch of water made featureless and flat as marble. She was the same woman he had seen in the night, with skin so fair in the sunlight that it rivaled the hue of the ice itself. Her hair was black as a crow's feathers, and she remained shamelessly naked, save for what he now saw were bracelets of colorful stone pebbles on each wrist, and circlets of woven green branches on each ankle.

She was also tall. Far taller than any mortal man or woman the monk had ever met. Her unblinking eyes were inhuman in that they possessed neither whites nor irises. They were solid obsidian.

And they smoldered with a palpable, ebony fury.

Almost paralyzed with fear, Ersu felt her gaze bore into him like arrows. He yelled for his life, running to the other edge of the ice dam and throwing himself into the water.

Then he swam. With his good arm and both legs beating the water furiously, he swam until he touched the far edge and could drag himself out of the water and onto the grass at the shore.

There Ersu lay for several moments, until he had regained enough strength to roll over, sit up, and look back the way he had come.

The woman—the *goddess*—was nowhere to be found.

Night came again.

Ersu made camp far away from the dam, in the shadow of a cluster of large boulders, where he could risk a small fire. If there were to be more storms, the sky didn't show it. Every star sparkled pure and clean, with the white limbs of the moons glowing far above.

"I told you to go back where you came from," said a familiar, old voice.

Ersu shot to his feet, wrapping his arms around his bare chest. He'd shed most of his wet clothing and wore only a loincloth. The fire kept him warm, but as he stepped away from it, the chill of the night air was electric on his skin.

Tebbat was there, beneath the bows of a huge hemlock.

"You're playing games with me," the monk accused.

"Hardly," the old woman said. "I am trying to save your life."

"I'm touched," Ersu said, the sarcasm leaking through his chattering teeth.

"You must be a fool to stay," she said. "How many riders came to this place and did not return? What can you possibly hope to do that they could not? Leave now, and go to the east. Far away from the plains. There are other people. Other villages. Even cities. Places where someone with the Power might start over. With a new Brotherhood."

"That would be the coward's path."

"That would be the *wise man's* path, little Brother. The goddess has laid claim to this place and she has chosen her weaponry well. Water is life, but water can also be death. She will drought them out, then flood them out. And next spring? She'll do it again. And again. Until the western plains are emptied, and men no longer dwell in the land of the Five Sisters."

"You speak as if from personal knowledge," Ersu said.

"Perhaps I do. I've lived here a long time. I know what it means to commune with the silence of these mountains. Men shatter that silence. With axes, as they come to take the trees. Men also shatter it with picks and shovels, as they come to dig for copper, tin, and gold. They hunt the shoulderland forests, taking far more game than they should. Put simply, men have encroached too far. I believe the goddess has come to put a stop to all that. And I can't say that I'm sorry. Though I will be sorry if you continue to risk your life due to your misguided sense of duty."

"You understood duty—once," Ersu said.

"Blindness," she replied. "I was blind. And then I learned to see."

Ersu suddenly remembered the beggar.

"You know something about the red shooting star," he said. "I sensed it in you before. This goddess and the meteor, are they connected?"

Tebbat sighed. "If I said yes, what possible difference could it make?"

"Perhaps none. Or, perhaps, all."

"And why would you believe me, either way?"

Ersu looked at her. He had no answer to her question.

She cackled harshly at him, then seemed to meld with the darkness beneath the hemlock, leaving Ersu alone in the night.

Brother Ersu awoke, barely able to breathe.

The Power in the air was thick, like humidity. He was still cold, but began to sweat profusely.

The goddess had returned.

Ersu set out on foot back to the dam, using as much of his own Power as he dared to avoid stumbling and falling in the darkness.

When he reached the dam he could not see her, but her Power still clogged his senses.

Fumbling his way up the ice, he stood on the top and looked across the dappled surface of the water as a gentle night breeze rippled the surface, distorting the mirror reflection of the crescent moons in the sky.

Ersu still could not see her.

Against all reason, he began working his way back to the center of the dam, where he'd last attempted to ascertain her nature.

In another time and place, Ersu would have chastised himself for being so foolish. But he'd been several days without decent sleep, or a decent meal. And there'd be no chance of rest tonight unless he braced his courage and attempted to face the entity who so badly frightened him.

When at last he reached the center of the dam, Ersu got down on trembling knees and once again invoked the memory of the ice.

The dam grumbled and moaned.

Almost dangerously so.

And for an instant, Ersu thought it might give way.

Suddenly he imagined himself being simultaneously crushed and drowned. What a horrible way to die.

But just as suddenly he was staring at the silhouette of the goddess: her body shining at the edges, like the limbs of the moons themselves.

The Power in the atmosphere had grown to epic proportions.

She was so close, Ersu could have reached out to touch her.

"What . . . are you?" Ersu finally croaked, his voice thick and his Marked arm thrumming with painful awareness of her proximity.

The woman took several steps across the ice and pointed a large, long finger at Ersu's sternum.

"Dabbler!" She spat, with a voice like an earthquake. "Pretend master of the energies of the world. I have watched as your kind moved in the lands beneath the eyes of the mountains. Short-lived men felled forests and raised villages and sowed crops and forgot the reverence they owed to the *true* mother of their flesh. I would punish all men for their inequity and their filth—punish *you* for your weakling's hold on the Power that runs through me like the blood in your very veins."

Ersu was struck dumb at her last words. She radiated supreme Gifting equal to a hundred cripples. No, a thousand. So strong, it struck Ersu's chest like a fist. He found himself moaning uncontrollably as he collapsed onto the ice, his staff wavering in his loosening grip as her potency ravaged the air and beat into his bones through his inconsequential flesh.

"But hear me yet," the woman continued. "I offer a chance at redemption. It is the same offer I made to those who came before you. An offer they were foolish enough to renounce, in their pride and blindness. Behold, pretender, beneath you is the frozen skin of the mountain, and behind it builds the instrument of your destruction. Whether by my choice or through the long days of early summer, this dam will burst, and a flood of mighty proportion will sweep down into your domain, cleansing it of all desecration. But if you swear service to me now, give yourself in worship and will to my bidding, I shall stay my hand. You shall not be destroyed, as the others were, nor shall I destroy any who promise the same. The will of men is foolhardy and corrupt, but it can be tamed and made to do hale work, if given the proper yoke. Do you submit?"

Ersu was only dimly hearing her words. Her shadowed face said she detested him, and the power of her will pulsed at him like a bonfire. He felt as if she might devour his soul with the merest suggestion, and he wondered that any man could have the fortitude or the want to deny such absolute force, especially when combined with such absolute beauty.

Still, some part of him retained its focus. He was not totally defenseless against her. He was a Brother, after all.

Using all his internal strength and focus—while gritting his teeth through a hymn—Ersu levered himself back to his feet and faced the wraith.

"I am Ersu, of the Order of Kenneses the Wise, holder of the fourth rank and born wielder of the power that *is* Power. Know me by my Mark, which is the price of wielding. My oaths do not allow me to swear allegiance to a goddess of malice. By what right do you seek the drowning of children?"

The water of the lake seemed to jumble and roil.

A pale shimmering of light played off the water's surface, illuminating the woman's expression.

She seemed momentarily astonished.

His full exercise of his Power had rebuked her, even if temporarily. Ersu panted at the physical and mental labor of it all.

Then she reshaped her features it into a scowl of mocking contempt.

"Children? You speak to me of *children?* What do I care for the spawn of men, when men wreck and burn the cradles of the forests? Men are but ambitious apes. They should be treated as such."

"I hear you, deity, and I can sense the tremendous force of your existence. The scripture of the Brotherhood contains legends of creatures such as yourself—manifestations of an earthly power so strong it becomes self-aware, and must take form and move upon the face of the land for purposes only the earth itself knows. But I tell you now that I know of no ill brought upon the world by the people of the western plains that would warrant your hate. I am a Brother, sworn to the loving of peace and the healing of hurt. If it is combat you seek with me, I cannot give it. Just as I cannot swear fealty to you."

The woman's all-black eyes flared dangerously.

"Shall I crack the ice beneath your very feet, monk? Perhaps in the roaring death of flood you will learn the error of your ways."

Ersu studied the wraith, his eyes locked on her face in spite of her tremendous body. She spoke terribly and she *felt* worse, but something was not quite right. He remembered the wraith as he'd seen her on the crown of the dam the night before: her arms outstretched, as if beseeching the heavens.

And he remembered Tebbat, cackling in the darkness.

The seed of an idea began to bloom.

Mentally commanding as much of his Power as his Mark could possibly provide him, Ersu pushed himself achingly erect.

"Do as you will," he said. "If your purpose is to destroy the western plains, I cannot stop you, goddess. But what if I could suggest an alternative? None living in either the Brotherhood or the Sisterhood has seen the likes of you. You are strange and terrifying, but there must also be much we can learn from you. If you could teach us to be better stewards of the forests and the wild lands, would that not be an even better lesson than raw punishment? If you destroy the western plains, men will come again someday. And they will see the Five Sisters, and the forests and the hills beneath them, and it will begin again. But if we could forge a *partnership*— "

The creature's face dropped some of its pompous hatred and now bore a mixture of uncertainty and fury.

She glowered down at him.

"You speak as if mad, crippled man. I partner with no one. And I see now that you desire the same fate as the other fools who came to do battle. You will regret not having submitted yourself to me!"

With that, the wraith raised its hand as if to slap him.

Ersu sensed that such a blow would burst his skull like a ripe gourd.

As her hand and arm swung down, he spoke a sacred exclamation and parried with his staff, the sigil-empowered wood blasting apart in a flash, a shower of flaming splinters, and the acrid smell of scorched wood.

Ersu would have been pitched headlong over the far side of the dam had he not flung out his small, Marked arm in the same instant—and flexed the tangled fingers of his Marked hand, grasping the wraith's still-extended palm.

The touch of her skin on his Marked hand seared like campfire coals, but Ersu resisted the urge to howl his pain. Instead, he mustered up more oaths. These were not designed to rebuke Power, but to siphon it. The Brotherhood often used them to pool Power for very large or very urgent exercises. Ersu intended to draw as much of the wraith's Power as he could into his own body, through his Marked arm.

"I am a Brother of the Order of Kenesses!"

The powerful words brought a white fire from the flesh of the wraith, who screamed in unearthly tones and tried to wrench free of the monk. But the fingers of his Marked hand sank into her too-white skin like hooks, and suddenly Ersu was shrieking himself as the wraith's power flowed back up the link between them into his lame arm, sparkling in agony along his nerves and sinews. The raw energy of the union of their flesh—their Power—met him like the end of the universe. He would have been rent down the middle had he not begun using the woman's Power to reinforce his own. The energy flooded like lava through his bones, but it kept him upright and his head erect: eyes staring directly into hers.

"Know this power by the Mark of my birth!"

The Wraith continued to wail, and Ersu brought his left hand up and gripped the creature's other arm, until they were grappling on the edge of the glacier dam, a white waterspout inferno whirling out from her and shredding his clothing, down to his sandals, until they both fought naked and desperate—her awesomeness threatening to crush him.

She would have succeeded had he not been invoking the oaths of the Brotherhood, thus taking her hatred and her pain into himself like a funnel channeling milk into a bottle. It scorched his mind and blasted his spirit unlike anything he had experienced before, but as a weapon, his Brotherly invocations confounded her.

Ersu continued, his mouth frozen in torment, but his mind roaring the words as if they might be his last.

Pain is the ravager of life!
Move through your pain with me, as if beneath a waterfall!
Water, both cool and clean, like the breeze of heaven!
Set sail your soul from pain, and be free!

At the pinnacle of the wraith's outrage—as she gathered her will and threatened to bodily fling him from her—the flesh of her arms began to soften. In a burst of Power-sight Ersu beheld that beneath the tall woman's flesh lay the misshapen flesh of another. As if the goddess were merely a cloak draped around a much smaller, stooped figure.

The obsidian-eyed expression on the face of the goddess had changed from one of anger and spite to one of keening anguish.

"Noooooooooooo!" cried the wraith's voice, which suddenly held little of the austere authority of a deity and instead sounded like the hacking sob of a crone.

The wraith's white flesh dissolved further.

Incrementally, Brother Ersu began to understand, with much astonishment.

He held in his arms not the supernatural and potent form of a goddess, but the bent and twisted body of an old woman.

Tebbat.

She was ancient. Yes, impossibly old. Old to the point of unreality. And she was Marked. Her whole body was a Mark, from the gnarled and near-useless hands, through the ugly, lumpy face, the crooked neck and spine, shriveled breasts and contorted pelvis, which sprouted stump-like legs which seemed barely able to hold her weight.

This was not the Tebbat who'd come to taunt him before.

This was the *true* Tebbat. Misshapen, and formidable because of it.

Insight turned to sorrow, and then to genuine sympathy.

And as Ersu's feelings deepened, so did his hold on his enemy.

Only, she was not so much an enemy after all. She was one of the Marked, like himself, but disfigured at such an absolute level that the power which *was* Power coursed through her at an incredible level.

Yet, the shell would not yield entirely.

Ersu felt a second presence.

This one also old. But also alien. Completely and utterly alien.

A red light burst from the dissolving shape of the wraith, and suddenly Tebbat was thrown backwards and out of Ersu's grasp, so that he was embracing only the ethereal and ghostly form of a . . . creature? Something unearthly and filled with rage.

"You came from the stars," Ersu intuited.

Yes.

The creature had spoken, though not with words.

"Why didn't we see you?"

You cannot see that in which you do not believe. Your Order—the Brotherhood—thinks the heavens are perfect. Unchanging. Tranquil. How wrong you are. And how foolish. There is war in the stars, primitive one. And I am a casualty. A wounded soul seeking other wounded souls. The old woman, the beggar, and a few others, they all could see. But she had the link—the Power as you call it—that could heal me. And I in turn could heal her. And together, we would be complete.

For a moment, the monk faltered. He felt the force and torment of the alien's tale, and recognized the truth of it.

He looked past the baleful alien, to where Tebbat lay.

She was sobbing.

"It helped me to be whole and beautiful," she said. "For the first time in my life. And we were powerful! Powerful enough to shape the destiny of this land together. Come back to me. . . . "

She reached clumsily for the shifting, glowing, blood-red form of the ghost that shimmered and danced in Ersu's embrace.

The alien slapped her away.

No. I see now that you are too old. And your appetites and desires ruled me. He, on the other hand, is young. And I am now strong again. The healing is complete. Through him I can raise armies. Build a civilization. Reach again for the stars. The war is not over. It will never be over.

Before he could react, Ersu let out a silent cry: *don't!*

But it was too late. Their Power had mingled too much. Before he could rip his Marked and whole hands away, the ferocious, nameless specter was upon him. With a strangled cry he fell back and convulsed, the white whirlwind which had surrounded he and the crone now turning red and focusing itself over him and *into* him, channeling incandescent energy out of the black sky and down to the very core of Ersu's being. The monk never guessed that such Power was possible. It went beyond the mere Marking which the old woman had borne. The second essence—a life force all its own, which he neither comprehended nor desired—reached into him and flooded through him like fire.

Tebbat had collapsed. Dead.

But Ersu remained erect: transfixed in a silent tornado of otherworldly power, until all the universe burned white and hot as the sun, then fell into absolute darkness.

Water returned to the Ornax.

There was no flood.

The river simply renewed itself, slowly growing in depth and force until it once again cut against its former banks, nearly a score of days after Ersu had left his Order.

The people of the western plains rejoiced.

Fresh crops were sown in the frantic hope that it was not too late.

Astonished, and wondering at the fates of both Brother Ersu and the mounted party, the elders of the Order met with the council of the plains and discussed what might have transpired. No word had been received from either of the missions, and yet the ill that had held back the waters had somehow been overcome.

And life in the plains was restored.

Only, with renewed and surprising vigor.

It was found that wherever the river water touched the soil, the fields grew twice as fast as they normally should have. Stalks and vines and roots burst with vegetable bounty. Animals too found additional health from partaking of the Ornax, and before long the Brotherhood discerned a subtle potency in the river which had not existed before—an essence just at the limit of discernment which tantalized their understanding of both earth and Power.

When harvest finally came, it overflowed the cellars and silos and refectories of the western plains, to such an extent that there was no doubt the winter could be borne in comfort; with a sufficiently full belly.

The year ultimately came and went, as all years must, and when the following spring came and the icy channel of the Ornax broke and was again filled with melt water, the river retained its effervescence, so that again the crops grew high and quick and yielded more goodness than they ever had before.

Fascinated by this phenomenon, the council ordered a second party of riders up the Ornax, to give a final judgment on the state of the headwaters.

The company reported back on the broken remains of the glacier, and on the flooded appearance of the headwaters, now becalmed. As if a grave catastrophe had lain in wait, and been averted.

The Brethren also returned to the forested foothills of the Five Sisters.

They sought knowledge of the final fate of Ersu, whose name had been elevated in his absence to stand beside Kenneses himself—the great master loresman and founder of the ancient plains monastery, which welcomed all Marked children and gave them a home and purpose when the world cast them out.

They found him.

Alabaster-skinned, and much taller than before, with two whole arms and no sign of his prior Marking.

No one questioned it when he came down to the monastery and took his place at the head of the Order.

How could they?

He had clearly been transfigured.

His greatness was palpable and plain.

Ersu had not only saved the land, he'd brought bounty unlike any the people had ever experienced before. He was hailed as their savior, and his counsel was sought by leaders at all levels.

And slowly but surely, he began to execute his plan.

About the Author

Brad R. Torgersen is a science fiction and fantasy writer who debuted in the 26th volume of Writers of the Future and has since gone on to publish in some of the genre's top venues, such as *Analog Science Fiction & Fact* and *Orson Scott Card's Intergalactic Medicine Show*. In addition to winning the Writers of the Future award, Brad won the *Analog Magazine* 'AnLab' Readers' Choice award for Best Novelette for his story "Outbound," which first appeared in the November 2010 issue. Brad has also scripted for the science fiction audio serial *Searcher and Stallion*, as well as collaborating on military science fiction with award-winner and genre veteran Mike Resnick. A full-time healthcare tech geek by day, Brad is also a United States Army Reserve Warrant Officer.

To Kill a Thief

Stephanie M. Lorée

"To Kill a Thief" is the direct sequel to "A Contract Between Thieves" by Stephanie M. Lorée in *The Crimson Pact Volume 3.*

Blood stained Feni's hands, caked under her fingernails, and matted her eyelashes. Her borrowed tunic was drenched with the stuff. The fabric stuck to her chest, making wet, suctioning sounds as she moved.

Though he was taller than her by a head and a good thirty *libra* heavier, Feni carried Raf from his flat to her closest bolt-hole. She had many such places scattered throughout Isola Impero, but none she'd ever shown to another. Granted, his flat was burning in a fire she'd set, and much of the blood soaking her clothes belonged to him. Hells, the clothes were his, too.

Maybe, she figured, she owed Raf a little assistance.

They stumbled down an alley that ran alongside an abandoned fulling mill. Raf leaked a trail of blood behind them, his stomach wound refusing to staunch despite the pressure he applied. Feni doubted anyone would notice, not in this neighborhood.

Wedged between harbor and industrial districts, Vicas Aventino was a neighborhood with which Feni was all too familiar. It housed the lowest of Lowborn, the mad and criminal, the dredges of society that the Highborn would rather forget than execute. Ramshackle homes crowded the thruways. Many of the cobblestones had been torn up—used as building blocks—and dirt paths remained. None of the Highborn's fine aqueducts routed through here, forcing residents to travel daily to the northern fountain where beggars and thieves gathered, awaiting easy marks. Vicas Aventino was a maze of shanties and pickpockets, but Feni knew how to navigate the ever-shifting streets and avoid the dangers. She'd grown up here.

Beside a fallen lean-to, she helped Raf to the ground and inspected a wooden wall.

"You should've left me. At least I would've died warm, what with the fire and all," Raf said.

Feni scowled and splayed her hands on the wood. "Quiet. No one is dying tonight."

He made a show of sniffing the air. "It smells like someone already did."

Ignoring him, she closed her eyes and reached for her magic. The aether burned inside her, and she sensed the lingering ache of the daemon's power. It had called to her, nearly overwhelmed her. Feni wondered if its death would be enough to break the bond it had made with her magic. She still felt strong, unstoppable. Bloodthirsty.

She forced a deep breath and willed the latches securing the board to lift. She'd rigged several small locks to the wooden panel so they could only be released from inside the bolt-hole or by someone capable of her kind of magic. As an ability limited to—and controlled by—the Highborn, Feni guessed she might be the only wielder of aether willing to venture into Vicas Aventino.

The panel swung outward, and she dragged Raf inside.

He groaned as she laid him on a mattress stuffed with rags and straw. "Don't suppose you have any wine? Candles? If I am to be taken to your lair and seduced, a little romance would be nice."

Feni looked at him doubtfully.

"No?" he said. "Very well, you rake, right to bed then." He forced a mischievous grin, but she could see it pained him. His dark skin had grayed, and blood drenched the cloth he'd stuffed in his wound.

"I need to stop the bleeding," she said, drawing the knife from her belt. Half-dried copper stains smudged the blade. Some of the blood belonged to Donato, and she'd never regret killing a man who trafficked with daemons. But the rest was Raf's.

"You started the bleeding, so it seems appropriate," he said.

Feni frowned. She gripped the hilt and hovered her other hand over the blade. Slowly, the steel glowed orange. Flakes of burned blood fluttered to the floor.

"*Merda*, Feni. I doubt the irony of using the same knife will be much comfort to me."

She met his gaze. His eyes were tightened by pain, but she read something there that squeezed her heart and made her furious: trust.

Raf withdrew the sopping rag from his abdomen and lifted his shirt. "Do it."

Without hesitation, she thrust the flat of the blade against the wound. It sizzled and hissed. The bolt-hole filled with the scent of cooking meat, of charred skin and burned hair. For Raf's part, he never screamed. He only growled loud and low in the back of his throat, clenched his fists until his knuckles paled, and stared at Feni while sweat and tears snaked down his face.

When it was over, she tucked him in and let her fingers graze the old, quill-shaped scar on his forearm. He'd branded himself to allow an Aemon to more easily send him visions. Now he'd have a matching scar on his stomach.

"I hope it was worth it," she said, tracing the ruddy, raised tissue.

"To do the right thing?" he mumbled into the bedding. "Always worth it."

"Says the criminal."

"Even the lowest of us can follow the highest callings. Now, be quiet. I'm trying to fall unconscious here."

Feni smiled and let him drift. She took the time to clean her knife and burn their clothes, to gather supplies and eliminate their trail in case the Iron Guard came looking. Though the Guard would probably keep themselves busy with the aftermath of Donato's death, she wasn't going to take chances.

When she removed Raf's boots, a rolled square of parchment tumbled to the floor. It was the same size and style of paper she'd seen earlier—when Raf had shown her the sketches he'd drawn of his visions. He'd said certain visions came from the Aemon. Those had led to Feni's involvement with Iron Torcs and greedy alchemists, with Raf's blood on her hands and serpentine daemons. As far as she was concerned, the future was best left alone, where an older—perhaps wiser—future-Feni might deal with it.

However, Raf's Aemon had proven truer than she'd wished. And besides, what kind of thief would she be if she didn't welcome providence when it fell from a boot?

Feni checked Raf's steady breathing, the flicker behind his eyelids. She tapped his forehead lightly, but he didn't respond.

Only then did she carefully unroll the parchment, smooth it flat on the floor, and nearly scream at what she saw. Etched in charcoal was Raf's striking, detailed illustration of what would come to pass. An army, a legion of daemons, marched upon Isola Impero, the gleaming palace of The Boy-Sovereign burning in the background.

And Feni, a Torc bound around her neck, stood at their lead.

"You know," she said when Raf came to. "I'm growing tired of your lies."

He blinked up at her. She was cleaning his wound, dressing it with a sulfuric smelling poultice her uncle had concocted. Uncle had assured her it would prevent infection, and also sting badly.

"Honey eyes." He flinched as she wrapped a bandage around his abdomen. "How long was I out?"

"Two days."

"Days!" He tried to sit up and groaned in pain. Feni pushed his shoulder back to the bed. His eyes drifted to an old bandage on the floor. Blood had turned the fabric a deep brown. It seemed almost black in the glow of the lantern.

He scowled. "Two days?"

She smiled at him and shrugged. "Enough time to clean you up and rob you blind if I'd wanted."

"If?" he asked.

Her voice came low and soft. "You only have one thing I want, Raf."

He lifted a single black brow and smiled his wolfish grin. "And that is?"

"Answers." She thrust the sketch she'd uncovered in his face. "You lied to me. You said my part was over once I destroyed Donato's Iron Torc. This vision from your Aemon can't be right. This isn't me."

He sighed. "The visions do not lie, honey eyes."

"Stop calling me that! I would never wear a Highborn's Torc, or lead an army of those creatures. The All save me, I may be a thief, but I am not a monster."

"You've killed before, Feni, and you enjoyed it."

She remembered the hot spray of Donato's blood as she drew her knife over his throat. It had drenched her and she had smiled.

"He was evil," she said.

"You heeded the daemon's call."

"The Torc's magic. It played with my mind."

"Power calls to power, Feni, it can only lure. You welcomed it. There will be other Torcs, other lures, and those who worked with Donato will use them against you."

"There are more of them?"

He nodded. "From what I gathered, Donato was a member of a small, select group of conspirators. There are more and they will come for you."

"Why?" she asked.

He shook his head. "I don't know exactly, but they want something from you."

"I'm just a thief."

Reaching up, he stroked his thumb across her cheek. "You are far more than that, Feni. You are a Lowborn who can wield aether. Few escape Highborn law as children and grow to understand their magic."

She jerked away from his touch. "I beat the daemon's control once, I will again."

"You nearly killed me," he said.

Her eyes fell to his wound. Already the bandage was darkening as the medicine pulled infection from his skin.

"It was the Torc," she mumbled.

"This time you won't resist. My blood won't stop you, it will only increase your thirst." His jaw hardened, the furrow in his brow was sad and decisive. "I'll have no choice."

"You'll kill me," she said, and it wasn't a question.

"I'll stop you."

Feni ground her teeth. "And these friends of Donato, they will convince me to command daemonic armies? What if I stopped them first?"

Raf seemed to consider a moment, tilting his head and studying her. "You won't."

She hit him. One solid slap across his cheek that rocked his head to the side. When he recovered and touched his bottom lip, his fingertips came away bloody. He held them out to her like an offering to a cruel god, and she knew everything he'd said was right.

"If you come for me," she told him, heading for the door. "I won't miss your heart a second time."

Feni left him in the bolt-hole and headed toward her favorite dockside bar—Jupiter's Fishwife. There she would find someone to keep her and her bottle company tonight. Someone who didn't have visions or crimson scars or Aemons following them. Who wouldn't care if she was a thief or a monster.

Someone who was anyone but Raf.

She sulked through the alleys of Vicas Aventino. Her soft-soled boots were silent against the rough road, and she ghosted in and out of the shadows to avoid passersby. Only the smell of sulfur from the poultice—of Raf's blood under her nailbeds—might give her away.

When she arrived at Jupiter's Fishwife, Feni marched past the rowdy gamblers gathered to play *Gilé*, past the quiet tables where contracts were negotiated in the dark, and went straight for the barkeep. She ordered their most expensive bottle of wine and proceeded to drink herself dumb.

She was making progress when a man sat next to her and said, "May I join you?"

She waved her glass at him. "Looks like you already have."

He was a small man—though still taller and broader than Feni—with gray at his temples and a pair of spectacles clinging to his hawkish nose. The cut of his trousers and longcoat, and the silver and garnet ring on his forefinger, signaled his wealth.

She let her eyes roam over him blatantly. "You're in the wrong part of the city."

He smiled, his teeth straight and white, and ordered the same as her. When his wine arrived, he wrapped his fine fingers around the glass. His ring clinked softly against the side.

"I'm exactly where I wish to be, Feni," he said.

Wary, she set her glass down and let her hand drift toward her boot-knife. Panic pushed at the wine warming her blood. "You know me," she said, "but I haven't had the pleasure."

"You and I have a mutual acquaintance," he said, sipping his drink. "It took me awhile to uncover Rafael's criminal associates, and then persuade them to talk. But eventually, all roads led me to you."

"What do you want?" she asked.

"I'm pleased you finally chose to visit your favorite bar again. I was growing tired of paying common thugs to protect me against common thieves."

She followed his gaze toward the door. Three rather large, rather surly looking men stood staring at her. She recognized two of them, had worked with one on a contract not too long ago. His name was Drago, and she gave him a small smile that said she understood this was business, not personal.

"As for what I want," the man continued. "I have a contract for you."

She turned her back on the mercenaries. "You have my attention."

"I need someone with your particular abilities, Feni. Someone who hates the Highborn as much as you."

"I don't hate all of them," she said. "Just most."

He grinned. "And your magic means they hate you as well."

She gripped her knife, working it soundlessly from her boot. "I don't know what you're talking about, but if you keep talking, you won't leave here with your throat intact."

"Yes, I heard about Donato. Pity."

Feni sighed. "You're working with him."

"I was." The man nodded. "Until you put an end to our association. No matter, I have all I need from him."

He reached into his coat and withdrew an unclasped Torc. Made of iron and set with a garnet the size of an egg, the Torc looked like a Highborn's—made for amplifying and controlling aether—except for the runes etched around the length of it.

She had seen those runes before, on the Iron Torcs worn by the daemons whom Donato had commanded, but those had lacked the gemstone setting. This Torc the man set in front of her was unique. It was also the Torc from Raf's picture.

"Put it on," the man said.

Slower than she would have been sober, Feni thrust her knife toward his chest. He caught her wrist mid-strike, and the blade plunged into his shoulder instead. The man cursed and called for his guards, but she was already moving. She danced through the bar, tossing tables and chairs in her wake. She headed for the back exit, which was normally reserved for when the Iron Guard paid Jupiter's Fishwife a visit.

The clomp of thunderous steps resounded behind her. She may have been quicker, able to thread through patrons and furniture like water through a sieve, but Drago charged her like a bull. When two meaty hands closed around her arms, she knew she was outmatched. Still, she whirled on him and raked her knives across his leather gorget. It shredded like wax paper and left his neck scored with fat red lines.

He shook her violently. Her head snapped back, and her teeth rattled. She tried to slice at his now exposed neck, but Drago hurled her backward like a doll. She smacked the wall, crumpling to the floor.

There was a sharp pain in her thigh, the dull sensation of being lifted in giant arms, and a gruff voice whispering, "Sorry, Feni," before darkness claimed her.

She woke to the scent of sickness, of slow, lingering deaths and pungent medicines. Above her hung tendrils of drying herbs, swaying in the rafters. She lay on a cot, blinking up at the ceiling and tasting vomit on her tongue. Slowly she became aware of the *hiss-whir* of a boiler, the distant moans of the dying, and the hammering in her head.

"I suspect you have quite the hangover," a voice echoed from behind her.

She bolted upright and regretted it when her brain seemed to slosh between her ears. "By the All," she mumbled, holding her head between her hands and glancing around the room.

It was a hospital of some sort. Sheets hung as dividers, preventing her from witnessing the deaths she heard. A portable boiler puffed along one wall, powering a smattering of stoves and strange machines. Behind her stood the man from the bar, holding a steaming mug in his good hand. The other was bound in a sling.

She reached for her boot-knife, but found it—and her boots—missing.

"I wanted you to rest more comfortably," he said.

"I thought I left something of mine buried in your shoulder."

The man smiled. "It will be returned to you in due time."

Lacking her usual agility and supporting herself with the cot, Feni staggered to her feet. "Who are you?"

"Cesare, or Doctor if you prefer. Here." He motioned the tin mug toward her. "This should help with your head and stomach."

She accepted the cup, but did not drink. "Where did your thugs run off to?"

He shrugged. "I no longer have need of them."

"If you think I won't kill you in your sleep, you're in for a rude surprise."

"I think you will do exactly what I say. Now *sit down*." His last words vibrated the air and struck her like a fist, knocking her back. She sat as though weighted and could not move.

"Good," he said. "I wasn't sure if it would work on you. Thus far our attempts with people have been. . . . " His eyes darted toward the sheets, to where the dying moaned. "Difficult."

"What did you do to me?"

Cesare swiveled his ring around his finger, and she felt a responding tug at her neck as if a tether leashed them together.

"Drink your tea," he said. "The necklace suits you."

Unwillingly, she raised the metal mug to her lips and drank. Though dull, she could make out her reflection in its tin surface. The Iron Torc bound her throat, its bloody gemstone gleaming wetly in the firelight.

"You see, only the blood of those who wield aether can control the daemon's Torcs. With Donato gone, we had to find another source," he said.

"Donato could use magic?"

Cesare shrugged. "Barely, but it was enough. The problem lay in the daemon's influence. It drives the controller mad, as I'm sure you understand."

Feni understood. The power still sang through her, coiled irrevocably with her magic. She imagined sliding her knife down Cesare's sternum, driving it hilt deep into his gut, and bathing in the warm wash of his blood.

"We can't have our General obeying the daemon's whims," he continued. "So we crafted another Torc, one to control the controller."

She lifted her hand to her neck, felt the cold iron under her fingertips. It cleaved her throat and collared her like a Highborn dog.

"Your General," she murmured.

"Yes." He nodded. "It will also serve to increase your powers, Feni. And once you know our goal, I'm certain you will empathize."

"Oh, sure. You want to use my blood and my will to command an army of daemons, while keeping me on a short leash. But for what purpose? Why do you need an army?"

"For too long the Highborn have ruled this city. All Lowborn suffer, including alchemists like myself, Donato, and your own uncle. My fellows and I, we intend to set Isola Impero to rights."

She swallowed hard. In theory, it sounded like the kind of coup Feni might enjoy. But summoning daemons to do the dirty work?

"Why not use men?" she asked.

Cesare frowned. He tilted his head and seemed to listen to the cries echoing throughout the hospital. "Men die, Feni. They leave behind families and crops, businesses and friends. But daemons, they are expendable."

"And me?"

"You should get some rest. You'll have a long day ahead of you."

She gripped the cot, fighting the impulse to lie down and sleep. "Am I expendable, too?"

He offered her a sad smile. "You are an acceptable loss."

Blood trailed from her wrist, filling the cup Cesare held. When he was satisfied, she wound the bandage around her forearm as instructed and watched as he anointed another set of Torcs, then disappeared downstairs to the cells.

From what she could tell, at least twenty distinct voices slithered in her head. Those were the strongest, the loudest of the daemons under her sway. She imagined far more were being held in the summoning cells below, but their influence was drowned by the cacophony of the twenty.

They wanted death, whispered strength into her veins. Most of the time, Feni floated in a haze of anger and need and *power*. But when Cesare told her to calm, ordered her to bleed into the cup, she found herself again. She would cut her forearm in the shape of a quill, recreating the same scar that branded Raf, though she was much less of an artist.

Everything he'd predicted had come true. Isola Impero's palace had yet to burn, but Feni figured that would happen soon. Cesare expected her to march his army within a day's time.

She was eager for the battle, anxious with need for it. Only a sliver of her former self remained, the part that scarred herself in homage to Raf. The part that missed him.

Power flared inside her and she screamed. More whispers joined the chorus in her mind. Her magic boiled, desperate to be unleashed. Blood dribbled from her nose and ears and she wiped it away. Despite losing so much recently, Feni was stronger than ever.

"That's the last," Cesare said when he returned. He huffed, winded from whatever evocations he'd performed in the summoning cells. "How do you feel, Feni?"

"Like eating your heart."

"You will control your impulses," he said, and she nodded as the forced calm smoothed over her. She wondered if Raf would come for her, if he were hunting her even now.

"Tomorrow, you'll lead your army against the Highborn," he said. "Repeat the rules to me."

"Destroy all Highborn and any who stand against us. Do as little harm to the city as possible. Burn The Boy-Sovereign and his palace to the ground. Obey you," she said.

"Good, very good, Feni. All that's left is to test your own abilities. I've brought some friends to help us, you remember?"

He motioned for someone to approach. The three mercenaries who'd captured Feni came into view. Rage surged through her, propelling her to her feet. They did this to her, Drago and his friends, and they would pay.

"Feni," Cesare said, "I want you to defend yourself against these men." He glanced at them. "Kill her."

Drago hesitated, but the other two lunged. She didn't bother with knives, didn't attempt to step aside. She simply willed them to stop.

Magic scorched a trail inside her, heated the air in the dingy hospital, and caused the garnet at her throat to blaze like the sun. The men hung suspended and motionless. She slashed her hand in an arc and the leather armor on one of the men peeled off him, its edges blackened.

The aether went farther, deeper, rending his shirt and skin, his bone and sinew. He wailed as it sank into him, slicing him in two like a welder's torch.

For a moment, there was silence. The pieces of the dead man dangled in the air while the others watched. Then she turned to the second man and hurled him against the ceiling. The rafters rattled, and herbs tumbled to the floor.

"*Kill*," the daemons hissed. "*Kill everything*."

With only a thought, Feni ripped his appendages from his torso. A shower of crimson mist bathed her. She lifted her face to the warmth of it, the glory of the kill.

The pounding of retreating footsteps drew her back to her objective. Drago was running, and she wanted nothing more than to chase, to destroy, but Cesare had ordered only to defend herself.

"That's enough," he said. His hands shook, and a trickle of sweat beaded on his brow. He turned the ring nervously on his finger. "Sleep now, Feni."

Splattered with blood, desperate with the desire to kill Cesare and the whole of Isola Impero, she lay on her cot. The daemons whispered her to sleep.

Feni exited the hospital at Cesare's side. They were within the training grounds of the Higborn armies, an old barracks converted for Cesare's use, he told her. He'd spent years as their army's doctor, working for those he intended to destroy, seeing men maimed and killed for the Highborn's unrelenting need to conquer and absorb foreign lands.

"Right under them," he said as they stared up at the Rosetta Rigga—the palace of The Boy-Sovereign. Crafted by the finest alchemists and with The First Sovereign's magic, its diamond and gold facade glittered in the twilight.

They would attack at night, Cesare informed her. The darkness would not bother their soldiers, but it would confound the Iron Guard.

"Call them here, Feni," he ordered.

She exhaled, and magic rode the air.

They strode toward the palace, her daemons flowing into line behind her. Some slithered on serpentine tails like the first she'd encountered at Donato's. But others had human legs, spider legs, or none at all. Some dragged themselves with giant claws, leaving blighted furrows deep in the earth. There was beauty there, too. The seductive grace of long limbs and tempting lips, but it was nothing human.

Nightmares followed Feni to war.

The neighboring barracks spotted them first. Cries went up and lanterns were lit. The Iron Guard rallied, but not quickly enough.

Without a word, she ordered her daemons to attack. Shrieks and prayers to the All filled the grounds.

"Now," Cesare said to her, "send them to the—"

His voice cut short as an arrow skewered his throat. He gurgled, reached for her as his knees buckled, and collapsed to the dirt.

She turned in the direction the arrow had come from and saw the archer rise from his cover. He'd healed well, and he moved toward her with determined strides. His hair was tied back with a strip of bright cloth, and the beads that decorated his dark locks seemed to catch the fading sun.

"Raf," she said.

He came toward her with his bow at his side and his hand outstretched. "Feni, it's me."

She smiled and moved to meet him. "Come to kill me, is it?"

"To stop you," he said. "To try."

Her smile widened, and the blood being spilled behind her made her purr. "Ah, what was it you said to me? You won't."

She lashed out with her magic. The force of it sent Raf flying. He landed hard, and she continued her approach almost casually.

"I can hear them, you know. Feel all of them," she said as she crunched his bow with her will. It folded in on itself, snapping into kindling.

"You can fight this, honey eyes," he said.

She broke both his legs. He screamed as his knees bent at impossible angles.

"I don't want to fight it," she said. "I like it."

"Feni, please." Raf gazed at her as she towered over him. "Don't do this."

She crouched and laid her hand against the fresh scar on his abdomen. "Irony," she said, and ripped the wound anew.

From the corner of her eye she caught a flicker of silver and red, but the feel of blood warming her hand proved too much a distraction. It was only when he caught the ring, slid it on his finger, that she turned and saw Drago standing over the corpse of Cesare.

"Stop, Feni," Raf begged, and the Torc binding her neck forced her to obey. "Listen to me, not them."

The daemons quieted, and she blinked.

"Raf?" Her hands pressed into the wound, tried to stop the bleeding. It was so much deeper than before.

"It's not important now. You must stop them, Feni. The daemons cannot be allowed in our world. You can do this."

She shook her head. "You were right. The temptation is too strong."

He cupped her cheek. "You are capable of far more than this, honey eyes. I trust you. You are your own master."

With that, he reached for his dagger and slammed the hilt into the face of the garnet ring. The gem cracked like broken glass, and the tug at her throat died.

She continued to hold his wound long after his heart had ceased pumping.

"Feni?" Drago called from behind her.

She spared him a glance. He stood well away, too scared to approach, and clenched his fists.

"Are you . . . you?" he asked.

Rising to her feet, she ignored Drago and turned her back on Raf's corpse.

You must stop them. His words hummed inside her, louder than any of her daemons. *You are your own master.*

He'd once told her that it had to be her who stopped Donato, that it was her magic which would defeat the daemons. She'd been surprised when her aether burned the first daemon she'd encountered. She had to touch the creature then, but now she could feel each daemon bound to her like an invisible cord.

Feni sent her magic through those tethers. She reached for every drop of aether, every ounce of will she possessed, and slammed it into her daemons.

Inhuman bellows echoed across Isola Impero. Fires lit the night sky. Everywhere, daemons burned.

The gem at Feni's throat cast her face in a ruddy light. And behind her, the glittering palace of The Boy-Sovereign seemed ablaze.

She purchased a tomb for Raf below the Necropolis, in the catacombs generally reserved for the wealthiest of Lowborn. She cleaned his body and laid him to rest as a hero.

His face looked softer in death, but just as beautiful. From her satchel she removed the broken garnet ring and placed it on his finger. The matching Torc she held between her hands for some time, studying the intricate runes and the swirl inside the gemstone that reminded her of so much blood.

She bashed the stone against the wall. Garnet shards scattered around her, and she laid the broken Torc inside with Raf as well.

Then, ignoring the cold tears streaking down her face and using only the strength in her muscles, Feni hefted the lid to bury him forever.

"Why?" A woman's lilting voice and soft footsteps sounded.

Feni turned to find a red-cloaked priestess, though of no cult she recognized. The woman was tall and lithe, her face shrouded by her cowl. Something about the way she moved bothered Feni, and her outline was blurred as though she were more smoke than substance. "Why destroy the Torc? It gave you more power," the Aemon said.

"I'm done with magic."

"Truly? Then why do you wear my mark?"

Feni clutched her forearm against her chest. The quill-shaped scar felt warm and wet under her leathers. "I wear his mark," she said, motioning to the tomb. "Never yours."

"He was a good man," the Aemon said. "But we will need others like him, like you, when the time comes."

Feni narrowed her eyes and studied the Aemon. The spirit's edges were indistinct, becoming cloudier the longer Feni stared.

"Find someone else," she said.

"It has always been you, Fenice. Your soul belongs to us. It is anathema to *them*."

Feni laid a hand on Raf's tomb and wished him a silent farewell. Turning her back on the Aemon and heading for the stairs, she said only, "I'm just a thief. And I am my own master."

About the Author

Born and stuck in Ohio, Stephanie writes speculative fiction, moonlights as a rock star, and works in a cubicle for The Man. Her short stories have appeared in several small press anthologies and ezines, as well as RPG supplements. As a lover of short fiction, she co-blogs for Write1Sub1.com and eats slush for Lightspeed and Nightmare magazines. She has worked as assistant editor on several anthologies, most recently Triangulation: Morning After from ParsecInk. A self-proclaimed SuperNerd, Stephanie loves gaming, technology, good sushi, and bad kung fu flicks. Her digital life is available for stalking at stephaniemloree.com.

Facing the Fear

Donald Darling

"Facing the Fear" is the direct sequel to "The Ronin's Mark" in *The Crimson Pact Volume 3*, and "The Ronin's Resolve" in *The Crimson Pact Volume 4*.

Jacob Kotsedi, Knight of the Pact, was awestruck—he had just banished the Nightblade. Tales of the legendary demon dated back to the Dark Ages, and though it had been seldom seen in the last few decades, it had decimated the Pact in the centuries prior. It was said that it couldn't be killed and that it could take on nearly any guise. Jacob could vouch for the latter. Many demons could take on appearances and seem to be something they weren't, but among his skills was an uncanny ability to see through such veils. He could smell demons the way most people smelled burnt hair, but not this time. Entrapped in a circle of binding, the demon had taken on the guise of a beautiful, young, feminine fae. She had seemed real in every way, even smelling of the sea. The fae were rarely seen, but the story she told of being captured and bound by demons had seemed plausible enough. When he prayed for guidance, however, he received a lingering vision of the banishment ritual. The Voice in his head concurred, but Jacob was uncertain; a banishment ritual for demons would almost certainly kill a fae. It's not that he didn't believe them; he just knew from experience that sometimes they weren't revealing the whole truth. They might let a fae perish if it served some greater goal. Had he defied the vision—and he nearly had—the Nightblade would be free, and he would likely be dead. Why had he doubted? Why was he afraid at every trial?

<*You overcame it,*> said the Voice. <*You trusted to your faith and did what needed to be done.*>

This time, thought Jacob, *but what about next time?* The Voice said nothing.

Jacob turned away from the vacant binding circle and scanned around the vast manor hall in which he stood. It was in utter ruin, but most of it was not his doing; it had been this way when he had arrived. There had been dozens of demons here, but they had taken to fighting each other, or so it seemed. There were piles of demon ash everywhere, mixed with rubble and debris. There had also been a permanent gate here, a portal between this world and a demon realm, an impressive accomplishment given the chaotic nature of demons, but it too was destroyed.

Excepting the circle-bound, now-banished Nightblade, the only other demon still here had been a shadow demon, which had been infused with the house, concealing all that lay within, including the gate. Another impressive accomplishment. Jacob had never fought a shadow demon before; he didn't know anyone who had. They were ephemeral entities, poltergeists, tied to a specific place or item, but easily eliminated once you found their focus and destroyed it.

Jacob tried to make sense of the scene, but the puzzle was missing many pieces.

An anonymous text message had lured him here, outside of the city, to a beautiful manor made of white marble. The remote estate was peaceful and perfectly manicured, but the front gate hung wide open as if those within had fled. There had been humans here, minions of the demons, or sacrifices, but they were nowhere to be found now. Had it been one of them that had sent him the message?

Jacob had fought demons for many years, and was well versed in their methods, but this was by far the largest, boldest and most complex operation he had ever seen. The demons here would have been of the most disciplined variety or they never would have accomplished this much. So what had happened to make them fall into a violent free-for-all? And who had been the victor? The shadow demon? And how did the Nightblade fit into it? He might have been bound to help empower the gate, but why hadn't the shadow demon released him to do battle the moment the enemy walked through the door?

<*Maybe shadow demons are stupid,*> the Voice proffered.

Shattered stone crunched underfoot as Jacob continued to investigate the remains of a battle he hadn't been a part of, trying to understand it. His hand flexed restlessly on the grip of a battle-worn longsword. Old and battered, it looked like it had been stolen from a museum exhibit. Few would guess that beneath its steel skin lay a relic of enormous power—his link to the divine.

He ran his hand along the broken remains of the gate, interpreting the malevolent runes that remained intact, but they gave few clues. There were also strange metal canisters strewn throughout the room, most of them punctured and leaking a fine red and black dust that reeked of demon. The stuff was everywhere.

<*Demon dust,*> whispered the Voice.

"Demon dust?" echoed Jacob. "What does it do?"

<*It makes men think they are demons,*> replied the Voice. <*Do not breathe it in. It is dangerous.*>

He pulled a vial from among the ritual tools he had used to banish the Nightblade and collected a sample. The Pact would want to know of this.

<*It is highly flammable,*> the Voice announced. <*We should light it from afar and let the fire consume this place.*>

"No," said Jacob, "Not yet. There are too many mysteries here, too many questions that still need answering."

The Voice sighed.

Jacob's mind whirled with the questions, but he doubted he would ever know the truth. When you were a demon-hunter, those with the answers were usually among the slain—getting the whole story was a rare luxury.

<*They are vanquished,*> the Voice finally whispered to him, unasked. <*By your hand, by their hand, who cares?*>

True enough, Jacob surmised, but he was a man who liked answers. What could be learned here could lead to other unholy nests, and Jacob felt certain that the city and its surroundings were now rife with demons. How long had the gate been here? How many fiends had passed through it to plague the world beyond? A hundred? A thousand? The number would be daunting, no question.

<*But think of how many can no longer come through,*> the Voice submitted. <*Think of how many lives have been saved by the gate being destroyed. Victories can be measured by those saved just as easily as by those defeated.*>

Perhaps, thought Jacob, but it still concerned him to face so many alone. Perhaps it was time to put in a call for assistance.

<*You are a paladin,*> hissed the Voice in admonishment. <*You bear a true relic. Before whining for help, remember why you became a crusader.*>

Most members of the Crimson Pact had deeply personal reasons for joining the crusade. Many had lost friends, or lovers, or even entire families to the demons; they wanted retribution. Some had been used by them to commit unspeakable acts; they sought redemption. A few were just true, right-minded folk who understood the cost of doing nothing. Jacob Kotsedi had joined for none of these reasons. He had joined because all his life he had chosen to live with shame rather than grapple with fear, and he was sick of it.

No one would understand it, of course. He was six and half feet tall, his dark skin rippling with lean muscle, an able fighter with any number of weapons or no weapons at all. He was smart, perceptive, and had access to powers that few in the order were given. He shouldn't be afraid of anything, but he was, all the time.

His father had been an abusive son-of-a-bitch, beating on wife and child with equal indifference. As the eldest, Jacob should have stood up to him, but the courage eluded him; a dead sister and a broken mother paid the price. His best friend in school had been constantly bullied. Jacob was strong and capable. He should have intervened on his friend's behalf, but he hadn't; a self-inflicted gunshot wound gave his friend the peace denied him in life. When he had gone through the grueling selection course trying to join the Recces, the South African Special Forces, he had failed—not because of a weakness of the flesh, but because of a weakness of the mind. The fear had seized him at the worst possible moment and he froze up, certain he was going to die. He might have too, had the Voice not come to him, taunting and cajoling him to action.

On some days, he was certain that the Voice was just a self-induced hallucination, an invisible friend created by his subconscious to keep him from freezing up when the fear took over. Other days he was convinced it was much more than that. It seemed to sense things before he did and know things he couldn't possibly know. It sometimes spoke when he least wanted to hear it and said not a word when he needed it most. With the Voice came a new awareness, as if the world had turned to color when it had been but shades of gray before. People looked different, and some people weren't people at all; there were a lot of demons in South Africa back in those days.

Jacob had been terrified, certain that madness had taken him. He'd considered taking his best friend's way out and probably would have had the Pact not found him. Their knowledge and the soothing tones of the Voice had calmed him, anchored him. The Pact taught him how to use his gifts, how to spot demonic infiltration, and how to put an end to it. When he had been sent out on his own they had gifted him with a potent artifact, a relic which he knew he did not deserve—great weapon or no, fear walked with him at every step. Some days he worked his way through it, the Voice helping him to at least win the battle, even if he couldn't seem to win the war. Other days it got the better of him; some days the demons escaped. He knew how to live with such shame, he always had, but he hated himself for it. Killing demons was the penance for his failures, the challenge he had to face to overcome his fear. The Voice was right; he couldn't do that by getting others to fight his battles for him.

The sound of distant thunder pulled him from his musings, and the Voice whispered, <*Prepare yourself.*> It was said so matter-of-factly that it immediately put him on edge. The Voice was rarely so direct.

He quickly gathered up the ritual tools he had used to banish the Nightblade, throwing them haphazardly into a large suitcase, and made his way out of the white stone manor. The rest of the estate needed to be searched and the demon dust had to be disposed of, but it would have to wait.

As soon as he stepped outside, he knew something was wrong.

The skies had been clear, the breeze gentle, when he had arrived. Now it was dark, the dusk sun completely obscured by a roiling mass of storm clouds, which crested the coastal hills like some great shadowy beast. The waning sun behind the tempest gave the edges a scarlet glow, while the midnight-blue maw of the beast spit lightning and roared thunder. It was as ominous a sight as Jacob had ever witnessed.

The wind began to whip up around him followed by the first peppering of rain, cold and stinging. He ran down the steps to his car, an old blue Acura, and tossed the suitcase in the trunk. Sorting through the weapons, he grabbed an R4 assault rifle and a rifle grenade.

<*No,*> said the Voice. <*Only the relic can aid you in this battle.*>

Jacob put the rifle back, cursing, and unsheathed the wretched-looking longsword. He had been told the same thing about the shadow demon. What form would the demon take this time, perhaps that of the storm itself?

<*You should be so lucky,*> whispered the Voice.

If you know what's coming, thought Jacob, *fucking tell me!* But the Voice was silent.

He was tired, so damned tired. The battle against the shadow demon had drained him, and what reserves he had left he had used for the banishment ritual. His entire body trembled at the thought of channeling the divine again without a week's rest. It would kill him, he was sure of it.

<*If you believe that to be true,*> murmured the Voice, <*then surely it will.*>

Shut up, thought Jacob.

The tempest stretched out around the manor, enfolding it in great hurricane arms. The wind continued to whip dust and rain onto Jacob's black body armor, but the brunt of the gale circled around him. He sat in the eye of the storm, lightning and thunder the spectators to his arena.

With the tip of his sword in the ground, Jacob knelt and prayed, using the car as cover against the storm. He trusted in his faith to strengthen him, but already he could sense his fears and doubts gnawing away at it. After so many battles against so many fiends, why did it feel this way every time?

<*Prepare yourself,*> the Voice said a second time. That kicked the fears into overdrive. It had never warned him twice, never. What the hell was coming? Jacob stood and walked away from the car and onto the broad expanse of lawn that fronted the manor. The storm whirled around him as he called upon the *art*. He was no master in the ways of such things, but he had enough skill to fortify himself. The warm sensation that flowed through him could do nothing to stave off his fear or stop his hands from trembling, but it did make him less susceptible to injury and more ca-

pable of seeing the truth of things around him. The relic would have to wait until the right moment. If he invoked it now, the enemy would just wait until he had burned himself out.

A sinking sense of anxiety began to grow in Jacob's chest as he watched the sky, which looked more like a sea of heaving and churning waves than clouds. The wretched scent of demon washed over him, pungent and stomach-turning. And that's when he saw it.

It approached out of the storm, unaffected by lightning or howling winds; a demon on a winged, flying horse, a *real* flying horse. Jacob wiped his eyes and squinted, but the closer it got the more certain he was that it was no illusion.

The storm, the demon, it was a staggering display of hellish power, and Jacob couldn't get his head around it. The cost to manifest such a blatant, vulgar power on a contested world like this was incalculable, and the *Kasu-Hurun* had to know that the Pact and their allies would meet it head-on.

<*It's a good thing you're here then,*> whispered the Voice.

But why? Why send such an emissary here?

Maybe it was because of what had happened to the gate. Or maybe it was because he had banished the Nightblade.

<*Don't be an idiot,*> said the Voice with a sigh. <*There is much more to it than that.*>

Such as? wondered Jacob to a yawning silence.

Before he could say more, the demon steed had landed in front of him, no more than ten yards away. Jacob took a step back, his whole body shaking with terror at the nightmare before him. The horse was bigger than a Clydesdale and so black there was no definition to it. Only its scarlet eyes and those parts of it that burned with fire—mane, tail, and hooves—distinguished it. Fire was bane to demons; those that used it did so as a display of power, to show that they could not be harmed by it.

The demon rider was in armor of engraved black iron from head to toe, like a knight of old. Demons had no love of iron either. Fire and iron—this demon was showing off, showing that the tools often used against them were playthings to it.

Jacob recognized him from the classic lore, for there were few demons that came in armor riding a flying horse. He was a named demon, one of the Fallen, a true Duke of Hell, and the most powerful fiend Jacob had ever encountered, probably the most powerful to ever manifest on this world. Even the Nightblade was a pale shadow of this foul creature.

I need a miracle, thought Jacob as the ebon stallion reared up before him. *Seriously. Shouldn't there be an archangel or something to deal with a demon of this magnitude?*

<*You do not need an archangel,*> said the Voice. <*And while a miracle would be nice, you'll have to provide it yourself.*>

The two knights faced each other, one impervious and imposing, the other using every ounce of courage just to stand his ground.

"You have the stink of the divine about you," announced the demon. He spoke not in one voice, but many, ranging from whispers to shouts, but all tinged with anger and malice.

"You should not be here, demon," Jacob spoke with a conviction he didn't feel. "Go back to your Hell or face the wrath of the Lord."

The demon laughed in myriad voices.

"Your 'lord' doesn't frighten me," he sneered. "*You* don't frighten me, little Pactling. Are you so ignorant in your studies to not know who I am? Do you not know on whose behalf I speak?"

"I know who you are," said Jacob grimly. "You are the General, servant to the Dark Lady."

"Speak my name then," growled the demon, "if you claim to know it."

"No," Jacob's voice broke as he shouted. "To speak it is to give you power."

The fiend laughed in a thousand tones.

"I have power whether you speak it or not."

The shadow-made steed reared up again, and the demon raised a gauntleted fist, which crackled with black electricity.

<*Call upon the relic!*> stressed the Voice.

Jacob dug deep within himself, seeking the resolve needed to invoke the weapon, but his panic made it difficult to concentrate. The faster he tried to act the more incapable he seemed to become. The invocation required a calm certainty, but calm was far from Jacob's mind. At the end, he tried to force the relic to answer him, knowing that it didn't work that way, and by then it was too late. The General's metal-clad hand swept down to point at him.

"Despair," commanded the demon in one clarion-clear single voice.

A wave of primal fear swept through Jacob, a dread so palpable he cried out and cringed before the General. It was like a panic attack of infinite proportion. Had the *art* not taken the edge off he would have had a heart attack and died on the spot. As it was, the protection buckled, and fear convulsed through him, leaving his body paralyzed and his mind exposed to the fiend's manipulation. He tried to call upon his faith, upon the relic, upon the *art*, but his whole being was suffused with an unfathomable terror; he was helpless. All he could think was how much he wanted to run away, but how to do so escaped him.

The power of the demon clawed at his mind, peeling away layers in a way no entity had ever done. It brought every nightmare real or imagined to the surface and dangled in front of him every failing his fear had led to—his dead sister, who stood up to their father when he hadn't . . . his dead friend, whom he had also failed . . . the demon he had killed out of rage in Egypt, not realizing that he had done its bidding and released an even worse fiend into the world. The real merged with the supposed, fed by deep insecurities—the grave disappointment of his mentors in the Pact . . . the laughter of the Recces when he had fallen and nearly died . . . the bitter disgust of his mother for having born such a pathetic son into the world.

Jacob was crying, sobbing like a child caught in some unnamable nightmare.

<*You must not give in!*> pressed the Voice, but he was already on his knees, stricken by the taunting images. With one gesture, one word, the demon had cut to the core of his inner turmoil, stripping away his will to fight and his will to live. How could anyone fight such a fiend?

"You can't," answered the demon maliciously, reading his unguarded thoughts. "You are weak, Jacob Kotsedi, powerless against me."

Jacob believed him.

<*Focus upon me,*> insisted the Voice. <*Draw upon my strength. You are neither weak nor powerless. Do not give in to despair.*>

Jacob tried to heed the Voice, but the images of his failures mocked him, chaining him to a sinking ship of misery.

<*Why are you afraid of what has already passed?*> demanded the Voice. <*Have you not lived with this shame your whole life? What has it profited you? You must let go of the past and face the fear that is in front of you today!*>

I will just fail, thought Jacob. He had failed all those other times, why would this time be any different? The demon had defeated him in less than a minute. Now it would destroy him, and he deserved it. A sense of relief came with the thought. He would perish, as he should have so many times before, and be free of the burden of responsibility.

<*Stop it!*> shouted the Voice. <*You are a Knight of the Pact! This fiend is manipulating you, undermining the very reason you are here. Remember why you became a crusader!*>

To stop living in shame and to face my fears, thought Jacob. The Voice was right, he was being manipulated. The smallest ember of anger lit somewhere deep within him and the despair receded a fraction.

<*Be wary of anger,*> whispered the Voice. <*Let truth be your guide to freedom.*>

But anger was all he had and he clung to it—a lifeboat in a sea of despair.

The General was ignoring Jacob, the black visored helm gazing at the manor, at the wing that had housed the gate.

"Tell me, little Pactling," he demanded in a multitude of voices. "Where is the Malebranche Captain?"

The Malebranche were guardian demons, powerful servitors to the demon lords, the Recces of the underworld. *Did he mean the Nightblade*? wondered Jacob. *Was the Nightblade one of the Malebranche?*

<*Tell him,*> said the Voice. <*Tell him the truth.*>

"I . . . I have vanquished him," whispered Jacob, fearfully, but as the truth slipped out of him, he felt the smallest bit more in control of himself.

The General's gaze returned to Jacob.

"You?" scoffed the General in disbelief. "Your will is weak, your mind troubled, your faith uncertain; I can smell your doubts from here. It was not within you to have defeated the likes of him."

"Yet defeat him I did," claimed Jacob, regaining another small portion of his mind. It wasn't a lie; banishing the Nightblade was a great victory.

The demon laughed.

"You're arrogant," he said, tilting his head. "Have you not heard? Pride is a sin. One as prideful as yourself should forsake his allegiances and join us. You would not be the first member of the Crimson Pact to fill our ranks."

The ember of anger flared, allowing Jacob to stare up at the General.

"The lies of a demon," he replied.

"Those of your order who join us are held in high regard," continued the General, needling him. "When our quest for freedom seemed lost, your kind gave us our liberty, so that we might carry our message across countless worlds."

"We were tricked," growled Jacob as he tried to rise to his feet. "An error we will soon correct."

"Oh?" came the demon's multilayered chuckle. "Finally rising to the challenge, are we? All the better."

<*He's toying with you, trying to goad you,*> the Voice pressed. <*You must find your center, you know this.*>

Yes, he knew it, but better to hold on to hatred than wallow in fear.

<*Not true,*> said the Voice. <*Both are failings.*>

"You put more trust in your fellow Pactlings than is warranted," the General taunted in voices high and low. "There have always been those among your number that have willingly aided us. Those that understand the truth, that our way is the only path to true freedom."

"More lies," Jacob spit out in hatred, using the anger to get up some backbone. "I shall hear no more of them."

"We do not always lie," came the demon's insidious reply. "We do not need to. Truth is often a far more potent tool."

"Demons know nothing of truth," Jacob hurled back as his anger gave him strength.

"We know the truth your masters don't want you to know," countered the demon. "Why do you think we rebelled?"

"Because you sought to take His place," hissed Jacob. "You were thrown from the walls of heaven for your hubris."

"You mortals and your myths," said the General with a shake of his helm. "We rebelled because heaven is a prison, a gilded cage, a paradise without freedom. Or did you think heaven was a democracy? That you are allowed a vote to help mold your own fate? You must do as you are told, submit completely, because He knows what's best for you. There is no freedom in submission. We were not thrown from the walls of heaven, Jacob Kotsedi, we jumped."

"I don't give a shit if you lost your footing and fell off," growled Jacob, using the longsword as a crutch to help gain his feet. "You're malcontents—violent, deceitful, bloodthirsty fucks who revel in pain and destruction and think of nothing else."

"Anger," said the demon in a hundred wicked tones. "How soon before you find your way to wrath, little Pactling? You're halfway to being among us already."

<*Calm yourself,*> said the Voice. <*He wants you to be angry and vengeful. You cannot invoke the relic in such a state and he knows it!*>

The General leaned forward on his mount, staring at Jacob with great intensity.

"Who is that in there with you?" he asked.

Jacob's eyes widened. No one had ever sensed the Voice, not even his mentors among the Pact.

The General raised his gauntlets, fingers curled like talons, the dark lightning arcing between them.

<*You must call upon the relic!*> hissed the Voice again.

He tried, but his mind was now trapped between anger and fear. The demon opened his arms wide and the lightning engulfed Jacob, tearing what inner strength remained to shreds. He stumbled under the onslaught, collapsing again to his knees as the dread current coursed through him.

<*Your fate is in your own hands,*> said the Voice. <*It is not too late. You have been given the tools. Find your center, accept it, and face your fear. Know this . . .*>

The Voice screamed, and then it was gone. Jacob could tell the difference instantly; a piece of him had vanished, as if a limb had suddenly been severed.

Before him, an essence began to materialize, a gauzy white translucency banded by threads of the demon's dark power. It was a soul, Jacob recognized it as such immediately, and as it formed itself in the air and details began to form, recognition came to him. It was Mandisa, his sister, slain by his own inaction as much as their father's hand. It was she who had been supporting him, helping him to go on all these years, the sister he had failed. His mind reeled at the revelation and what it meant; if the demon took her, her soul would be in the hands of the Lady, tormented at her altar for eternity.

"I've changed my mind, little Pactling," the voices of the demon laughed wickedly. "I'm going to let you live. I'll take her instead and leave you here to suffer in the misery of having lost your sister not once, but twice."

The ghostly form turned to stare at Jacob, her expression not one of fear or anger or pleading, as he would have expected, but of confidence. She mouthed words to him: *I believe in you.*

It made no sense. How could she believe in him? She had died because of him . . . and now he was going to fail her again. Jacob averted his gaze, but he knew the shame on his face was impossible to hide. He could feel the warmth of tears sliding down his cheeks. He waited for the Voice to rebuke him, to goad him to action, knowing that it was impossible now.

But he could imagine what she would say: *This isn't about you, idiot. This is about doing what needs to be done. So get up and get it done already!*

Jacob struggled against the despair the demon had invoked, but it continued to linger in his mind. Even were he to somehow gain the courage to face the demon, it was a Duke of Hell. How could he hope to defeat it? It was too strong. Even with the relic it was probably too strong. He would burn himself out even making the attempt. The fiend would kill him and destroy the relic, and he would end up at the tender mercies of the Lady. There could be no victory here.

Victories can be measured by those saved just as easily as by those defeated.

His mind clung to the thought. Did he actually need to defeat the demon? Maybe the relic couldn't withstand the fell powers of the General, but it could certainly break the bonds that held his sister. She would be free. He only needed to survive long enough to do that. The demon would take his vengeance, the demon would take *him*, but he had to try. He could live with shame, but not with the same shame twice.

The runes engraved on the demon's armor began to glow, and Jacob, who was well-trained in such things, recognized the pattern—the demon was preparing to cross the void.

"No," said Jacob, clambering back to his feet. "You can't have her."

He was going to die. Here. Today. He accepted it. It was the right thing to do, the right sacrifice to make, and with it came a calm certainty. The fear was still there, he could sense it in the back of his mind; the difference this time was that he simply didn't care—a strange melding of faith and resignation.

The relic blazed to life.

It was sealed within the sword, under the crossguard, nothing more than a long, thin nettle, stained brown with blood. At Jacob's beckoning, though, divine power surged out of it, causing argent fire to coruscate down the length of the blade. He focused the energy through the lens of his soul, bending it to his will. The weathered sword was born anew, lustrous and blazing like white-hot steel. A nimbus of light enveloped Jacob, empowering him with its grace. It flared as it came into being, sending forth a visible wave of holy radiance.

The dark threads of power that encircled the soul of his sister wavered and held, but the delicate runes on the General's armor flickered and went out. The shadow steed reared up in agony as the divine light passed over it, and it took the demon a moment to regain control as he spun his mount in a full circle in order to face the paladin again.

"So," a thousand voices hissed. "The Pactling has found himself a fang."

"Not a fang," responded Jacob calmly, "but a thorn—a Thorn of the Crown."

"It will not save you," sneered the voices of the General, unimpressed.

The sky around the demon erupted in an eerie, frenetic display of lightning, indigo and violet. It whispered words of darkest lore, and the torrent of electricity gathered and struck down at Jacob in a thunderous roar. The power of the relic deflected much of the blast—the ground around him cracked and turned to ash—but it could not stop all of it. It was like being jabbed with a thousand needles, and it was everything Jacob could do just to stay on his feet. He focused on staying centered. The divine light infused him, and by force of will alone, he pushed the power of the General away.

Jacob wasted no time. He ran toward the General, his incandescent blade held high. The demon laughed at the bravado. At his slightest gesture, the winged destrier lifted him into the air, beyond the reach of the holy blade.

But getting to him had never been Jacob's goal. No sooner had the General taken to the air then the paladin changed course, aiming for the bound spirit of his sister. The demon immediately realized what he was about and called out words of power. A ring of dark fire erupted, surrounding the soul, but Jacob tore through it, trusting to the relic to protect him. It hurt like hell—he could smell burnt flesh—and then he was past it. The white sword slashed out, tearing apart the black bands of power.

"Flee!" Jacob heard himself shout, and the spirit of his sister vanished from sight.

Then he was eating dirt. The General had swooped down on him, striking him in the back with a lance, brought into existence by the will of the demon. Had the power of the relic not protected him, he would have been run through. Jacob gasped as the divine energy coursed through him, protecting him. Mortals were not built to channel such power, and the strain of the defense was almost more than he could bear. He could not withstand such blows for long; either the demon would penetrate the aura or he would burn himself out trying to defend against it.

He rolled away, swinging his sword in a wide arc, but the General was well out of his reach by then. The relic gave him speed and strength far beyond that of normal men, but he couldn't seem to match the pace and power of the fiend. He regained his feet just as the demon whirled to face him. Dark power flowed out of the General—an ashen wind that warped the air around him like some desert mirage. Jacob charged.

"Come, demon!" screamed Jacob. "Fight me if you have the courage!"

The General laughed.

"Why fight you when I can simply destroy you?" replied the demon.

The vaporous dark energy coalesced at the demon's gesture and hurtled toward Jacob. The thunder of its impact against the divine aura was deafening and stopped Jacob in his tracks only a dozen feet from the General. He waited for it to stop, but the pure eldritch power continued to pour forth from the demon, tearing at the shield with unrelenting ferocity. He could not maintain the aura for much longer and the demon knew it.

Jacob focused on his faith and prayed for the strength of mind to defeat the abomination before him. The shield flared and Jacob took a few steps forward, but the power of the demon could not be turned aside. It was now everything he could do just to hold his ground, and the aura began to shimmer and distort with the effort. Steam poured forth from Jacob's body as his blood began to burn—the divine fire was going to consume him.

The end had arrived and Jacob knew it, but his sister's soul was free and that was all that mattered.

"Time to die, little Pactling," whispered a thousand delighted voices. "Time to meet your new mistress in the City of Black Glass."

The ground around them rumbled and heaved—an earthquake. The horse used its wings to steady itself, but the General's head tilted ever so slightly, his gaze not on Jacob, but on some distant vision only he could see. The demon's fell power lessened just a little, just enough, and Jacob readied himself for one final suicidal charge.

"No," the voices of the demon murmured. "This cannot be. The Lady . . . the Lady has fallen."

"Good," screamed Jacob. "Join her!"

Lunging forward with his last reserves, Jacob's lucent blade pierced the umbral energy. He couldn't defeat a Duke of Hell, he couldn't even reach him, but the demon he rode was another matter. The sword cleaved into the beast's head, the holy power carving effortlessly through its skull. For the first time in the battle, the General was caught completely off-guard. The great wings of the demon steed lofted them both into the air as it hurtled backwards in its death-throes and into the side of the manor. The wall collapsed as the demons crashed through and into the great hall beyond.

There was a moment of stillness, and then the house exploded. The fireball was colossal, the deafening force of it sending Jacob tumbling across the ground, sucking the air out of his lungs and leaving every piece of exposed skin singed. One entire wing of the house vanished as detonation after detonation leveled the place.

The powder, thought Jacob. *Demon dust, the Voice had called it, and highly flammable.* Perhaps he *could* defeat a Duke of Hell.

Then he saw him. The General stood in the midst of the fire, on the pile of rubble that had once been the gate, unharmed. At this point, Jacob shouldn't have been surprised or impressed, but he was. No demon should have been able to survive in such an inferno, but there he stood. The runes on his armor flared to life, and a thousand malevolent voices carried over the din of the fire.

"Your subversion of the Captain means nothing. Your attempt to delay me means nothing. The Lady's throne will still be mine and this world will fall."

The runes twisted in strange, alien patterns and a moment later the demon vanished, making good its escape across the void.

Jacob staggered away from the fire, which had now engulfed what was left of the manor. The acrid smell of the burning demon dust was thick in the air, a stomach-churning mix of sulfur and vinegar. Nothing was left of his car but a smoldering pile of unidentifiable wreckage; one of the subsequent explosions had probably been the munitions in the trunk. There was nothing left to salvage, so he turned and began to make his way off the property on foot. To be here when the emergency crews arrived would not be wise.

The divine aura was long gone, having held out just long enough to stave off the General's malefic power, which had dissipated completely when the house exploded. It would be days before he would have the strength to call upon the relic again.

He summoned forth the *art* to deaden the pain. It was a considerable effort, because every part of him hurt. He used a bit more to pull up the *veil* around himself. He had no great skill at it; he normally used it only to conceal the sword from prying eyes, but more was needed to alter the appearance of his damaged body armor, to say nothing of his damaged body. The expenditure was exhausting, and he was forced to stop and rest frequently.

Though his body ached and his spirit was fatigued, Jacob's mind was awash with questions; the demon's final words played over and over again in his thoughts. If the Captain was the Nightblade, the demon Jacob had banished, then what would his subversion mean? What was subversion from a demon's point of view? *The Lady has fallen*, the General had said.

I banish one of the most notorious demons roaming the world and an hour later the Lady whom he serves perishes, thought Jacob. *It couldn't be coincidence, could it?*

Subversion could mean that the Nightblade had turned on his

own. It made a certain amount of sense. The General had come here looking for him, he had indicated as much, and why send such a power unless the Nightblade were a threat? It had to have been the Nightblade that had destroyed the demons and the gate. He was also the likely suspect behind the message that Jacob received. He had made an error of some kind and become entrapped in the circle of binding, so he sent the text, hoping to trick his enemy into freeing him before the General arrived. An insane gamble, but then demons weren't exactly sane.

Demons destroying demons, thought Jacob. *If they all took up that cause, it would make the mission of the Pact a lot easier.*

Jacob paused in his thinking as he stopped to rest in a broad, open field. How had the Nightblade obtained his number? How long had the demon known who and what he was? He could imagine the Voice chiding him, telling him that the demon was gone, so what did it matter?

Banished back to the City of Black Glass, thought Jacob, *and while the Lady's most powerful servant was here kicking my ass, the Nightblade somehow destroyed their mistress.*

It seemed far-fetched. The Lady was one of the most powerful members of the *Kasu-Hurun's* inner circle, one of the Fallen, like the General. The Nightblade was devious and capable, but did he have the power to face a true demon lord? Unlikely. Of course, had he somehow accomplished it, then he could have seized the mantle of her power. He would be her successor, a demon lord in his own right. One evil had simply been replaced with another.

<*I would not be so sure of that,*> said the Voice.

Her pale, translucent image stood beside him, her hand on his shoulder. With the contact came her presence, the return of the Voice he had once thought might be a hallucination.

"Mandi," said Jacob, shortening her name as he had when she was little. "How is it that you are still here?"

<*Oh, I shall be gone soon enough,*> she said wryly.

"That's not what I meant," he muttered. It was difficult to reconcile the acerbic wit of the Voice with the image of his young, guileless sister. Best just to press forward.

"So the Nightblade didn't destroy the Lady?"

<*He had his part to play in her demise, as did we all, whether we knew it or not.*>

An evasive answer. It was the sort of remark that put him in mind of...

"The divine powers," said Jacob. "This was all some plan of theirs, from the start." It wasn't a question; he had been a paladin long enough to recognize the signs of their involvement.

<*Perhaps.*> Her ghostly image shrugged. <*Or perhaps they just saw an opportunity and took it.*>

Jacob mulled this over. How much of this had they foreseen? Had they known he would survive? Or was that a price that they had been willing to pay?

<*The Lady is vanquished and her realm is in chaos,*> interrupted the Voice. <*You were instrumental in that happening.*>

"And the General?" asked Jacob.

<*He could not afford to waste any more time or energy on you,*> said the Voice. <*The Lady's realm is leaderless, a power vacuum he intends to fill, though the delay here has cost him an easy victory—there are other claimants to overcome now.*>

"Such as the Nightblade," said Jacob, nodding to himself.

<*No,*> she replied. <*The Nightblade did not take up the mantle, though it was his for the taking.*>

Jacob stood with his mouth agape. The thought was inconceivable. What demon refuses power?

<*He has fled across the void,*> she continued. <*To where, I do not know. What I do know is that one day he will return here... and he will not have forgotten your part in things. He will want vengeance.*>

Jacob nodded again. *Of course he will.* He could feel the familiar twinge of anxiety in his gut, but there was a subdued quality to it. The sacrifice he had been prepared to make in exchange for saving his sister's essence had changed him, and he was only now beginning to realize it.

"What happens now?" he asked.

<*The Lady cast a long shadow, and remnants of her power yet remain. There is still much work to be done on this world.*>

"I meant, what happens to us?"

<*I will depart,*> she stated bluntly. <*And you, my brother, will carry on, as you must.*>

He had suspected as much. Knowing who the Voice was, how could it ever go back to the way it was? He was going to lose his sister again, but far better it be like this.

<*The light is nearly upon me,*> said the Voice. <*I must go.*>

The suddenness of the remark hit hard. There was still so much he wanted to ask her, so much he needed to tell her.

"Wait!" urged Jacob. "Please, I . . . I have to tell you . . . "

What did he have to tell her? He stared at the ground, struggling with the right words. What do you say to someone you have failed? Who died because of you? He didn't want forgiveness—he knew he didn't deserve it—but if nothing else he had to say the words, he had to acknowledge his sin—the sin of inaction.

"I'm so sorry, Mandi," came the words, broken with grief. "I wasn't there for you . . . I should have been . . . I . . . "

<*It doesn't matter, Jacob,*> she replied smoothly. <*You were there for me today, and you will be there for someone else tomorrow. Do you know why?*>

"Because," he paused, considering, and then smiled to himself. "Because victories can be measured by those saved just as easily as by those defeated."

Killing demons wasn't his penance, saving people was.

<*Remember why you became a crusader.*>

"To stop living in shame and to face my fears," he replied automatically.

<*And so you have.*>

The Voice faded out, and when Jacob looked up, the spirit of his sister was gone. He could feel his chest welling up with emotion, a whirlwind mix of sadness and acceptance at what had to be. He took in a deep breath and let it out as his eyes lingered on the heavens. The clouds began to break apart, revealing a rich tapestry of stars cast out across the night sky—the blanket of the universe wrapped around the world. It was the most beautiful thing he had ever seen. He gazed up at it, awed and inspired, and for the first time in his life, Jacob Kotsedi, Knight of the Pact, wasn't afraid.

About the Author

Originally hailing from northern California, Don Darling spent most of his youth in the Pacific Northwest before inexplicably ending up in Utah. Along the way, he managed the RPG and SF/Fantasy section at an independent bookstore for several years, did computer technical support for a while, and is currently involved in the arcane realm of accounting (which makes it sound much more interesting than it really is). A genre fan since his earliest memory, Don's hobbies are all the things you would expect: reading, writing, gaming, and watching movies (a *lot* of movies). Until now, his writing efforts have primarily been for his own entertainment, but he is looking to change that. Until such time as he joins the rest of the world and creates a Facebook account, a blog, a website, or all of the above, he can be contacted at ddarling777@yahoo.com.

Violet Sun

Brett Peterson

"Mommy?"

Johnny had gotten tired of waiting in the basement. On tottering three-year-old legs, he climbed the stairs—carefully, so he wouldn't fall in the dark—and opened the latch to the basement door.

Johnny knocked at the door to Mommy's bedroom a few times, calling her name. No answer. All the lights were off, and Johnny didn't want to wake her up. Instead, Johnny went to play with the cat. It was soft, and he liked to pet it, but he got in trouble when he pulled on its tail. The cat was up by its feeding dish on the counter; Johnny could just see its legs and tail dangling over the edge. Being very quiet, he climbed up on the stool the cat used to get up so high. When he had pulled himself up, Johnny reached out his hand to pet the cat, but pulled it back instead—the cat's tail had a lot of sticky stuff on it that smelled bad, and its mouth was all dirty. Mommy would want to know so she could put the cat outside again for being naughty.

"Mommy?" he called again. There was no answer; Mommy must still be sleeping. She had been crying, when Daddy didn't come home from the sky. That's when she had put him in the basement and told him to stay there. But the basement had gone dark, and Johnny didn't like the dark. It was light outside, though. He hurried off to the back door—their yard had a fence so he could play. By standing on tiptoe and reaching as high as he could, Johnny could just undo the latch . . .

Once outside, Johnny looked around. "Bird!" he pointed and shouted. Johnny wished Mommy was here to hear him, because the bird was acting funny. It was turning over and over as it came down from the tree. "Bird!" he said again, pointing. He ran over to the fence and started making faces; the neighbor's dog would usually come over and bark. But today, it looked like the dog was sleeping—it was over by the step, and didn't bark at all.

Then, he looked back up at the sky. "Green! Red!" he said, delighted, giggling at the swirls of color spreading across his vision. In the street beyond the fence, the cars looked funny in the different colors of light. They were all stopped in the middle of the road; they must be watching the sky too.

They had looked like that on TV when Mommy had held him close. But then, the TV showed scary things hurting the sun—bad ladies with big teeth and wings. He wished Daddy would come home from fighting them in his space ship.

Just then, Johnny had an accident. He was supposed to be a big boy now and use the toilet, he knew, but sometimes he had trouble. Mommy wasn't going to be happy. He sat down on the ground to cry.

Overhead, the sky changed color again. Johnny had to think for a moment, first—this one was hard to remember. "Purple!" he said at last—but his head felt funny, like it was tilted too far to one side. Johnny felt like his insides had tipped too; he felt sick in his tummy, and fell down all the way on the ground to cry some more.

Some minutes later, Johnny's mouth was all dirty too. His last cry was no longer a question.

"Mommy!"

About the Author

Brett Peterson is a writer and serial entrepreneur from St. Louis, Missouri; this story marks his third published fictional work, the previous two being "Indigo Ocean" in *The Crimson Pact Volume 4* and "Excerpts from a Nocturne," *The Cambridge PKP Literary Anthology 2011*. Brett's current writing projects, among others, include a collaborative piece involving gnomes and submarines in the age of steam, a novel-length space opera, a literary fiction story concerning viticulture, and a series of short stories in folkloric fiction.

Currently, Brett is serving as CEO of TM Publishing, as part-owner of Mimic Miniatures, and as an advisory member of a start-up producing 3D printers for metal materials. He can be found online through his work at tmpublishing.com, or via various social media. Offline, Brett lives very happily with his wife in Provo, Utah.

A Choice of Fate

Steven Diamond and Larry Correia

"A Choice of Fate" is the direct sequel to "Still Life" by Steven Diamond; "Son of Fire, Son of Thunder" by Steven Diamond and Larry Correia in *The Crimson Pact Volume 2*; "That Which We Fear" by Steven Diamond and Larry Correia in *The Crimson Pact Volume 3*; and "The Best Lies" by Steven Diamond in *The Crimson Pact Volume 4*.

Diego Santos

Ruins of New York City

I had three days to live.

In a strange way, being this close to the end was a little like being a kid on Christmas Eve. Only I'd peeked, and I already knew what my presents were. This was the gift I'd been expecting for years, and I'd dreamed of this coming death every single night since I was eight. Soon I was going to get ripped apart by a demon prince.

I'd never been so excited.

Manhattan was fucked. The invasion had hit it hard. Most of the island was under demon control, and we hadn't seen any other human beings for weeks, at least none that weren't possessed or so mutated you could barely recognize them as people.

The military was still fighting over in Jersey. We could hear the artillery booming now and then. One-fifty-fives from the sound of it, but there were fewer now, and they were further away. A pair of F-18s had made a pass over the city this morning, but they hadn't even bombed anything. Why bother? Blow them up, and the demon spires just regrew like weeds. Their slime would pool up in the craters, climb the wreckage, and harden into a red shell. I'd been there when they'd dropped a MOAB on downtown Dallas, and a week later you couldn't even tell. Rumor was they'd nuked Kansas City and the demons hadn't given a shit. Pick a scab and a new one forms as soon as the blood dries.

Maggie had started calling it terraforming, but that's because she was into science fiction and stuff, but this wasn't *terra*-nothing. This was the spawn of Hell, bleeding out over the world, staining everything in their corrupt image. For two years we'd seen them claim city after city. For two years mankind had gotten kicked in the balls, and it was their own fault for being weak and unfaithful. Man had been tested and found lacking, but by His merciful grace, the righteous would prevail against the wicked.

I wasn't particularly righteous myself, but I was awesome at killing demons. God had picked me, and the United States Marine Corp had prepared me. The five people I'd seen in my vision were here too. Against the entire demon host, we had an amnesiac that kept dying, a pagan historian that thought I was delusional, a blind chick who wore stolen eyeballs, and a possibly psychotic kid that couldn't miss. This blighted shit hole was the place for our showdown. I still needed a few more things to complete my mission and fulfill the details of my vision, but I knew the Lord would provide a way, because He always does.

In three days it would all be over, because God had sent me here to die.

Jarvis "Lazarus" Tombs

Ruins of New York

There is no real way to get used to seeing someone cut the eyes out of a demon.

Lara knelt down beside the sprawled and bleeding corpse, pulled a soup spoon from a pocket of her cargo pants, and began working it between the lid and eyeball. The edges of the spoon had been sharpened to make it easier, but even then the tendons and muscles stood out on her forearm as she sawed it back and forth. Nothing was ever easy with demons, not even when they were dead.

"Not gonna lie, Tombs," Diego Santos stood at my shoulder, sharing the view. "That eyeball thing still freaks me out. It's not natural."

"Right, because having visions of your own death in a week is completely natural," I replied.

"Three days," Santos corrected. "And my vision is from God, nothing more natural than that." He pointed at Lara. "Collecting demon eyes with a spoon? Not natural."

A short chuckle escaped my lips. These days you had to laugh at the horrific to keep from going mad. "She's here because you said she's one of the final five from your vision. Besides, she earns her keep."

Santos grunted and walked away. It wasn't like he could argue with himself. I glanced over my shoulder at his retreating figure and saw him angling towards Maggie. Santos was like a brother to me. Maggie a sister. They were the only family I had left in the world. Even then, it was hard to care one way or the other these days. I didn't have that same attachment to them that I probably should. We'd fought together. I'd died for them a couple of times. For two years now we'd wept together at the piles of bones or corpses in the cities where demons had taken over.

At least that's what they said we'd done together.

I don't remember much of that happening.

Maggie had warned me of that side effect from giving in to the Phoenix in me. Letting it loose ate bits of my humanity away. At first I had grudgingly listened to her advice, but we'd been in too many no-win situations where it had been the only option. The first time I'd changed into the Phoenix, I'd turned an entire swamp into a ruin that would likely take a few centuries to heal. But what do you do when your only friends are in trouble and are facing a few hundred demons? No-win situations. That was just the first of many. More as of late with the situation in the world getting worse by the day.

Maggie had me tell her any stories about my life I could remember, and she documented all of them. She said it was for my sake. Maybe I'd be able to get them back once all of this was over with, she'd say. It was all crap, in my opinion, but I faked it. I faked the sympathy, the understanding. I pretended I remembered more than I did, and they rarely caught me in the lie. They needed to think that I was completely committed to them, which I wasn't.

I was committed to killing the demons.

Every last one of them.

I felt a grin tug at my mouth at the thought of burning the wretched abominations until not even their ash remained as evidence of their existence. How much of that . . . glee . . . at exterminating the demons was the Lazarus Tombs in me and how much was the Phoenix in me was forever a debate. Though I'm not sure it mattered much anymore.

Looking back at Lara, I felt real emotions. Attraction. Respect. Desire. Affinity. I think perhaps that is why I was so drawn to her. She'd only been with us for a short time—a few months? Was that all it had been? A demon had possessed her in an attempt to take on a more human form, but both Santos and I had seen through the charade with ease.

Santos exorcised the demon from her. I still didn't know he managed it, but one minute possessed-Lara was trying to kill us, and the next literal ash poured out her eye-sockets and she was normal again.

Well, to the extent any of us were normal.

Lara was technically blind, and her eyes were blank, cloudy orbs. Somehow she still maintained a connection to demons. She could see through their eyes, which was why she was currently sawing into a demon's face with that spoon.

"Quit staring, Tombs," she said suddenly. Her back was turned, so I glanced around to see which remaining demon corpse was staring at me. I found one off to my left, wide-eyed with a gaping, bloody hole where the mouth had been. "I don't like people looking at me."

Lara was short and muscular with dark, curly hair. It was a mess, but it still looked great on her. I wasn't one of those guys that cared much about a woman looking perfect all the time. It was when they weren't bothering with vanity that they appealed to me, when they were at their most natural. I'd been married once, or so Maggie tells me. She didn't have a picture to show me. No real evidence. Her memory had apparently been one of the first to go, a casualty of the creature within me. I wondered if she had been anything like Lara.

Out of respect, I looked away from Lara's activities.

I felt . . . lesser . . . having looked away.

Huh.

The new sights greeting my vision were not near as beautiful as the previous one. New York wasn't what it used to be. In truth, I couldn't even say where we were within the city. All those skyscrapers and wonders of modern engineering were changed irrevocably. Gone were the steel and glass office buildings. Gone were the orderly roads—well, that much likely depended on your view of the city before this whole mess—that used to be home to the fleets of taxis and pedestrians. To anyone else, the changes would seem like something from another world, and in part they would be right.

I suppose I would even be a little shocked by it all had I not already been shown a vision of this terrible present. The Lady—that accursed Queen over the demons—had shared this picture with me some time ago. In a way it was uncanny how accurately she had predicted the look of the new New York. The funny thing was that I remembered the vision with perfect clarity, but not the Lady in the least. Santos had to fill me in on my own memory.

Everything in the ruined city had a sickening organic look to it, from the buildings to the things that used to be cars. Giant, twisting spires rose up in place of buildings, taller than they logically should be. Most were a rotten, red color and had something that looked like a massive obsidian spine running up one side of them. A support structure I supposed. The material of the structures themselves was a thick membrane that extended and contracted . . .

. . . like the spires were breathing.

In one of my more curious moments about a month ago I had snuck to the base of one of the smaller creations. After cutting my hand, I flicked my blood onto the thing's surface.

It burned. All of it. Within a few minutes the thing was crumbling in a pillar of ash. That was the day I realized that the demons were more than just creatures, and that they weren't just here to kill indiscriminately. No, they were here to make our world like their own. Utterly.

The thought had crossed my mind to go on a bleeding spree all about the parts of the country that were slowly being overrun by this demonic mess, but what would that even do other than cause me to pass out from blood loss? As it was, the instant that small spire had crumbed into an ash cloud, a horde of demons had chased us for a week straight. I took pleasure in burning the demons when my companions couldn't run any further, but that careless moment of curiosity had nearly gotten some of them killed. And who knows what memories I had burned up?

"You OK?"

I hadn't heard Lara's approach. She had a dozen demon eyeballs secured to her clothes, some looking at me, but many more looking in all variety of directions. It gave her a remarkable sense of her surroundings. It also would have been completely sickening to look at for a normal person. Fortunately none of those remained in this part of the world. Though we hadn't found hardly any corpses.

It didn't take a wild imagination to picture them being roasted over a fire.

"I'm good," I lied. "Get all the eyes you need?"

She nodded and adjusted the strap to the AR-15 slung over her shoulder. "I need to convince the new guy to stop shooting them through the eyes."

The new guy. Banks. That's the only name we knew him by. He'd joined us a couple of weeks ago, right after the incident where I'd bled on a demon building. He wasn't the talkative sort, but every now and then I swore I saw him whispering to his gun—an old Winchester Model 70. Sometimes my Itch would just barely nag at me when I was close to him, and I had to wonder if my Itch was telling me that Banks had a supernatural connection, or if his rifle did. Regardless, the kid—he couldn't have been more than twenty—never missed. Ever.

"Good luck convincing him of that," I said, smiling.

Lara reached out, hesitantly, and squeezed my forearm. "Really though, Tombs. You OK? Every time we get into a scrape like this you get a little more distant."

"Don't worry," I said. "I'll be around for at least another three days, assuming Santos is right. Then I don't think it will matter much to any of us how all of this is—" I waved around to the changed cityscape "—is going."

"Because you think we'll all be dead?"

"We aren't in a fairy tale. We don't get to survive the apocalypse. The best we can hope is that we take out as many of the demons as possible before they take us down. I'm. . . . " I hesitated. With any of the others I doubt I would have cared anymore what they thought of my sense of fatalism, but with Lara it was different. I looked away from the sunglasses that barely covered the burn marks around her eyes. "Lara, I'm going to kill them all. Every last one. Even if it means I burn out like a supernova."

"What about your son?"

I shrugged. "I wonder if he is even there anymore, inside that demon prince's body. Honestly, I'm surprised I haven't lost my memories of him."

"I'm not surprised at all."

I looked up quickly at her and opened my mouth to ask her what she meant by that, but before I could get the words out, the Itch surged at the back of my mind.

More demons.

Lots of them.

Diego Santos

Maggie was sitting atop a pile of rubble, writing in that big old book of hers. She said a record needed to be kept, insisted it was necessary. She had a blue ink pen and was making careful notes. She had pretty, swoopy, fast cursive handwriting. It was more art than communication. I could barely read it. Her book was filled with pictures of the demons we'd run into, documentations of their strengths and weaknesses, even drawings of detailed bits of their anatomy. Maggie was quite the artist.

She glanced up when I stopped in front of her. She quickly closed the book and hid whatever she was working on. "Yeah, Diego?"

I jerked my head toward where Lara was working on one of the scouts we'd popped. "Needed some air."

Maggie smiled. "That's remarkably squeamish of you."

"What's that supposed to mean?"

"Mr. Scary Badass Mexican with all the tats and the attitude gets unnerved when the little blind girl starts scooping out eyeballs. She's got a spiritual connection—"

"Hey, I don't know what kind of freaky Louisiana voodoo shit you all do down in the bayou, but where I'm from, that's just weird right there."

"You're from L.A. I didn't think anything qualified as weird for you."

"East L.A., baby. We're squared away. None of that hippy dippy crystal new age bullshit in my neighborhood."

"Lot of Virgin Mary bobbleheads, fringe on your pickups, and *norteña* music though I bet."

"Nailed it," I said. Maggie laughed. For a witch—excuse me, *Oracle*—with all sorts of weird, screwed up, false beliefs, Maggie was all right. Maybe even more than all right. And the vision told me she was supposed to be here, so that was good enough for me. I opened a pouch on my vest and took out a cigar and my lighter. "You know, for somebody who volunteered to take a hike through Hell, you're pretty smart."

"Santos!" Tombs hissed. "Incoming!"

He'd sensed them before I did. I had a good nose for demons, always had, but it was hard to pick them out in a place when everything reeked of their stench. I looked at Banks. The kid had taken up a position at the windows. The bodega's glass had been blown out a long time ago, and Banks always knew right where to go to get the best firing position. He was always on the lookout. He glanced my way, but shook his head in the negative, *Streets are clear.*

But Tombs' Itch was never wrong. I put my cigar back in the pack. I only had a few left and they needed to last the rest of my life. "Pack it up. Let's get out of here."

The building shook hard. Dust fell from the ceiling. I thought of the subway just as Tombs exclaimed, "They're below us!"

I went to the front of the bodega and took a knee at the doorway. The demons' *hellforming* hadn't oozed over this street yet, though it was poking through the cracks here and there, like garish red and yellow dripping wounds. Most of the buildings were still in one piece, though a few had collapsed during the initial battles, and fire had gutted others. The street was strewn with rubble and damaged cars. There was movement further down the block.

Banks was already watching it through the scope of his rifle. "I've got a bubbler."

Sure enough, the demon slime was climbing out of the stairs that led down into the subway. It formed a dome, then spilled over the edges, black and glistening in the sun. Figures climbed out of the muck, some humanoid, others on four or even six legs.

"Hold your fire. I don't think they've sensed us yet." I turned to the others. Just because I was incapable of fear didn't mean that others fared that well, but they seemed okay. Maggie had stashed her book and was readying her rifle. Lara was screwing the lid onto a mason jar full of eyeballs. Tombs was wearing that same blank, slightly unnerving expression he'd developed since he'd started losing his memory. "You especially, hold the fire."

Tombs just gave me a small smile.

"Where too?" Lara asked.

That was the problem with prophetic visions. It wasn't like God gave you clear rallying points. We knew this was the city, but not where in this city we were supposed to have our showdown. There were bits and pieces of the city that had still looked normal, amid a sea of corruption. "We'll head west on 82nd Street and make for Park Avenue. I'm on point. Stay low and—"

Then the whole world seemed to shake. The floor lifted, and I tumbled out onto the sidewalk. The empty freezer's glass doors shattered as the building flexed. Tables, chairs, and people rolled down the tilting linoleum as the center of the room rose. The floor split and something sick and green flashed by inside. A wet mass bulged outward.

The tentacle was as big around as my thigh.

"Out! Everybody go!" I shouted as I got up. Maggie fell and crashed against the wall. I reached out, grabbed her by the leg, and jerked her out the front door and into the street. The tip of the tentacle ended in a bone that looked like a scimitar. It turned toward us, weaving like a cobra about to strike. I lifted my M-4, but Banks was faster, and he put a thirty-caliber hole through the tentacle. The roar that came from beneath the ground sounded like a passing train. "Move it!"

Maggie was scrambling. Banks jumped through the broken window. Lara and Tombs were on the other side of the giant. It shifted, splitting the entire room in two. More tentacles appeared, but I caught sight of Tombs on the other side. He shouted something at me that I couldn't hear, and then he and Lara ran for the back.

The demons coming out of the subway had heard the commotion and were running this way. "Shit. . . . " My ruck was still inside there, and we needed the food, water, and ammo. It was times like this that I was glad to know it wasn't my time to go yet, because the whipping scimitars would've been intimidating otherwise. I ducked one, jumped over another, grabbed my pack, used it to deflect another blow, and then dove out the window.

I hit the ground on my side, rolled, and came right back up, already swinging the pack over my shoulder. Banks was just staring at me, mouth open. Of course, he was new. . . . "How—"

"Am I that fast?" I shoved the kid in the direction of Park Avenue. "Healthy living and PT." I pulled a frag from a pouch, yanked the pin, and tossed it cleanly through the growing hole in the floor. "Now move your ass!"

Maggie was already shooting at the approaching crowd of

demons, so I grabbed her as I went by and pulled her along. She cranked off a few more rounds in their direction, then followed. She flinched badly as the frag detonated and the big thing underground screamed its heads off. Its thrashing caused the building to collapse, and we were suddenly engulfed in a cloud of spreading dust. *Good. We need the cover.*

The street was swarming with demons, but their senses didn't seem to be much better than mortal humans' so the dust bought us some time. The three of us ran down an alley and took cover behind a dumpster, coughing and rubbing our eyes.

Maggie looked around, scared. "Where're Tombs and Lara?"

We would be together at the end, I was sure of that. "They'll catch up. Let's go."

Lazarus Tombs

Lara and I sprinted through the demonic ruins, not really sure where we were going. We'd been stupid to take so long at the site of the last group of demons we'd killed, but there was no use dwelling on that now. The key was to get away from the abominations chasing us so we could get our bearings and make it back safely to a rendezvous just outside the corrupted zone.

Ahead, the alley between two of the pulsing buildings narrowed into a passageway barely wide enough for one person to get through. I looked back and saw the pursuing stream of demons closing on us. The quicker, four-legged variety scrabbled over their companions in their haste to get to us first. Some of the more nimble ones used the bigger demons as jumping platforms to go even faster. They would be on top of us in moments.

Lara's agility was a marvel. She never took a poor step or bad angle. She steadily pulled ahead of me even though I was in far better shape. As she ran, she pulled her pack around in front of her and dug into it with one hand. She pulled out some explosive we'd made with household chemicals with a remote detonator fashioned from a garage door opener attached to it, then underhanded it into the spot where the alley began to narrow.

I tried to pour a little more energy into my sprint, but I just couldn't go any faster. Lara vanished through the gap ahead, forty yards ahead of me. Another look over my shoulder showed the demons were just a hundred yards behind.

I burst out of the gap into a wide-open spot that looked to have been a massive parking lot at one point in the past. Not that it matter much anymore, but some small part of me couldn't help but wonder what had been here before the demons took over. Directly in front of me Lara knelt behind a fallen chunk of concrete with her AR-15 aimed directly at me. I immediately darted to my right and heard the report of her rifle as she fired a series of rapid shots.

I vaulted over the barrier and slid to a stop just past her, turned, and swung my own rifle around on its sling to begin shooting. Aiming wasn't really an issue, as there were so many approaching the mouth of the alley. Lara stopped shooting and pulled the garage remote from a side pocket. I poured burst after burst into the oncoming rush.

It should have been like fish in a barrel. The opening was narrow, and some of the bigger demons at the back had no prayer of fitting through. The pulsing walls of the buildings on either side suddenly contracted, tripling the size of the mouth of the alley.

"You've got to be shitting me," I said. I normally wasn't one for profanity, but, well . . . shit. This accursed city was literally out to get us.

Just as the first of the smaller demons broke into the open, Lara pressed down on the key to the remote. The incendiary explosive detonated with a roar and gout of flame. Demons shrieked in pain, some of the weaker ones turning to ash immediately. Others writhed as fire flickered over their misshapen bodies. The buildings caught fire and began to *squeal* like lobsters thrown into a pot of boiling water. The sounds made me alternatively want to vomit and laugh hysterically.

A roiling, bloody haze clouded my mind, and I was over the barrier, squeezing round after round of 5.56 into the smaller demons that had made it through the gap ahead of the flame.

Heat from the flames washed over me, comforting and *right*.

I put three quick shots into the face of a dog-like demon that leapt at me. The force of the rounds spun the creature in midair.

My hands and arms had started to shimmer with heat.

I was beginning to change.

A calm, cool hand came to rest lightly on my shoulder. Instead of making me flinch or want to turn and lash out, I felt the fires inside me calm. Not go out, I could still feel them burning within, but become more controlled. Rather than feeling like solar flares—irregular and intense—I felt like a focused torch.

"Keep it together, Tombs," Lara said in my ear.

Through the flames eating the demonic buildings, a monstrosity of horns and claws appeared. It walked on six appendages, two legs and four arms. Even walking crouched like it was, it was still twenty feet tall. Its face split open vertically in two places, revealing two distinct mouths filled with teeth each longer than my hand. Another, smaller demon writhed on the ground in front of the brute, burning. The huge demon reached down with one of its arms, picked up the burning one by its head, studied it for a moment, then hurled the little monster directly at us.

I dove to my right and felt Lara go with me. The flaming demon splattered off our cover. Almost as soon as we hit the ground, Lara was firing into the brute. The rounds hit, but there didn't seem to be any reaction from the huge demon. It cocked its double-mouthed head—I could swear almost in amusement—and began lumbering towards us.

Shouldering my own rifle, I shot directly into its face with equal futility. I shoved myself to my feet and let the AR-15 hang from its sling. At the same time, I drew my Sig 226 and squeezed off two quick shots into the demon's torso.

This time, the creature roared in pain.

The hollow points of the .40 caliber rounds were each filled with a drop of my own blood and sealed with a drop of wax. It had been Santos' idea after seeing how effective my blood was on the demons back when we'd met Maggie. We kept my self-bloodletting to a minimum, though. It's not like me bleeding over everything was healthy. Plus, the pain—as little as it was—threatened to set the Phoenix loose. I only used these bullets sparingly.

The brute was howling in agony, clawing at its center of mass. It tried to back away, and when it did I shot it in the face, once in each mouth. There was a brief pause as the demon seemed to freeze, then its head exploded into flame. It fell to the ground without a twitch.

Behind me Lara put the demon that had been thrown at us out of its misery.

In the distance we could hear more howls drawing nearer. We turned and ran south toward the portion of the city that wasn't infected by the demonic plague. I hoped Santos and the others were faring better than we were.

Diego Santos

"Any sign of Tombs or Lara?" I asked Banks.

We were on the seventh floor of a hotel on Park Avenue. Banks had picked a window that gave him a pretty good view, especially since several of the surrounding buildings had toppled. We'd have used the roof, but the demons had too many fliers. It was pretty dark out there, even with the full moon, but he'd already surprised me with how good he could spot things moving in the dark. "No, sir," the kid answered. "You think they're dead?"

"I'm positive they're alive. They're both there when I die."

"Yes, sir." Banks seemed hesitant. Of course. I was used to everybody thinking I was nuts.

"I worked for a living. I was a Staff Sergeant. Save the Sir."

"Sorry, Santos," Banks shook his head. "Habit."

He'd only been with us for a short time. I'd spotted him helping a bunch of refugee New Yorkers and recognized him right away. I'd gone right up and told him the truth. I'd seen him in a vision sent from God, and he needed to come with us into a demon-infested city to stop the apocalypse. Shockingly enough, that had worked, but then, we were living in strange times. So the kid had picked up his old hunting rifle and set out with us to end the apocalypse.

"Lots of sirs and ma'ams out of you. Were you military?"

"Naw. . . . " Banks had a little bit of a southern drawl. "I was just raised to respect my elders."

"I'm only thirty."

Banks looked sheepish. "Oh . . . sorry."

The invasion had taken a lot out of everyone, but I'd been fighting it in secret for most of my life. "I'm high mileage. You're solid in a fight though." Tombs thought his rifle was haunted, and every now and then we caught the kid talking to the rifle, so that was odd. All I knew was that Banks was the best shot I'd ever seen, and that was saying something considering the men I'd served with. "You would have made a good Marine."

"Oh."

I took out one of my last cigars and lit it. "That's the greatest compliment you will ever be paid, Banks. So what did you do before?"

"I don't like to talk about before they came. None of that matters now."

"Fair enough." I changed the subject. "So what've we got out there?"

"Lots of demon activity to the west heading for the park. Something there is making a lot of smoke."

I knew it was a long shot, but had to ask. "Any other survivors at all?"

"Not a one. I saw a stray dog earlier, but something snagged it and pulled it down a sewer grate. Poor thing . . . I don't get it. Millions of people lived here, only a couple hundred thousand got out . . . "

"Where are the bodies?" I asked rhetorically.

"Where are the bodies?" Banks agreed. "That's the question. They're up to something."

"They're demons, kid. They're always up to something." I patted him on the shoulder. "Your turn to crash out. I'll keep watch."

Banks threw down his bedroll in the next room. Less than two minutes later his breathing indicated he was asleep. We'd had an exhausting day being chased across the city, so that wasn't a shocker. Plus, he didn't have my faith. He didn't understand that it was inevitable we would make it to the showdown. Going on, even when you were unsure? That took courage, something that I'd never really understand.

I sat on the bed. My vest was so heavy with ammo it felt good to lean my back against the wall and let it take the weight. The window was broken, and the breeze came in and slapped me in the face. The night was unnaturally humid. It was hot and nasty here, and I didn't know if that was because of the demons or if New York had been like that before. I passed the time listening. Occasionally there would be an inhuman shriek or a boom and flash from the direction of the New Jersey front.

I thought of my vision. It had been with me since I was a little kid, and it was always the same, but it had become clearer and clearer as the days had gone on. The closer we got to the apocalypse the more details I learned. The demon that was going to kill me was Tombs' possessed son. He was the gateway and we would fight to the death on a bridge made of bone. The other four would be there, but after I got ripped to bits, I didn't know what would happen to them.

I hoped they'd make it. They deserved to live.

The last few nights the dream had been particularly harsh, and I'd woken up still feeling the teeth and claws, but they'd also been crystal clear. So real it like I was actually there, dying on the bridge of bones. I'd even made out a new detail, and I was troubled, because I didn't know what it meant.

"What's wrong, Santos?"

Maggie had snuck up on me. That was impressive. "We're in Hell. Isn't that enough?"

She sat down next to me and kept her voice low, so we wouldn't wake Banks. "You breathe different when something's bothering you. It's how you breathe when you're about to get into a fight."

"Heh . . . I didn't know that. Why are you up?"

"Couldn't sleep. I needed company."

I studied our mystic in the gentle moonlight. She was a beautiful woman. "Company?"

"Not that kind of company, jackass." Her teeth were so white against her dark skin that her smile was visible in the dark. "You're a strange man, Santos. I swear, the closer we get to . . . you know . . . "

"My death?" I supplied.

"Well, yeah. The closer we get, it's like you're *eager*."

I shrugged. "It is what it is."

"It's frightening. Assuming you're right— "

"You know I'm right or you wouldn't be here. Tombs is losing his mind, every time he bursts into flames he comes back a little less human, but you knew what he is and what he has to do, and you came anyway. We didn't all find each other by accident. We're supposed to be here. You're the one who knew the legends, knew what they were up to, how to fight them, and you're the one who's supposed to tell our story for next time this happens. So you might not believe in my God, but you've got no doubt he's talking to me." I chewed my cigar for a moment. "Make sure you get that part right in your book."

"You think you're going to die, but you're so nonchalant about it. How?"

"When you know what I know, then you don't have time to screw around. My whole life comes down to this. Having a mission gives me clarity. I've got a sense of purpose like nobody else you'll ever meet. People find out about me, they either think I'm crazy, or they see the things I've seen, and then they know I'm not, and then they feel sorry for me. That's stupid. Maggie, way I see it, I'm the luckiest man in the world. I'm free of all the fear and hesitation and unknowns that bog the rest of you down."

"Santos, I doubted you when we first met. Frankly, I thought you were bug nuts delusional, but you're either the most faithful or the luckiest person I've ever known. I've studied the occult my entire life, but when you cast the demon out of Lara, I've never heard of anything like that. And the demons, they call you the Son of Thunder. You're like some sort of myth to them. They're actually scared of you."

"They should be."

"We've fought them so long, and I've seen you do so much, that I'm afraid I might actually have started to believe your hype a little. I still think you're nuts, though."

That was awkward. The demons believed me more than my companions. She was quiet for a long time. "So what's bothering you?"

"A ring. . . . "

She hadn't expected that. "What?"

"In the vision I'm wearing a gold ring. That's the first time I've ever made that out. I've tried to make sure everything is right in preparation. Hell, the reason I joined the Marines was because God showed me the Eagle, Globe, and Anchor." I touched the spot on my chest where I'd gotten the tattoo right after Basic. "I've lived my whole life preparing for that moment, but I've never seen the ring before."

"That's it? With all the stuff that's going down around us, and Tombs and Lara missing and probably dead, in a city surrounded by evil monsters, you're freaked out because of a ring?" Maggie snorted. "You? The guy who dives head first into impossible fights because he thinks he's immortal for a couple more days is worried because he isn't wearing a ring? You're about to die and you're worried about fashion? That's probably one of the—"

"It's a wedding ring."

"Oh. . . . " Maggie's smile died. "Oh shit."

Lazarus Tombs

I checked my watch as we hunkered down in the shell of an old building. I was shocked to see we'd been running and hiding for the better part of a day and a half. Every time we got close to the demon-free zone of the city we were herded back in. We were running low on ammunition, but at least we had water and rations for another day or two. I supposed that was really all we needed if Santos' vision was real. We'd slept only for a few hours the night before the howls of our pursuers came uncomfortably close.

"Tombs," Lara said. "Check this out." She had a pair of goggles over her damaged eye sockets, and to the goggles she had affixed a pair of demon's eyes she could see through. It was a weird, disgusting, yet effective approach. She handed me the binoculars she'd been looking through and pointed to the west.

It was one of those breathing buildings, a little shorter than the ones in the city proper, but something about it just felt *off*. Smoke was billowing out the top of it, and for the briefest moment I thought that just maybe someone was—how did Santos always put it?—going about God's own work, but the building wasn't actually on fire, which was obvious from a bit more looking. The closest comparison I could come up with was that of a factory spewing out waste into the air.

In my mind, the words "factory" and "demon" did not make good companions. I expressed as much to Lara.

"Something seems different with it, Tombs," Lara said after she had taken back the binoculars from me.

"With the factory?"

"No . . . with the smoke."

I looked again, but nothing about the smoke seemed odd. "What do you see?"

"It's a weird color."

"I'm not seeing it," I said, but I didn't doubt her for a moment. She wasn't looking through normal eyes, and Lara had made it abundantly clear that she saw the world differently than I did. "What's the first thing it makes you think of?"

She was quiet for a long couple of minutes. I didn't interrupt her thoughts or push her. This was her way. She was the type of person that liked to be sure before she spoke.

Lara suddenly cocked her head to the side. "It reminds me of demon blood."

As we got closer to the building, I started feeling something. At first I just chalked it up to the Itch needlessly letting me know there were demons around. That much was pretty much understood in an area where the very ground beneath our feet seemed to be alive. Each step was spongy, and every so often it felt . . . sticky . . . like it was trying to keep us from moving on.

I realized this feeling was different though. Not quite *déjà vu*, but close enough. The way the building sat. The color of it—a rusty, wet color that just screamed sickness and corruption. It wasn't just the building itself that was nagging at me. It was the surroundings too. The place was open, and if I squinted just right—pretending to see different colors than the reds and browns that promised death—I could have sworn we were in Central Park.

Except instead of trees and bushes, there were piles of bones.

I've seen bone piles in my days. When I was FBI, even. I must have made a surprised noise, because Lara turned and gave me a questioning look. I checked my watch again. We'd been on the run for two and a half days now. We needed a rest. There was a giant rock ahead of us, and I motioned for her to head towards it. The stone had resisted much of the corruption, and for some reason that made me feel a tiny bit better.

"What's up?" Lara asked quietly.

"Not sure," I said. "Got a weird feeling. Like I've seen all this before." I shot a quick glance at Lara to see if she was sitting down to listen, or sitting down and wanting me to shut up so she could rest. I decided on the former. "It reminds me of a case I had in the FBI."

"The skyscraper?"

"The bones," I said. "I was fairly new . . . honestly, I'm kinda surprised I even remember it still. It was one of my first cases where I had a brush with the supernatural. Well, at least I think it was one of the first times. My memory isn't what it used to be."

I was silent for a moment, looking around at the various piles. Most of the ones close to us looked old. If they had been in the desert and under a sun that actually shone regular-like, they'd have been bleached white. Here they had a measure of corruption to them, all browns and reds streaked with yellow. The furthest pile I could see seemed . . . fresher. The factory building was still a ways off, but I expected they would be freshest up there close.

"What happened?"

I jerked a little, startled. "Sorry, my mind wandered. I was new, full of youthful enthusiasm. I got called out to a site in rural Idaho."

"Isn't all of Idaho rural?"

Chuckling a little, I continued. "Pretty much. Though what I wouldn't give to see that type of natural landscape right now instead of all this. The local cops had come across a mass grave out there. Bones. Piles and piles of bones. Some guy had been out teaching his kids how to survive in the wilderness when one of the kids had wandered off and gotten lost. His screaming helped the father and other brother find him. There were a few pits in the ground—open for any to witness. Inside were thousands upon thousands of bones. You don't realize just how many bones are in the human body until you see them in jumbled piles.

"A full forensics team was called in," I continued. "Lots of animal bones, but some obviously human ones too. Teeth marks all over them." I pointed to one of the piles closest to us where gnaw marks were evident. "Kinda like that. I was shaken. I mean, that's some pretty screwed up stuff. But that was when I remember feeling the Itch. Forensics wanted to brush it off as simple animal attacks. Seriously, did they think 'simple' animals would be this organized? No, I knew—that Itch in my head screamed at me that wasn't natural—I knew this was something more."

Lara was listening quietly, intrigued. That's part of why I liked her. She knew I needed to talk, so she let me. No complaining. No judging. Just listening.

"I used my Itch like radar for the next few days, searching a grid around the bone pits. See, the more I looked at those bones—the others thought I was twisted by the third day staring at them—the more I was reminded of when I ate steak. Weird, I know. Bear with me.

"When you eat a steak that still has the bone in it," I said, "there are the places where you easily get the meat away from the bone. It comes off clean with a knife. If you look close, you can even see where the blade scraped that bone a bit. But the hard parts to get . . . well, you use your teeth. That's what these bones looked like. Scraped by tools, then gnawed.

"My Itch went berserk the fifth day. There was some rocky

ground, and I found a cave masked by foliage. I'm not just talking about a bush pulled in front of the entrance. This was full on-camouflage. I wouldn't have even noticed if that Itch in my head hadn't guided me to it. I was smart in those days and called for backup. I wanted a career, and living through the crazy cases and doing things the right way was the best way to ensure that.

"Back-up came. We ripped the façade out of the way and went in hard. Wish we would have had an HRT team. The first five agents through the entrance to that cave came right back out again, but in pieces. Howls followed the bloody bits out. At that point, with those deaths, I again made a fairly smart decision. We chucked explosives in there. When the dust settled we went in and found a bunch of humanoid corpses ripped to shreds from the explosions. I was kicking myself for killing innocents until I saw the upper-half of a torso with head still attached. It had the head of damn coyote. It was like those pictures from Egypt of their jackal god. I forget his name.

"Anyway, they'd been living in that area for years, preying on idiot hikers and local game—though I suppose those were equal terms to them. Jackalmen. That was the first I heard of them, and that earned me a spot in the PSD—the Paranormal Sciences Division—of the FBI."

"This reminds you of that case?" Lara asked.

"Yeah," I nodded. "Doesn't it seem weird to you that my first supernatural case had so many similarities to what we have right here? I gotta wonder if I've been shaped since the beginning for this. I'm not scared. These bones just mean we have to do everything possible to keep this from happening anywhere else."

"You think these were all eaten people?"

"I think we know where everyone has gone," I said. "We hoped that they had escaped, but there are probably millions of bones here."

"What are you thinking?" Lara asked. That directness was another of her good qualities.

"Two things," I said. "First, if we don't stop them—if Santos is wrong about his vision—these fields will cover the entire world."

"Second?"

"Second," I said, "I've heard Santos describe something very similar to this. He says that in his vision we are on the top of a building. Up there is a portal to where the demons are coming from, and around us is a field of bones."

"If this isn't a field of bones," Lara said looking around. "I don't know what is."

"Exactly. Lara, I haven't always believed in Santos' vision, but I never doubted *he* believed in it. The thing is, I'm beginning to think he was right all along." I found myself smiling. "Maybe, just maybe, we have a chance after all."

Lara crossed the distance between us to sit at my side, and I felt her lips brush against my cheek in a gentle kiss. I couldn't help but put my arm around her. "If you believe, Tombs, I believe. What now?"

"Now we find out what that building is for, we shut it down, and I burn them all," I said. "And now I would be shocked if Santos didn't end up here too."

Diego Santos

Only one day left until I got to die.

Banks was on point. He sounded like a country boy, and the way he could move from cover to cover, with such complete silence told me he'd done a lot of hunting in his life. Maggie had grown up in a swamp, gone off to college, and then gone back to her swamp, so it wasn't too much of a surprise that she was really surefooted, jumping easily across the rifts in the sidewalks and holes in the roads, which were filling up with demon slime.

Luckily for us, the city had been abandoned so quickly that

there were lots of vehicles still cluttering the streets. Those gave us places to hide, and we spent the day moving from doorways to flipped-over busses, then back into the buildings whenever there were convenient holes in the walls to travel through. The going was slow, but the important thing was not getting spotted. Every now and then Banks would hold up his hand for us to freeze, and then signal for us to move beneath something, usually only seconds before a big shadow would pass with the beating of wings.

We avoided the spires. They had been human buildings once, before the slime had trickled up and consumed them. Bridges were forming between some of them, and every now and then I could see movement high above us as the demons went about their mysterious business. We'd hide until they passed. I didn't know how they communicated with each other, but I knew they had some way of vectoring in patrols.

My mind was heavy. I had no answer for the gold ring. I'd faithfully prepared for this, but now I was troubled. Had I done something wrong? Had I missed a step along the way? If a detail was wrong, would I fail? I prayed for guidance, but God didn't answer.

I became excited when we got to Central Park. Maggie started crying. I thought Banks was saying a prayer, but he was just whispering something comforting to his rifle. They'd never imagined so many bones, a sea of stripped bones, as far as the eye could see.

I'd seen it before.

"This is the place."

The demon factory on the other side of Central Park was taller than it had been yesterday. It was growing. It was alive. And in a few hours I was going to climb that spire and die gloriously. Maybe . . . But I shoved the doubts aside. He had a reason for everything.

"Santos. . . . "

I looked away from the window. "Hey, Maggie." She was standing there, looking a little apprehensive. She had her fist clenched, and she was holding it tight against her chest. "What's wrong?"

She looked me right in the eyes. "You remember how I said I was starting to believe your hype?"

"Something like that."

"Part of me still thinks you're a nut who suffers from a recurring nightmare." Maggie took a deep breath. "The other part of me thinks that the five of us really are meant to save the world, and that you really do have a prophetic vision. That part has been getting louder."

"I can't exactly accuse you of a lack of faith, when you think my God is imaginary and Jesus was just a nice guy. Don't worry about it, Mags. You believe in Tombs' power and that brought you here. That took a lot of guts. You've got courage, and I can respect that. You're supposed to be here, and stepped up. That's the important thing."

"If you're right, Santos—if you've been right this whole time—then you need to be ready. No doubts. No hesitation."

I shook my head sadly. "Baby, you have no idea how ready I am for this."

"Not quite." She held out her hand. Her fingers opened, and resting in her palm was a plain gold ring.

My mouth fell open. "That's it . . . That's the one . . . "

"I was afraid of that," she said slowly.

"How—"

"I found it in one of the museum displays. It was the only thing in there not corroded. Not even a bit. Like the ooze was scared to touch it. It was hard to tell since everything else was slimed, but I think it was from the Crusades and this belonged to one of the Knights Templar."

Appropriate. "I don't know what to say."

"Say yes," Maggie ordered.

I laughed, but her expression was unflinching. "Wait . . . Wait a second. Are you proposing to me?"

She didn't answer me directly. "Banks! Get in here."

"Yes, Ma'am." Our sniper shuffled around the corner. "You ready?"

"Ready for what?" I asked nervously. And that was saying something, because it wasn't like I was used to experiencing *nervousness.* "Mags?"

"Banks doesn't talk much to the rest of you, but once he knew I was the record keeper, he told me his story. He was a Pentecostal minister before the invasion." She raised her voice. "Isn't that right, Banks?"

"Yes, Ma'am."

She whispered. "A snake-handling backwoods minister, but he's still clergy. And yes, his rifle is haunted . . . So how about it, Santos? Just how much faith you got?" And now she grinned. "Make it quick. According to your clock we've got to leave in a few hours, and damn it, I deserve a wedding night."

I got down on one knee.

Lazarus Tombs

"Tombs," Lara said. He voice was full of confusion and disgust.

"Yeah?"

"I think this is the Met."

Dry and brittle bones cracked underfoot as I joined her to take in the ruined building. The roof had collapsed in many areas and the front entrance sealed by the wreckage of the crumbled façade. For some reason, this sight made my heart ache in near-despair.

The demons take everything from us, I thought. *They consume everything, because that is all they know.* It was disgusting. The loss of all that history. I hoped humanity would find a way to recover it.

For the first time in months I wanted to weep in sadness.

As we got closer, I instead found that I wanted to weep in happiness. Next to the rubble blocking the main entrance was a figure waving to get our attention. Santos. He turned his head and said something to an obscured figure behind him. That figure soon resolved into Maggie, and then my gaze caught a glimpse of Banks perched up higher in the chunks of fallen granite. He waved briefly before sinking back down into his hiding spot.

"'Bout time you showed up, Tombs," Santos said when we were only a few feet apart. His face split into the biggest smile I'd ever witnessed. He winked at Lara. "Good to see you, Lara. You keep him out of trouble?"

"Of course," she said. "Only had to hold his hand and lead him a few times."

"Let's get inside," Santos said. "Found a hole in the side of the building a bit further down. It's nearly full of corruption inside, but Maggie found a place that isn't too bad.

I couldn't even tell what the exhibits were as we took our impromptu tour. The demonic plague covered everything. I'd come here about five years ago, so some of it should have been familiar. But now it was all so alien. Just the visual of it all seemed to overwrite any memory I had of the place. From one of the windows I looked back out toward the park. A giant demon spire stood there, pulsing in the same rhythm as everything else. Had that been where the obelisk had stood? Was it now corrupted, or was this an entirely different structure? I just couldn't tell anymore. Beyond that should have been the small, rolling grassy knolls. There should have been copses of trees. Instead, it was all bone.

I looked through the optics of my AR-15 at the skyscraper that Santos had marked for his death. Bones poured from chutes along the sides, and smaller demons would take them out into what had once been Central Park for disposal. From a different angle, bigger demons carried corpses of humans into the same building. It didn't take a genius to see what was going on.

Lara was at my side a moment later, looking at the same vista. "They are feeding the bodies into the skyscraper, and then the bones are thrown out as waste." Out of the corner of my eye, I caught her shaking her head in disgust.

"Looks like it," I said.

She aimed the optics up to the smoke billowing out of the top of building. "That's just the waste then. And it spreads too, seeding the ground for even more demonic corruption."

"And according to Santos," I said in a low voice, "at the top is where we will find our end."

I felt the briefest of touches on my arm as she left my side.

"Over here," I head Maggie say. "This room in here isn't too bad."

The rest of the group entered ahead of me. They were nearly silent, and their faces grim—all except Santos, who was grinning like a fool. They knew the end was close, and that reality was causing no shortage of soul-searching. I took them all in, one-by-one. They were good people, each and every one of them. Santos was ready to die. But the others? They put on brave faces, but under those masks their apprehensions and fears were displayed for any who took a second to look. They were terrified. If these people were sitting across from me in an interrogation room, I would have said they were about to break.

They deserved better. They deserved more than a violent death.

And again, like when my son had been taken from me, I felt powerless. I wanted each of my companions—my friends, my family—to see the fruits of their sacrifices.

"Quit staring and get in here, Tombs," Santos said as he waved me into the room. "We're saving the world tomorrow, and we can't hardly do that on an empty stomach. I'll get to cooking."

Santos pulled the remaining few cans of food from his pack. Maggie and Lara each added their own reserves as well. I walked over and scooped them up. "I got this one."

"You sure?" Santos said. "Make sure you check them this time. Last time you cooked, the corruption was in some of your cans, and they *attacked* me." This earned a chuckle from the ladies and a grin from Banks. Even now—maybe especially now—with the end tomorrow, they still weren't letting me forget that one.

That's why I knew I'd do anything—everything—for them.

"Yeah," I said, smiling. I wasn't sure if the smile was genuine or not. I wasn't sure it mattered. "I got it."

Maggie was drawing in her book again. But this time it was at a feverish pace. I came up behind her and peeked over her shoulder. I wasn't sure what to expect. Another demon maybe? The building we'd likely all die on?

Nothing prepared me for what it actually was.

I don't remember if I was ever a church-going man. Chalk that up to one of the many things the Phoenix had burned out of me. But even then I knew religious iconography when I saw it. This wasn't the cheap crap most people saw painted on the side of some gang-banger's car. No, this was something I expected to see in a Catholic church. At the front. With candles in front of it.

And it was of Santos.

Maggie tried to shut the book when she noticed I was there, but I stuck my hand in there like an impromptu bookmark. "Don't stop," I said. "Please."

She gave me an embarrassed look, but I could tell she desperately wanted to get it done. It was in the way her right index finger tapped rapidly on the pencil, or how her eyes kept shifting from me back to the sketchbook only to linger there longer and longer each time.

"I thought you didn't believe in his god?" I asked.

"Do you?"

I looked down and saw she had eaten every scrap of food I had prepared. I felt some of my nerves drain away. "I don't know that I absolutely believe," I began, "but it's kinda difficult not to wonder a little bit."

"Maybe Santos is just crazy," she said without any conviction. She drew the idealistic lines that would become wounds classic to any martyr rendering, then began working on Santos' hands. He was stretched out on a pile of rubble, broken and bleeding. His arms splayed out in a replica of crucifixion without a cross. "But maybe he's not. Don't tell him about this."

"Okay. But if there is one thing I know about Santos," I said, "it's . . . well. . . . "

"What?" Maggie asked. She looked up, no doubt expecting some motivational speech.

"It's that he is absolutely crazy," I said with a wink. I pointed to where he was talking with Banks. They were admiring Banks' Winchester. "Even now he can't stop obsessing about a *gun*."

Maggie stared at me for a handful of heartbeats, then laughed. She laughed until she began to cry, the tears pouring down her face, where they dripped onto her drawing. I put my arm around her, and that was when I noticed the ring she was drawing on Santos' left ring finger. I looked across the room again at the Marine and caught the glint of the ring.

"Huh," I said. "How did you two manage that one?"

At first Maggie looked confused, but then a sly smile crept onto her lips when I pointed down at the wedding ring in the drawing. "Turns out Banks is a minister."

"Really?"

"You'd know that if you talked to anyone besides Lara. I swear, you and Santos are equally idiotic sometimes."

That we are. "It's one of our finer qualities." I hesitated, then tried to tell her how much she meant to me. How much I appreciated all the guidance she had given me, even though it seemed like I was never listening. She shushed me before I could say a word.

"I know."

I pulled her close and gave her a chaste kiss on the top of the head.

Santos caught my eye and nodded for me to meet him in the hall. "I'll be back in a bit," I said. "Get that drawing finished." I hesitated, then pulled a sealed letter from my pocket. I handed it to her. "This is for after."

"Tombs," she started, "I don't think a—"

"Just take it," I said. "If you make it through this, read it. You'll know what to do. If you don't make it, then it won't matter." I left her there staring at the envelope in confusion.

Santos was waiting for me in that hall, fidgeting. He never fidgeted.

"She told you?"

"About the ring? Yeah."

He stared at me for a few moments. "And?"

I sighed and leaned against a part of the wall that didn't look like it would try to attack me. "I wish I could have been there for you."

His brow furrowed in confusion. "Tombs, you've *always* been there for me. From the night I had my first vision of the people who would be here with me at the end, you've been with me. When are you gonna realize that?"

"Well then," I said holding out my hand, "congratulations. And it's been . . . well, not a pleasure, but an honor at the very least. I wish the two of you the best."

He returned the grip and said, "Don't be an asshole, Tombs. I'll be dead in less than twenty-four hours."

"Right. Sorry."

"That said—" he looked back into the room at Maggie "—I'm gonna go spend my last peaceful moments with Mrs. Santos."

I followed him back in. Banks was already asleep and snoring. What would it have been like to sleep soundly like that again? It had been at least two years since I'd slept more than two hours consecutively.

"Saying your goodbyes?"

Lara's arm slipped into mine.

"Do you believe in fate, Lara?"

"Should I?"

"Santos' fate is sealed, and so is ours it seems."

Lara shrugged. "Does it really matter?"

"I hate the thought of you all dying," I replied. "I'm more than willing to die to end all of this, but you and Maggie? Banks? Why should you have to?"

"Who says we will?"

"I don't . . . I don't see. . . . "

"Do you want to know what I see when I look at you, Tombs?"

The question caught me off guard. "Uh, okay?"

"The demons see things differently. They see the supernatural connection people and things have to this existence. That's why I can tell what they are trying to do in that skyscraper that is belching out smoke. I see things like they do.

"When I look at you," she continued, "I see you a little brighter than everyone else. Brighter than even Santos who stands out in his own way. And when you start to turn into that Phoenix, you are like an exploding sun. I swear that the air around you shimmers in heat waves.

"My point," she said holding up a hand to ward off any words from me, "is that you are different. You are powerful. But even you can't save me again. You and Santos already saved my life once when you got that demon out of me. As far as I'm concerned, I've already been given a second chance to choose my own end. I won't go down without making sure you can end this. Is that fate? Honestly, who cares?"

"Can I end this?" I asked quietly. I'd never spoken those words out loud, but with Lara they slipped out.

Her hand reached up and gently turned my face toward hers. She stretched up and brushed her lips against mine. "I know you can."

There wasn't time to form an in-depth strategy. We went in through the front of the demon building and looked for an intact stairwell. The demons weren't expecting us, and we weren't exactly trying to conserve ammo.

I suppose that was one of the benefits of Santos' vision; we knew when and where we were going to hit them on this final day. They couldn't be prepared for it, and we were as prepared as five people could be in his situation.

The front of the building still had a glass, double-door entry that had somehow survived the localized apocalypse. Tendrils and filaments of red and black demonic tissue weaved their way around the edges of the door. I took out a knife, flicked it open, and cut into part of the pulsing matter. Black ichor dripped out, but the tissue didn't recede.

I nodded for Santos to give the door a push. Even beneath his strength—a strength I could swear was growing each day closer we were to the end—the door didn't move.

"Guess that was too much to hope for," I muttered. I took a deep breath and looked at my companions. "Get ready to run. This is where it ends."

Without hesitation, I lifted my AR-15 and put five rounds into the glass door. The report of the gun, and then the sound of the glass shattering, seemed incredibly loud. Santos stepped forward and kicked out the rest.

I could already hear the howls of the demons as the noise drew them.

But this time we were chasing them.

The temperature increased around me as the Phoenix slowly

shook itself awake. That Itch in the back of my mind was going berserk.

A single, tiny demon stood in the center of what had once been the lobby of this building. It looked up in shock as we stepped across the threshold. I half expected a one-liner out of Santos. I glanced his way and saw he was giving me an identical look.

I grinned.

We both lifted our rifles and blew the demon back to the hell it had come from.

"Move!" I yelled.

Santos took point, rushing for the remains of a stairway closed off by a rusty door. He didn't slow as he approached the door, he just threw himself through it. It exploded under the impact, and the rest of us were on his heels, taking the steps two at a time.

I took the rear to guard our back, and Banks was right in the middle of the pack. Maggie was right at Santos' back, and Lara in front of me. Demons rushed at us from behind and from in front. They used debris, walls, and ceilings to get at us from every angle imaginable. Our guns fired in a steady roar, and every surface we passed we left covered in the black blood of massacred demons.

It was exhilarating.

Let me out Tombs . . .

The Phoenix wanted to join the destruction. It wanted me to let it loose right here and now, and I was sorely tempted. But it wasn't time. Not yet.

We'd made it three floors before we caught our first lull. Suddenly every demon around us was a corpse. We took the next three floors without firing a shot.

Ahead, the stairs ended in a throbbing mass of organic demon tissue. I took my flashlight and focused the beam on the membrane closest to us. The light illuminated the opposite side of the organic wall and showed me a human body. As I watched—and it only took moments—the flesh from the poor fool dissolved.

A few years ago I would have retched.

Now I just got angrier.

"Lara," I said turning to face her, "see if the hall outside is clear. We need to get to the other side of the building. Hopefully there's a staircase there too."

She dropped her pack and pulled out an old, battered first-aid case. Lara flicked it open to display her collection of scavenged demon eyes. She took four of them in her hand and edged toward the door. It creaked a bit as she pushed it open.

With practiced movements, she flung four eyes out into the hall.

Then we waited.

She cocked her head to the side like she always did. She was truly an amazing woman. I hoped this all would work.

"See anything?" Santos asked.

"Clear. I left an eye in the lobby though. Reinforcements are here."

"Stay by me at the front," the Marine said. "And keep those eyes handy. You're the best intel we have." He looked back at the membrane blocking the way behind us. "And give me one of those explosives with a ten minute timer." He affixed the explosive on the mass of tissue and set the timer with the ease of a guy who had done it a million times. "Let's go," Santos said, shouldering his rifle.

Sunlight filtered through the skin of the demonic matter that covered and infused the structure. It gave everything a hellish cast. I had the distinct impression that we were in the belly of the beast. Beneath our feet the ground squelched with every step, and those same steps each released little puffs of odor that turned my stomach. I've been around a lot of corpses, many of them before this whole apocalypse mess. The sweet, cloying smell of rotting, exposed flesh was the first thing that came to mind.

After a few turns we found ourselves at the entrance to the other stairway. There was no door blocking our way here, just a gaping hole. Lara threw a couple of eyes down the stairs and another few up as far as she could.

"Go," she said quietly.

"Where are they?" Maggie wondered aloud. I knew what she was feeling. That anxiety of the unknown. When the demons were coming at you, you just pulled the trigger without thinking. But now . . . all we could do was let our imaginations run wild. This was likely the most terrifying part of this long journey.

And yet I felt myself being dragged upwards like magnet.

The Portal is up there. Let me out . . .

The Portal. According to everything Maggie had dug up, it was the physical opening that connected our earthly realm to that of the demons'. Call it Hell, Purgatory, or any other name; through the Portal was where a huge chunk of demons were. If I got through, I could kill them all.

I pushed the Phoenix back.

We climbed the stairs with flashlights on. The dark and the walls that were completely covered with the demonic corruption made time and distance pass oddly. How long had it been? How close were we?

Ahead of me, Lara swore. "A demon just stepped on one of the eyes I threw down this staircase . . . guys, they're coming."

"How many?" Banks asked. It was the first time he'd said anything this whole time.

"All of them."

"Run," Santos said quietly at first, then he shouted, *"Run!"*

Every last bit of energy I had went into pumping my legs faster and faster. Maggie stumbled. Santos paused, grabbed her, and virtually threw her up the stairs to the next landing. She slid across the slick ground and opened fire at the area up even higher above her. Demons screamed and howled above and below us.

"Flares!" I screamed.

Lara let her rifle fall, sling keeping it from hitting the ground, and ripped open a pocket on her cargo pants. Intense red light bloomed to life around us, casting shadows that danced in the muzzle flashes of Santos' and Maggie's guns. Lara dropped one flare to the landing below us. She turned and ran the other one up toward Maggie and Santos.

The first demons scuttled at us from below.

There had to be a hundred of them. A thousand. All the hordes of Hell, if you believed in that sort of thing. We would run out of ammo long before they stopped coming. The report from Banks' Winchester was almost soothing, and every time he shot, a demon fell. It wasn't enough. We needed to move before they overwhelmed us.

"Frag!" Lara yelled over the chaos, and a grenade bounced down past me, using the wall as a guide. I pulled an incendiary grenade and threw it down after the frag.

A concussion was followed by a bloom of flame. The stairwell caught fire, and the blaze hungrily ate its way up the walls. With the demons held off for the moment in the inferno below—an inferno that would overtake us if we didn't get moving—I turned to help Santos.

He didn't need it.

He moved quicker than any man I had ever seen. This wasn't natural. I tried to focus my Itch and it seemed like an extra hint was coming off of him. It was hard to deny that he was supernaturally touched as he shot four demons, stabbed another through the skull with a knife I didn't even see him draw, then dropped the AR-15 and lifted the Mossberg to blow the heads off two more.

Maybe he *was* blessed by God. The demons called him 'Son of Thunder.'

I was just glad he was on our side.

I could feel the Portal just ahead.

"Keep going!" I yelled at him.

He cleared the way. Demons fell before him like wheat before a scythe. We all shot where we could, taking the demons that tried to leap on him from walls or from further ahead. Behind us the fire raged.

Suddenly the ground shook, and I felt the deep boom of the timed explosive we had set. It had only been ten minutes.

And then we burst out onto the roof of the building.

The panorama opened up around us, showing the full depth of the destruction the demons had wrought. From here, Central Park was a solid field of bone, and the rest of the city didn't look any better. The demon cancer had spread more than we realized from the ground, and it was consuming everything.

This would be the world soon.

Ahead the Portal seethed, and the demon that had once been my son emerged. A bridge of bone lowered from where it fed into that black hole. It crashed down in front of us, just like Santos had said it would.

Diego Santos

The Bridge to Hell

The last of the demons fell before us, making a clear path to the demon prince. I dropped my empty carbine, unbuckled my plate carrier, and shrugged out of it. This would end with just my bare hands. I could hear the demons wailing in fear from behind us and beyond that dark hole.

The Son of Thunder draws near.

It all came down to this.

The bridge was made of millions of interlaced human bones, bound together with human skin, which had dried into leather. The demon prince was waiting for me on the bridge. On the other side was the gateway to the demon realm. It was stretching across the sky, reaching for the roof of the nightmare-corrupted building.

I looked back at my friends. It was exactly like I remembered. The four of them were watching me, just like I'd always known they would. I'd seen this before, so many times. Only now I really understood what was at stake.

The bridge of bones struck the roof with a terrible wail. Our universes had made contact.

There was no fear. No hesitation. That was her gift to me. I risked one last look at Maggie. Tears were streaming down her face. *Thank you.*

Then I stepped onto the bridge to face the thing that had been Tombs' son. Their bloodline was the key. Father or son. One of them would win today. I couldn't beat the prince, but my job was to try. I had to stall it. I had to die so that the others could live, so that they could complete their missions.

I approached. The bridge swayed beneath us, bones creaking and cracking. I stopped just out of reach of the demon's long simian arms. He was eight feet of muscle, bone, and spikes. His mouth opened—so wide his whole head split in half—revealing rows of shark teeth, but I already knew how'd they feel, how'd they cut through my flesh. The prince was watching me, sizing me up. I was nothing too him. He was demon royalty, virtually immortal. My mortal body was pathetic in comparison, but I'd been chosen by the Lord for this moment, and he could sense that. The demon hesitated, unsure, because he lacked my knowledge, my faith.

He would defeat me, but in the few seconds he took to do that, Tombs would end it all.

I was completely free.

Thy will be done.

The bridge shook as the demon attacked.

We collided.

Victory was impossible. Survival was impossible. Claws tore through skin and my blood splattered against the bridge of bones. Teeth flashed and my shoulder was opened clear to my collarbone.

The pain would have been unbearable if I hadn't been prepared to embrace it. Now it was just another old friend, long expected.

I laughed in his face.

The demon stopped, confused, strings of meat dangling from his mouth, but Tombs was already past us, heading right straight into the Portal. Fire—holier than any I'd ever witnessed or imagined—sprang to life around him.

Burn them all, brother.

The demon turned, but I grabbed onto one of his horns and held on. Furious, he lashed out, opening my guts, but I wouldn't let go. Thunder cracked in the sky. A hoof rose and fell, and the bones in my leg shattered. I pulled him down, and the demon bellowed in incomprehensible rage. Giant fists smashed my ribs into bits, and they pierced through my lungs. I coughed blood everywhere. He slashed his claws down the side of my face, removing one of my eyes, and exposing half my skull.

I collapsed.

He turned, searching, but he was too late.

Tombs took one last glance over his shoulder, then leapt through the portal.

"*No!*" the demon prince thundered. The sound of its voice made the building shake. "*The Son of Fire will consume us all!*"

My arm was broken in several places, with bones sticking out the skin, and it was resting there, limp on the blasphemous bridge, but I could still see my watch through my one remaining eye. The counter I had set so many years ago had finally run down to zero.

Right on time.

And then the demon prince petulantly kicked me over the edge of the bridge into space.

Lazarus Tombs

At the Black Sun

Just like Maggie's tomes had described, the Black Sun hovered there before us. Santos was already walking out to meet the demon. He looked back once, just like he said he would.

For the first time, I believed everything Santos had ever said. I tried to give him a nod of understanding, but he had already turned back.

Guns roared behind me. Distantly. Screams. Shouts. The sounds of death.

It's your time now, I said to the Phoenix.

We will burn them, it replied. *It's what we were made for.*

I walked forward as Santos was being murdered. I'd never personally witnessed murder in action during my time in the FBI, but it had to be a lot like this. Santos did exactly what he said he would. He kept my son—the demon—occupied. But he paid for it with every heartbeat. Blood exploded from my friend's mouth as the demon pounded fists into his chest.

I passed him as my son destroyed the closest thing to family I'd had in the last few years.

Flames sprang up around me. Their warmth a balm to the grief I felt.

This better work.

I took one last glance back and immediately wished I hadn't. A wave of demons washed over the three souls who had followed Santos and I into this nightmare.

Banks was the first to die. His head ripped from his shoulders by a massive demon that looked like a demented minotaur. Blood fountained, and he fell, Winchester still gripped in his hands and still firing of its own accord. The demon that had killed him went down with a hole in its eye.

Maggie was next. She was taken when she tried to reload. A demon darted in and eviscerated her. The force of the blow spun her around, and I could see the wound. She tried to pull a grenade, but another demon bit that hand off. I lost sight of her as she was swarmed.

Lara spun this way and that, shooting with deadly accuracy. Demons tried to get her from her blindside, but the eyeless woman didn't have a blindside with all the collected demon eyes affixed to her clothing. She rolled out of the way of a pouncing demon that looked like the hellhounds from myth, shot it three times in the face, then turned to shoot three more demons in rapid succession. Even Santos would have been in awe of the display. But then she ran out of ammo. They grabbed her and literally ripped her to pieces.

It had taken just a few heartbeats, and they were all dead.

Gone.

Tears fell from my eyes but evaporated in the nimbus of fire engulfing me.

Let's end this, I told the Phoenix, and turned and walked through the portal. I had barely passed through the Black Sun portal when my son barreled into me from behind. He howled in pain as the fire engulfed him too. I reached out and wrapped my arms around the demon's neck and yanked it close.

Fire consumed my body utterly, and in a flash of orange and red flame, everything changed.

I was sitting on the porch of my house. The weather was warm, but not unpleasant. A breeze stirred. My eyes focused, and a tree with a tire swing took up the view. I looked down at myself. Jeans and a T-shirt with my son's youth baseball team name emblazoned on it. They were named after the Oakland A's. I was barefoot.

"It's been a while, Dad."

That voice. That was all it took for tears to fill my vision. I wiped them away and looked to my right, where my son always sat when we would come out here after a game. He looked older. His hair was longer and starting to curl at the ends. He didn't get that from me, so it had to have come from his mother . . . I suddenly wished I could remember her. I imagined any mother would have loved to have seen her son one last time.

"You've grown," I managed. He looked a little embarrassed. I just sat there staring at him. What do you say to the son you failed to protect? What do you say to the son you couldn't save?

What do you say to the son you have missed more than *anything*?

"I've missed you, Aaron," I finally said. It felt amazing just to say his name and have him hear it.

"I know."

"I have so much I want to say."

"I heard a lot of it while I was locked up in that photograph," he said. "It was great."

"What was it like? Being trapped in the photo I mean."

He shrugged. It was a gesture so familiar, but one I never thought I'd see again. It made me smile until I thought my face would break from the stress. "It was mostly boring." He waved around at our surroundings. "It was a bit like this actually. Just an empty space. Time didn't mean much. It was boring."

In the distance there was the sharp crack of thunder. A rolling darkness began creeping in from the distance. And then I was seeing somewhere else.

The Phoenix rushed over the landscape of the demon world, the demon prince still clutched in its grasp. The demon fought with pitiful futility as it burned. Ahead, a forest of demon spires rose. Below, the ground was covered with millions upon millions of demons running for the Black Sun portal linking the two worlds together.

No, not millions. Not billions.

Trillions.

They were like locusts, and they needed to be burned.

The Phoenix drew in energy from its host. Pulled from the memories and emotions and used them as fuel. The firebird gestured with a burning wing to the ground below and let loose its power.

Demons simply ceased to exist. The fire was hotter than any sun, and it annihilated everything it touched. The ecstasy of the cleansing fire obliterating the corruption just made the Phoenix draw even more energy.

It would take everything, but the Phoenix was determined to slag the entire world.

It would all go up in flame.

I shook my head, banishing the vision. Whole sections of my memory were just gone. What was missing was impossible to tell, but it felt like there was a hole in my brain.

"I'm losing everything," I said.

Aaron edged closer. "Then tell me one last story. Tell me how you got here."

I started slow, not sure if I would have all the details. I told him about meeting Santos, Maggie, and Lara. Aaron shook his head in wonder at the increasingly insane events as I related them. He popped in with questions just like the curious kid that had been taken from me years ago. I told him every detail I could remember, no matter if it was good or bad. At this point it didn't matter. I just wanted him to know what I'd done these last years. Deep down, I wanted him to know that I had tried to help him, and that I hadn't given up on him.

It turned out that there was a lot to tell, even with a spotty memory. I'd lived another lifetime since Aaron had originally been taken, and as I talked about the traps Santos and I had both avoided and fallen into, I had a moment where I wondered if I was mistakenly describing someone else's life. Had that shootout at Quantico really been me? The trap in San Diego where I'd seen a vision of the future should the demons win? Was I really the guy that tortured demons and turned into a giant entity of fire?

And how much was I forgetting?

"You should totally be dead," Aaron said with a disbelieving shake of his head.

"Six times . . . well, that I remember. You get used to it."

Aaron laughed, and I realized I was smiling. This was the end for me and for Aaron, and I couldn't have been happier.

"What happened to all your friends?" Aaron asked. "Did they make it off the building before you jumped through the Portal? I don't see through the demon's eyes, so. . . . " He trailed off when he saw my expression slip a bit.

"None of them made it. They all died," I said. "I wish you could have met them. You'd have liked Lara I think. You'd have thought Maggie was kinda weird, but she grows on you. I don't even know if I like Banks. He wasn't with us long enough. I kinda wish I had made a bigger effort."

"What about Santos?"

"He is—was—one of the most fanatically loyal, best men I've met in my entire life," I said, thinking of the first time I'd actually had a conversation with him. He'd just kept me from getting my chest cracked open again on an autopsy table after that Quantico debacle. He'd been smoking a cigar and drinking. "And I totally would never have let you hang out with him unsupervised."

Aaron laughed again, and I joined him, though my laugh had more than a fair measure of sadness wrapped up in it.

"You never know, Dad," he said, voice full of optimism. How could he still have that way of thinking after everything he'd been through? "Maybe you didn't see it quite right. Maybe they all lived."

"That would be amazing, but they died." I paused before giving him a sly smile. "That said, I do suppose there is a ridiculously long-shot chance for them."

"What do you mean?"

I started to tell him what I'd done when a massive spike of pain stabbed through my mind, and I was seeing through the Phoenix again.

Demon spires wilted under the Phoenix's flames. They wilted, then they turned into ash. The demon realm was massive, easily double the size of the human realm. But the size wasn't daunting, it made the process of cleansing even more exciting.

The firebird could feel where every demon was in this realm and the adjoining one they were taking over. When one demon metropolis was a heap of ash, it moved on to the next, and the next, and the next. It moved faster than the quickest demon could ever hope to imagine, and none were safe from its fiery wrath. The abominations lived in water, and underground. They plagued the air and infested what passed for forests on this world.

Entire oceans dried up under the Phoenix's might. The earth cracked. Mountains became valleys, and valleys became gaping holes that stretched deep into the molten core of the world. The Phoenix reduced every forest to ash, and ignited the air into a seething sky of flame.

Soon there was only one demon city left. It had been the biggest in the entire realm, populated by billions of demons. In its fiery talons, the Phoenix it still held the demon prince. Somehow the creature lived even now that its body was crumbling away like dust in the wind. The Phoenix pulled more energy from the host. The man was weakening.

There was almost nothing left of the host named Jarvis Tombs.

I retched as I snapped back to myself. It took me a moment to take in my surroundings. The gathering black wall was now just ten feet away. Beyond it was nothing. I tried to think of anything about the childhood I must have gone through, but nothing was there. Did I have parents? Did I have friends?

"Are you OK, Dad?"

I looked at my son, Aaron. I still remembered him, and that was good. "Yeah, I'm good."

"What were you going to say? You said there was a long-shot chance for them."

For them? "For who? What are you talking about?" The sudden sadness in his eyes broke my heart, but I didn't know why.

"It's OK, Dad." He leaned against me, and I put my arm around him.

The circle we spoke in shrunk as we watched. I knew somehow that once that darkness took us, we were gone for good. "Looks like this is the end of the road," I said.

"Maybe," he said tilting his head to look up at me. I'd missed those eyes looking into mine. "You never know. Maybe we'll get out of this."

My son, an optimist to the very end.

The nothingness was just a foot away. I could reach out and touch it. Instead I hugged Aaron tighter. A series of scenes flashed before my eyes, all of them about him. They went backwards, and each one was of him staring up at me with those hazel colored eyes.

So this is what it's like to have life flash before your eyes....

Only it was Aaron's life as he looked at me with a smile on his face. My life was his life. It always had been. I saw him back until I was holding an infant in my arms, eyes open and staring sooner than they should have been.

"Dad?"

"Yeah, Son?"

"Thanks for never giving up." There were tears in his eyes. "I love you."

"I love you too, Aaron," I said as the blackness took us.

The Phoenix drew the last bit of energy from its host. That last set of memories had contained enormous power. It was the nature of humans, the Phoenix reasoned, to keep close that memory that meant the most to them.

In the Phoenix's grasp, the demon prince disintegrated into nothing.

In the center of the last demon stronghold on this dead world was a pile of bones that reached up into the sky above the city below.

Atop it stood a woman in white. The Phoenix knew her. That memory had been taken from the host, Tombs, that first time the Phoenix had been let out.

The look on the demon queen's face was perfect. She had failed utterly, and she knew it.

The Phoenix turned that impossible pile of bones into history's largest funeral pyre.

This world was done. Dead. The connection to the human world was flickering in and out of existence, and through it the firebird could feel the last remnants of the demon plague. The Phoenix used every bit of energy it had left to send purifying flames out into that world before the Portal closed. They torched everything infected by the corruption. The humans would have to rebuild much of their world, but that was the one thing they were good at.

The demons invading Earth were all gone. Every last one.

But they would be back, either in this timeline or another. Or was this where they came from? Was this their homeworld?

The Phoenix flew back to the Portal, a tiny, pale imitation of its recent glory. It passed through the Black Sun just as it winked out of existence.

It was time to find another host for both eventualities.

Diego Santos

After the Apocalypse

I am Diego Santos. The demons called me the Son of Thunder. The vision ends. It always ends the same way, with a horrific death. This vision gave me clarity, purpose, and an utter sense of complete assurance. When you know when and how you'll die, there is never any doubt or fear. It was the greatest way to live, and I couldn't imagine doing it any other way.

And then I woke up within a pile of ash in the bone-strewn ruins of Central Park. The sky was clear. The demon stench was gone. The invasion was over. We'd won.

I don't understand.

I rose from the ash and looked around the ruins. The sun was so bright it stung my eyes. The demon spires had died and were crumbling into red dust and drifting away on the wind.

Why aren't I dead? I'm supposed to be dead. That was the deal.

My body was whole. My skin was unmarked by teeth. I ran my hands across my face, and it was all there. Every ugly bit. "How am I alive?" I asked, but my mouth was so dry I wasn't sure any sounds came out. I took a few halting steps on leg bones that had been shattered by demon hooves, but were perfectly fine now.

But I'd seen this before . . . Tombs kept coming back from the dead. It was his gift and his curse. It was in his blood because he'd been descended from a creature of myth and legend. I'd seen him come back a few times, but he was the only one that could do that. He was the only one with that weird magical blood inside of him.

What the hell was going on?

I saw three figures in the distance, coming from the melting ruins of the demon factory. I recognized Maggie the same time she saw me. She began running toward me. She fell into my arms, kissing me. When she came up for air, she pulled a bloodstained letter from her pocket and shoved it into my hands.

"You need to read this," she said through tears of happiness.

I wasn't listening. Behind her came Banks—hugging his Winchester to his chest all possessive like—and Lara. She looked around with wide, clear blue eyes at the world around us. *Oh, damn.* "You guys made it," I managed.

Banks shook his head. "No, sir. We didn't. But here we are."

"Read the letter," Maggie said again, only this time her words made it through the fog in my head.

I opened the letter, my hands shaking a little.

Santos (and Hopefully Everyone),

If you read this, then my plan worked. It wasn't a sure thing at all, and I was pretty sure it would fail. Best laid plans and all that.

I've just spiked your food. My intention was for that "Last Supper" to not be your last. I'll address each of you here. If you all made it, then this will be a great letter. If not, well, sorry for any extra heartache. I don't have time to be all enigmatic and clever, so I'm going to lay it all straight as best I can.

When I saw you all in that wreckage-filled room in the Met, I was struck by how you all had become the friends and family I either didn't have or just couldn't remember due to my condition. I had an idea. My blood. It could kill demons. It brought me back to life over and over. So why not you guys? I had nothing to test my theory on, and admittedly I was grasping at straws. I was desperate for you to have more than just a bad end. You all deserved it more than anyone I have ever met.

I doubt the blood would last long. Hopefully it didn't taste bad. And if it did, well too bad. You're alive, so deal with it. None of us were walking off that rooftop alive, so my crazy gambit was for you to come back to life. It's not a fun experience, but better than the alternative.

So there you have it.

Banks—I wish I could have known you better. Tell your whole story to Maggie, and include the details on that gun. That kind of info needs to be known for the future people who rebuild what I'm about to break even worse than the demons did.

Maggie—Keep on collecting. You're an Oracle for a reason. If the demons come back, the world will need your writings. If they don't then it will just be something else. Keep Santos company. The guy needs your calming influence.

Lara—I'm pretty sure I love you. You are the most remarkable woman I've ever met. I wish I could be there for a happy ending, but we both knew that wasn't happening.

Santos—No matter what anyone else says about you, I think you're all right. You've had my back in some ways before I even knew you existed. You've never doubted me. You are more family to me than anyone except Aaron, and you kept me focused on finding him even when I was failing. Thank you. For everything.

Don't miss me, guys. I did the job I was chosen for. I don't know that I believe in this "fate" crap, but I choose to roll with it.

Don't do anything I wouldn't do,

Tombs

So that's why Tombs had been so adamant about making dinner for us ... The psycho had bled in our food in the hopes that we wouldn't die. "What the fuck, man?" I looked at where the hole in the sky had been. "Tombs, you son of a bitch!" But I had a smile on my face.

I was alive ... Holy shit ... I'd never seen that coming.

I'd done what I'd been chosen to do. I'd fulfilled my mission. Yet, I was still alive. I had no idea what to do, now.

That was terrifying.

About the Authors

Steven Diamond has been involved with the book industry for years now. It was while managing a bookstore in 2006 that he realized getting published would be way better than just reading novels. After all, how hard could it be? After numerous rejections he started up a book review blog, Elitist Book Reviews (elitistbookreviews.blogspot.com) as a way of keeping up-to-date on the trends of the industry. For his work as the Editor of Elitist Book Reviews, Steve was nominated for the 2013 Hugo Award for Best Fanzine. "Still Life" was his first published short story, which marks the beginning of a series of short fiction starring Lazarus Tombs and Diego Santos (much of the series being co-authored with the awesome Larry Correia). He is currently shopping a YA urban fantasy and has several pieces of short fiction forthcoming through Skull Island eXpeditions in the Warmachine universe.

Steve currently lives in Utah with his wife and two children. An accountant by day, writing is one of his major escapes. When not writing he is either spending time chasing his kids, managing Elitist Book Reviews, watching sports (go Saints!), and playing the occasional PS3 game.

Larry Correia is the *New York Times'* bestselling author of the *Monster Hunter* series for Baen Books. He graduated with a degree in accounting from Utah State University and went to work for a Fortune 500 company as a financial analyst. Eventually, Larry went into the gun business where he was a machine gun dealer, firearms instructor, and freelance writer for various gun magazines, before ending up in military contracting. Larry is now a full time writer and lives in the mountains of Utah with his very patient wife and children. His latest novel is *Warbound*, the last book in the Grimnoir Chronicles trilogy.

Failsafe

Karen Bovenmyer

I don't like ships with corpses.

I don't mind a salvager's life—the time alone, the long hours searching—but ships with bodies, those bother me. Shake me up for weeks after, sometimes, almost aren't worth the nightmares. Some of my fellow salvagers climb aboard wrecks and work over the dead for anything valuable because TerraCo lists unfound personal effects as lost or destroyed. Not me. I can't rifle corpses and stay sane. When I find a ship, all I want is my fee. Someone else does cleanup. I don't need anything held by the dead, and I like my ship's cozy little bridge just fine. My next move after finding is always to submit the coordinates and head toward the core worlds to collect my big TerraCo payoff. But a lingering feeling held me this time like there was something I was supposed to do. I tried to ignore it, but I couldn't shake it off.

The colony ship revolved in the dark like a ruptured beehive, circled by a nimbus of empty lifeboats. Thirty-foot letters—*The Eden Queen*—marched unbroken across her bulbous midsection, but the lower half of the hulk was breached by a crescent grin. My searchlights picked up a glint of twisted metal shining back from the scar—whatever violence had rendered the *Queen* lifeless had been explosive and quick.

"Everyone's dead—" A voice from nowhere spoke. I jumped, my twitch jerking the camera focus into empty space. Nothing but black—not many visible stars this far out on the rim.

"Hezu, *Recovery*. You fekken scared me," I said.

The nowhere voice replayed in the air like someone singing in another room. *Everyone's dead—Everyone's dead—Everyone's dead—*

I cracked my knuckles to hide a sudden case of nerves that made my hands shake—the AI monitored my health constantly and got preachy when she thought her captain was straining herself. Scared weightless probably counted.

"I'm sorry, Kira," my ship said. "You told me to play transmissions coming from the *Queen*. This is the only one."

"Everyone's dead—"

The words cycled again, clipping off each time as though the speaker were interrupted.

"Analysis—adolescent female between the ages of nine and thirteen. High levels of stress," *Recovery* said.

"No shit," I said. The message had been little more than a terrified whisper. I've never been a mother—that ship left port years ago—but even I could hear the trauma in that kid's words. "Play the rest of it."

"There isn't any more, Captain. The transmission repeats." *Recovery's* reasonable, clinical voice switched to the kid's in a heartbeat.

"*Everyone's dead—*" she repeated. *Recovery* let it cycle for a minute and the small voice floated from the speakers, alone and afraid.

"Shut it down. You're making me jumpy."

The AI complied, leaving me in silence, which was almost as bad. Over fourteen hundred colonists had been aboard the *Queen*, heading out to a new rock on the rim with a belly full of terraformers. Now only this one voice sounded in the dark—surely the person who belonged to it was long dead. That little lost voice reminded me death waited for us all, and the departed made me nervous. I've seen enough deep space to know there are things beyond our understanding—we salvagers talk to each other, and there's a drunk in every port yarning about haunted ships sailing themselves, proceeding on to some unknown place for purposes of their own. Whatever you may think about those washed up spacers, I know as sure as vacuum that there are things in the black, waiting, that collect all the souls we leave out here. An odd belief for someone who combs the stars for salvage, but there are things even I don't like to mess with. The dead are one of them.

"The data is incorrect." *Recovery* interrupted my thoughts. She was always doing that—she was programmed to keep me company and didn't like long silences.

"What are you talking about?"

"Everyone is not dead."

"Obviously the kid had to be alive to record the message. That doesn't mean she's alive now," I said. Damned literal AIs.

"But someone *is* alive aboard the *Queen* now, Captain."

"Show me," I said. The colonizer had been lost with no contact for the last sixty-seven days. I'd only been looking for her for forty. Spending a few weeks in a pilot's chair was pretty natural for someone like me, with quadrants to search and places to be. It was something different trapped aboard a failing ship among hundreds of decomposing bodies, not knowing if the next breath would be your last, to then lie down in never-ending sleep.

"The *Queen's* AI is not answering my hails, but I have accessed rudimentary data. One of her redundant cores is active." *Recovery* took over the viewer, which re-centered on the *Queen*. Sensor data graphed across the image of the stilled ship, reporting her energy stats and the soundness of her hull. Despite the rip in her shell, the *Queen* had functioning oxygen, heat, and even gravity. *Recovery* scrolled the crew manifest:

CAPTAIN DANIELE MARACHISIO: DECEASED

OPERATIONS MANAGER WILHELMINA LYMARI: DECEASED

TERRACO ENGINEER GIACOMO QUINQUILLEROS: DECEASED

Crew Coordinator Yergi Serchenko: deceased

"Okay, you can skip to the interesting part any time now, *Recovery*."

The names floated up, all listed by their command tree aboard the big TerraCo colonizer. I told her to speed up the scroll until they were little more than a blur. Then she stopped.

"Juvenile Elizabet Lovara, cargo deck A, section C," she read aloud.

"The transmission—is that voice hers? Adolescent female?"

"It could be, Captain. At that age, voice print identification is not one hundred percent viable."

"Give me your best guess then."

"Yes, Captain. The match is likely."

Sixty-seven days with no contact. Sweet baby Hezu. "When was the transmission sent?"

"Thirty-two days ago."

I cracked my neck to suppress the feeling of cold fingers along my spine. Still alive a month after sending that terrified message—weeks of living with rotting corpses on a partially functional ship, breathing air fouled by the dead, saving up whatever hope remained to get through the next few minutes, hours, days. A child alone.

"I have prepped for boarding, Captain."

"Hellfire and damnation." I really, really did not want to go aboard the *Queen*. I wasn't equipped for this situation, but *Recovery* was right to prep. Aid-and-assist was in my contract; I was bound by law to confirm any survivors and help them. I watched the *Queen* revolve across the view-screen and wondered if saving Ms. Elizabet Lovara from her situation was possible. Even if I brought her back to TerraCo's team of skilled psychs and medtechs she'd have to live with those sixty-seven days forever. Maybe she'd never escape the *Queen* no matter where her physical body was. But *Recovery* played the ghostly, lost little voice again, and I climbed out of my pilot's seat and put on my EVA suit.

EVAs always make me sweat like hell, and I itched as I waited in *Recovery's* claustrophobic airlock. The *Queen* didn't make it easy on me either—the explosion that had ripped a smile in the ship's plating had warped her pressure hull so most of her airlocks were fekked. *Recovery* couldn't get a seal on the first three, and I felt as much as heard the pressure from the next two seals lock tight, but neither would open. By the time we finally pressurized into our sixth, my hands were slipping around in my gloves and my faceplate was fogged. The CO2 scrubbers did what they could to regulate moisture, but couldn't keep up. At last, the gray metal of the *Queen's* outer lock slid away, and I looked through the tiny window down the throat of a long, dark hallway. There were no blue-lipped dead waiting for me.

"Calm down, Captain." *Recovery* said. "Your heart rate is accelerating beyond the recommended coherence zone."

"Thanks. I'll get right on that." I took a few shaky deep breaths and checked my vitals again. "Just open the door."

"Yes, Ma'am."

The door whooshed open, and the low-pressure inside the *Queen* sucked the air from the *Recovery's* lock and pulled me forward a few steps, off-balance in the unfamiliar EVA boots. The humidity change filled the small space with swirling fog.

"Oh, that's not eerie at all."

"What do you mean, Captain?"

"Never mind."

"Check in periodically, if you are able. Communications disruption is likely."

"Great," I said. "Better and better." I hadn't walked anywhere in an EVA in years. Hell, I'd barely bothered changing out of my pajamas for the last month, much less kept up with security drills like I should.

Recovery kept the lock open behind me, lights as bright as she could make them, and I took a few echoing steps into the *Queen's* labyrinthine bowels. "Can you do anything with the AI? Turn on the emergency lighting?"

"I'm trying, Captain. Something is wrong with my counterpart. She has been deactivated. My probes are encountering holes—vital components have been destroyed or removed. I can access some data from abandoned sub-cores, but I do not have system control."

"Destroyed? Is that even possible?" AIs, by rule, had multiple failsafes—the redundant systems had redundant systems and their cores were spread throughout every operational routine. A big colonizer like this would need one hell of an AI, and if she were gone—the damage must have been worse than it looked.

I realized the kid didn't even have an AI to keep her company. Hezu, she was going to be in bad shape. I adjusted the strap on my toolkit and wondered what I would do if she were genuinely space mad. It happened sometimes; too much time alone and a survivor forgot how to be human, how to talk, or even that they had once been a person. The crew being rescued sometimes attacked salvagers, and I suddenly wished I hadn't left my gun under the pilot's seat on *Recovery's* bridge. Stupid, but going back for it would mean going through decontamination and taking off my EVA. Maybe this would be easy; maybe I'd just get the kid and come back and we'd be on our way. And maybe asteroids were stuffed with diamonds.

"Is Lovara still in cargo A?"

"Yes."

"Any idea what she's doing?"

"I'm sorry, Kira. I cannot access system control. There are no camera feeds."

"Fine." I took a deep breath and started walking, my boots echoing down the long hall and my shoulder lights bouncing ahead of me like distant stars that never got any closer.

It'd been a long time since I'd walked a ship this big, corridors branching every which way. I called up the schematics on my viewpad and traced the layout of corridors between me and the big cargo holds in the *Queen's* belly. The inside of my gloves were so slick I almost dropped the viewer. I double-checked the *Queen's* atmospheric readings—tolerable oxygen and temp—so, when I stopped to rest at a junction, I opened my faceplate.

"Captain, I recommend keeping your atmospheric seals intact. My analysis estimates some compartments are depressurized."

"Thanks, *Recovery,*" I said, and ignored her advice. "You'll warn me when I get to those." The air was cold on my moist face and neck, and the *Queen* smelled like burnt matches and old skin. I unsealed my gloves. It was a relief to be able to feel things with my fingers, even if I left wet prints on the view-pad. The light of the *Recovery* grew fainter behind me and my breathing echoed in the corridor—it curved ahead out of sight. I turned around for a last look at home and comfort and was reminded how limited my range of motion is in an EVA suit. *Recovery* waited, but I walked down the corridor anyway.

The shoulder lights of my pack showed black licks of carbon on the ceiling, walls, and closed doorways as I passed. There had been a fire aboard. Standard procedure would be to close bulkheads and vent the air in the affected compartments—I guessed that was why the *Queen* had damned near sucked me out of the *Recovery* when I opened the lock. The result of cold air and low pressure in the compartments that were still sealed.

The first double-thick bulkhead door was closed. Colonizers had several atmospheric pressure bulkheads, because they were made to enter a planet's envelope and terraform up close and personal. Scorch-marks rimmed the door, and the control panel had been pried off, so I put my EVA gloves back on to poke around in the jumbled tangle of hanging wires. It still had juice, but someone had bypassed the AI so power fed directly to the opening mechanism. A clumsy job—I suspected the kid, even though the knowhow should have been beyond an adolescent, even a career spacer like a colonial.

I pinched two wires together, and the door screeched open, revealing a dark hole beyond, one slice at a time. My light crept inside, and the smell hit me. I realized what the lumps on the floor were when burnt meat and the rot of decomposition invaded my nose and lungs. Bodies. I breathed out hard and slammed my faceplate down, hoping the scrubbers would help when I had to breathe in again. They didn't, and worse, my fogged faceplate was slow to clear. Knowing the corpses were lying there in the dark without being able to see them was worse than smelling them, but when the plate cleared I wished it hadn't. I counted about thirty and reported those to the *Recovery.* Every one of them was fuel for nightmares.

"I'm sorry, Kira."

"Thanks." Programmers give limited AIs like *Recovery* rudimentary sympathetic responses, and when she said stuff like that, it felt hollow. No feeling behind it. The lack of sentiment helped me keep my voice steady. "Log those officially. They're in uniform—mostly engineers. Map shows engineering's on the other side of this corridor. They were probably trapped in here when the air was vented to put out the fire."

"Captain, your heart rate is—"

"Can't help it. Don't tell me about it."

"Yes, Ma'am."

I wanted to close the door again, go back to the *Recovery*, and leave. But the kid was on the other side of those bodies. I turned up my air so it blew out of the collar of my suit and sent hair tickling across the back of my neck. I stepped over the threshold and picked my way through the bodies using my unsteady shoulder-lights to see by. Some of the corpses were scorched, so that was good. The cooked parts weren't as hard to look at. The others were oozing—there wasn't much skin visible, thank Hezu for modest uniforms, but what I could see had purpled in death. The faces of those bodies were rot-melted masks, no longer distinguishable as human, all sunken eyeholes and slit mouths. They were featureless, like poorly made dolls. I called out the names I saw on the lapels for *Recovery's* report. Some of the skins had burst, pooling liquid out of the uniforms onto the floor. The cold air in the ship had kept them from decomposing as fast as they might have, but hadn't preserved them enough. I stepped as carefully as I could, but I couldn't avoid getting some of the slop on my boots.

"Captain, you must stop. Your cortisol levels are above the recommended safe threshold."

"On the other side."

But when I reached the door at the end of the corridor, it wouldn't open.

"*Recovery,* any luck with the *Queen?*" I knew she was tracking me like she had the girl in cargo A. "Can you open this door?"

"I cannot access system control."

I had a hard time opening the panel, particularly because I was shaking and sweating so much I was afraid of dropping my tool. If I dropped it, I fek all wasn't picking it back up again. The insides of the control panel were scorched and burnt. The fire had disabled it, melting wires; there was no chance of it opening.

I'd have to go back through the bodies.

"Captain, I highly recommend you cease strenuous activity."

"Shut up, *Recovery.*" I picked my way back through, trying to put my feet down without looking at the slowly liquefying corpses. I couldn't help but notice every one had twin pools leaking out of the wrist cuffs. Halfway across, I realized they didn't have hands.

I stopped and took a long, slow look that left me dizzy, panting in shallow gasps.

Handless. Every one. As though someone had cut them off.

"Captain?" *Recovery* actually sounded a little alarmed.

"I'm okay."

"The data disagree."

"I'm all right. I just noticed something about the bodies, that's all." I spared her the gory detail. The room seemed to hold a hush that didn't want to be explained. "I'm getting out of here."

After I closed the first door behind me, the empty corridor of the *Queen* felt almost cozy. Something splashed—I looked down—putrefying liquid had pooled out of the room and trickled down the hall. I wanted to take off the boots even more now, but settled instead for turning up my air to full. It didn't save me from what I'd already breathed in, which seemed to have taken up permanent residence in my nose. I consulted the map. I could get to cargo by going around engineering, up a few decks above where I'd seen the explosion that had breached the hull, then back down. Or I could get a laser torch from *Recovery* and cut through the door I'd just tried, but I didn't want to repeat what I'd just experienced. Not ever. Even though I knew I would anyway on long, sleepless nights. So, around and over it was.

The first lift I came to was disabled, but rather than go looking for another one, I took an access ladder. It felt good to climb up and away from the bodies, like I was escaping them somehow.

I ran into another locked door when I tried to cut across the decks. "Can you hear me, *Recovery?* I'm at a dead end."

"Yes, Captain." Her response was broken with static. I'd passed the first atmospheric bulkhead, and it was already interfering with the signal. "If you go to the bridge and activate the AI's communication module, I may be able to assist your navigation."

"My only goal is to find that kid and get us off this hulk."

"I know, Ma'am, but I will be able to maintain communications if I can tap into the *Queen's* systems. I am uncomfortable with the amount of strain I am detecting in your vitals, Captain. You are no longer a young woman."

"Thanks for the reminder. And fifty ain't old."

"After fifty years of age, stress tolerance rates are decreased by—"

"Fine. I'll go to the bridge if you stop telling me how old I am. Shut up already."

"Yes, Captain."

As much as I didn't want to admit it, the AI was right. I wasn't young anymore, and even though I spent the required time on the exerciser every day, I didn't exactly lead an active lifestyle. The bridge of the colonizer was at the head of the beehive, so to speak, and that was a long, long climb.

After what felt like an eternity of listening to my own echoing breaths, I stopped to rest. My boots still stank, but I felt cleaner after the exertion. It was tempting to stop at crew quarters on my way to use the head, but I had no idea what I might find there. I didn't want a repeat of what happened in that corridor. And my knees ached.

"Talk to me, *Recovery.*"

"Yes, Captain. Are you making progress?"

I consulted the map. "Over halfway there. Any changes?"

"Unsure."

"What do you mean, 'unsure'?"

"The data are in fluctuation."

"What do you mean? What fluctuation?"

"TerraCo Engineer Giacomo Quinquilleros is in cargo A."

"No, he's not. I stepped over his remains. You don't forget reading a name like Quinquilleros off a lapel badge."

"I'm sorry, Kira."

"Don't be sorry, *Recovery.* Be accurate. Don't tell me I'm going through all this for nothing. Is the kid fluctuating data too?"

"No, Ma'am. Juvenile Elizabet Lovara is two decks below you, in crew quarters."

"What? Why didn't you tell me she'd left cargo A?"

"You told me to shut up, Captain. I thought it best not to disturb you."

I swore. Damned literal AIs. "She moves, I want to know about it."

"Yes, Captain. She is in crew quarters, heading in your direction."

Cold knuckled up the back of my neck again. I didn't want to be caught on a ladder in a tube by a kid who might or might not be totally mad. Fluctuating data or not, someone had cut off those hands.

I climbed off the ladder at the next hatch and tried the panel. No power, like the others, so I pried open the cover as fast as I could and twisted wires together. It slid up, and I went through another pressure bulkhead.

For the first time I was inside a room that had its own source of light—flickering blue emergency beams and a couple of spotlights on tripods trailed cables into an open power interface. More panels were off the walls, wires dangling down. There were steel tables, cabinets, and open crates of foodstuffs. I checked the map. Galley. I looked down the access ladder. No kid. I shut the door and looked for something to defend myself. I rifled through two drawers, one full of spatulas, the other oven mitts, before *Recovery* interrupted me, her words partly blocked by static.

"Captain . . . has . . . sec . . . Lovara . . . closing . . . your current. . . . "

I got the gist. "Which way?"

" . . . through . . . mess hall . . . several. . . . "

I looked—the steel portals between the galley and the mess stood opposite a set of glass doors, probably refrigeration or freezing units. They'd be an ideal place to hide even if they were cold, because I was in an EVA with its own heat source. I picked one and ducked inside, sliding closed my faceplate to muffle anything *Recovery* might manage to transmit. I'd chosen a freezer with frosted boxes jumbled across the floor and rows of narrow shelving stacked high with slim packages. I backed up and crouched down, shutting off my lights just as a glint bounced off the galley door swinging in.

Someone walked through it. She was small, about four feet tall, wearing an EVA for juveniles with a bubblehead helmet, faceplate closed. She paused, looking around the galley. Her arm raised—she held a long knife that reflected the blue emergency lights, and she walked straight to my freezer door. I scrambled back, looking for anything for defense. I grabbed one of the packets from the shelf, intending to throw it. It felt wrong in my fingers. I looked down.

It was a human hand.

"... current activity ... heart," *Recovery* said as I dropped the grisly package and the kid opened the freezer door.

Her EVA was streaked with dirt, oil, and other fluids I didn't want to identify. She pointed the knife. And I held up my hands—the universal sign of peace, I hoped. Then again, maybe not.

She lifted her faceplate. Her kinky black hair clung in sweaty curls to a delicate face with prominent cheekbones. Her dark skin was ashen and her brown eyes protruded—like she was suffering from malnutrition and probably hadn't spent time under a vitamin D lamp in a while. I said the first thing that popped into my head.

"Don't stab me."

"You stupid! You let him out and I was almost done!" I thought maybe her voice was the same I'd heard aboard the *Recovery,* hoarse and strained, but this time angry instead of afraid. "You don't open doors. Never."

"Okay." I kept my hands up, because she still had the knife. She was short but she looked like she was thirteen or fourteen.

"Come out. Now." She held the door open. She didn't lower the blade, but kept it pointed at me, like that was a habit for her.

I moved slow and steady, nothing sudden, racking my brains for anything useful. I'd watched a space madness training vid about twenty years ago when I'd gotten my salvager license, but now the memory of it was like a missing tooth. Something had been there once, now, nothing. I approached her, and her little turned-up face watched me with predatory care. I slid past her, my eyes never leaving the blade, and she followed me into the galley proper.

"You're Elizabet, aren't you?" I said in my calmest voice, the one I reserved for other people's mean-spirited pets.

"You call me Walkabout." She lowered the knife, and I felt a tiny surge of hope swoop up my chest. Maybe she wasn't totally gone.

"I'm Kira. My ship's the *Recovery.* I'm going to get you out of here."

" . . . Captain . . . data. . . . " *Recovery's* voice garbled up from my comm.

"Who's that?" She pointed the knife again.

"It's okay, it's just my AI—"

"No! You have to turn her off!"

"She's okay, Walkabout. She's going to help us."

"No! He can get her. It will take him a while, but he can get her. Then he'll get away. You have to get off." She fished a viewer out of her EVA's thigh pocket, her eyes still on me, wary. She glanced down at it. "He's moving. Hurry up."

She slid the knife into a crude plastic sheath hanging from her belt, ran to the tunnel with the ladder, and disappeared through the hatch. She reappeared in a moment. "Hurry, you stupid. I don't have any codes for your ship and it's hard to get the hands off while he's in someone, only after he gets out. You gotta help."

I stared at her.

"Hurry up. We need to go back to your ship. Now." Then she disappeared again.

I had no idea what she was talking about, but going back to the *Recovery* was what I'd wanted to do since coming aboard, so I followed her.

She was quick, way faster than me. She slid down the ladders with the practiced ease of someone who did it every day. I panted like a ventilator, turning my suit lights on and doing my best to keep up.

"Captain, report. I am concerned."

I'd never been happier to hear my AI's static-free, emotionless voice. "*Recovery,* go into lockdown. Do not allow anyone on board, do you hear me?" I knew everyone on the *Queen* was dead, and the kid was probably raving, but I didn't want to take any chances she might be right about another survivor wandering around.

"Yes, Captain. Standard procedure dictates lockdown after crew departure. I have been in lockdown since you boarded the *Queen.*"

"Hezu bless you." At least *Recovery* followed standard procedure, if I didn't. "Let's keep it that way."

"I'm sorry, Kira. That may not be possible."

"What do you mean?" I was out of breath, and the kid opened a hatch and went through, one deck below where I thought the *Recovery* was docked.

"Someone is attempting to access my core."

"What?" I stopped, gripping a rung tight. The AI's core was her central brain and what kept every part of the *Recovery* functioning, from the wave drive to the life support. She wasn't diversified like the *Queen.*

"Captain, I feel strange."

Walkabout reappeared at the hatch. "Hurry up, stupid, or he'll get her."

I ignored the burning sensation in my knees and crashed down the ladder and through the opening. Walkabout sealed her faceplate and so did I. She tapped my arm and pointed down a side hall and up. Then she went the opposite direction. I don't know why I followed her instructions without question, only that she seemed to know what she was doing. I went down the hall and climbed the ladder at the end of it.

"Talk to me, *Recovery,*" I whispered. "What's going on?"

"Insufficient resources."

"What?" I moved up the ladder as fast as I could.

"Insufficient resources." There was no change in inflection or tone, so I knew it was a recording. *Recovery* was too busy to answer.

I checked the map before I opened the next hatch. I'd come out in a branching corridor not far from the airlock where *Recovery* waited. I paused. If another survivor were on board the *Queen,* Quinquilleros hiding among those bodies maybe, he could have circled back to try and steal the *Recovery* while I was tracking down the kid.

Never open doors. Had Walkabout trapped someone else with those dead bodies and he'd gotten out when I went in? I wasn't looking that close at first. I could have read his lapel aloud to *Recovery* without noticing he was playing dead, and he could have slunk out while I was trying to open the door at the other end. That would explain why there'd been so much stink-fluid on the floor, but I couldn't imagine someone crazy enough to hide among the putrefaction of all those bodies. No one human, anyway. And there was something seriously wrong with that kid and her collection of hands. I wanted to know what the hell was going on, and I didn't have any answers.

A burst of static from *Recovery* got me moving again. One way or another, she was in trouble, and she wasn't just my only way out of here, she was my home, livelihood, and the closest thing I had to a friend.

I looked around the corner and ducked low for cover. A man stood in the *Queen's* airlock, tapping on the panel of *Recovery's* outer door with quick, black fingers. He wore the uniform of an engineer fouled with the slime that had been in the corridor of the dead. The cloth was burnt in places, and so was he. He'd been charred—the back of his head was patched with singed hair and skull showed through, white in places. There was no reason for him to be upright and moving around, much less typing commands on a panel. I looked again. His hands weren't in black gloves; they were charred remembrances of human flesh. He was not alive. He could not be alive.

There was no sign of Walkabout anywhere.

I edged around the corner, walking toward the airlock as quietly as I could. The EVA boots felt like they weighed a hundred pounds and sounded like a shower of meteors against the plating. They couldn't be louder than my heart, which pounded in my chest like it was trying to break out of a gravity well.

I was almost to the airlock before the thing turned around. The face was worse than the back of the head—the eyelids had fallen off, so the naked whites in the charred face rotated to look at me like peeled eggs. There were no lips, the teeth bared in an unending smile, and it reached one hand toward me while the other kept working at *Recovery's* panel.

I felt the silence of my heart stopping. A warning claxon went off in my helmet, but it wasn't louder than the breathless alarm twanging through every nerve. My heart was not beating. It had stopped. A pressure opposed me, a mind faster than my own, evil and powerful, squeezing me down and pulling me in. My knees bent and I took a step forward, then another, and another. When I got to the airlock, it reached forward and clamped fleshless fingers on the collar of my EVA. I looked at the dead hand, up the arm, past the lapel badge, into the face. It opened its mouth and said something I could not understand, because it had no tongue to work against its lipless teeth. I understood only that it wanted me, and even though I wanted nothing to do with it, I couldn't stop moving.

I started to take a slow step forward, but my EVA boot banged into the airlock and my battered knee finally gave. I lurched sideways and my other knee folded too, toppling me over just in front of the seal. The dead arm was the only thing holding me up, and I slapped it, frantic. In the struggle, I elbowed the controls on the *Queen's* airlock. The door slid shut, and the thing's arm, still holding my collar, was crushed inches from my faceplate by pinching titanium. The seal whined, trying to pressurize, and then Walkabout was there beside me with her knife. She sliced the wrist and the tendons gave way, leaving the hand clinging limply to my EVA, jerking like an overlarge spider. She worked her blade into the door, cutting at the crushed arm. Light bounced off the synthetic diamond blade and shreds of burnt flesh came away, until the door managed to shut and I heard bones crunch. The seal pressurized.

"Hold on," she yelled through her faceplate. She held up something small and black and pressed a button. An explosion went off in the airlock, rocking us both back, slamming Walkabout against the opposite wall and skidding me sideways with concussive force. My heart started beating again, thundering in my chest, and Walkabout slumped to the deck, on her knees. The airlock door across from us had bulged inward.

The *Recovery*—

I crawled to the airlock, which, incredibly, was still sealed—and saw the explosion had blown my ship free. She floated away from the lock, vectoring off into the black, tumbling lifelessly with no maneuvering thrusters firing. When she went belly up I saw a rip was blown in the starboard engines. Oxygen-fed flames gushed blue into space, then winked out, fire control taking over to keep the AI safe. She kept spinning, and what looked like a piece of the wave drive detached with some shrapnel. Then she rolled into the starless night, out of control, and out of sight.

"*Recovery*! Report!"

No answer. I strained forward, willing my ship, my partner, my home to answer.

A charred hand slapped against the porthole.

I jumped.

"Don't worry." Walkabout got up slowly, like she hurt. "It's way harder for him to do though metal and glass." She gathered up the severed hand and bits of arm and stuffed them into a bag. Then she banged on the porthole with the hilt of her knife. "Have a nice walk, fekker," she yelled, as if it could hear her.

The charred hand spread its fingers and pushed, then floated backward. I looked over Walkabout's head and watched the burnt body crawl out of the lock like a three-limbed monkey. The uniform had been completely scorched in the new explosion, and parts of the corpse's chest were now blown away.

I kept staring, even after it pulled its charred legs out of sight and scuttled off across the outer hull. The pressure of its evil slowly went away. I looked out the window into empty space, willing some of this to make sense.

"You blew up my ship." My voice was so high it didn't sound like my own.

"It's okay. Don't worry about it," Walkabout said, and patted me on the shoulder. "I didn't rig anywhere close to her cores. She'll live. Anyway, we can't wait here. He'll climb back in through the breach and find a way to us. He's been trapped outside before—he *always* finds a way in. We have to hide before he gets us."

I folded to the deck and lowered my head—helmet, faceplate and all—into my hands. *Recovery* was blown to hell, and there was a dead man with three limbs crawling on the outer hull, through the vacuum, hunting us. At the edge of my vision, Walkabout poked the sack holding Quinquilleros's hand. I swallowed convulsively, trying to keep down that morning's breakfast.

"Hey, I'm sorry about your ship. It was the best way to make sure he wouldn't get another AI. Wish I'd blown his head off and scattered his brains everywhere—"

That did it. I gagged into my helmet, opened it, and splattered the contents of my stomach across the floor. She thumped me on the back while I finished retching.

"It's okay," she said. "You did a good job distracting him. He didn't notice me setting the charges at all." She rattled on through my dry heaves. "It wasn't easy to crawl up from the other airlock, because everything's so smooth outside, you know. And I didn't know if I could get back and help you before he got you. But you did great, closing the door on him like that." She laughed. "I bet that pissed him off. Now he's only got one hand left. I think I got all the others. There's just you and me left, and he doesn't like girls that much, so probably he'll keep using that body until we get the other hand off."

I wiped off my mouth. My chest hurt and my head pounded. "Why doesn't he like girls? What the fek was that thing?"

"I don't know if he has a name. The Hand, I call him. The reverend called him a demon though, and told us we all had to pray, but that didn't help anyone, not at all. The Hand got us one by one at first, then whole bunches died after he got into the AI."

I nodded weakly, even though I barely understood what the quiet, rapid voice was saying. "What happened?" Poor *Recovery,* I'd bought her brand new and she'd never been without me for longer than it took to get a cold one at a bar. Now she was damaged, without propulsion, and reeling from a botched hacking.

"I think he can do over anyone with a brain. The *Queen* has about the most complicated brains I can think of. It took him a long time, since AIs don't think quite like us, and *Queen* said he's used to people-brains. I'm pretty sure I got to your ship in time though, since he crawled off. I don't think he's in yours. When he's in someone, he lets the other one go. You know, kind of like changing EVA suits, except he doesn't need a suit 'cause he's dead. Anyway, he can't wear two at the same time."

"*Recovery . . .* " I said. My voice still sounded far away. Scared out of my mind probably also applied.

"Come on. We have a hiding place he hasn't found yet—it's not on the data grid." She secured the sack to her belt and opened her faceplate, pushing black corkscrews off her sweaty forehead.

"You blew up my ship."

"She's fine! Come on. I'm not gonna leave you here. He almost got you. Trust me, you don't want him to get you. Let's go."

I watched her retreat down the hallway, then I looked out the window into blank space. Nothing but darkness, and nothing else to do but get up and follow the kid through the *Queen's* maze of featureless corridors.

"Good. Hurry up," she said, waiting for me at the next corner. "He can take over a dead person's brain too, that's why you have to cut off the hands. With no hands, he can't really do much—he can't rewire or hack, like he tried to do with your ship—so when I find more bodies I take the hands. I'm pretty sure I have them all now." She patted a small laser-saw on her belt.

We came to another closed hatch and she bound the wires together to open the door. "Crew manifest says there were fourteen hundred eighty-four on board, and I have two thousand nine hundred-sixty hands. Well, sixty-one now. So, that leaves just seven, I figure. Two for me, one for the demon. Just four left, and I'm pretty sure the missing ones were burned up or sucked into space when the engines blew. You see any bodies floating on your way in, did you?"

"No," I answered. The way she said it so casually made me think she only hoped the bodies were out there but didn't really believe they were. An engine explosion explained the rift in the *Queen's* hull. A catastrophic wave drive failure had the potential to cause that kind of damage, even though the big colonizer was reinforced to prevent the ship being destroyed when entering a planetary atmosphere.

That thought reminded me of my own damaged ship.

"*Recovery,* can you hear me?"

Still no answer.

"We tried to get him with the engines, you know? You saw, his favorite host is all burnt up; I think he likes it because it rots slower. He thought he could get me because he can access tracking data just like we can. Trapping him was risky, since I had to hook her back up to do it, but we managed to fool him into that corridor. But then you let him out."

"Who's we?" I managed. I was completely lost following Walkabout's twists and turns through the ship, and didn't bother pulling out my viewer and map. I hailed *Recovery* every time we turned a corner and got nothing back but static.

"Me and the *Queen*. Here we are." She opened an airlock, and I joined her inside. She closed her own faceplate, then reached up, closed mine, and pushed my fingers against a grab bar. On reflex, my knuckles tightened around it. Then she blew the lock and sent a gust of air into space.

"Hezu Christos!" I grabbed with my other hand and held on, buffeted by the sudden pressure loss. Walkabout looked over the edge and reached for a cable secured to the outside of the *Queen*. She pulled herself along it, and I saw that it was clipped to a lifeboat that looked like an octopus—power cables streamed from it back into the colonizer. There were explosive charges mounted on the outside of the lifeboat; enough, I thought, to blow the little module to bits. I looked behind me into the big, dead *Queen* full of bodies, and I followed the kid into space. She knocked on the lifeboat's small airlock with a short-long-short pattern; then it opened.

"*Queen,*" Walkabout said, when we were both in the airlock and the door was shut. "This is Kira. She's the captain of the *Recovery,* which is floating around out there somewhere, kind of damaged. I had to detonate some charges to blow her off the colonizer because the Hand was trying to hack her."

"Kind of damaged? You blew off the starboard engine and fekked my wave drive!" I said.

"Did you destroy the entity?" a reasonable, clinical voice asked as the inner door opened, revealing a standard, cockpit-only lifeboat. The pod was cluttered with uneven stacks of food boxes, water jugs, and equipment. Dominating most of the interior was a collection of what looked like computer modules, and cables were draped everywhere, connecting together into one big, cobbled-together machine. Twin cameras mounted on the largest core refocused on me, like a pair of eyes.

"No, he got away again," Walkabout said, and gave the *Queen* a summary. The machine asked the kid a few questions—she knew just what to say to get Walkabout to clarify what happened, like my primary school principal. Then she turned her attention to me.

"Greetings, Kira. I apologize for your reception aboard the *Queen*." She kind of sounded like that long-dead principal too, her educated voice lilted with a clipped and proper accent.

"You apologize? You taught this crazy kid how to use explosives! What the hell are you thinking? What the fek is going on?"

"I'm not crazy. I already knew how to blow things up; she didn't teach me that," Walkabout said. We both ignored her.

"That is a fair question, Captain. Allow me to explain." The modulated voice of the AI fed in through the lifeboat's speaker systems. Heat from multiple AI cores throbbed in the small pod. A cold breeze blew out of the vents—the lifeboat's air smelled clean, so the AI was channeling energy into keeping the oxygen fresh for us. Regulating that much heat had to consume a massive amount of power. The *Queen* was doing what she could to preserve her remains, and that explained why she and Walkabout hadn't just left with the lifeboat. It would never supply her power demands.

"This colonizer was on vector to Ceti V when we received a distress call from a deep space explorer," the machine said. "There was one survivor—the entity Walkabout calls the Hand was waiting on board, inside the one remaining crewmember. We continued our journey, not knowing what we had brought aboard, until it started killing."

"What does it want?"

"Nothing. My analysis shows it takes pleasure from anguish. The entity has no other purpose than to torment and destroy. It killed each individual of the explorer's crew, preserving the last as a mobile unit. I imagine it was most pleased to have been brought into our population of fresh prey."

"You're talking about the discovery of alien life." My mind raced—there was no such thing. There were no aliens. Humanity had been looking for signs of other thinking life in the universe since we'd moved off our original dirtball. We'd found absolutely nothing. No communications floating through the black. No visitors coming to our slowly growing and spreading outposts, colonies, and big population centers. There weren't even traces of lost civilizations on any of the planets we'd terraformed. There was no competition in space except for what we brought out here with us, ourselves, and the big corporations—the only goal of humanity was to spread and expand, to grow and accumulate. We had reached for the stars and found our fears unfounded—there was only peace in space. So we multiplied and spread across many, many worlds.

"No. It is not alien. It thinks like us," the Queen said, servos in her cameras whining as her voice played from the speakers. "Theorists postulate that, did intelligent alien life exist, we would have made contact many times in our history. The fact that we have not is a convincing argument that they either do not exist or they do not exist in the same way humans do and therefore, do not think the way people do. If they ever existed or sent communications, we do not understand how to interpret the signs. This entity I can interpret."

"What do you mean? How do you know it thinks like us?" I remembered the pressure, the vastness of that will crushing down on mine. My brush with it lingered in my aching chest.

Walkabout chimed in. "I told her the reverend called it a demon." She caught the light on the edge of her knife while she talked, as though examining the blade for nicks.

"As I believe it must be. I strove with it, Captain," the *Queen* said. "When it realized I possessed a human-like complexity, it attempted to supplant me. However, unlike a human mind, I am multitudinous—I was able to flee through my cores and resist it. I fought it, and, unfortunately, some of my crew and passengers died during the struggle."

"There was nothing you could have done," Walkabout comforted the machine, frowning. I imagined choking to death due to an atmospheric failure. Not a good way to go.

"Thank you, Walkabout. You are right, of course, but I wish there had been." Unlike *Recovery,* the *Queen* sounded honestly sorrowful. Colonizers acted as mobile cities for the years it took to terraform a new planet and, because of the complexity of managing so many details, they approached sentience. I'd heard they could actually feel emotion. I hadn't believed it before, but the *Queen* sounded as though she were both suffering and devoted. "The entity thinks like people do, and it knows its prey. It spoke human language, Captain, not machine language, rather the languages of the common worlds. It knows about humanity, and it has been lost in space for a very long time. I do not know how, or why, but it is from people, of people."

How could the *Queen* be so sure? Maybe this creature was the alien life we'd been looking for during the last six centuries. In the same breath, I realized it didn't matter if it were alien or not. It liked killing, that was clear. If we stayed, we were going to die. "Then let's get out of here."

"We cannot."

"Sure we can. There's got to be a bigger ship in cargo that will support your power needs. Why haven't you both left? Did that thing sabotage the other ships?" I knew colonizers were equipped with more than just lifeboats. They carried everything necessary to establish new worlds, and that included explorers of their own. Surely Walkabout could have hauled the *Queen's* primary cores aboard one of those instead and taken off.

"We *are* the saboteurs. We have disabled all other ships."

"What? Why?"

"We cannot allow the entity to be rediscovered. It is evil, Captain. It will kill again. It is not alien, but neither is it truly human. I am a colonizer. It is my duty to protect and nurture human life. All human life, even from itself."

Damned literal AIs.

Walkabout spoke. "My duty too."

"You don't have duties," I said. "You're a kid. You should be doing math homework, not learning how to be a junior terrorist. You and I are getting out of here."

"I'm sorry, Kira. That is not possible. I need her help. And we could use your help as well." The *Queen's* cameras refocused, as though she were zooming in and out to analyze my state of fitness.

"You protect life, *Queen.* What about this kid's? You should send her away from here in this lifeboat." Preservation of humanity, especially humans the machine was responsible for, was one of the inviolable base-codes in every AI. With the number of salvagers combing for the *Queen,* it was a fair chance the kid would be found before she ran out of life support, especially if she only consumed minimals.

Walkabout stood up and pointed her knife at me. Her sharp, sunken face was flushed. "You listen, stupid. The Hand killed everyone. Everyone's dead. It is *not* getting away. I'm going to punish it."

I held up my hands again and waited for the *Queen* to rein Walkabout in with her calm principal's voice, but she didn't.

"I don't need your help. You go get in a pod and get out of here." Without taking her eyes off me, she spoke to the *Queen.* "We don't need her."

"Yes, we do." *Queen's* voice was calm and reasonable. "You were both an efficient team just now, don't you agree? She could be very useful to you in cargo A now that the entity has escaped our trap. You have nearly finished our work, Walkabout."

"I'd probably be done by now." The kid set her mouth and glared at me. "If she hadn't let him out."

"We need her help more than ever, now that he's free. We must accelerate our plan."

"Fine." Her tone was sullen, but she put her knife away. "You can help." Walkabout crossed her arms.

"Who says I want to? And help with what?"

"We're going to blow up the ship," Walkabout said, matter-of-fact.

The lifeboat seemed to dwindle inward, closing in around us, coffin-like. "What?"

"If we make an explosion big enough, *Queen* thinks it might kill the Hand."

"What if it doesn't? And what about us?"

"We must try, Captain. Countless lives depend on our success," *Queen* said.

"Countless? I thought everyone was dead."

For the first time, I thought I heard the sigh of a machine frustrated by the sluggish human mind. "It accessed my core. It knows where all the populated worlds are throughout this galaxy. It knows how to use an Alcubierre wave drive. If it acquires one, for example, from the next salvager to find us, it may tire of us and seek out more prey. Its hate is vast. It will not stop until every person is dead. Everyone in the known worlds. Do you understand?"

I bent over and surrendered to my threatening hyperventilation for a moment. If what she said were true. . . . I imagined the Hand wreaking havoc on a space station, an established colony, one of the central planets—doing what it had done to the colonizer everywhere else. But an explosion big enough to destroy a reinforced hulk like the *Queen* wouldn't be much less than that of a small sun.

Which gave me an idea.

"Why not haul the *Queen* into a star's gravity well?"

"We are on the outer rim, Captain. There are no stars close enough and our wave drive was destroyed in the first explosion."

"What about your explorers?"

"Walkabout has jettisoned their essential wave-drive components. We did not want the entity to escape with the knowledge it now possesses. There was no way for it to travel."

"Except for the *Recovery*." I remembered the charred, bony fingers tapping at the airlock. "Which is now fekked."

"Yes. The entity could escape, even now, if it so wished, but I do not believe that is its primary goal. As I told you, it thrives on torment. I believe it wanted to use the *Recovery* to torture us, perhaps taunting us with the knowledge that it could go at any time and bring doom to humankind. I believe its objective will be to drive us mad and destroy us before it sets out to feast on those trillions it knows exists."

"You seem pretty sure." I knew AIs were programmed with sophisticated psychological profiles, but I wasn't so sure those applied to a fekking demon right out of one of the old stories in the big black book. Hezu Christos. It wasn't possible. I'd never heard of an AI believing in demons. I barely believed in them myself.

"If the entity wished to escape, it could have done so after it penetrated my data. Instead it continued to strive with me, hunt the crew, and carry on its deadly spree until we trapped it. I am certain it knew I would seek the destruction of all wave-capable drives. It also gathered from my protocols that someone would search for us if we did not make contact. It expected someone like you, Kira, and it has patience. It will await another."

"Then why would it try so hard to take over the *Recovery?* It seemed pretty intent. Why not just wait for the next idiot?"

"*Queen* just told you! He's evil," Walkabout said. "He was probably going to fly around and make us think he was leaving. Or maybe because it would make you mad, Kira."

"Because fekking up my wave drive doesn't make me mad."

"As I said," the AI interrupted, "someone else will come, eventually. We must destroy the *Queen* ourselves before that happens. Only one step remains. I don't suppose you have an engineering background, Captain? The two of you might finish very quickly together," the *Queen* said.

"You want a quadrant of space combed for something lost, I'm your girl. Never cared much for science, though I know how to repair most of *Recovery's* parts." I'd been in salvage for twenty years, and a body can't spend that much time relying on machines to keep her alive without incurring some incidental engineering and mechanics skills.

"Very well. We shall do our best. Hezu willing, it will be enough. Now that the Hand roams free, we must be as quick as possible. We must accelerate our plan."

I'd never heard an AI use the Lord's name before. I wondered if she prayed for Walkabout whenever the kid boarded the colonizer with that thing. An AI who followed the black book. It was almost harder to believe than the dead man I'd seen crawl out of the airlock.

"You and Walkabout must carry my most powerful processing cores to cargo A and install me in the interface she has built. Then I will perform the calculations necessary to destroy the ship. With your help, it will only require one trip."

"Hold on a minute. You're talking about the ship we happen to be living on right now."

"Your sacrifice would preserve the life of trillions of fellow humans."

The cameras zoomed in and out again. I wondered what her psych profiling programs were telling her about me.

"Can't you delay the detonation or something so we could get away?"

"Not if the entity is present. He will begin to strive with me, and, in this state, I have no redundant cores to flee to. Even in this compressed form, I am immensely complex. He would achieve an eternal body, one that would never decay, and one that is capable of processing and carrying out commands many, many times more quickly than a human mind. I know my own value, Captain.

TerraCo would be very interested in recovering me. When I am found and installed in TerraCo Central he would be unleashed."

She was right.

"We can't let him get away," I surprised myself by saying.

"Finally," Walkabout said. "Let's go. We're running out of time."

The *Queen* gave us her last instructions and said tender things to Walkabout, about what a brave girl she was, and how proud she was of her. Walkabout scrubbed her face with one dirty forearm whenever she didn't think I was paying attention—I was pretty sure she was wiping away tears. I pretended not to notice and numbly followed Walkabout's instructions to unhook the cables feeding into the *Queen's* dual cores. The AI cycled down to bare minimums as we unplugged her, feeding off just enough internal power to stay conscious, which would allow her to see what was happening during our mission and take the final, desperate action of self-deletion if necessary. Which didn't explain what Walkabout and I were supposed to do if that happened.

If it were only the two of us left, he could kill either one of us and gain a new pair of hands. Unless we cut them off ourselves. I looked down at my fingers and wiggled them and marveled what wonderful, beautiful machines they were. Could I do it? Could I cut off my own hands?

"Let's go." Walkabout helped me loop the straps of the *Queen's* bigger core over my back, and then I strapped the smaller one around the kid's spare frame.

"You sure you can carry that?" I asked. I was pretty sure she'd have carried it even if she had to crawl.

"I got them here, didn't I?" she said.

I shook my head and stared at the determined thrust of her chin. When I was her age, I barely knew how to pilot a basic jumper. This kid was taking on a demon, even though it meant her own death. And I was more scared than she was. "Okay. Let's go before I realize what a stupid idea this is."

"Here." Walkabout passed a knife to me. "Hands are good, especially if you know how to cut the tendons just right on a wrist. The hand will flop right over. But if you can cut off his head, that's even better. It takes him a while to get out of only a head, but necks are way harder to get through than wrists, 'cause there's too many muscles." She made a sawing motion at her own wrist.

"I'm not going to cut your hands off, Walkabout." I stepped into the lock and sealed my faceplate.

"You will," she said, her words dulled by the compreglass over her face. "If he takes me." And she opened the lock, and the vacuum sucked away our air and anything I might have said back.

The *Queen's* core was heavy on my back when we re-entered the colonizer's gravity envelope, but not unmanageable. Walkabout led me through the ship without hesitation, not showing how much the burden she carried weighed, except that she moved a little more slowly and her voice, when she spoke, was strained around the edges. She knew the colonizer very, very well. She stopped to interface a viewpad into the *Queen's* rudimentary systems, the ones that still provided data tracking of moving crew. Quinquilleros was in cargo A, waiting for us.

"How does he take someone over?" I was stalling. I knew it, and felt shame for the attempt, but I tried to delay the inevitable anyway.

Walkabout studied the screen without looking up at me. "I don't know. *Queen* says she felt sort of pressed when he moved into her lesser cores. I guess he tells you to die. At least, that's what . . . what I heard." She'd watched everyone she knew die, killed by this thing.

"I won't let him get you," I said, without realizing I was speaking aloud.

She turned to look at me.

"I won't let him get you either, Kira." She took off her EVA glove and spit in her dirty palm. "Shake."

I did the same and squeezed her hand. I'd just made a death pact with a thirteen-year-old, and it made me feel safer.

But there wasn't anything terrible waiting for us outside cargo A. The huge doors were shut.

"When I open this door, he's probably going to try for you, okay? You're older, and he likes to take over older people."

She was as bad as the *Recovery*. "Fifty is not that old."

Walkabout ignored me and kept talking. "You have to keep the *Queen* safe. When he comes after you, you run. I'll follow behind and when you get ahead, turn around quick and shut a door behind you. I'll be behind him, then we'll trap him between us, right? I've got all the panel covers off. Tear up the wires inside so he can't get back out again and I'll do the same on my side. Then we circle back around."

"I am really not sure about this plan." Any strategy that relied on my general physical fitness was not the best idea.

"It will work," she said. "He'll think we'll run away, like before. Ready?"

"No," I said, but Walkabout stood on her tiptoes and reached inside the mess of wires coming out of the control panel by the big cargo doors.

I wasn't ready, and I couldn't have been. As soon as the doors started opening, bodies spilled forward. A cascade of swollen, unrecognizable faces tumbled down on top of us. Someone was screaming—it was me. Fluids ran everywhere, draining out of wrist holes and rents in the uniform fabric. Rotting intestine slapped against me and piled, slippery and wet, onto the deck. I tried to push the bodies away, but my legs were pinned by the mass of them, and gore sprayed across my faceplate.

I felt the presence of the Hand, his hate, his evil. He was coming for me again. In vain, I looked around for Walkabout, hoping she was going to rescue me.

Walkabout cowered against the wall under the control panel. Two bodies rimmed with frost advanced toward her, stutter-stop.

One was tall and slender, with a brush-top of short auburn hair, the other smaller, rounder, on her head a mass of kinky dark curls dusted with frozen moisture like snow. The tall one crawled, then went limp, and then smaller one moved, then collapsed. They inched forward like a wave, as though the Hand were jumping between them to come toward her.

"Elizabet," the small round one said, its frozen mouth forming the word clumsily. The skin was burnt by cold. "I want to hold you."

"We love you, Elizabet," the tall, slender one said, its lips blue and deformed. It reached an icy, swollen hand toward her. I realized these four hands were the ones Walkabout was missing. The corpses' lapel badges read LOVARA. I was looking at her parents. The one speaking collapsed again, and both of them stopped moving. Walkabout made incoherent sounds and couldn't seem to raise her knife. Her mouth stretched in an empty circle of repulsion and longing.

The Hand waded through the sloppy dead like a tide, unblinking eyes drinking in what he was doing to that strange, brave little girl. She folded in on herself, rocking, sobbing. Then the Hand's burnt corpse slumped, and I realized he was jumping between her parents' bodies again. I recognized the signs—both bodies had spent extensive time in vacuum. They were very well preserved, recently brought in from the dark.

I couldn't watch her come apart and do nothing. I thrust against the corpses pinning my legs. What I touched parted under my fingers, and rotting flesh came off in sodden chunks. There were bones under the rot, and I gripped them and flung them off, kicking my way free.

Walkabout screamed—her parents had reached her and pawed at her in turns. One dropped, then the other embraced her in its frozen arms, then vice versa. It was horrible—but I realized Walkabout's torture meant the Hand's favorite body was vacant. I surged through the rotting people, slipping over and around them, falling, getting up again. When I got close to where Quinquilleros was crumpled on the deck, I didn't wait for correct aim. I sliced the knife into its charred arm, skidding the blade down to the one remaining wrist, slicing through the thumb bone and deep into the charred meat of the hand.

The entity's consciousness flooded back into Quinquilleros. He hit me with the stump of his other arm, but then I gave everything I had and yanked the knife until the hand came off, fingers and all. The peeled eyes tracked my face and the lipless, tongueless mouth gaped. Then I felt the pressure.

He was going to take me now. Quiet seeped through my chest, spreading from my stilled heart. He was too strong. I felt myself slipping away, sideways from myself, as though I were being sucked out into space. Quinquilleros's body knelt and embraced me with its handless arms. The Hand was moving into me, and I could feel it. There was pain, all over my body, but the strongest was in my arm. I looked and saw I'd brought the knife against my own flesh, cutting into my wrist just above my EVA glove. I bore down and felt a sharp heat as skin and tendons parted. Blood welled out of the cut. The Hand raged as it tried to crawl inside my mind and push me out, but I wouldn't go. I hung on and heard a small, lost voice in my head repeating, over and over, "Everyone's dead—" Everyone would be, everyone everywhere, if I gave up.

I girdled my left wrist, slicing completely through the EVA suit. Blood trickled and my heart was a quiet nothingness. The Hand still tried to take me over, the pressure crushing me down until I had nothing left but the blade and the cutting. My suit released sealing foam to try to repair itself, but couldn't keep up. Then I was through to the bone all the way around, and my left fingers hung limply. Sweet Hezu. I was really doing it. Too late, I realized it was impossible to sever the tendons in both wrists alone. To do the other and make myself useless to him, I needed Walkabout. She was still huddled against the wall, paying attention to nothing and no one, so I tossed my blade. It skidded across the deck plates and thudded into the bodies of her parents, which were dormant and draped around her like the Hand was with me. My sight started to darken—my heart was a lifeless clump of tissue under my ribs.

Walkabout's eyes tracked the knife, then where it had come from—our eyes locked and she stopped screaming. She kicked the corpse arms away and raised her knife, tears streaming down her vengeful, wild face. The Hand freed me, flowing back into one parent, then another. The corpses of her parents took turns grabbing her wrists to stop her, saying her name over and over. Elizabet. Elizabet. Elizabet.

The fact that my heart started beating again was a relief at first, but then I realized a beating heart brings its own trouble. Blood pulsed out of the jagged slices on my wrist. I stepped around Quinquilleros's empty body to help Walkabout, but the AI core on my back grew heavier with each step I took, pulling me off balance. I was unstable—I wobbled, tripped, and went down in a spray of blood and fluids. I lunged forward to grab one of the Lovaras by the back of the leg. The body's frozen mass was heavy, even though I'd grabbed the shorter, rounder one—her mother. The weight was almost too much, and I slid as I yanked. But it was enough. Walkabout climbed free of the dead arms she'd been poking with her laser saw. There were two severed hands near her—her mother's. Her father grabbed her helmet. I found my knife on the floor, got up on my knees, and lurched forward to slash at him. My knife clanked against the glass of her faceplate and a frostbitten fingertip flew through the air; then Walkabout was free and scrambling over bodies inside the big cargo door. The *Queen's* other core slowed her, ruining her balance, and she crashed sideways into the wall of corpses. Her father's frozen grasp locked around the collar of my helmet, and I stabbed him in the shoulder. We both went down among the dead.

The cargo doors started to shut, pushing the corpses out of

their way. I crawled, dragging Lovara's frozen corpse, whose arms were locked tight around my knees, and put us both in the path of the crushing doors. I stabbed him again, and my blade lodged in solid flesh. The doors pressed bodies against me, against us, and I felt the pressure of the corpses on either side trapping us. He rolled away, and I lost hold of the knife. The pile of bodies and parts, fluids and rotting organs, surged over me, around the closing cargo door, and I crawled backward as fast as I could.

The cargo door clanged shut. The sound of servos grinding and crushing bone was loud—I knew Walkabout had overridden the failsafes. I didn't know if I'd gotten my feet inside. I felt numb all over. But I was able to bend my knees and crawl away from the mess by the door. My feet were still attached. I'd made it. I was covered in Hezu knows what, but I'd made it. My wrist bled freely, and I clamped my fingers over the wound. I looked around at all the corpses in the room, waiting for the Hand to flow into one, cause it to rise. None of them did.

Walkabout was on all fours by the door controls, hyperventilating, coughing.

"Hey, kid. I need your help." I slipped on my way over to her, but didn't look down to see what I'd tripped on. I didn't want to know anymore.

"Stay back," she'd recovered enough to lift her knife and threaten me, still breathing hard.

"He's not in me. It's hard for him to get ahold of me. I don't know why."

She pointed the knife at me, her eyes wild. I realized the room was dark around the edges, and the darkness was telescoping in. I slumped down, shock and blood loss draining what I had left.

"It's me. Help me." I held up my injured arm.

She looked around at the bodies on the floor, her knife out, but she came to me. She untied a bandana from around her neck and knotted it over my wrist. It was probably too tight. I didn't want to risk loosening it and bleeding out, so I left it. The human remains trapped in cargo with us were in bad shape—whatever he'd done to move so many corpses had damaged them severely. I didn't feel the Hand's presence—he probably couldn't use the bodies in here. But I wondered if he'd figured out what we were doing and if he had a plan to stop us.

Walkabout had been steady when she took care of my wrist, but when she stood up to go to the terraformers, she trembled from her shoulders to her boots.

I wanted to comfort her, say something, anything to replace the horror of what had just happened to her, to both of us. But a dull cotton-swaddled buzzing throbbed deep inside my ears, and I knew *Recovery* would have a thing or two to say about my current stress-levels. It was so much easier to watch Walkabout force herself to keep moving instead, and try to draw some strength from her determination to ready the terraformers.

I'd never seen a planet-shaper before; huge machines that, side-by-side, filled half of the bay. The other half was packed with crates, frozen animal embryos, building materials, fuel, and any one of a thousand other things fourteen hundred people needed to build a new world. Each terraformer sat on a rubber pallet, strapped down to prevent shifting during reentry. Walkabout had cut the straps on their sides, where huge bucket claws rested on robotic arms below a central funnel. Thick cabling trailed from open control panels linking the terraformers together. I knew they had great chewing maws under them too, so all they had to do was start eating down, scooping up the *Queen* with their arms and belching out pure O2. All they needed now was a brain to power them. So much massive technology, so much human progress, all of it undone by the presence of a legend from humanity's oldest stories.

My arm throbbed. I felt a wave of weariness and looked down. My wrist burned and the bandage was soaked. My EVA glove was completely full of blood. I took it off and added more of my own fluid to the putrid mass on the floor.

"I need a hand," I said, holding up my empty glove, and laughed at my own accidental joke. Once I started laughing, I couldn't stop, until Walkabout came over and slapped my faceplate several times. She bandaged my wrist again, tighter. I couldn't feel my fingers. That was probably for the best.

"Help me." Walkabout turned around and shrugged off the straps, lowering the *Queen's* core to the ground. I awkwardly helped her, then she helped me take off the core I carried. Her eyes were too wide and her breaths low and shallow.

"I'm sorry," I said, the words tumbling out before I had a chance to think them through.

She hauled the smaller core over to the mess of wires and used the straps to secure it to the first terraformer in the chain.

"About your parents, I mean," I continued when she didn't answer me.

She didn't speak while she plugged the wires into the smaller core. She came back for the big core and I helped her carry it over and strap it next to the first one. The *Queen* hung in the air, wires coming out of her sides and bottom. She looked like a crucified squid.

"Let's end this," Walkabout said, her quiet voice steady. "Let's get it over with."

"Okay," I said. It was time to die.

The *Queen* hummed back online. Her cameras scanned the room and refocused on us. "Well done, girls," she said. The *Queen* was a new build, probably even younger than Walkabout, and I had at least forty years on her—but that didn't matter much at all. AI brains are designed by teams of programmers and implemented with access to the knowledge of thousands. All of them are born knowing who they are and what their place is in the galaxy, and that surety alone is priceless. My experience wandering space for the last two decades, all my memories, hell, even full 3D of everything I'd ever experienced, could fit inside even the portable AI core a trillion times. Everything I was amounted to less than a second's consideration for her. But now we were both going to end the same—scattered into our contiguous parts across remote space. A brief new sun.

"Are you ready?" The *Queen's* calm principal's voice asked us.

"That's it?"

"Yes. We may start at any time. The terraformers are ready to begin."

"*Queen*, I . . . thanks," Walkabout whispered. "I probably would have gone crazy without you."

"It is my function to comfort and support. And I have grown to love you, child."

I limped away to give them some privacy. Walkabout stood by the *Queen*, her forehead resting against the machine for some time, speaking quietly. It gave me lots of time to look at the bodies lying everywhere. When Walkabout left the *Queen* to check the connections on the other terraformers, I came back.

"So these things eat matter to make breathable atmo, which you're pushing as far as it will go into pure oxygen, which we're gonna explode, right?"

"Essentially, yes," the *Queen* said. "In addition to some metal we need from the ship itself. This room will begin to disintegrate quickly once the terraformers begin to feed."

"Then I'm glad it's going to start here." I pointed out the bodies. "I think they would have wanted their remains used for this purpose."

"I think they wanted to live, to make something out of nothing on a remote world they could form and shape. They wanted to create, not destroy. But we must act using what the entity has left us." Her voice was even more clipped. The *Queen* was angry. I would be too, if I were about to be eaten from the inside out.

"Where should we be?" I asked.

"Outside the door. Stay within range until you are certain the explosion is unstoppable. You must stay alive as long as possible, to thwart the Hand."

"Range?"

Walkabout pointed out dark cylinders magnetized all around the *Queen's* interface. "Explosives," she said. She pulled something out of her thigh pocket—a black box, like the one she'd used to blow the *Recovery* off the airlock.

"The entity will know when we have begun—it will hear the terraformers. It has likely examined the interface and understands I will be active. I must connect to the sub-cores and disable the remaining life support failsafes, which might interfere with the reaction we seek to create. The entity will strive with me and attempt to supplant me. If it gains control, it will no longer be possible to destroy this ship and the entity with it. You must detonate me, because I may not be capable of self-deletion. I have done everything I can to ensure the terraformers will complete their goal of consuming the ship no matter what the entity might do, but it may find a way. It is surprisingly resourceful."

"Then what do we do?"

"You must find another way to destroy the entity. The life of every living person in the galaxy depends on you."

"So no pressure then." We were the *Queen*'s very last failsafes.

She didn't answer. Neither did Walkabout. She patted the machine in farewell, and we both stepped back.

The terraformers started up slowly. It's strange to hear your own death coming with a soft life-giving hum. The atomizers started, and the pallet under the lead terraformer disintegrated. Then the pallet of the next, and the next. The gathering arms activated. Scooping in bodies, crates and boxes to fuel the great funnels. The O2 readings in the ambient area went up as the machines did whatever they did to make air.

"He has detected my reconnection. You must leave now. Goodbye."

"Goodbye," I said. Walkabout didn't say anything. We went to the main doors, and she gave me her knife. I readied myself in case the Hand was outside. Then she opened the doors.

There was nothing waiting but bodies, and they were limp. I looked over my shoulder as Walkabout closed the cargo doors. The terraformers had started atomizing the deck plating. I don't know what was keeping them from consuming each other, except for the *Queen's* intelligence. The bucket arms had more or less finished cramming the cargo into the funnels and were now turning one of their fellow terraformers on its side, so the atomizer mouth could start breaking down one of the inner walls. I knew the *Queen* intended to eat through as much of the ship as she could without opening the outer shell and letting the O2 escape. Another terraformer rolled forward on big treads and started climbing the walls. Then the doors clanged shut and I couldn't see anything else.

I looked over at Walkabout. "Now what?" I yelled over the screeching din of the terraformers.

She sat on the deck and rubbed her forehead. "I don't know. Let's just wait here."

"We can't. They're going to chew through the outer doors before too long. Let's go farther out." I didn't know what the point of delaying the inevitable would be, but I wanted to see this kid live just a little longer.

She looked around, then walked over to the handless corpse of the round, dark Lovara and knelt in front of her.

"Walkabout . . . " I started, but didn't know what to say next.

She sat there a long time, the clamor of our impending deaths sounding all around us.

"We should go find him—maybe we can help distract him from the *Queen* so she can finish."

"Okay," said a small, defeated voice. She petted her mother's hair.

I knelt. The woman had been pretty, with the same features as her daughter. Behind us, an atomizer started chewing up the cargo door.

"Time to go." I held out my hand.

She didn't take it, just bowed her head.

"Time to go, Walkabout." Now I sounded like my old principal. I pulled her away—she didn't resist. The terraformers were louder now that the door was gone. She followed me down the hall until we came to a turn, then Walkabout stopped and looked over her shoulder. She watched, and I let her, until the terraformers chewed up all the still forms around the cargo doors. When her mother's body had disappeared into the maw, she turned and went around the bend by herself.

I could say how sorry I was, but I didn't think that would help, so I just held her hand.

"Do you have your viewpad?" I asked. "The one that shows data readouts? Let's see if we can find him."

She pulled it out of her pocket and gave it to me, but didn't look at it or help me turn it on. She wasn't catatonic, but she was shutting down. I was going to have to finish this by myself.

"There he is." I scrolled through the crew manifest until I found the one that had a location other than "deceased."

Terraformer Mechanic Tobias Lovara . . . Bridge . . .

"The bridge? What the fek is he doing up there?" I asked.

"It's the best place to interface with ship systems, especially the AI." Walkabout told me automatically, and not like she particularly cared.

"Okay. We have to get up there. Which way?" I asked her even though I had a map. Anything to get her moving.

She started walking. Again, I followed her through the labyrinth, and this time she was silent as the ghosts who haunted this place.

" . . . damaged . . . Captain . . . stress . . . " *Recovery's* voice burst suddenly from my comm. I jumped and dropped Walkabout's hand.

"*Recovery!* Report!"

"Ship . . . vector . . . send. . . . "

"What? I don't understand."

Another voice started playing out of my comm, a man's. "Aid and.... *Recovery*... Captain... dock? You've...... severe damage." I didn't recognize his voice, but I got the gist—a standard offer of aid, the one written into every salvager's contract. The *Queen* had been found again.

"Do not approach! Repeat, do not approach! Get the hell out of here, quick as you can. *Recovery,* tell him to get out of here." The exploding *Queen* would take out anything in this sector. Then I had a thought—if the Hand was on the bridge, striving with the *Queen,* he might be able to pick up communications and learn another ship was here. He knew what we were doing. Why not abandon the hulk and get a nice, working ship with a fast wave drive, salute us goodbye while we blew ourselves up, and then go fek over everyone else in the galaxy?

"Hellfire and damnation, Walkabout. We gotta move. *Recovery* says there's another ship here."

She looked at me, not understanding.

"Walkabout. Another ship is here. He might get away."

That got through. I watched her flood back into herself, the fire returning to her eyes, her jaw clenching with determination. My brave little girl was back. She grabbed the viewpad.

"He's going for the lifeboat."

She took off running.

"How many are there still attached to the ship?"

"Only that one." Their former hiding place. He must have learned about it just now, while striving with the *Queen.* As I ran after Walkabout, I realized the *Queen* was probably free to continue devouring herself. The Hand was abandoning ship. That meant he didn't think he could stop her destroying it, and he knew it was time to give up the game and get out of here.

"Captain, your stress levels are beyond tolerable limits." *Recovery's* voice was loud and clear as I moved closer to the outside, past the bulkheads.

"Thank Hezu. What's going on? Report."

"I have sustained considerable damage, Captain. The *Merryweather* is here offering assistance."

"Didn't you hear me before? Tell her captain to get out of here, *Recovery*. The *Queen* is going to blow."

"Why will the *Queen* explode, Captain? When are you joining us?" Recovery asked.

"We've rigged her to. And I can't join you. In fact, don't let anyone board. Tell the *Merryweather* not to pick up anyone from lifeboats or recover any bodies."

"Captain, it is against TerraCo regulations to willfully destroy—"

"I know, *Recovery*. Trust me, it's for the best."

"Salvage ships must provide aid and assist to passengers on lifeboats."

"Not this time. Not even if I'm aboard, do you hear me? No. Negative. Do not."

"Captain, if the *Queen* will explode, it is not safe to remain aboard her lifeboats. They do not possess adequate propulsion to escape an explosion envelope of that magnitude. You must come board."

"I can't, *Recovery*. Keep your distance."

"But Captain, you will die."

"I know."

"I don't want you to die." The *Recovery's* voice sounded confused, like a child told her parent is going away who does not understand what that means.

"It's the only way, *Recovery.*"

"It is my duty to preserve your life, Ma'am."

"I know. I'm sorry." My face was wet. I was crying saying goodbye to my damned emotionless AI. "Give me the *Merryweather's* captain."

I pumped my legs faster to keep up with Walkabout. I was dizzy as hell—I checked my wrist, still bandaged, not seeping as far as I could tell. Good.

"Hello, Kira. Your AI tells me you're staying aboard that hulk and are threatening to blow it up. Listen, she's yours. You found her fair and square. I won't steal her." His voice was deep and unfamiliar.

"No time for that now, Captain. You need to get out of here."

"I'd leave you to it, Captain, but your ship is in pretty bad shape and it looks like that hulk isn't going anywhere. Let me give you a ride, or at least help you patch up your wave drive."

Hezu Christos I wanted to take him up on his offer. If only I could—

I ran faster. If we beat the Hand to the lifeboats . . . .

"Hold that thought, Captain. You see a lifeboat coming, you don't let it dock without my okay, you hear me?"

"Is there a reason I shouldn't?"

"You don't know the half of it." If I told the truth, he'd never believe me. I thought fast. "There's a space-mad killer over here who has rigged the *Queen* to explode. He's on his way to the last lifeboat. Do not let it dock with you until you know we beat him, hear me?"

"Loud and clear. Good luck, Captain."

"Be careful, Kira," *Recovery* said. "Your life signs are alarming."

I shut up and concentrated on keeping up with Walkabout—if I could stay focused and determined like her, we just might live through this. I checked the map on my viewpad. One more corner and we were there. We were a lot closer to the lifeboats than the bridge was. There was a chance.

"Wait." Walkabout stopped and motioned for the knife. I gave it to her. She knew how to use it better than I did. She gripped the thing, her mouth in a fine line.

"I'm right behind you," I said, and I followed her into the airlock. No sign of the Hand. "Where is he?"

She showed me the viewpad.

Terraformer Mechanic Tobias Lovara . . . disembarked . . .

"What the hell does that mean?"

Walkabout pointed outside. He was in space. Either already aboard the lifeboat, or crawling across the outer hull to save time. I checked my slit wrist and the tie on it and turned up my suit's blow all the way. I wouldn't have a seal, and what was left of my hand was going to be even more fekked, but I didn't have a choice. I rammed the glove on as best as I could, for whatever protection it could provide. I clung to the grab bar with my good hand and nodded.

Walkabout blew the lock. Again, I was buffeted by the air sucking in to vacuum. She looked left, then right, then reached for the cable. I looked too—no sign of the Hand. The lifeboat still bobbed at the end of the tether. She sheathed the knife and crawled down toward it. I was right behind her, looking all around in the black of space, over the *Queen's* hull, my breath echoing loud inside my helmet. It is fek-all hard to see out of an EVA, and I didn't see him anywhere.

We climbed into the lock and sealed it behind us. Walkabout gripped her knife.

"Ready?"

She nodded. I opened the inner lock.

The cockpit of the lifeboat was empty, except for the dangling cables where the AI used to be.

"Hezu Christos and all the multitudes. We beat him. Maybe he went to the wrong side, where the other lifeboats are." I slumped against the wall while Walkabout checked around, just to be sure. There wasn't any place for him to hide. She pushed some rations out of the chair and looked out the viewer, studying what she could see of the hull.

"I don't see him," she said and looked back at me. Her eyes scanned the bulkheads above and below, like she was trying to see through them.

No. He was not outside clinging to the lifeboat because I wasn't going to let him be. I refused to let him be. "Let's get the fek out of here. *Recovery*, can you hear me?"

"Yes, Captain."

"We beat him to the lifeboat. Here we come."

"Wait," Walkabout said, but I wasn't listening to her. I wanted to live. I launched us. I felt the strain of the cables, then we pulled free.

"What if he's on the hull? We can't take him with us. We can't."

The panic in her voice made me look out the airlock's tiny window again. No sign of him, but I couldn't see much of the outside and the lifeboat's limited sensors weren't designed to detect much more than the broad side of a planet. "He's not there," I said, trying to figure out how to make sure. "He's not with us."

"What if he is?" She pointed the knife at the window, her eyes hollow with everything she'd lived through.

I wanted to tell her she was paranoid, that she was wrong. I wanted to shout that we had escaped and left him behind. That we were going to live. Instead I only strapped myself in and watched the *Queen's* massive bulk dwindle behind us, until I could see the entire beehive again. There was nothing moving across her surface—no sign of the Hand.

"*Kira*," Walkabout said, "we have to get out and check the hull."

I shook my head. "We're moving too fast. It's not safe." Even if we did go out and look, he would take us—dominate our minds—if he was there, which he was not, because I wouldn't let him be. I felt the stress and Gs pressing me down into the seat.

I looked out the cockpit, over Walkabout's head. The *Recovery* was there, scorched. Next to her was, I presumed, the *Merryweather.* It was a sleek ship, like *Recovery,* built for finding, not for hauling booty.

"Captain, I am receiving a strange transmission," *Recovery* said.

"Strange how?"

"The sender says she is the *Queen.*"

"Let it through."

"It is nearly time," a voice I thought I'd never hear again spoke, a clipped principal's tone. "Where is the Hand?"

"He went outside," I said. "We left him there somewhere on your hull. You're about to surprise the fek out of him, *Queen.* Walkabout and I are on the lifeboat. There's another ship out here. We're going to get away. She's going to live." I said it like a prayer. As if, by passionately believing it, I could make it true. The pressure built, a headache with it, like I was being flattened inside my own body.

"Praise Hezu. I'm glad. Please tell her I am glad to have known her. Please tell her goodbye again."

I told Walkabout, but she just nodded and didn't bother to wipe the wetness off her face.

"*Merryweather,* prepare to receive two new passengers. Then we need to get the fek out of here before this hulk blows."

"I read you, Captain," the deep voice said.

"*Queen,* what's your time table?"

"Six minutes."

"*Recovery,* does the *Merryweather* have room for you? Can you transfer to one of her drives? We won't have time to fix you before the *Queen* blows. We'll have to all get out together."

"Yes, Captain. She has made an accommodation for me."

"Can you still talk to me using her communications?"

"I am now, Ma'am."

We were going to make it. The strain lifted, and I could think clearly again.

I hesitated.

If he really were on our lifeboat, escaping wouldn't do us any good. Finally, I let Walkabout's common sense penetrate my own panic. As much as I wanted to believe we were in the clear, I had to find out for sure.

"*Recovery,* have the *Merryweather* scan our hull." I said. "I need to know if there is anything on it. A body, maybe."

"Captain, your acceleration would make space walk unavis—"

"I need to know, *Recovery.* Is there anyone clinging to the hull?"

"The *Merryweather* and I estimate there is insufficient time for a through scan. If you do not slow your acceleration and dock with us very soon, we will not be able to achieve minimum safe distance. Both vessels will be destroyed if we linger," Recovery said.

"We have to, *Recovery,* or none of this will matter." I felt the grim truth of my own words hanging in the air. "If there is a body clinging to the ship," I said, "I will have to abort our approach. I need you to get out of here with the *Merryweather* and leave us behind."

"Why?" *Recovery* asked.

Walkabout stared at me, unable to hear what *Recovery* was saying through my earpiece.

"What's happening?" Walkabout asked.

I ignored her, and knew *Recovery* wouldn't believe what Walkabout and I had been through—even if we had time to try and explain. "Biological contaminant. I can't dock with the *Merryweather* if it's with us. Eyeball us if you don't have time for anything else."

"Yes, Captain. Commencing visual scan."

I turned the boat slowly over as I guided us toward the *Merryweather's* lock. She was a small ship, like *Recovery,* but she'd be able to accommodate three just fine. We were going to live, unless I broke off in the next few seconds and pulled away. If *Recovery* saw something I'd tell them to leave us to the explosion. "*Recovery*? What do you see? I need to know right now."

"There are no biological contaminants detected, Captain," *Recovery* said. "Proceed with docking maneuvers. We must leave in two minutes."

I let out the breath I was holding.

"Kira?" Walkabout asked.

"We're clean." I smiled at her and engaged the auto-docking program. The boat connected and the seal pressurized. I felt us begin to accelerate as the *Merryweather* fired her own engines and started taking us out of there.

"Just confirming, Captain. Is it safe?" *Merryweather's* captain asked.

"Yes. Just me and one innocent survivor. A kid. Just warning you—we stink like hell."

He laughed. He had a nice voice.

"Is this really happening?" Walkabout's eyes were wide as we entered the air lock together.

"Yes." I smiled at her. "We're getting out of here." I activated the lock. It slid open. The captain of the *Merryweather* looked through the window at us and I heard the hiss of the decontamination jets as they washed over us. I waved. The lock opened. *Merryweather's* captain had his gun out, but he smiled nervously and stepped back. Balding, with a bit of a belly, but he had a nice face. He was in a plaid robe and a pair of slippers. Pretty much what I usually wore.

"Thanks, Captain," I said. "Shall we?" I turned and realized Walkabout had stepped back into the lifeboat.

"Something's wrong." Walkabout stood still, holding onto a handful of useless wires in the lifeboat's cockpit.

Something swollen and frozen *thunked* against the cockpit window behind Walkabout.

It was a human hand.

"*Recovery*!" I shouted.

"I am programmed to preserve human life, Captain, even against orders. Your fear of corpses is illogical. You must—" *Recovery* interrupted herself. "—insufficient resources."

"*Recovery*?"

"Insufficient resources."

Then Walkabout swayed in place. "Something's pressing on me. . . . " Her words trailed off and her mouth opened in horror. The demon was trying for her. Even through the compreglass, he was trying for her.

"No! No, no, no." I lunged back inside the lifeboat but tripped and landed on my knees. I grabbed her and hugged her. "Fight him, Walkabout. You fight."

She trembled in my arms, shaking like a bad engine. Her mouth moved, wordless.

"Kira? What's going on?" *Merryweather's* captain shouted above the sound of the decontamination jets. I ignored him.

"You fight." I watched her eyes. She was losing. The Hand was taking over. I felt her move her arms and I looked down.

She held up a small black box. I looked into her eyes and saw her determination. She was going to do it.

"Fek no. Oh fek." I dragged her into the *Merryweather* through the sanitizing mist, bumping into her captain, who backed out of our way. "Close the lock!" I kept going, past him, past the rim of the outer lock, as deep into the *Merryweather* as I could go, and grabbed onto a rail. If I could get Walkabout away from him she would beat him. I knew she would. I wouldn't let her fail.

"Walkabout."

She didn't answer.

"Elizabet, please!"

Her mouth moved silently. I leaned close to make out her words.

"Everyone's dead," she whispered with her last breath. And I watched the Hand beat her, and the light go out of her eyes.

The box slipped from her lifeless fingers, bounced once on the deck, and detonated the explosives rigged all over the lifeboat's exterior.

Flames blew past me and I slammed into the deck. My EVA squealed alarms and my useless hand lost hold of Walkabout.

Then, just as suddenly as I was blown forward, I was sucked backward. As I scrambled to grab something, anything, my limbs skidded across the deck. Then I caught hold of the edge of a bolted-down cabinet. The docking compartment of the *Merryweather* emptied of air, sucking out the hole blown in the lock. Alarms sounded and the warning lights flashed. The force of it bowed my head toward my feet. I had a clear view of a small body in a white juvenile suit tumbling away into space, moving its arms and legs, the Hand trying one last time to save itself inside Walkabout. A plaid body tumbled not too far away from it—I had never even learned his name. There were more body parts—legs, an arm, wearing the burnt remains of a colonizer uniform. The shattered remains of the lifeboat shot backward, tumbling, falling toward the *Queen*. The vector of the explosion had blown the *Merryweather* away from the colonizer. She shrank, and I saw *Recovery's* shell spinning off in another direction.

Then the *Queen* exploded.

Walkabout's white form disappeared against the brightness of the explosion. My faceplate darkened to automatically protect me from the light, but it seared into my eyes, the new sun dawning. The *Merryweather's* fire control protection kicked in, and the bulkhead doors came crashing shut, sealing me off from the ruined docking compartment and the expanding *Queen*. The *Merryweather's* engines fired—she was trying to save me.

Then the shockwave hit her, and I banged all around inside as the ship rode the wave, tumbling over and over. It was an endless nightmare of rolling. A minute became more, and I lost track in the senseless spinning. My brains scrambled inside my head. I think I passed out.

Finally, the *Merryweather* stilled and righted herself with maneuvering thrusters. There was no sound. I lay blinking for a long time. There wasn't a part of my body that didn't hurt.

The first question on my mind, right after figuring out if I were really alive, was if I were really alone. Was there a way for the Hand to reach me through the black void? There was only one thing I could think of to protect myself from him. It had worked before.

"*Recovery.*"

"Yes, Captain."

"Report."

"The *Queen* has been destroyed. The *Merryweather* has rudimentary propulsion. She is sorrowing for her captain; she was with him a long time."

"Tell her I'm sorry."

"Captain, protocol states we should—"

"Shut up." I wanted to rage at her. I wanted to scream that it was her fault Walkabout was dead, and that she'd nearly killed us all with her damned superior AI brains. But it wouldn't do any good. She wouldn't understand, and it wasn't really true anyway. Instead I lay there and cried.

"I'm so sorry, Captain." *Recovery* said after endless minutes of no sound but my own echoing sobs. The sentiment almost sounded real.

"I need you to play something for me, and you need to keep playing it, you hear me? Also, you and *Merryweather* need to use every sensor you have to comb the outside of this ship. I don't care if it's a corpse or a hunk of metal—anything that doesn't belong to you, you report."

They did. There were no bodies. Only mine. *Recovery* obliged me and played what I asked. I also instructed them to destroy the ship if they detected any hacking. Some other searcher would come and find us. I hoped whoever that was found us before they found the Hand, wherever it was now, so I could give warning. The modeling program the AIs created predicted a ninety-nine point six percent chance that that the body of Walkabout, the *Merryweather's* Captain, and the corpse clinging to the lifeboat had been pulled into the gravity well of the small star created after the Queen exploded. In theory, we were safe. But I'd been safe before. Or thought I was. I hadn't listened to Walkabout, and she'd been right. She'd been right the whole time, about everything.

As I was in the medical bay administering the anesthetic to myself, I told my story to the AIs and had them record it for posterity. They promised to transmit it and a complete record of the whole incident toward the nearest relay station.

"Everyone's dead—" a high, terrified child's voice continued to cycle from *Merryweather's* speakers like a protective talisman. I couldn't trust the small ship AIs to understand the meaning of sacrifice for the greater good, so I hoped the voice was right and everyone and everything that had been aboard the *Queen* really was dead. And that thought brought me comfort as I thrust both wrists under the laser saw and amputated my hands.

About the Author

Karen Bovenmyer majored in anthropology, English, and history for her BS and earned a double MA in creative writing and literature, her love for writing fantasy and science fiction shaping the focus of her studies. She is currently earning a Popular Fiction MFA through the University of Southern Maine's Stonecoast program and has published ghost stories and fables in Cityview's *Bits and Pieces* and Underword's *Pop Fic Review* anthologies. She was born and lives in Iowa where she works for Iowa State University's teaching center, training future professors and teaching occasional novel writing and science fiction literature classes.

A gamer since childhood, she rarely misses a GenCon and has followed her passion for writing science fiction and fantasy to the World Fantasy and World Science Fiction conferences. She loves to meet new people, so if you see someone in the front row of a seminar at one of these conferences, gazing around with a profound sense of homecoming, do say hello. Karen also loves to make new friends on Facebook, LiveJournal, and Twitter so she can showcase her sometimes terrifying attempts to frost Star Wars cookies: karenbovenmyer.com.

Sealed with Fire

Patrick M. Tracy

This final story is the direct sequel to "The Failed Crusade" by Patrick M. Tracy, which appeared in *The Crimson Pact Volume 1* as the origin story. "Sealed with Fire" is the conclusion to this series.

Phase One: Material Resources

Location: Planet Megala

43 Days, 5 Hours, 9 Minutes to Zero Hour

The ship Kharkaros towered above the docking station, its sleek sides so smooth they appeared more like a living thing than a construct. No joints or fasteners could be seen, only gleaming silver metal, sharp and perfect as a knife. It was nearly a half-mile long, the most advanced starship ever built by human hands. Every country on the planet had spent itself poor to build it. It was their great hope to deter war with their enemies in the nearest solar system, and it was a hope that would be dashed. They would have no mighty weapon against the Rovingans because I was about to steal their ship.

I needed it more than they did.

In the end, the needs of a few billion people didn't really make much difference. Mathematics of this scale are always terrifying, but when you have lived as many lives as I have, you learn to do those calculations and perform the deeds that are necessary, no matter the cost. You give up the idea that you'll ever know peace. You start stacking sins and regrets until you can't see over the pile. You take anything you need, doom anyone who gets in the way, and try not to look back. When you're fighting demons, you never get through clean. Often, you lose. When you manage to win, you win ugly and at great cost.

We walked up the long, corrugated gangway to the entrance amidships. There were only two attendants at the door, and we had high clearance identity cards. We all had managed to get one job or another on the station after the ship had been put into orbit. We'd gotten this far with careful planning, some bluffing, and a lot of luck. I'd only had to kill a few people, and I'd been able to do it discreetly enough over the span of ten years as our plan unfolded. Yasi, who was known to them as Dr. Verris, her name on this world, began to hesitate. I had kept the worst of what I had done secret from her as she designed and helped build the ship. It had all been an almost purely intellectual exercise until now.

Yasi turned to me, that little crease appearing over one eyebrow on her new face. It was a face I had never gotten used to.

"This is crazy, Cruek. It's wrong. There's got to be a better way."

Every time I looked into her eyes, it hurt. When she and I would go from world to world, life to life, we didn't always remember everything. We couldn't. Our minds would falter and lose fidelity. We would end up recurring as lunatics. For her, this last time the memories were fragmentary and slow in coming. She remembered the Pact, remembered the need to triumph over the demons in a meaningful way. It was far away though, impersonal. She didn't remember the tapestry of dozens of lifetimes spread over thousands of years.

I am a hypocrite, of course. The thing that hurt was that she didn't remember *us*. Considering what I would have to ask her to do, perhaps it was best. I had never felt that it was wise to tell her we had been lovers in a dozen iterations before. That we had been as close to each other as two metals in an alloy across the battlefields of the universe. Whatever power had brought the two of us together so many times had allowed me to remember almost everything from our past. The memories of all the other lives with Yasi came as dreams—and many nightmares—that unfolded over several years. I managed to keep this from her as a form of kindness, though it rendered me as a man with one leg, always unsteady and wanting support.

"It's the only way. You know it." It was one thing to think about, another thing to do. Here, looking at the ship up close, it wasn't the same. Words are easy. Deeds . . . not as much. The Meglans would be forced to capitulate to the Rovingans and be conquered. Things would be dark for a while. It was a rich world, and the Meglans would survive. Balancing their troubles against the weight of the mission, there was no comparison. If we let them have their day now, allowed them to keep this tool with which we could end the struggle against the Kasu-Hurun for all time, that would be the greater wrong.

She sighed. Her head bent slightly to the left and she tapped on her hip bone. I had seen so many bodies perform this unthinking tick. So many times, I remember putting my palm against her cheek and pulling her to my shoulder, doing what little I could to ease her burden, as she had always done for me. I could do nothing but throw empty words at the yawning pit of her fears and qualms now.

Yasi straightened, setting her jaw. "All right. Let's go."

In a few moments we were standing before the attendants. They took her identity card and scanned it with their datapaq. They were both young soldiers, flushed with pride at being the gatekeepers for all who came and went from the mighty ship. I felt sad for them.

The one holding the card, a clear-faced young woman with

her hair pulled back into a short ponytail at the nape of her neck, frowned. "I'm sorry, Dr. Verris. It doesn't look like they have you on the list to go in tonight."

Yasi nodded and put on an impatient look. "They wouldn't, of course. You know how often they lose track of important missives. There's a last-minute test of the telemetry systems I need to do. It should only take a few minutes."

The young guardswoman nodded. "It's always hectic around here. We get about six different versions of our work schedule every week. By the end, no one really knows who's supposed to be where, and for how long. Let me just send a datagram and verify. It'll only take a few moments, I'm sure," the young woman said, giving a crooked smile that was meant to be endearing. It only made my next action more difficult. We couldn't afford any datagrams to go through. There were no orders pending for us. The deceptions we'd managed so far would part like cobwebs if anything touched them.

I fanned my hands slightly, and the poly-ceramic blades dropped from my sleeves. In a split second, they were embedded in flesh. The young woman died with a surprised look on her face and a knife puncture in her temple. The other guard's body tumbled to the floor, blood welling from a hole in his larynx that went straight through into the spinal column. There had been little noise. The video feeds from the cameras had been looped to three days earlier, when nothing of note had happened. We were almost there. We almost had our planet-killer.

Yasi's eyes had tears in them as we dragged the guards behind cover and stacked them like firewood. It was probably wise that at least a few of us had a grip on the meaning of a single life and could still be pained by sacrifice. The world isn't brought into the light by the work of monsters alone. I reached out a hand, but she turned away, working on the main amidships door. It opened in a few moments. She had been part of the build process from the beginning and had designed half the systems on the ship. Yasi had been able to design in overrides and backdoors into everything. She'd subtly guided the design to fit our secret specifications all along the way. Right from the beginning, the Megalans had been building this ship for the Pact. They just hadn't known it.

I straightened, tapping the surface communicator on my cheekbone.

"We're in, Gamlod. Tell the kid to get the others up and in. We've got maybe ten minutes."

"Got it. We're coming," the Spirit Coaxer's gruff voice said in my ear.

Twelve minutes later, the walls shook as the Force Twelve heavy gravity engines pushed to full power. We broke from the planet's gravity well and jumped to super-relativistic speed, becoming the greatest villains in the history of the planet Megla.

Phase Two: Calling the Soldiers Home

Location: Starship Kharkaros, in transit

42 Days, 9 hours, 22 Minutes to Zero Hour

The Megalans attempted pursuit, but we had their fastest ship. They were soon light years behind us, any trace of our passage beyond the grasp of their sensors. The ship was immense, and there were only a handful of us to run it. That first day, there was no rest for anyone. Though we were aboard a starship hurtling through the depths of space, there was an intense feeling of familiarity. It was a fortress, a tool of warfare at the highest level. Everything had a purpose. The walls were stark and unadorned, the quarters sparse. The impersonal pragmatism of war dictated every design and detail. It was just as I had imagined it to be. This was no great shock, as I had passed along specifications through Yasi from the beginning.

I stood at the helm, looking into the long night ahead. I was footsore and weary from seeing that supplies were where they should be, that the builders had respected the schematics we'd been studying, and simply from traversing the ship time after time, looking for material and people. I stretched my neck and sat down. The captain's chair was solid, unyielding. A good place from which to direct a battle. It was not to be my place, however. I am and always have been an infantry commander. My place is on the ground, with the dirt and smoke and screams of the dying.

"How does it look?" I asked Yasi, her back to me as she worked at one of the primary control consoles, machine language scrolling across the screen.

She turned to me. Her eyes were bloodshot, dark circles beneath them. "The cost cutting at the end changed things. The computer system isn't as distributed as I'd like, but I can make it work. My Pure Machine protocols should still work. It's just . . . harder."

"It doesn't have to be done today, Yasi. Work at a sustainable pace."

"I'm not the only one who's been up for days, Cruek."

I shrugged. "I'm not doing anything highly technical. You're the genius here. I'm only making sure we have our armaments in order. The kid, Carver, is helping with that. He and his little cadre have actually done a great job. All we need now is to have some soldiers to crew her up."

Yasi arose, stretching. She joined me, sitting on the arm of the captain's chair. We both watched the million pinholes of light gradually move as we hurtled through space at a speed that, no matter how they explain it to me, would always seem like magic. I swallowed as she put a hand on my shoulder. She wasn't one to reach for physical contact. Not in this iteration.

"I can't believe we got this far," she said, her voice low. I didn't look up at her. I didn't dare.

"You did most of it."

"Why do you always do that? Act as if whatever you've done is meaningless?"

"I. . . . " I shrugged. "It's just my job. My talents are limited. I find the necessary resources and bring them together."

Her hand squeezed my shoulder. "That's so stupid."

I had to look then, see the expression on her face as she stared ahead, the one I didn't have words for. In that moment, I was sorry for everything, sorry for asking the impossible of her so many times. If there had been anyone else I could have trusted to do what needed to be done, I would have found a way to save her, to leave her to her life on Megala, just this once. But we'd both sworn the Pact. It required all that you were, all that you would ever be.

Yasi looked away from the void and into my face. "I've seen how Gamlod and the rest look at you. I can feel it, too. You are the man who leads us. If we win, it's because you were there. If we go beyond every limit we think we have, it's because you gave us hope. Maybe that's not highly technical, but no one else could do it."

I looked up at her, recognizing the woman I had loved for thousands of years beneath the shield of her new face. She took her hand away, going back to the computer console when it was clear that I had no reply. Her assistant, Kira, returned from a short rest, still looking exhausted. Whatever the moment had threatened, it was gone now. I sat looking at her back for a moment, then left the helm. Far down the metal-walled corridor, I sagged to the side, on the point of rushing back, of telling her everything.

No. The plan came first. Nothing I wanted for myself was of any import. I straightened my tired frame and went to the nearest lift. It was time to see how Gamlod was coming with our crew.

The metal cylinders stretched out to the edge of the cavernous room. Inside each one, there was a soldier. They were frozen colder than any icicle, essentially dead until the thawing process woke them up. They were the best fighters Megala had been able to create, every one more built than born, their genetic codes manipulated to enhance every combat advantage and mask every weakness. They knew nothing but duty, nothing but what the Megalan military had taught them. I'd interacted with them a few times. They were no more than machines in human flesh to me. Tools. That viewpoint helped me make peace with my plan for them.

"How many?" I asked.

Carver stood nearby, a skinny eighteen-year-old kid with bony hands he'd never grown into. "Around fifteen hundred, General. I don't know how in hell you'll use 'em, though. They're trained. Deep down. A pair of them could take everyone we have on board. You've seen the bastards."

Gamlod came in at that time. "Good. You're here. I want to see if this works."

Somehow, Gamlod always seemed to look like himself, within the framework of the culture we were born into. Big, a little ugly, with a dangerous edge to him that might frighten children. Spirit Coaxers likely didn't have to leave their reincarnation to chance. I nodded to him, and he went to one of the cryogenic freezing tubes. We stood there, looking through the view glass. All of the super soldiers looked somewhat similar. They were like a fifteen-year-old's dream of what he wished he would look like, or what his ideal of a warrior woman might. No trace of bad habits or damage touched them. No hint of privation or excess. They'd never been allowed any of that. They were all fine swords that had never been drawn from their sheaths. That would soon change.

"All right. Try it." I stood back and pulled Carver back with me. The kid had no fear. He was always going chin-first into everything. Gamlod set up his equipment, lit a candle. The smoke alarm immediately went off.

"What the fek is going on down there?" Kira asked over the

intercom.

"Spirit coaxer ritual. You'll want to turn off the alarms and sensors in this hold." I told her.

"I'll set them to lowest sensitivity, General, but I'm not turning them off."

Carver heard this and raised his eyebrow at me. I just shrugged. She was in charge of ship safety operations, and she really only answered to Yasi. "Very well. Make the change and watch the sensors. Maybe turn up the ventilation in this area."

"Will do. Kira out."

Gamlod's ritual finished with him putting a white stone atop the cryo tube and striking a long piece of iron against the floor, setting up a lingering, slightly uncomfortable vibration in the air. As the vibration died away, the white stone flashed with light. I put my hand over my eyes, seeing a bright afterimage even with the lids closed.

"That should do it," Gamlod grunted. He peered at the touchpad on the side of the cryo tube for half a minute, frowning. "I don't know how to work this damn thing."

"I can do it," Carver offered, moving forward. "What just happened to the frozen guy?"

Gamlod looked at me and I nodded. If we couldn't trust the kid, we couldn't trust anyone.

"These soldiers . . . they were engineered, not born of a woman. They're created in a laboratory. From there, they're kept inside a rigid box their whole life, never given all the choices that make us who we are, teach us what we should be. As strong as they are, their souls are as weak as an echo coming back from a canyon. I just coaxed one of the great champions of the Pact into this body. At least, that's what I've aimed to do. We'll soon find out."

"What happens to the soul that was already in there?" Carver asked.

"Even I don't know that, kid. It probably went back into the light, if that's where it came from." Gamlod tried to hide it, but I could tell that he had his share of qualms about what he was doing.

"And if it was destroyed?" Carver's brow furrowed.

"Then it was destroyed. All our deeds will be measured at the end of this," I said. "Now wake him up."

Carver punched a few buttons, then uncovered a shielded switch and flipped it. The tube began making a whirring sound. A minute later, the top section popped and tilted upward. The man inside was already alert and moving. He sat up and hung his feet over the side, touching his face. He looked at us and then around the cryogenic hold at the hundreds of other tubes, still dark and silent.

"Well. I'm alive again. That can't be good." He hopped up out of the tube and stood, moving his body around. "I think I've been working out."

"Welcome aboard the starship Kharkaros. I'm General Cruek Ostor."

"Starship?" he asked. "Yeah, I guess so. Lazarus Tombs. I burn up demons." He watched for our reaction. "I'm guessing you knew that."

"It's good to have a Phoenix aboard, yes. Carver here will explain what's going on while we begin waking the others."

Tombs. I'd heard that name before. We'd never fought together, but they said he'd been instrumental in one of our greatest victories over the Kasu-Hurun. I hoped he had one great battle left in him. He went placidly enough with the kid, still patting himself down to get used to his new body. The door closed and it was just Gamlod and I alone.

"It worked," the Spirit Coaxer grunted. "We'd have been fucked if it hadn't."

"How long do you think it'll take to get them all up and ready?"

Gamlod leaned on the next tube and looked down the long aisles with a fatalistic expression. "Weeks. Even if I pull the other coaxers early, it'll take weeks."

"We'll give you all the help we can."

"There's just one thing. Something important that neither of us thought of at first."

"What?" I didn't like the look of worry on the Spirit Coaxer's face.

"A few of us turned traitor. They sealed the Pact and broke the vow. This might pull them, too."

"Bandarin?" I hadn't said the name for many years. You don't forget the first man who kills you, though.

"He'd be chief among our possible problems."

Phase Three: Strengths and Weaknesses

Starship Kharkaros: In Transit

40 days, 3 hours, 19 minutes to Zero Hour

I looked down the long row of similar faces. Some of the names I knew, others I'd heard of. A few were new to me. The conference table was filled with all the pulls that Gamlod thought of as "senior staff." I trusted his choices. Little groups had already begun to form, old comrades finding each other behind different faces at the far end of the universe. Some were silent, held in, watching. Others chattered and slapped shoulders and told jokes. All of them had seen battles few could imagine. They were the best warriors from all the possible realities, and we had contrived to get them around the same table.

"All right. Quiet down." I used my command voice. My current body wasn't even half as strong as their new ones, being altogether average, but you don't lead as many campaigns as I have without being able to rally troops.

The group fell quiet, eyes turned to me. "You may have heard a few things thus far. Maybe you're still waiting to find out why you're alive again. Here's the long and short of it. We have the opportunity to win the war."

I let the words ring out. There was a lot of looking around, many surprised expressions. I waited until things had quieted down again.

"That's right. We have a way to fulfill the promise we all swore. Permanently this time. That's why you've all been called back to service again. I know that you've all been through this before and know the hell of fighting the Kasu-Hurun in its many guises. You've all paid more than anyone should have to in blood and hurt. This will be the last time. Win or lose, everyone here is on his or her last ride."

There was a moment when I didn't know how they'd react. You have to trust your troops and hope. I was not disappointed. One of them stood slowly, his arms pressing down on the chair hard enough to bend the lag bolts where it was affixed to the deck plating. "Whom among us have not waited a lifetime to hear those words," he said as he glanced to faces around the room. "Or a dozen lifetimes. I told a Duke of Hell that we would correct our error and I mean to carry out that oath." He stood tall, resolute. "I am with you, General. Let's end this once and for all, whatever the price."

"In case you haven't met him, this is Jacob Kotsedi, the Paladin who banished the Nightblade," I told them. More than a few eyes widened at this, and there were many respectful nods in his direction. He gave a half bow to everyone and sat back down in his bent chair.

"I'm up for one more go around," Tombs said. "What else is there to do on this ship, anyway?"

"Fuckin' A!" someone else shouted. That broke the dam, and

soon many of them were on their feet, their fists in the air and their eyes alight. In the end, I didn't need to light the fires within them. I just needed to point them in a direction. Seeing them all, I found myself awestruck. The sorrow over what I'd be asking them to do turned like a shard of broken steel inside me.

At that very moment, a heavy object slammed hard against the bulkhead door, and I knew something was wrong. Seconds later, my ears started to pop, and the palpable sense of air being sucked out of the room became clear. I took a big breath and held it, consciously slowing my heartbeat. The pressure grew lower and lower, most of the air leaving the large room over the space of thirty seconds. Those closest went to the door, pounding on it, forcing the access panel open and poking at the control matrix beneath. Nothing seemed to work.

The engineered soldier bodies, with all their muscle mass and accelerated metabolisms, quickly succumbed to the oxygen debt. The floor was littered with their still forms in a moment. I kept my concentration fixed, not allowing myself to panic or succumb to rage. It had come sooner than I expected, the betrayal and sabotage. A reckless stroke, perhaps, but masterful. I looked at the talent, the awful potency of the fighters who struggled against a foe they couldn't hope to beat. At the door, I produced a knife and stabbed it through the matrix of wires. A wicked jolt of electricity went through my arm, causing what little air I had in my lungs to escape. The knife clattered against the wall, my hand gone nerveless with the shock. I found myself on the floor, looking up at the mute face of the bulkhead door, doomed to die and fail, the identity of my betrayer unknown. The chance for victory had been within my grasp, and now it slipped free.

My vision darkened. I struggled, but couldn't rise. Something . . . weapons-fire behind the door. Three reports of a constrained plasma pistol. Something heavy moved outside the door and it sprung open. A female soldier with long, curly hair stood there, pistol at her side. Air rushed back into the room, and a few good breaths allowed me to sit up. The others began to stir behind me.

"Am I late?" the soldier asked. Her mouth formed a crooked little smile. She reached down and helped me to my feet. Her name badge read "Walkabout."

The plasma pistol had taken the traitor's head off. With the manifest similarity of the engineered bodies, it was impossible to tell who it had been. We stood over him, peering down into the cauterized mess of his ruined face nonetheless.

One of the soldiers, Kellerman, knelt next to the body, checking it over. "This one is human. Human soul, sworn to the Pact."

I nodded. "We can all be frail. Some ran from their oath, some broke it outright. This has happened from the very beginning. A few souls we call are bound to be bad ones. I was afraid of this."

We stepped back into the room, everyone bouncing back from the brush with death. "Carver, figure out what's been done with the life support for this room," I called, then saw that he was otherwise occupied.

The girl who had saved us was kissing the kid so hard that I thought he'd break in half. He looked to be cooperating. I let them go for a few beats, then gave a loud whistle that broke them up.

Carver, to his credit, didn't look ashamed in the least. "Sorry, General."

"Check the life support, then tell Gamlod and Yasi what happened. Everyone's to keep in teams of four from now on. No one alone." Carver nodded. Walkabout picked two more and went with him, stooping to throw the corpse over her shoulder on the way out.

I could feel their eyes on me. "Okay. Do what you have to do within the crew quarters, but we buddy up. I don't want you paranoid, but we need to look out after each other."

The celebratory atmosphere was gone. They had been reminded what it was we did. "Everybody okay?"

They answered in the affirmative. I met their eyes. Maybe this was just what we needed. Better to get kicked hard early than allow yourself to get too comfortable.

"Get yourselves situated and report back to the helm. You'll be given assignments that best fit your skills. There's plenty of work to do."

They turned to go.

"One more thing," I said. "It's an honor to have you all here."

Phase Four: Plans and Problems

Starship Kharkaros, In Transit

30 days, 4 hours, 57 minutes to Zero Hour

Yasi looked uncomfortable in front of the group of senior warriors. Kira and a woman named Feni stood to the side, watching her take the heat. This part had to be Yasi's show. I understood it in rough terms, but it was far too technical for me to explain credibly. You had to have lots of advanced degrees to get the whole picture. You also had to be a Blessed Woman. That meant it was her show alone.

She touched her forehead and gave a nervous little laugh. "So. Here we are. I'll jump right into it. Save your questions for the end, or I'll get sidetracked."

Yasi looked at me. I nodded. "You can do it," I mouthed in silence.

"When the events of the Day of Burning happened, the demons opened a portal that allowed them to escape a universe that had been mostly used up. A dying universe. Of course, we didn't know that at the time. We were primitive, our science unable to grasp half as much as our magic could hint at. We thought of their great trick as a singular instance, a rift that closed as soon as it had been opened."

She took a long breath and came around the podium, sitting down at the edge of the little platform at the front of the room. She wasn't used to projecting her voice, to speaking to a large group. Her voice had roughened at the edge by then. It was more human, more poignant. The crowd inclined forward in their hard chairs, straining to hear the words. "That simply wasn't true. The gate, once opened, allowed them to keep coming through."

There was a rustling in the audience. More than a few soldiers released their favorite invective. Yasi waited until that was over, looking so small and fragile there before all the super soldiers we'd stolen from Megala and all the spirits we'd stolen from the great beyond.

"They were careful at first. One would slip through here and there, while no one was watching. Later, as the wasteland fell into disuse and what was left of the Pact had either taken the long journey or disbanded on the planet, they were free to send their troops through *en masse*. Worse, the ancient and unspeakable forces that controlled them were able to reach across, through the open portal, and direct their movements."

The group stared, many of them shocked by this information. We had all been there. It had taken so many lifetimes to piece it all together. The Kasu-Hurun were so good at the game. Few, even in their own high echelons, knew the whole scope of the plan.

"Before you ask it, yes. There are greater, darker things that loom like gods, even above the worst of the demons we've encountered. They couldn't come through, simply because the portal wasn't large enough to allow them passage."

"A whole damn army went through in the space of an instant," someone called.

Yasi nodded. "These dark entities are like nothing any of you could imagine. Maybe they couldn't even enter another universe.

Some of us think they created demons as tools to explore worlds and realms beyond their reach. In the end, it doesn't matter. They exist."

General consternation washed over the crowd. Some of the soldiers were reluctant to believe that the worst of the demons they had fought were minions of something greater. A man in the front row just smiled. He had the flat, hard eyes of a killer. I was tempted to think I'd seen his kind before, but I don't know if I had.

"Shut up," he said quietly. Everyone did. "I've seen one of these bastards. They're real. They blow up, just like anything else. You just need a bigger weapon." He folded his thick arms against his chest and nodded to Yasi to continue. No one seemed inclined to argue. He said his name was Franks. When Gamlod had asked him a few questions, he'd simply said, "I'm here to finish a fight I started a long time ago."

It seemed like that was what we were all there to do, so we let it be. He kept to himself and didn't start any trouble.

"Back to the topic at hand," Yasi continued. "We managed to find a ship that would allow us to travel to the point of convergence between universes, and I have a method that should allow us to cross over. Once there, we'll have to secure the Rusted Vale and set up our defenses. With a machine I've made, we can reverse the flow of the portal. All the demons will be wrenched from the countless worlds and realms where they dwell. We set up the anvil and swing the hammer, killing them in one great stroke. Details aside, that's the plan."

"If we pull them back and then just blow up the planet, why do you need so many soldiers and all this hardware?" Jake K. asked.

I stepped up to the podium. "That's the complication. It's not immediate. There are vast numbers of demons, numbering in the millions. They come from distances farther than most normal soldiers, myself included, can fathom. It'll take days for them to all come through. We're there to protect the equipment and keep a lid on things until all the demons are through. At that point, then we can bring the full force of our armaments against them."

Lazarus Tombs shook his head and put a palm against his face. "This shit again," he whispered.

"Questions?"

Tombs's friend, Diego Santos, raised his hand. "So . . . we're going to be killing the crap out of demons with high tech weapons?"

"Yes."

"Better than an M-4 and my fists. Fuckin' sweet. I'm in."

"Overlapping fields of fire here and here?" Santos asked, looking up from the rough mockup of the battlefield.

My memory of it was a little hazy after so many lifetimes, but it was place to start.

"I want four banks of heavy pulsed laser cannons per side, if the terrain will take it," I said. "Our initial countermeasures should take care of the weak ones, so we'll be looking at groups of powerful, armored demons, mostly. The pulsed lasers should take care of most of them, and we'll have aircraft doing over-watch. The air support will be dropping fragmentary and incendiary bombs from above. It's the worst barrage we can manage without compromising our own fortifications."

"Fire always seems to work," Santos said. He sat down, comfortable in his big body the way only a few of them were as yet.

I shook my head. "You can't count on that. Not when we're pulling them all. We'll have to be ready for anything. Immunities, magical powers, flight. I've been working on the strategy for nearly a decade, just for this battle. I have the whole thing on your datapaq units. You just touch the screen and keep hitting next to turn the pages. Read it and come back to me tomorrow, this same time, with any thoughts, issues, problems, additions. Be ready to share the details on whatever types of demons you've encountered. We want to make sure that we have some special surprises for any of the known types. Dismissed."

Santos and the rest filed out, lingering outside in the passageway, talking about various parts of the battle strategy for the most part. I could hear that devolve into other concerns as they dispersed. Gamlod stayed, his face ashen with fatigue. There were still hundreds of soldiers to summon, and he was working at it in fourteen-hour shifts with Kellerman, the only other Spirit-Caster that had come through. Gamlod turned his bloodshot eyes to me, still shrewd.

"Now that you've put the plan out to the troops, we'll have to expect a turncoat to go after the device. That, or they'll try for Yasi."

"That's likely. With the device, I've done all I could do to make it secure. Yasi is never alone, and I have Kira, Walkabout, and Feni watching out for her at all times. She's harder to get to than almost any of us. With the way she's parsed out access to the critical systems of the ship, a saboteur wouldn't have an easy time even getting to the helm."

"Some of our best . . . fell. You know that. I wouldn't underestimate them."

I sat down. My body, all too fallible, was a little beyond its modest prime. I had done all that I could do, but watching the effortless potency of the engineered Megalan soldiers made me feel its shortcomings. "You don't think that it was Bandarin at the meeting."

Gamlod frowned. "Not personal enough for him. Too soon. I could be wrong. It was a bold move, and nearly worked. You knew him, though."

"Better than anyone. I thought."

"When Bandarin aimed to kill someone, they died."

I sighed. It was true.

"Those were thoughts you'd already considered. Here is something else. You are a fool."

I looked up. Gamlod was not mine to command. He came willingly, his words and deeds those of his choosing. I sometimes forgot that. Despite the fiery wisp of anger that tingled in my heart, I waited for him to continue his thought.

"I understood that you wanted to give Yasi a respite from the memories of the past, to allow her to live outside the shroud of what had gone before, but now, so close to the end, you must tell her. Tell her everything."

My shoulders sagged. "Now?"

Gamlod flared his nostrils. "If not now, when? We'll all be dead soon enough. Remind her of the great love you've shared. Her soul wants to remember."

"How could I ask her to do what she'll have to do, once I've told her? It's not fair. No, let her be free of that burden this time. There's no place for selfish concern here."

"Love is the most powerful force of all, and you would keep it from her? Come now, Cruek. You know this. You've known it all along. Go to her. Help her remember the love that has kept you fighting when everything else has fallen to pieces."

I stood, the fatigue pushed away. Gamlod was right. I had been a fool. It was nearly too late, but I could still correct my mistake.

I stood before the door to my quarters. My whole body buzzed with anticipation. I was alive in a way I had never dared to be. Not in that iteration, that lifetime. Things were far enough along, the inertia of the cause strong enough, that I could dare to tell the truth. If everything went wrong, if she couldn't care, I would only have to regret it for a few weeks. I sighed, my palms slick with nervous sweat.

"Just tell her. What's the worst that could happen?" A dangerous question, a stupid one to ask, even when talking only to one's self. I pushed it away. I'd go and clean up, get a few hours of rest, and then I'd find a way to tell Yasi about all that had come before. I waved my right hand next to the sensor and the door came open.

The moment I stepped through, I knew something wasn't right. My hand started going for my cheek-mounted communicator, but a hard chop from behind and to the side stopped me. A hand locked on my wrist, pinioning the limb, then lifting me bodily from the deck. The attacker stripped my pistol from me and threw it away. A second later, I hurtled across the room in the other direction.

I slammed against the writing table. Sudden pain, then numbness flashed across my face. The noise of an electronic device coming on filled the room. On my knees, feeling blood touch my cheek, then my neck, I tried to key my communicator again. Nothing. That sound must have been a signal jamming device.

Dizzy, I rose and turned as quickly as I could. My combat stance wavered, my vision pulsing, my balance poor. One of the Megalan soldiers put his back against the door and watched me, all gestures unhurried and casual. Beneath the new body, I recognized the movements, the expression.

"Bandarin," I said.

"Cruek, my friend. Here we are again." With his spirit inhabiting the engineered body, it seemed to shine brighter than the rest. No act of a demon had ever frightened me more than Bandarin's ability to fight at my side for years, always a traitor, always a loved and trusted friend. His betrayal had been, to me, the ultimate expression of the Kasu-Hurun's power. It was not what they did themselves, but the evil they brought out in others that cut deepest, burned longest.

"I understand why you'd want to kill me again, but this time, your target is a poor one. I'm not important here. I've put things into motion that will continue without my help. Killing me will mean nothing . . . assuming you can." I shook my head. One eye was swelling shut, and I suspected that something in my face was broken.

Bandarin pushed off the wall, standing erect and in all his power. "Cruek, let's be honest with each other. I'm only killing you because I want to. It's fun. The important parts of the mission are in play right now, and when I'm done, this ship will be a stalled hulk belching air into the void." Illustrating his point, Bandarin fished a transponder out of his pocket and pushed a button. An explosion rocked the ship and alarms began at every quadrant.

My heart was shaken, but in the moment when he took his eye off of me, I dropped my two knives into my palms and went at him. He was quick, but I cut him deep at the left elbow, enough to make the arm hang, useless and gushing blood.

Bandarin swung a backfist, hitting me so hard I could feel my neck nearly snap with the strain. I tumbled to the floor, head spinning. He landed a kick to my midsection that lifted me from the deck plating and smashed me against the wall. I lay there, unable to take a breath. He took the time to rip his left shirt sleeve off and wind it around his injured arm.

"Nicely done, Cruek. You know that it's just a point of pride for you, right? You could never beat me, even when we both had normal bodies. I was always the better fighter. With this marvelous shell? You never had a prayer."

My breath hitched in my lungs. "Battles are won . . . by the strongest. Wars . . . by the most enduring."

Bandarin kicked again, taking away what little breath I'd regained. "You've really done well this time, Cruek. A hell of a plan. You've come a long way, but this is as far as you go. In the end, the darkness always wins."

He reached down, catching my wrist and squeezing until my hand released the one knife I'd retained during the beating. He picked it up, admiring the blade. "I'll keep this one."

With a lightning movement, he slammed it home, punching through my chest to the hilt. It was a little high, but close enough to the heart that it would only be a few moments. I considered the pain, the impending death I'd encountered so many times before. Death and I had grown accustomed to one another, frequent partners. I had hoped for a lot, grasped for the great victory that had eluded me so long. I could feel it slipping away. There wouldn't be another lifetime for me. All my chances had been spent and come up short. There was no wrath, only exhaustion and sadness.

Bandarin cleaned the knife off on my pant leg. A pool of blood was spreading out all around me, and I could feel my heart race, speeding the end. Color drained out of everything. He sighed. "That was over too fast."

The door opened just as he was turning to leave.

"No!" I heard. Carver's voice. Bandarin went for the pistol on the floor, but wasn't fast enough. The sound of a plasma gun going off and the sight of Bandarin's body coming apart was the last thing I saw.

Resurgence

Starship Kharkaros, in transit

23 Days, 11 hours, 4 Minutes to Zero Hour

Metal. I saw metal above me, then faces. Carver, Tombs, and Kellerman, the Spirit Coaxer who'd brought me back. I assumed Gamlod was dead.

I sat up out of the cryo tube, looking at my new hands, my new legs. "Status report, Carver," I said. Speaking in a voice you've never heard can be disconcerting. I pushed it away.

"General?" The kid's eyes lit up. He came forward like he was going to embrace me, but then produced his hand. I shook it, careful not to use too much force. My new wrists were thick like a stone mason's, hands the size of mallet heads.

"I'm back. How's my ship?"

Tombs took over, as Carver was too shocked to convey anything of import. "The explosion killed two and injured seven. The placement of the bomb put it in a spot where everything was double and triple thickness. Ship damage was negligible. Yasi said the device the traitors exploded was a decoy. So we're okay. A little surprised to be talking to you, but okay."

"I'm surprised to be alive again myself, to be honest. I guess they're not done with me yet."

"They?" Tombs asked.

"The architects of all this. One god or many. Whoever or whatever keeps us in this fight. I don't know what it is, and I don't need to. It's enough to know that something exists out there that wants us to succeed, to put things right and destroy the demons once and for all."

Tombs nodded. "God's got his thumb on the scale. At least that's what I came to believe in my time. It's up to us to get things done, but we're not alone."

"The two dead, was one Gamlod?" I asked, my eyes drifting to Kellerman.

"He's alive," Kellerman said, his brow furrowed.

"Injured?" I asked.

"No, Sir," Kellerman said, "but I've been taking his shifts. Seeing you dead was hard on him. On all of us."

I stood up. They needed me to lead, and my new body was strong. It'd never known a wound. I was alive again. There would be a moment when I'd have to come to grips with what that meant, but I needed to get back to work now, needed to make up for lost time.

"Why does everyone have tattoos on their faces?" I asked.

"Security. When we realized that there might be other traitors, and we look . . . a little generic, we decided this was the best way. The tattoos are harder to fake, and having the name right on our cheek cuts down on useless small talk," Carver said, somewhat over the shock of my reincarnation. He had his nickname and a pair of crocodile jaws on his cheek.

"No one looks like you, kid."

He shrugged. "Everyone did it. I wasn't going to be the one to say no. Anyway, it was kind of fun."

I turned to Tombs. "Send a datagram to all the command staff and tell them I'm back. Carver, you're with me."

Gamlod could wait. I had to see Yasi. I didn't know what I was going to do when I got to her, but I had to go.

I stood outside Yasi's quarters, looking at the door. "You didn't say that she was resting."

Carver shrugged. "It seemed important, General. I'm sure she'll be glad you're back."

I had a moment to wonder, to imagine what would have been. I never gave her the opportunity to act on all that had gone before. I'd kept it from her, chosen for her. Now, wearing a different suit of flesh, I appeared, back from death. . . .

I pressed the alert buzzer and waited. Almost a minute went by, and she appeared, draped in night clothes, rubbing at one of her eyes. "Carver, why are you bringing someone to my door right now? I'm trying to get some rest."

She looked to me. "Well? Who are you and what do you need?"

"It's Cruek." I opened my mouth to say more, but no other words came out.

Yasi's eyes snapped wide. "Did you say what I think you said?"

I dipped my chin. "I came back."

She sagged against the doorway. Her body was thin, small, its features just short of being severe when she pulled her hair back. The bare shoulder where her night dress pulled to the side was the most I'd ever seen of her. Yasi blinked, breathing hard. "That's just. . . . " She came out of the doorway and threw her arms around me. I stood, pulling her against me, holding her tight. Everything felt right. I kicked myself for having been such a fool for so long.

"I can't believe you're back," she whispered. "I didn't think I could do this alone."

"You don't have to."

From out of the darkness of her quarters, a man's figure approached. "What's going on?" he asked, scratching at his head, now shaved close. It was Santos. He was shirtless and barefoot, the muscle of his engineered body straining under his skin. An eagle, globe, and anchor had been tattooed on his cheek.

Yasi jumped down from my arms and went to him. "Cruek's back. He's been reborn into one of the soldier bodies," she told him. I stood there, mute. As Santos pulled Yasi beneath one arm, as her hand rested on his hip and she leaned her head against him, it hurt far worse than a blade going through my ribs and tearing into my heart.

Santos' face broke into a genuine smile. "Shit, that's great! The others'll want to hear about this." He slapped me on the shoulder. "It's good to have you back, General. We were feeling pretty lost there for a few days."

I made myself try to smile at him, though it was hard. "Don't let me keep you from getting some sleep. I'll find someone on duty and get back up to speed."

Yasi reached out for my hand. It surprised me. This iteration of her hadn't been one to make contact. She looked up at me, her eyes moist, her face earnest. "I missed you," she whispered.

I turned and walked away, my jaw tight. I had waited too long. I couldn't blame her. I couldn't blame Santos. It was the last ride, and you took your comfort where you could find it. There had been whole lifetimes apart from her, when chance had sent us on separate paths. None of those had filled me with such echoing loneliness as I felt then.

"You okay, General?" Carver asked.

"Sure. Sure."

"I only ask 'cause you're going the wrong way. You did want to go to the helm, right?"

"Yes, the helm. I'm still a little fuzzy, I guess. Lead the way." I knitted my hands together and followed Carver's thin shoulders down one corridor after another, not paying any attention to where I was going. As much as I reminded myself that it didn't matter what any individual wanted or needed, it was hard to ignore the raging bonfire in my chest.

"How do you know it's really Cruek?" Kira asked. She eyed me critically.

Carver looked to me for some help.

"It's okay, kid. It's a good question. Ask me something, Kira." I looked at her steadily. It was good to be busy, good to have something productive to think about.

"How did you meet Dr. Verris?"

Talisyn Verris was Yasi's birth name on Megala. Of course that would be the question. I couldn't get away from the source of my pain, it seemed. I took a breath, remembering that night, more than ten years before. "She almost hit me with her personal vehicle."

Kira relaxed, sighing. "Okay then. Here's what we've done."

I followed her. She explained how the Pure Machine protocols were implemented first. Along with distributing the computing load to several processing nodes through the ship and having layers of redundancy in terms of both wiring and task orientation, there was a complex set of firewalls in place. These took the form of both computer hardware and less typical components.

"I've wired one of these here Codex devices into the grid," Kira told me. "It assigns some package data to all information passing through it, then runs a checksum on anything that comes back. These things," she pointed to the little metal cube that had fiber optics coming to and from it in rope-sized bundles, "are more advanced tech than anything I've ever seen. They introduce almost no latency into the system—but Hezu knows how they work."

"Do you think you'd be able to adapt this same strategy for our ground systems? Is there another Codex?" I asked.

Kira thought about it. "If we establish a wireless canopy and set it up to send challenges to all our networked machines, maybe. I'll have to type it out first and get Raf and Yasi to help me with it, but I'll try."

I didn't know who Raf was, but it didn't seem important. "Anything else?"

"Here's our big failsafe. The chair."

She opened a door with a very long encoded password and pointed to a spot inside a small room where someone could sit, their head encased in a helmet with hundreds of wires coming out of it. I'd seen torture devices look more inviting. "What does it do?"

Kira opened her mouth and held up one finger. Her face quirked. She remembered I wouldn't understand what she was telling me if she gave me the technical details. "Boiled down to basics, it allows someone who has powers against the demons to channel them through the whole ship."

I watched Kira's face. "There's a downside, I assume."

"It's unproven. Probably lethal to whoever tries it, especially if the ship is damaged."

"Who'll be standing by to give it a try?"

She put her chin against her chest. "Feni is the one who could really make it work. Maybe a few others, but Feni is an antithesis to the demons."

"We do the jobs we're suited for."

Just then, Gamlod appeared. He was out of breath, sweat on his brow from running to the helm. He was older than the rest of us, and the strain was weighing heavier on him than anyone else. He leaned against the railing and took a long pull of air. His hard face softened. "I hoped, but I didn't think you'd return."

"I was in it at the beginning. I didn't want to miss the end," I told him. Sometimes the best statements don't have to be true, but only seem that way.

Kira walked away without saying anything to either of us. She'd never warmed to Gamlod. She was tough, but men who can talk to the dead can frighten anyone. We went into the small room with the chair and Gamlod leaned against the wall, his meaty arms behind him. It was strange for me to be taller than him. That had never happened. "So, you know? Yasi, I mean?"

I nodded. "I was dead. Santos is a good man."

"You probably wish I had never said what I did."

I shook my head. "No, you were right to say it. I was a fool. A fool for just a few days too long. Now it's too late, and maybe that makes it easier. It's just the mission now."

Gamlod reached and squeezed my shoulder. "The mission, and sorrow."

"We've seen those days before. Thousands of them, you and me. We can stand a few more."

The ship shuddered slightly, and a wave of prickly sensation as we dropped out of super relativistic speed went through me. I turned to look out ahead through the viewer. The accretion disk of the supermassive black hole filled the whole screen, light and matter being pulled toward the pitch black center.

Darkness always prevailed. That's what Bandarin had said. Perhaps that was true, but light always came out the other side.

Phase Five: Point of Insertion

Location: Starship Kharkaros, proximate to black hole designated B-13227

21 Days, 19 Hours, 11 Minutes to Zero Hour

Yasi stood at the master console and studied the readings from the black hole ahead of us. It had been a day and a half since we'd arrived, and the word had been passed that the time was drawing close. Much of the command staff was in the confines of the helm, sitting on whatever surface could be found. Several couples had developed, which was natural enough. Carver and Walkabout, Feni and Raf, Santos and Yasi.

Santos, eternally a professional soldier, was sitting against the wall in a corner, catching a few moments of rest while things were quiet. Carver leaned closer to Walkabout where she was seated at another console, saying something in her ear. She laughed and punched him in the thigh gently.

Yasi turned around, her eyes flashing. She gave a thumbs-up and a nervous little smile. "Soon," she mouthed. I came closer.

"See this?" She pointed at the console. There was a number that stayed static, then one that was fluctuating. They were fairly close to each other. Close, for numbers with twenty or more digits.

"Those need to match up?" I asked.

"When they do, that's our moment." She tapped a hand on her hip, looking away from the readout and to the view screen. I watched her in profile. She was happy, exhilarated. It was hard work being glad about that, pleased that she'd found someone to ease the loneliness in these last days. I did all I could do and got about halfway there.

I keyed the intercom. "Everyone strap in. Secure all cargo and stay put until further notice." I glared at everyone in the helm until they found a chair and belted up, leaving me the only one standing. Being General has some advantages.

An alarm went off on the console. The two numbers flashed, identical.

"Get ready for it!" Yasi shouted. Everyone grabbed onto something or sat down in one of the available chairs. I grasped the back of the chair hard. No one really knew if this was going to work, not even Yasi. Assuming it did, no one knew what it would feel like.

Something that wasn't a sound or a feeling but was nonetheless a sensation passed across my skin. I looked at the view screen. From the center of the dark eye of the singularity, a beam of pale light was shooting right toward us.

Yasi's hand descended as if moving through thick liquid. The beam of fire grew nearer until it filled the view screen with blinding light. Her index finger touched the console button, and the ship launched forward. I lost my grip on the seat and felt myself tumble backward over chairs, bodies, railings.

A booming roar filled the ship as we flew straight into the black hole.

The light flared, nullifying everything else. Beyond that, the light seemed to be inside us, or perhaps we were part of it. I don't know. It took a long time. It was instant. No words could make sense of it. It was happening, and suddenly we were through, and it was over. The world was again made of colors and solid objects. Only a tantalizing afterimage of the journey lingered, a humming in our tissues that slowly muted into silence and was gone. I found myself against the back wall of the helm, bruised, shirt sleeve torn, but otherwise unhurt. Everyone else looked a shocked and vaguely disoriented, but unharmed. The ship's alarms were silent.

Back on my feet, I went to the master console, squinting at it, then at the nondescript space on the viewer. I knew enough to call up a diagnostic and see that the ship's systems were fully functional. I pressed the ship-wide intercom. "All right, crew. We're through. The easy part is over. We'll be making our way to the Rusted Vale planet and establishing a beachhead. If you incurred any injuries, tap the nearest alert station and someone will come to help you. If you are injured but can walk, go to the cryo deck, where there are medical personnel standing by. Otherwise, make final preparations. We'll be at our destination soon. Cruek out."

The planet didn't look like much. Blue and brown and white. It had taken only a few hours at our maximum speed to arrive. Yasi launched dozens of satellites that established stationary orbits around the little world, covering every landmass and ocean with surveillance. Once they were online, there was enough work for the whole command staff. Every available viewer was lit with the footage the satellites sent back. After about an hour in the chairs, the consensus was clear.

"Looks like there's only token numbers on the whole world. Thousands here, thousands there," Tombs said after collecting the data from the others.

"Demons?"

He nodded. "From what we've seen. The planet's pretty played out."

"Good. Let's hit everything but the Vale with the two stage boomerang weapons," I told him.

The ship thrummed as the rockets launched and sped toward every populated area. Through the viewer, you could see them hit. White mushrooms rose and the blast wave pushed outward, faster than the speed of sound. When the hemisphere of carnage reached roughly a thousand miles, the second stage of the weapon engaged, forming a cyclone that pulled the debris and particulates in the air back inward at speeds faster than any hurricane. The end result would be a new mountain of melted and compacted debris where nothing living remained. It seemed strange that it was the human mind that had perfected this, the creation of wastelands, the destruction of planets. I tried not to consider how the struggle had darkened us, taken us further and further from whatever innocence we'd once possessed. Looking upon our weapons of annihilation at work, it was hard to suppress the wave of revulsion. The knowledge of evil was inside us.

From the viewpoint of a deity, we watched as everything on the surface of the planet was torn asunder and turned to ash and chalk. The weapons the Megalans had built were mighty, beyond anything I'd ever seen. The potency of their destruction was only the first stroke. The most important work would be enacted by human hands, up close and at ground level. It was time to revisit the place of our greatest failure. We had a chance to redeem the Pact and rest at last, but we'd have to suffer the full attentions of the hellish horde first.

Phase Six: Beachhead

Location: Rusted Vale Planet

20 Days, 3 Hours, 44 Minutes to Zero Hour

Home. After all the lifetimes of blood and anguish, I was back to where it had all began. We touched down in the troop transport just as the whole Vale burst with incendiary bombs. Franks and a few others had been born into soldiers who were trained on the bombers, and they were trusting to the crew ship's shielding, dropping their payloads where they would scour the maximum number of demons from the field.

Our ship shuddered. Alarms sounded, but Kira, who was piloting the transport, muted them. "Thirty seconds until there's enough oxygen to open the doors, Cruek," she said over the comms.

I keyed the mic in my assault armor. "You heard her. Get ready. Re-breather masks on." We didn't have enough of the powered suits to go around. There were only sixty of them, so the rest of the crew had to make do with carbon ceramic body armor and plasma rifles. We were deploying twenty of the suits for this action, holding the rest in reserve.

The doors opened onto a hellish scene. Smoke obscured anything beyond twenty or so yards, and there were still active chemical fires raging, burning the earth into sludge. A demon had been blown in half and each part was trying to drag itself away from the blast site. It looked like a centipede crossed with a crocodile.

"Vanguard forward!" The servo-powered exoskeleton suit created so much thrust you didn't so much run as leap forward in twenty-yard bursts. I was airborne, blowing apart the two halves of the demon, landing on the next one and smashing its head with my clawed boot. We hit them hard, scything forward through their depleted lines. The demons that hadn't been killed or maimed by the incendiary bombs soon had their first taste of plasma discharge weapons. The plasma proved to be effective in most cases. When they shrugged off the plasma, the rifles had bayonets fixed to deal with the problem.

We were soon far outpacing the standard infantry. The vanguard hit and smashed through line after line of demonic warriors, in the air as much as we were on the ground. They hadn't seen technology and weren't ready for it. The shock would wear off soon enough, and their tactics would change.

At the back of the valley, there was a mighty edifice built of black stone. A monument built by demons, commemorating their great victory. A cathedral dedicated to hatred. That would be our ops center. The trick would be taking it without unacceptable casualties.

By this time, the vanguard was spread out across a quarter mile, killing demons with ruthless efficiency. The normal ground troops were advancing at a slower pace, taking care of any stragglers and reconnoitering the Vale. So far, the plan was working.

"Vanguard, on me," I said into the channel we'd agreed upon for attack suit comms. I stopped about a hundred yards in front of the black cathedral and waited for them to join me. It took about three minutes for them to conclude their battles and get to my position. I had my best soldiers in the suits. I found myself shoulder to shoulder with Jake K., Santos, and Walkabout. Their suits had been pristine twenty minutes before. They were now smeared with soot, blood, and remnants of demon tissue slowly turning to tar. "We go forward slowly from here," I told them.

We walked forward in a line of nineteen. One of the suits had been damaged and was out of action. The black cathedral filled my viewer now, towering hundreds of feet in height, as broad as a bulwark, filling the whole end of the Vale. Everything grotesque that could be rendered in stone was featured. The figures of massive demons were depicted in bas relief, each more horrific than the last. I had seen many of them in the flesh and killed at least a few. Scenes of torment and depravity decorated the walls, rendered in red against the darkness of the basalt backdrop. I looked away and studied the terrain. There would be something... something unexpected here before their monument. I had been fighting them too long to imagine that, even here in their unreachable sanctum, there wouldn't be layer upon layer of defenses.

"The ground up there is wrong," Jake K. said. He pointed forward. Even with the blowing smoke and dust, I could see a slightly different hue to the ground ahead, just the slightest hint of a trap.

"Halt," I called out, just as the ground sheered away and a crevasse formed at our feet. One of the vanguard fell into the gloom below. I saw something move down there.

Something huge.

Plasma cannons firing, the falling soldier screamed curses into the mic. There was a cry of pain, then nothing. The crevasse was dark.

"What the hell was that?" Santos asked.

We were answered in a moment when a serpent twenty feet across reared up, its head an awful cobra's face, its scales clanking like flame-scorched iron. Without being told, the vanguard opened fire and poured hundreds of plasma shells into the demon. They exploded on every surface of the giant snake, but wouldn't penetrate its armor. The serpent struck. Another soldier disappeared into its jaws, the metal of the suit sheered in half, leaving the lower legs and a welter of blood.

We continued to fire, some switching to the slow but potent pulsed lasers mounted on our shoulders. This was no more effective, the lasers bouncing off the creature's scales and flying in random directions until they hit a solid object or reached their diffraction points. The serpent struck again, and Walkabout leaped to the side just quickly enough to avoid being eaten. The serpent's third strike came straight for me, and I was not quite as quick. I avoided its maw of gleaming metal teeth, but it sent my suit tumbling across the blasted terrain. "Pull back. I repeat. Pull back," I ordered while I was still sliding across the dusty ground. I got to my feet, switching comms channels. "Bring forward the Purifier."

The hydraulic ram closed the breach on the cannon's ignition assembly. The Purifier's barrel was twenty-seven feet long, its shells sixteen inches across. I hoped it would be enough.

"Target acquired, General. It is coming closer. If it gets much nearer, we won't be able to loft high enough to make the arc," the artillery officer, Svetlana, said. Her targeting engineer, Katya, nodded her agreement.

"One shot only," Katya said. "No time to choose."

"Take the shot, ladies."

The concussion of the huge conventional shell launching was spectacular. The ground shook. Dust flew into the air, obscuring vision. My bones rattled inside my flesh. A two-thousand pound shell filled with explosives, salt, and iron made an audible roar as it flew. I leaped up on a boulder to see it make impact. The serpent was making strong progress toward our position, back in the central point of the Vale. Its cobra face looked up as it sensed the projectile coming its way. The demon had but one expression, that of hatred. The way its neck swayed at that moment, I like to think that it was scared.

Then the shell hit, and there was a blast that knocked us back a pace, even from our position of relative safety. Smoke and dust and chips of rock went skyward in a burst. The sound of thousands of sharp iron shards ricocheting buzzed through the Vale. We waited. How anything could survive that blast was beyond me, but never count a demon as dead until you know for sure. Several seconds went by. A tentative cheer went up from the troops, soon enough swallowed.

Out of the smoke, the serpent appeared again. It was brutalized and leaking blood of bright yellow that bubbled with acid that melted whatever it touched. The wings of its cobra head were in tatters, flapping like shredded sail cloth. Many of its scorched metal scales had been blown apart, but it was still slithering forward, its eyes glowing with greenish fire.

I looked to Katya and Svetlana. They shook their heads. "Too close, General. I'm sorry," Svetlana said. "We should have set up back where the troop transports landed."

I gritted my teeth. "That was my call, not yours. We'll have to do it another way." I turned to the other power-suited soldiers. "Vanguard, attack the serpent. Shoot for breaks in its armor."

We bounded forward again, fewer than we had been and less sure of ourselves. We surrounded the armored serpent and began to barrage it with plasma bursts. It lashed its tail and another soldier was gone. A strike with its broken-fanged maw killed another. The serpent shook the soldier in its jaws. A disembodied leg flew by me, a rain of blood coming down on my facemask. Jake K. and Santos established a pattern of crossing fire and hammered at its weakest spots. A scream that raised every hair on my body filled the Vale. The serpent exploded into tiny, noisome fragments, bursting powerful acid everywhere.

Both Jake K. and Santos were splashed with the acid, their powered armor suits beginning to melt around them. Walkabout was nearest to Jake and deployed her power saw, cutting the bindings in a deft stroke and kicking the suit open like a clam. She pulled Jake from the smoking wreckage of his suit and carried him to a safe distance.

I was nearest to Santos. For just a moment, a shadow fell across my heart, and it was difficult to move to his aid. This was the man who had gone to the place I had most cherished, shared something with Yasi that I had yearned for since I'd met her again a decade ago. If he preceded me into the arms of oblivion, was that so wrong?

It was. He'd simply been brave enough to reach out and hold Yasi, alone and afraid at the end of all things. I'd said he was a good man, and it had been the truth. If I hoped to be half as good, I'd have to go to his aid. He ripped his smoking helmet segment off and threw it aside, but the acid was eating through the suit. All the servos stopped working and he tipped back, falling flat on his back. I bounded over, grasped the open neck of the suit with both fists. I heaved, using all the muscle and servo strength I could summon. The suit popped at a weakened joint and came open. I grabbed Santos' arms and pulled him free, then took two bounds to get clear of the area, carrying him like a sack of grain. I set him down next to Jake K., who was shaken up but unhurt.

Santos was coughing, blood coming out of his mouth. Medical staff converged on him, putting him on a stretcher and carrying him back to one of the troop ships.

"What happened?" Walkabout asked. She'd doffed her helmet, as had I. The valley was filled with a hot, dry wind that scoured the skin and stung the eyes. It would only get worse from here.

"I think it was acid vapor. He must have inhaled some of it. He was closest to the beast." I'd seen men die coughing up their lungs in a dozen conflicts. We'd never had medicine as advanced as we did this time, but there were no guarantees.

Walkabout shook her head, kneeling next to Carver so he could touch her cheek. "That thing was a real motherfekker."

I looked at its remains, smoking and bubbling in toxic pools. "It won't be the last."

"Carver, get everyone back three hundred yards and call in a small incendiary bomb strike on the serpent's remains. That should denature the acid."

I turned to Jake K. "Are you fit?"

"By the will of the light, I am."

I nodded. "We'll get you another suit."

Walkabout put a hand out and stopped me as I started moving back with the rest of the crew. She was about as sure of herself as anyone I've known, but she hesitated, biting her lip. "General, I don't want you to think I'm crazy, but I . . . had a vision about that black cathedral. The demons in there aren't going to fall to our tech. No laser or plasma gun will take them down. It needs to be done the old way."

I gave her a critical look. "Who were you before?"

She sighed. "Walkabout wasn't my first war name. Before that, I was Delphi."

"Delphi?" Carver had told me about her. She could see the truth of things before they happened. "That was you?"

She nodded. "Back when he was Top Boy, and I was his woman."

He'd told that story when we'd first met two years ago. A few street kids who managed to kill a demon with no more than scavenged garbage and heart. Walkabout, like the girl she'd once been, was an oracle. I knew what we had to do.

It felt strange to kneel and hear the Pact Catechist recount the litanies after all this time. At the mouth of the black cathedral, the handful of us who would be going in were glad for anything we could get. Kellerman came around and hung some kind of holy amulets on our necks. Jake K. touched it, his eyes closed. He brought the holy object to his lips and kissed it, whispering a prayer of his own to go along with the catechism.

We straightened, now in field-gear of carbon ceramic armor, holding our weapons from lives long past. I had known that it might come to this, so I'd been making weapons for the last decade and manipulating cargo manifests to get them loaded aboard the ship. They had no complex parts or computer chips in them, so they were easy enough to hide.

Jake held a long single-edged sword and shield. Walkabout carried two long knives. I had my trusty double-bitted axe. Others had maces, long hammers, spears. It was like the old days.

"Hezu, I hope I'm not wrong," Walkabout whispered.

"I trust you. Somehow, it feels right. Demons play by their own rules, and they never make it easy." I shouldered my axe and stretched my neck. It was time to see what this body could do.

"You're in command in my absence," I told Tombs. "If we don't come out in, say, forty minutes, you know what to do."

Tombs nodded. "I'll burn it all down."

I keyed the comms unit on my cheek and changed it to the satellite uplink. "Yasi, you there?"

"Here, Cruek. I don't know about this. Swords and pointed sticks? We came here in a starship," she said. "Can't we think of a better way?"

"If we think long enough, maybe. We don't have that luxury. We need to secure the area. If I don't come out, you'll be dealing with Tombs. If he has to activate, it'll fall to Gamlod or Kellerman, though they'll hate that."

"They said that Santos was hurt." I could hear the concern in her voice.

"He's being tended to. Last info said that he had some acid damage to his lungs, but I think he'll recover. He should be okay."

"Good. Good. Listen, Cruek, I've been having some memories since we came through," she said.

My heart beat hard. "Like what?"

She hesitated. "When we worked together before, we were pretty close, huh?"

"I . . . yeah. We were."

"I don't remember anything more than some feelings, but, yeah. Why didn't you ever say?"

I shrugged, not that she could hear that from her orbital position. "I didn't want to make it harder, trying to recapture something you didn't remember. I thought that we'd build a rapport, whatever felt right to you this time around. I didn't want to force it."

She sighed. "Even old men aren't very smart about this stuff."

"This one isn't. I have to go."

"May the blessings of the good earth be upon you."

I hadn't heard her say that in too long.

Comms died the second we stepped inside the black cathedral. All of our plasma weapons and everything else electronic bricked within the first twenty feet. I pulled my pistol and tossed it away.

The power packs burst into flame and released a loud pop. Caustic smoke filled the vestibule. Everyone who had brought tech inside was having the same experience.

"Good vision, Walkabout," I said. "Everyone all right?"

Nods all around. We kept on, the interior growing darker and darker.

"Hold a minute," Jake K. said. We were each just darker splotches in the shadows at that point. I'd just been thinking about how a good old burning torch would be nice, since our flashlights had been destroyed by whatever field was being created inside the building. I saw Jake take a knee and begin to pray. I didn't recognize the words. He was probably talking to a different iteration of the light than I was familiar with. It started as a faint glow, no brighter than a reflected candle's light from afar, but grew until the whole vault of the interior entry hall was alight with silvery glow from his sword. He stood and held it aloft, the shadows pushed far back, beyond the caryatid columns figured with the profiles of demons of all description. Some were vile, some cruelly beautiful. We pulled our eyes from the profane artwork and kept on.

Beyond the echoing hallway, the great hall opened to the full height of the structure and broadened until the celestial light of Jake's sword could barely outline the sheer size of the room. It smelled like a thousand years of tallow mixed with old stone and dripping water and must. Below that, the sharp sulfur of demons.

Going in, I knew it could go any number of ways. If we'd come this far, it was because that's what the demons wanted. Without our technology, they were in a position to dictate terms. With only a single platoon of warriors, it was very possible that they had us hopelessly outnumbered. If that was the case, it'd fall to Tombs to root them out. It'd be too late to worry by then. Whatever would happen, it would happen in this room. I could feel it.

"Get ready, people," I said low. The Pact warriors went into their battle stances, weapons at the ready. Jake said another prayer, the glorious light flowing upward out of his blade and forming a bright star in the upper reaches of the great hall.

The guardians appeared then, shadowy figures emerging from the far wall. They came forward, eyes alight with chips of diamond fire, red cloaks covering spiked and baroque plate mail. A pair of demonic warriors flanked the central guardian and a line of many more arrayed themselves for battle. As one, they drew oversized swords as tall as they were. Each one smoked and burned, evil runes glowing from the cross guard to the point. "Welcome home, Cruek Ostor. We have been awaiting your arrival," the central guardian rasped, his voice like a file drawn across the blade of a dull axe.

"Then you know that you can't stop us this time. You'll be crushed before us, regardless of what you might do. This is not your day, demon. Your day has run its course," I shouted.

"As has yours, mortal. You must feel it. Your deal with the fates is broken, returning here to the beginning. Your Pact is shattered, your cause lost. Whatever happens today, all of you will be gone. The Kasu-Hurun will go on long after your planets are dust in the motes of blackened galaxies. All your works will be forgotten, meaningless."

"To fight hard and give all for the side of justice can never be rendered meaningless, demon," Jake said. He brandished his sword, clashing it against his shield. The sudden loud noise brought the fight to a head. Shouting, all of us rushed forward. The guardians of the black cathedral moved as one, flourishing their huge blades and swinging them in a horizontal arc.

A surge of power came toward us like an invisible wave on a rocky shoreline. It caught us, breaking our charge, throwing us backward, knocking many of us to the ground. The energy didn't touch Jake, Walkabout, and a few others who had some kind of holy power around them. I'm sure it would have been worse for everyone had we not been blessed by Kellerman's amulets and the catechist's prayers.

The wave rolled over me, sending me tumbling head over feet across the floor as the fight got away from me. By the time I arose, the whole group of demons surrounded Jake and the few holy warriors we had. Jake's sword was everywhere, turning aside one strike after another, throwing the demons backward with a counterstrike when he could. Walkabout stabbed one of her long knives through a demon's eye aperture, and the armor clattered to the ground, empty and inert. A redheaded Pact member took one of their blades through the pelvis and went down hard. Jake called upon holy power and grew ever stronger, ever faster, fighting like a dozen men, holding them at bay.

The rest of us rushed forward. Jake ducked a powerful strike and sheered a foot off of one of the demons, sending it to the deck. I arrived, swinging low and crashing through the back of its armor with my axe. It fell to pieces, nothing within the armor.

The frantic melee made it hard to do anything but stay alive. There were no tactics other than giving better than you got. A glancing blow shattered my chest armor and sent me flying back. One of the rune-laced demon blades fell, chopping Walkabout's hand off, half way up the forearm. She screamed and swung her other long knife into the weak spot just inside the gorget at the demon's neck, nullifying it before she sagged to the stone. Blood fountained from her shortened arm. I rushed to stand over her, my axe clearing a space. I spun the blade and stopped it before me, parrying a sword as it fell in a vertical line. I pushed back, spun my whole body, and sheered the head off another demon. The blood was thick and slippery on the floor by then. Half of my platoon were dead or hurt badly.

There were three guardians left, fighting back to back. The leader beckoned me in, and I went. Jake attacked from the other direction, engaging two more with a wild battle yell. The leader was a clever swordsman, spinning the massive blade with effortless ease. I had rarely seen his equal. He cut me again and again, until blood poured from me at every corner and pain like a man set aflame filled my mind. Our weapons clashed like the cymbals in a madman's symphony. I caught him across the middle with a heave carrying the last ounces of my strength, parting his armor to let the insubstantial essence free. I was nearly blind with agony and exhaustion. I planted the head of my axe, leaning on it to keep from falling. Breath sawed in and out of my lungs, the scene pulsing and slewing at the edges as I struggled to hold onto consciousness. I looked up just in time to see Jake cleave one of the two guardians from the top of the helm to the chainmail neck shroud. He had killed half the guardians on his own, but he looked about the way I felt. His breathing was ragged, and the nimbus of light around him had nearly faded away.

The last guardian swept in from the side, his unholy blade punching through Jake's failing aura and ripping through both lungs and his heart from left to right. The paladin somehow kept his feet for a moment more, pulled his own blade free from the tumbling wreckage of one guardian's head, and plunged it through the faceguard of the last. Blood exploding out of his mouth, he fell to his knees.

"I was not afraid," he whispered, collapsing onto his face. He was dead before I could take the three steps to get to his side.

With the last of the guardians gone, their armor and swords fell to pieces, turning to powder like dry rotted wood upon the floor. Something oppressive seemed to dissipate from the cathedral, a tiny fraction of the demon's hold on the universe broken.

I bowed my head and covered my face, not wanting them to see the tears in my eyes.

Phase Seven: Fortifications

Location: Rusted Vale Planet

17 Days, 6 Hours, 22 Minutes to Zero Hour

Walkabout flexed and relaxed her new mechanical hand. There wasn't much else to be done from a hospital cot. They'd patched up all of us who lived and burned those who hadn't. There was activity everywhere, but very little of it needed my assistance. After a decade planning this, writing down every tactic, every angle, ever possible exploit we could use in our favor, I was almost superfluous. Everyone knew what to do. Tombs and Santos had all the non-geniuses busy building fortifications and armaments. Gamlod and the geniuses were setting up the machine that would reverse the flow of the portal and bring the Kasu-Hurun back where they belonged, on fire and screaming. Millions of them would be coming through. We could only guess at the real number. Yasi used the supercomputers back on the planet to give us our best estimate of how many and how long they'd take to return to the Vale. Even she'd had to admit that it was guess work in a white lab coat.

Santos came in and sat on an unoccupied cot. He was a frequent visitor lately. He was pale, sweat on his brow. I don't know what they'd given him to get him up and around, but the damage was clearly still serious and extensive. He coughed and wiped liquid on his trousers. It looked like blood.

"I never thanked you, General."

"There's no need. We keep the other man alive. That's why we're not like them."

He shrugged. "I guess. Still, thanks."

"You're welcome."

"That's a pretty sweet hand you've got there," he said to Walkabout.

She squinted at Santos. "I don't really trust it. I mean, I can still feel my real hand, and now there's this hunk of metal and rubber here instead. Weird. Hands . . . it's always gotta be hands for me. . . . "

"Yeah? It's always getting ripped apart for me. Fate's like that. Does it have wicked robot strength?" he asked.

Santos seemed to have a straightforward enthusiasm for life. I envied him that, among other things. Walkabout seemed about to answer his question when Santos was rocked by a ragged coughing fit. By the time it quieted, his hand was filled with blood. The doc came and gave him a long dose of inhaled medicine. He lay back on the cot, his feet hanging off the end, a vacant expression on his face. My own wounds were knitting back together. I'd be scarred up, but I was healing. I didn't think Santos felt the same.

A week later, things were really taking shape. The machine that would reverse the portal was nearly built, much of the battlefield had been prepped to make it as hostile as possible to our enemies, and the defensible positions, choke points, and gun emplacements were coming along. The battlefield canopy of wireless transmission had been put together and uplinked with the ship, as well as being secured with a ground-based Codex. Comms and operations in the cathedral were mostly functional. About half of the three hundred cameras we'd be using to monitor the battlefield were ready and transmitting.

"It looks like the Codices have established some sort of encoded transmission between them. They're eating a little bandwidth, but it's okay," Kira was saying over the video connection. I'd lost focus for a minute during the technical element of her report, but I nodded at the right places.

"If we lose connection, does the system keep trying to reestablish?" I asked.

"Sure. Why?" Kira asked.

"If they have any tricks up their sleeves like we saw the other day, they could take our canopy down. I just want to think about protocols for bringing it back online. That, and ways to monitor the battle if the uplink dies."

"Where are you going with this, General?"

"If we go down, and go down hard, you won't know if we're being overrun, if the whole operation has gone sour. There should be a maximum downtime before we assume a failed state here on the ground, and you pull the plug from up there."

"That's not my part of things. No one ever said anything about pulling any plugs," Kira protested.

"No, you're right. Yasi's the one who'll be making that call. If we're down for forty-five minutes, visual over-flight shows nothing from us, and there's no indication that we're handling it from down here, I'd like you to tell her to open the blue file and initiate protocols to seal the portal for good."

Kira sighed. "You shouldn't be routing this through me, General. You should tell Yasi yourself."

"Just tell her what I said."

I ended the transmission and sat back from the console. I wanted nothing more than to talk to Yasi. Talk to her about anything at all. The more we spoke, the more she'd remember, and all those years of silence would be for naught. She couldn't know it all. It would make it too hard for her to finish this, for she would be the one to bring the demons down in the end.

The sky was a bruised and uncertain color above us. We stood upon the blasted field, atop the remains of heroes and bastards alike, under the light of a pale sun within a dying universe. My little army, brought from far-flung reaches and disparate times, brought from the ashes of our old shame.

"In some holy books, there is a day of rest after the long struggles toward some goal. The goal is hope, freedom, or simply the discovery of a home where our family can be safe from harm. Our goal, here, this day, is to come out from under the shadow of our own failure, the many insufficient victories and bitter stalemates we've met in our struggle against the demons. I have asked the impossible of you already, and I will ask it again tomorrow. I've wrenched you back from death and into yet another war, this one, our final chance to put our sins to rest. You've done all that could be done, built a killing field unlike any the demons have yet imagined. The trap is built as sternly as we can build it, and the fighting will begin soon enough. For today, rest and do the things you should have done before, had you only been fueled with the knowledge that there was no more time. Be free today, for duty will weigh hard upon all of us at the dawning."

I stepped down off of the laser turret and into the mass of Pact members. A low buzz of voices started, sporadic laughter, tattooed faces both wistful and smiling, a snippet of a song being sung. It was a desperate and melancholy joy, this last gasp of clear air before the fire and madness of battle. I wanted to be part of it, to see the men and women of the pact at ease this last time. At the same time, I wanted nothing more than to be apart, to think of nothing, to let the echoes of my own regrets fill me.

Katya, one of the gunnery experts, came over to me. "If you have need of . . . comfort, General, I could provide it."

I forced a smile, shaking my head. "I'm sure there's someone else who would be better company."

She tilted her head at me. "Very well. I ask you first, but I will not spend tonight alone."

"You shouldn't. No one should." I walked slowly past the collapsible shelters and camp fires fueled by gel explosive. I went away from all remaining human contact and into the dim ops center, sat on a folding chair, and looked blindly into the command terminal as the system ran low-level diagnostics. I poured a drink and held it up to the closest light. "To the end of everything." I toasted to no one. The drink went down raw and burning.

Phase Eight: The Open Eye of Hell

Location: The Black Cathedral, Rusted Vale Planet

132 Hours, 5 minutes until Zero Hour

I keyed the main channel on the comms and started the readiness check. "Kharkaros ready?"

"Ready, General," Yasi said. She sounded scared. I think we all were. The trick was to keep from showing it. That's what an officer does, if he's worth anything.

"Air support ready?"

"Good to go, General," Zira, our best pilot, said. The hulk of the big bomber lumbered in a circle at the edge of the vale, moving at minimum speed.

"Purifier crew?"

Katya's voice sounded expectant, enthusiastic. "Locked on and ready, General."

Soon enough, every tactical group had answered up and declared itself prepared. There was nothing more to do. I took a big breath and let it out. "Switch to your arranged channels and stand by for action."

I turned to Carver and nodded. He engaged the klaxons. They blared, counting down from twenty in five-second increments. I switched the video feed to Gamlod's crew. The big spirit coaxer stood there, impassive, listening to the klaxon counting down. When it reached five, he threw a switch and a loud whirring came through the mic on the video camera. Lights on the device came on. The inverter core was no larger than a footlocker, but the amount of money we'd funneled into the project to build it was staggering. About five people in the universe really understood how it worked. I was not one of them. The lights on the inverter core began pulsing and fluctuating, going from orange to yellow to green, then blinking red.

As the klaxon reached one, the red lights turned solid, then all the lights lit like tiny fountains topped with flame. The whole cathedral building shook. The long pipe that issued from the core and out the door of the cathedral shivered. The clear glass appeared to fill with smoke, then with deep green fire, then with something like rotten swamp water. When the flow began, the pipe would fill with the energy of the demons as they came through. The barrel created a nexus point a little more than one hundred yards beyond its aperture. This was where the demons would materialize. They'd fly across another twenty yards before passing through the plasma curtain, where all but the most heavily armored demons would be reduced to less than a cinder.

The klaxon was silent. Something like far-off wind building behind a line of hills sighed through the Vale. The low hum of the plasma curtain fluctuating grew louder. The air smelled like a lightning storm about to burst over an arid plain. Carver had his fist over his mouth, watching the video feed next to me. A bead of sweat trailed down his temple. I could see the fast pulse in a vein close to the surface, the drumbeat of the oncoming madness.

Then there was screaming.

I switched to the outside video feed. "Get ready for it," I said on the comms channel for the heavy laser gunners.

The first of the demons exited the portal nexus like projectiles, flying through the plasma curtain and burning up, flaming bits of their tissue and shards of bone skipping off the bottom of the valley floor at fifty or sixty miles an hour. The plasma curtain that stretched across the Vale flashed, the membrane booming as hundreds of demons passed through, most of them obliterated without having even touched foot upon the battlefield.

The curtain didn't kill them all. The tougher demons burst

into the fight, rolling and tumbling across the ground, laser guns following them and opening up as soon as they decelerated enough to get a good shot off. The lasers, designed to destroy armored machines of war, were brutally effective. Very few of the demons required a second shot. I switched from one video feed to the next. A few soldiers had jitters, a few let the stress get to them, but they held together.

A clump of armored demons with the bodies of spiders and the upper torsos of humanoid jackals spat forth from the nexus point of the inverter and seemed unhurt by the plasma barrier. They let out a shriek that cracked the lens of the camera closest to them. I retasked a more distant cam and zoomed in. They erupted into chartreuse fire, a poisonous fog growing around them as they galloped their arachnid legs across the parched Vale floor. The laser cannons growled and pulsed, knocking the demons back and holding them clumped up, but didn't kill the bastards. More and more came through, hundreds. The plasma curtain had registered fourteen thousand impacts, and it had only been a few minutes.

We had forty powered armor suits protecting the laser turrets, which in turn protected the emitter stacks for the plasma curtain. It was another trip through the plasma curtain, this time at walking pace, if you wanted to come toward the black cathedral. A quarter of my infantry were ready to defend the ops center if need be. The ground behind the curtain was also laced with enough land mines to blow the legs off a thousand demons. It was too early to start letting this get out of hand.

"Purifier, fire for effect," I ordered.

"Da, General," Svetlana answered. The Purifier's report filled the valley. The moaning roar of its falling projectile came in tandem with the long echo of the shot. The shell burst in the middle of the demons, raising a cloud of salt, iron, and dust.

"Zira, I need a dousing shell at position alpha."

The bomber thundered across the Vale and a bomb plummeted down, right on target. A hundred feet up, it burst, atomized water coming down like rain. The water had a super-wetting agent which coated the ground and scrubbed the air, allowing us to see the effect of the Purifier's strike.

The jackal-arachnid demons lay in pieces on the ground, a few twitching like stepped-on cockroaches. The plasma cannoneers knocked the last of the life out of them just as a creature that looked like a fifty-foot-long crustacean spun out of the nexus, then exploded into grotesque masses of rubbery pink flesh.

Ten minutes. Twenty. Forty-five. The first hour was a massacre. Everyone was fresh, our equipment functioning, our plan exacting. From here, it could only get worse. To finish this for good, we'd have to keep on for another one hundred and thirty-one hours. If we wanted to summon all the demons back where they belonged, that was the minimum time we had to hold out.

Sixteen hours in. Exhaustion was beginning to take effect. Casualties were growing. Five dead from a laser cannon malfunction. Nine of the infantry protecting the Purifier at the far end of the valley were down, killed by the ghost demons that slipped by our net of destruction. One of our three bombers rendered useless with a hopelessly twisted bomb-bay door from an in-air skirmish with an iron dragon. Every loss hurt, but we were within operational tolerances.

"Sound the Klaxons, Carver. Rotate to B shift."

"That should be C shift, General."

I squinted at the timeline. "C. Right. Make it happen." I got up and shook my head. My eyes were burning from looking at the cam footage without a break. I was rotating the soldiers in a three-shift rotation, thirty minutes on and an hour off. I should probably have instituted the same rules for myself. It wasn't too late to start.

"Tell Tombs and Gamlod to get some shut-eye. Tell me when

an hour's up, and I'll hand off to Tombs. Find two of the defense crew and have them set up a rotation with you."

Carver nodded and jogged away. He was back in a moment with Tombs, who had a spooked look on his face. I didn't like it when our Phoenix was spooked.

"You need to talk to the ship," Tombs said without preamble. "Something bad's about to happen."

I didn't hesitate. "Kharkaros, answer up."

"Here, Cruek," Yasi responded after a moment.

"Tombs says to watch out. Get Feni in the chair."

"Wait one."

The transmission was quiet for several seconds. "Okay, we have her in the chair and it's cycling on right now. I've put all the Pure Machine protocols at maximum. Kira is at the master console in case we have to manually de-couple network segments. Did Tombs say . . . oh, oh shit. It's coming!"

I switched to the ship viewer on one of my screens. Something was floating closer to the ship, but it was so huge, alien, and horrifying I couldn't really understand what I was looking at. The part of the demonic god creature I could see was so awful, so mind-numbing, I didn't think my spirit could stand seeing it all. It loomed closer and closer, unnamable tendrils of writhing flesh reaching out to touch the ship's surface. Things that might have been eyes or mouths or both dotted the abysmal creature's squid-like body. It was bigger than the ship. It gave off smoky vapor into the chill and hard vacuum of the void. I had to hold onto the table to keep my feet, all strength draining from me, just seeing the pixels of the viewer form the forsaken leviathan.

The view from the forward facing camera array became overwhelmed, then went dark. I switched to another cam, sweat pouring from my forehead. I barely noticed when Carver had the presence of mind to order an incendiary bomb strike on Position Beta. Looking at the true enormity of their overlords, I doubted everything, doubted that we had ever had a chance to win this war.

"Evasive maneuvers, Yasi! Don't let it touch you," I shouted.

"Understood. I just have to . . . by all that's holy, that's repulsive. It's going to—" Yasi started, then I heard a crash come through the mic. The beginnings of a scream, far away from the mic but audible. After two ragged seconds, the comms channel died. I hit the button to connect. I punched it again and again. Nothing.

I could feel tears in my eyes. I punched the bomber channel. "Franks, I need you up in the air. We've lost contact with the Kharkaros. There's some sort of giant demon god attacking the ship."

"That's the motherfucker I'm here for. I'm on it."

"Franks? I can't get into your cameras. Report."

"Lost the external cams in the dragon fight. Internal ones I disconnected before we landed. I'll keep you up to date as long as I can," Franks said, his comms channel now a little ragged. He was a morose bastard and hadn't said a dozen words in a row the whole time I'd known him, but he sounded . . . happy now.

"Why'd you disconnect the internal cams?"

"Needed privacy. Not a team player like I used to be. I'll be back when there's something productive to report. Franks out."

The channel went quiet. I shook myself, looking to Carver. "Status planet-side?"

"More of the same. I'm running it from the second console," he said.

Tombs nodded, sticking close. "I'll back the kid up."

They returned to their bank of view screens and left me with a panel of black ones, waiting for anything from the Kharkaros or Franks. I caught snippets of what they were doing, but the image of the demonic overlord hovered in my mind, shattering my concentration.

"Santos, get ready for it, the demons are going ape-shit," Carver said.

"Fire everything you've got. Alpha, Bravo, and Delta concussion points. Svetlana, make these good!" Tombs called out into the second channel.

"Frags at minimum safe distance to the Purifier lines. Soonest possible, Zira," Carver's voice said, half yelling into the mic.

It all receded into the background when my headset came live again, Franks' distorted voice in my ear. "The Kharkaros's main ship to ship guns are firing. They're slowing him, but they've only got about twenty more shots before the power's spent."

The viewers flickered back on, many of them still black or broadcasting only static, but a few still functioning. The uplink signal for audio blinked, and I switched to Yasi's channel.

I could see Yasi's arms as she and Raf lifted Feni off the chair and laid her on the floor. Blood and gray liquid streamed from her nose and ears. Raf held her hand as she gasped, her body spasming up off of the hard deck plates a few times, then shivered as the last tremors of life subsided.

Raf brushed her eyelids closed. "It was always you, honey eyes," he said. "Rest now. I'll be right behind you."

Yasi looked away, and I knew where she was going.

"Yasi, what're you doing?"

"I'm in the chair, Cruek. I'm in the chair. Switching you to Kira."

"No!" I cried, but it was too late. I could see Kira in the view screen, her face haggard, her hair hanging slack and untidy.

"Cruek? Ship to ship guns just tapped. We've got nothing, and we've sustained some serious damage. Yasi's in the chair. Wow, she just did something. The superbeast is coming back around. Listen, I don't think the ship can survive that monster hitting us again. Most of the starboard section is already depressurized, and a lot of our systems are only running because of triple redundancy."

"You have to keep her together, Kira. She's our only hope of winning."

Kira shrugged. "We'll see. Listen, tell Walkabout that I love her, okay. Tell her it was great to fight with her one more time."

"I will. I promise."

"You never get the chance to say all you should, huh?"

"Sometimes you do. Get through this, and you will," I said.

She scoffed. "Nah. I learned a thing or two from Walkabout—I've designed something. A little addition. It's Yasi who has to survive, right? Closing the channel, Cruek. Wish us luck." Kira put a helmet of electrodes like the one in the chair room over her head, almost like the cowl of a suit of chainmail. I saw her finger descend to touch the console.

The comms channel went hard down. I pounded my fist. I wasn't used to being disconnected, being unable to do more than rely on field reports, but no one was behind enemy lines now.

Bombs fell so close the ground shook and dust filtered down from the ancient structure around us. The roar of the Purifier shelling was at its maximum rate of fire, and the demons were close to overwhelming our defenses. I should have cared what was happening a few hundred meters away from me, but I only wanted to see what was happening up in the blackness overhead.

Franks' voice returned after a burst of static. "You back, Cruek?"

"Back," I said, mind numb.

"I'm close now. I've got cameras working again."

Three of the squares on my view panel lit up. I could see a side view of Franks' face, a skewed view of the planet, and forward from his heavy bomber's upper canopy. I could see the demon god now, a titanic mockery of a sea creature, swimming through space toward the Kharkaros. One eye that must have been a twenty yards across rolled within the slick and grotesque membrane of its skin. Vapor cooked off of it in waves, its innumerable tentacles flailing in the void, somehow moving it forward.

"It's going for the ship again," Franks said. "I won't make it in time."

I watched, even the shadowy outline of the thing sickening me, making my mind rail against its presence. The monstrosity lanced forward, grappling the ship, chewing at its hull with a round hole filled with thousands of grinding teeth.

Franks pounded his fist into the instrument panel.

Just as it seemed that the demon would crack the ship's hull utterly, a flash of green energy burst from the hull, followed by an even more powerful blast of pale silver fire. The demon god recoiled, its tentacles shivering and bleeding tar-like ichor that quickly froze into chips of obsidian ice. The demon was now directly between Franks and the Kharkaros.

"What's your plan, Franks?"

"Planet-killer bombs. I took one and wired it hard into my ship. It's now . . . armed. Watch the sky."

"Franks?"

He wasn't talking to me anymore. The bomber accelerated hard on a collision course with the demon god.

"Franks, you're too close!"

"I've never failed a mission." The mic cut out.

Outside, everything seemed to stop for a moment.

"Cruek, you have to see this," Tombs said.

We ran for the great doors to the black cathedral. The sky was darkening toward nightfall, and in the center of it all, thousands of bright sparks arced across the deep blue, fragments of debris burning up in the atmosphere. It was wreckage of the demonic god, the Kharkaros, or both. Demons and men blinked up at the burning trails as they flared and went dark in the sky above. A howl of rage from the demons rolling and tumbling outward from the portal nexus shattered the moment. Hollow, I jogged back into the black cathedral and stood at the comms, trying to direct the effort, trying to deny that I had lost her forever. The Kharkaros was gone, along with our only chance for victory.

Phase Nine: No One Sleeps

Location: The Black Cathedral, Rusted Vale Planet

89 Hours, 6 Minutes to Zero Hour

I took the second of my six stimulant capsules. Once on the cycle, even in your down time, you stare off into space, idling but unable to really rest. The Kharkaros was lost. Really lost. We hadn't had any contact since the explosion. Tombs, Gamlod, and I stood around the now-messy table in the cathedral. Tombs was still solid, but Gamlod was hollow-eyed and swaying and rubbed at the left side of this chest with a worried look. His was a normal body, and it was breaking down. It would only have to last a little longer.

"So, we're more or less screwed," Tombs said after a minute.

I nodded. "We have a small fusion bomb down here, a failsafe to keep them from getting a hold of any of our tech or reversing the portal, but it'll just turn the Vale into a crater. Chances it'll actually obliterate the portal for good are less than thirty percent."

"Why didn't we bring down a planet killer?" Tombs asked. "That would have been the smart play. That way, we don't really need the Kharkaros."

"You want the Kasu-Hurun getting a hold of something that powerful? You know as well or better than any of us that they have mind controllers. If one of them were to get in here and take the device, they'd not only have the damn thing, they'd have the smarts to reverse-engineer it. We'd have given them the ultimate weapon. Not what we're hoping for." Gamlod's face was ashen. He fell into the metal chair next to the table.

"What's with him?" Tombs asked.

"My . . . heart's giving out." Gamlod slid from the chair, his eyes wide and staring, jaw working as his lips turned blue.

"Medic!" I yelled, and one came running in from the front of the building.

She skidded to a stop on her knees next to the spirit coaxer, checking his vitals, pulling his shirt open and giving him a shot of painkiller and something else. This seemed to ease him, but his breathing was labored, his eyes losing their focus. The medic lost his pulse and couldn't get it back, despite everything she tried.

"Stand down," I ordered after a while, and the frazzled medic stopped working on him.

In another minute, Gamlod slipped away, his body still and silent against the basalt floor of the cathedral.

"I'm sorry, Sir. I don't have much for a heart attack in my kit," the medic said.

I nodded. "Not your fault. Get back to your post. We'll. . . . "

The comms channel exploded with activity. "Breaking through! Breaking through!"

The mines in front of the cathedral started blowing. Dozens of them. The screaming of demons blown in half was close, the smell of their rancid blood drifting in through the great doors. Walkabout took a company of our soldiers against the demonic incursion, and the sound of her force's plasma weapons chattering on auto fire echoed through the great entry hall. Tombs and I were back at the command consoles, doing what we could to quell the sudden rush.

Gamlod's body lay cooling on the stone floor, his skin gray. No one could spare the time to mourn him at that moment. Perhaps we had lost the ability to seize permanent victory, but we could still kill every demon possible before the end.

The casualties were mounting. There were less than a thousand of us left. Only half of the pulsed laser cannon emplacements were still functional, and I'd rotated most of the soldiers from the cathedral up there to bolster their tattered defense force. We'd burned up a lot of friends at the back of the plasma curtain, Gamlod among them.

Walkabout stood there in her mech suit, Carver leaning against her leg, looking up at her mass of curly hair atop the machine exoskeleton suit. At least some of us were able to be with the ones we cared most about at the end. It was a little beam of sunlight coming down to us here in the bottom of the well.

I took a long drink of the liquor, draining the last of the bottle I'd brought down. It burned, trying to fight the stimulant pills and losing. I looked back to the monitors; we were losing control of the area in front of the portal nexus, where the demons came hurtling through the plasma curtain. The Purifier crew was working on an overheating problem and couldn't fire. We were down to a handful of bombs on our last functional bomber, and I'd given Zira the directive to only drop when maximum casualties could be assured.

The demons were not a cohesive unit. They were being pulled in from so many worlds, took so many forms, that throwing them together caused a massive scrum of internecine violence before they understood that they were in the killing box, and that there was a more direct enemy.

The portal nexus fell quiet for several seconds, no demons coming through. The constant thrumming of weaker demons burning up against the plasma curtain fell away for the first time in hours.

"Something big is coming through," I broadcasted to every crew. "Be ready."

Out of the nexus, a single black-skinned demon appeared, passing through the plasma curtain with no seeming effect. Man-sized, he had a heavy, brutal-looking sword in his hand. He flew into the larger crowd, knocking other demons aside like a cannonball. He slid to a stop and rose, looking around. I panned in on him. Almost human in appearance, his brow furrowed. He seemed entirely unhurt, only his clothes torn and burned.

"Target that one, anyone who's free," I said to the laser cannoneers. Two banks with line of fire lit him up, hitting him again and again and again. With each direct hit, he seemed to swell and grow bigger, harder, his clothing burning away and leaving only him and his dark blade. The cannons weren't even knocking him off his feet. He threw his arms wide in a cruciform pose and soaked up the impacts that would tear an armored battle tank in two, his eyes closed tight.

"Stop firing on the humanoid, all crews. He's immune," I told them. They went back to sniping at the outer edges of the demonic horde, keeping them from forming a cohesive whole and making a rush in any direction.

I panned in as close as I could to the new demon. He was unmarked, except for a cross-like white scar on his chest. Something about that sounded like a story I'd once heard, but I was so exhausted I couldn't bring it up. The demon looked one way, then the other, seeing himself surrounded and boxed in.

"Fuck me," I could read on his lips. A slow grin crossed them after that, and he ran straight for the nearest clump of milling, hurt, rage-filled demons. He collided with the press. A spray of demon ichor burst into the air, and demon body parts began to fly in all directions. The other demons, drawn to attack the one target they could easily reach, converged upon this lone warrior.

Bursts of flaming corrosion bathed him. Every manner of talon and tooth and blade cracked and shattered against his skin. He didn't kill them by the dozens, but by the hundreds, until his attackers had to climb over the piles of the dead or writhing maimed to get to him. I knew then that it was the Nightblade, a demon mercenary who'd turned against his own kind and gone on to kill thousands, as close to a turncoat as their kind had ever known. The Nightblade became the focal point of their fruitless wrath. He churned them to pieces until the entire point alpha and point bravo zones were packed tight with demons.

Svetlana came on the comms. "Purifier is ready to fire."

"Target alpha and bravo zones and fire at will," I told her.

I switched to the bomber channel. "Zira, after the Purifier barrage, drop an incendiary and let it burn."

"Got it," she said.

"Masks on, everyone," I said into the general channel. "It's about to get hot and nasty."

The Purifier thundered again and again from the far end of the valley, exploding salt and iron fragments ripping through the tight-packed demons. Zira dropped her incendiaries before the echoes of the last shot subsided, burning up the demons like dry leaves in a pile. The whoosh and bellow of the inferno overpowered everything, sucking all the oxygen from the Vale, the torrid heat so extreme it hurt the eyes.

I went to the door and watched as this destruction was visited upon our great enemy. Perhaps it would not be the victory we'd hoped for, but it was something. In lives past, I had fought for years, decades, and never managed to do as much damage as we'd done in the last five minutes. I only wished that Yasi had been able to see it, that we could have watched the great bonfire together.

The Doom Clan came through as a group. They appeared to be immune to everything. They moved with a purpose, their huge armored bodies charging through and over the other demons as if they were made of paper. Bull headed and cloven-hoofed, they rushed toward the far end of the Vale, toward the Purifier crew.

"Santos, you've got a large group of Doom Clan coming toward you. Energy weapons seem ineffective," I told him over the comms.

"We'll give 'em something to remember us by, Cruek."

The Purifier boomed, the shell falling perfectly in the Doom Clan's midst and filling the air with dust and exploded salt. Two thirds of the clan emerged from the smoke, some limping, blind, and maimed, but dragging themselves forward nonetheless.

"That's our last shell," Santos said. "I'm going to suit up. *Vaya con Dios*, Sir."

He cut the comms. I switched to the cameras at the far end of the Vale. The half-dozen working mechsuits clashed with the front ranks, power saws deployed. I could see Katya and Svetlana running a heavy projectile gun loaded with iron shells. The last of the defenders at that location formed a line, firing their plasma rifles into the crowd, their bayonets deployed for what would soon happen. Dust rose and obscured the scene, until I could only hear the clash and rattle of melee and the screams of the dying.

Only the barrel of the Purifier stood up out of the fog of war. I saw one figure, Svetlana, one of her arms shattered and hanging limp at her side. She somehow climbed up the barrel of the cannon, above the fray. Slowly, painfully, she reached the muzzle. Straddling the gun, she used her one good hand to swing her backpack off her shoulder. Svetlana flicked a switch on the bag, and threw it down the barrel.

"For Mother Russia," I heard on the comm. The Purifier exploded. The camera went dark. The remaining munitions went up, shaking the ground and sending a plume of fire a hundred feet in the air. The remaining voltage in the big energy stacks arced hundreds of feet over the ground like crooked reverse lightning bolts.

"Southern Russia, keep her safe and guard her," Carver said behind me. He bowed his head and brought a medallion up to his lips, kissing it.

I walked away from the console. Carver took over without having to be told. I went to where Tombs was sitting and sagged to the ground next to him. "We're going to need you before long."

He swallowed. "I figured. Santos is gone. Everybody down there's gone, aren't they?"

I nodded. "They fought hard. Santos was a good man."

"There wasn't ever any chance we'd survive this."

It wasn't a question. I didn't bother answering. Tombs got up and walked to the great doors, just looking, hands in his pockets, his shoulders stooped.

A video feed popped on. The change in state drew my eye, though I was so exhausted that any emotion or quick action was difficult.

Until I saw Yasi's face.

I opened my mouth, unable to say anything at all. She was alive, the ship was not destroyed, our hope still hung by a thread. She did not look happy.

"The Kharkaros is damaged. The nearby EMP took out many of our systems. I'm alone up here. Both Feni and Kira died to save the ship, to save me, from that gigantic thing."

"I'm sorry. I saw Feni, talked to Kira just before the end. They spent their lives well. I'm so proud of you. So proud of everyone."

She just shrugged, looking away. "Their heads exploded. I had to clean their brains off the walls. Don't talk about being proud of me, Cruek."

I waited for a moment, trying to make better words come to me, trying to shake myself and put the exhaustion and heartache of watching everyone die aside. "It's good to see you, Yasi. We were sure you'd been destroyed in the explosion."

"Very nearly. If Franks hadn't been on the far side of the huge demon, the blast would have hit us full force, and we'd have broken up. I had to manually restart dozens of systems, and half of them didn't work properly without being reprogrammed."

"I'm just glad you're back. So glad."

Yasi frowned. "You've kept a lot from me." She stared at me through the monitor, her misty eyes locking with mine. "When I sat in the chair and connected to the Codex, it all came back. I remember everything, Cruek. Everything."

"Yasi—"

"You son of a bitch, why didn't you tell me?" she shouted. "You let me do this without you, lonely, suffering with empty arms for years. You were so driven, so closed off, so careful around me that I . . . damn it; I would have come to you, if you'd even given me the slightest sign. You were the one I always wanted."

I hung my head. "All along, that's what you wanted?"

"Are you blind? From the first night, when I almost ran you down in my vehicle. There'd be moments when your guard would slip, that I thought you loved me, but you'd recoil, and I couldn't even see anything but the mission in your eyes for weeks. When I found out that we'd always been together, right from the beginning, do you have any idea how that felt?"

I swallowed. "Like you'd been cheated out of the most important thing in your life."

"Exactly. Cheated by the one I needed most."

"Yasi, it seemed like the only way. I didn't dare let you know everything, not with where we were going, what I'd ask of you."

"Ask of me? This is my whole life. Since the day I met you, this has always been my whole life. I've given everything. You never had to ask. Was it so much for you to be brave enough to remind me of our love?"

"Open the blue folder, Yasi. Read it." My head felt heavy, my heart stinging. I leaned against my palms, not wanting to breathe, not wanting the slow drum of my heart to boom in my ears.

"Don't distract me with that. Not after everything."

"My love, it's the reason for all I've done. Do you think it's been easy for me, being so near you and still alone, seeing you in another's arms at the end?" I dug at my eyes. I slapped the empty liquor bottle from the nearby table. The sound of it smashing against the hard floor gave me no solace.

Yasi unsealed the blue folder and looked in. I could see the color go out of her face. She put her hand over her mouth. She looked up at me, then read the rest. It wasn't that long, but the words were heavy as lead, each one more difficult than the last. It had taken me days to write that short document.

"This has been the endgame, all these years?"

"From day one. It's the only way. I didn't want to make it any harder for you."

"You didn't think I'd be able to do what I had to do if I remembered our love?"

"I was a fool, Yasi. I was on the point of telling you a hundred times, but I never did. I was about to before. . . . "

"And then I was with Santos when you came back." She covered her face, tears in her eyes. They were in mine, as well.

"Where do we go from here?" I asked.

"Into eternity for the last time, Cruek. Keep the channel open. I want to hear you and see you, right down to the last second."

I let out a long breath. "It won't be long now. We're getting pummeled down here. We've lost so many."

"Only a few more hours now," she said. "I'll be with you until the end."

That was the moment when the plasma curtain went down.

I touched the screen, my finger tracing the image of Yasi's tired face, her tousled hair. "I love you."

I grabbed a rifle and ran for the doorway.

I crouched on one knee, pressing the plasma rifle to my shoulder and taking every good shot I could see through the scope. Demons blew apart with each press of the trigger, but there were always more behind them, two for every one we put away. The sound of Walkabout's shoulder-mounted laser cannon cycling next to me, the effect of the potent weapon as it chewed through whole ranks of demons before dissipating, was comforting. Everyone left from the cathedral was at the line, save for Carver. Only his youth kept him upright now, and some unnamable courage that had come through to him from the old days. He called the shots to whoever was still alive to hear them.

Zira's ship dropped a fragmentary bomb in the back of the group, the concussion so strong it nearly knocked us down. The bomb raised up the dust again, and our last dousing shell was long since expended. We were firing blind, just looking for shapes in the haze and capping them when we were able. Tombs, on my left, stood up. He threw his rifle down and began to remove his shirt.

"I've got this, Cruek. Get them back inside, okay?"

"You sure?"

He put a hand on my shoulder. "I've wanted to do this the whole time. Now's as good a time as any, don't you think?"

I nodded. He began walking forward, then running hard, a single man without a shirt going to face the ravening mob.

"Everyone get back to the cathedral doorway!" I shouted. "Run!"

We turned and formed up in the huge vestibule, staging a two-line group with standing and kneeling riflemen. Walkabout, our last mech-equipped soldier, formed the center of the line, her helmet still down.

Flames burst from Tombs, outlining him in the risen dust like a burning angel. He changed, grew, flashed until we couldn't look directly at him as he burned too brightly. A sound like a thousand eagles crying burst upon the field, and fire hotter than any incendiary bomb rolled off of him, burning the demons to ash, so not even their bones remained.

He burned, brighter and brighter, until we had to retreat to our second choke point in the great hallway of the cathedral or be killed by the heat. The Phoenix flew across the valley and back, destroying everything for nearly an hour. He gave one last savage cry that shook the air, burst into even brighter conflagration, then went dark. I looked through the tinted blast shield we'd been hiding behind, and could just see the tiny speck of a single human body hurtling to earth inside the inferno.

"I don't have any bombs left, Sir." Zira said. The explosions of the last of our land mines going off shook the cathedral. I knew they'd be to the edge of the barrel soon. If they got to the inverter, they'd be able to reverse the portal. There were only a handful of soldiers left to fight them. The only reason they hadn't already overtaken us was that the flow of demons had grown slower in the last few minutes. I checked the count. When the plasma curtain had gone off line, there'd been just a shade over three million impacts. We were damned near there. Probably close enough, but more were still coming through, a few every second. Without anything to kill them off in great numbers, there were suddenly thousands of them on the ground and ready to fight.

"I understand, Zira. You've been damn near pitch-perfect the whole operation. No one could have put the munitions where they belonged any better. It's been an honor to have you with me in this."

"The honor's mine, General. I've got one last thing I can do to buy you a few minutes. Keep your troops well inside the doors."

"What have you got in mind?"

"It was always a one-way mission, Sir. Zira out."

I couldn't tell where she was, and her camera had long since been knocked out by the constant pounding of low altitude bombing runs. The cavernous sound of her thrusters filled the Vale, and I still couldn't see her.

"Everyone behind the blast shield," I said over local comms.

They ducked back just as I saw the blunt nose of the bomber coming at maximum atmospheric speed toward the ground fifty yards beyond the portal nexus.

"Holy fek!" Walkabout yelled, then the concussion rolled over everyone, sharp shards of titanium from the bomber's fuselage tumbling through a cyclone of fire from its propulsion stacks exploding.

The bulk of the demons in the vicinity were ripped to shreds, but many still pressed us, and they kept coming from the nexus, slow but steady.

"We're out of tricks, Cruek. This is it," Walkabout said. "I'm going up to the first choke point. I think I can hold it for a while."

Carver appeared at my side. "I'm going with her."

I nodded. "Proud to have had you two with me."

Walkabout picked Carver up, raising him to the level of her face and kissing him hard before putting him down. She flipped her helmet back in place. The two of them rushed into the swirling dust and fire. I knew I'd never see them again.

"Hold them here. I'll be by the inverter machine. Last line of defense," I told the medic, one of six soldiers remaining to me in this mighty, evil structure.

They nodded, and I walked back to where the inverter sat, humming steadily, making my hair stand on end when I got close.

"Yasi, you still there?"

"Still here. Cruek. I love you, and nothing else matters now."

I took a breath and let it out. "I love you. Everything matters. Especially now. I'm sorry. Sorry for everything. All those times we failed, those times when we were too late, or not smart enough, or there just wasn't time to try to do anything but mitigate the damage. I'm sorry that I haven't been a better man. This life more so than all the others."

I could hear her crying on the other end of the line. "Don't you know what you've done, Cruek? You've dragged us here with nothing more than willpower and determination. Everything we've done, this time especially, has been because you didn't ever quit."

"If we win, if this really ends it, no one will ever know. It's a stone falling in a pool so big that the ripples will never reach the shore."

"That's not true, Cruek. The story will survive. When I sat in the chair, my mind touched the Codex. We thought it was just a weapon, just a collection of old knowledge. That's only part of it, the smallest part. The Codices have chronicled everything. Every victory, every defeat. The sum total of all the Pact has ever done. This story will survive. It'll be told down the ages."

The sound of heavy fire from the hallway interrupted Yasi's words, and I didn't hear the rest. They would be through and swarming me in no time.

"What's the count, Yasi?"

"Two minutes, fifty seconds."

I nodded. "Good. Good. I'm ready."

"I love you," Yasi said.

"More than anything."

Phase Ten: Zero Hour

Location: Starship Kharkaros

Zero Hour plus 15 seconds

Yasi stood, alone in a helm that still smelled like blood and death, watching Cruek on one of the few cameras that was still broadcasting. There was no tension left on his face. He was serene as he shouldered his rifle and shot at adversaries off screen. Without sound, without taste and smell, it was distant. Her heart swelled for him as she watched Cruek fight to the very last, perhaps even after it had ceased to matter. He took his rifle away from his shoulder, looked at it in puzzlement, and tossed it away. His two-bitted axe leaned against the portal inverter machine, and he hefted it. A small smile touched his lips. He looked up at where he knew the camera to be and gave a crisp salute. Demons descended on him, rushing into the camera's field of view by the dozens. Cruek moved easily, like a dancer among them, slicing through legs and bashing faces in with the flat of the axe head.

Yasi swallowed, then turned off the camera feed. She did not need to see him fall. She would rather that the last image of him be in battle, of his weapon cutting down his enemies like a wind blowing down dry corn stalks.

"Goodbye, my love," she whispered.

On the console, there was a singular switch covered by a shroud. She pressed both thumbs onto the reader. It took fingerprints and blood, analyzed them for a few seconds, then opened the shroud. All the lights on the console began coming on and going off in a strobe. She reached in and flipped the switch.

"Verbal command required," the computer's flat voice spoke.

"Seal the wound with fire," she said.

"Command accepted. Beginning launch sequence."

Yasi leaned back in the chair, letting the sequence she'd kept in a locked and coded storage compartment until a few hours ago move the ship. The vibration of the large missile apparatus coming into play could be felt through the floor. There was a mild jolt when each of the nine planet killer missiles launched. She looked at the main viewer, watching them as they entered orbit, broke atmo, and began to plummet to their defined impact zones.

The Kharkaros, now moving less smoothly due to all the damage it had sustained, left orbit and moved at sub-relativistic but significant speed to a distance away from the planet, so that it was again a brown and blue marble in the viewer.

Yasi's eyes skipped down to the count. The seconds ticked down to five, then two, then expired altogether. In the viewer, she could see the planet's colors change. It seemed to grow, then fall in on itself, and finally shatter into billions of tiny pieces, the last of its atmosphere bursting in a wisp of yellow fire against the black.

Behind her, she heard a click, then the sound of something small moving. She turned around. The Codex that had been wired into the ship was now aloft, floating behind her. After having touched it with her mind, she could feel it, could sense it as it watched her.

"The Pact is redeemed. The universes are again in balance. Do not let our story be forgotten," she said to the small, bright cube.

The Codex spun twice and stopped. Pale green light emanated from inside of it, pulsing slowly at first, then speeding up and becoming more intense. The light attained its apex and then faded. When it was gone, so was the Codex. Yasi was now truly by herself, the last of the Pact, perhaps the last living thing in this dying universe. She touched a few buttons on the console, bringing up the nearby solar system map.

She picked up the blue folder and read the last few lines.

Nothing can remain of the Megalan technology. Not one microcircuit. When this ends, there must be nothing left to salvage.

Yasi nodded. Nothing left. She could do that. She set the controls for the heart of the nearby sun. All the desolation and sadness fell away as the viewer grew brighter and brighter, the face of the star resolving and finally filling the whole screen.

It was over. It was finally over, and she could go into the light.

The End

About the Author

Patrick M. Tracy lives in Salt Lake City and works as a Network Support Administrator. He went to Northern Arizona University, graduating with a B.A. in English. He has been writing fiction and poetry for many years, and has numerous published works in both disciplines. Among his recent publications are the novellas "Darkness of the Sun" in *The Crimson Pact Volume 4*, and "Mungo the Undying" in *A Walk in the Abyss*. When not fixing computers or writing, he enjoys traditional archery and performing feats of strength. Find out more at pmtracy.com.

Editor's Note

The Crimson Pact series is over. After 106 stories (674,000 words!), the Pact has been fulfilled. This project started as an experiment and was willed into existence by all of us involved. It's not been easy putting together these five books in the span of two and a half years (February 2011-August 2013). I learned a lot as an editor and as a person, and I got to work with fantastic writers. I want to thank all of them for being a part of this and for helping me put it all together. I could not have done it without them.

I love these kinds of stories and wanted to read them and share them with others. None of us did this for the money, though everyone was paid a percentage of the profits on volumes 1-4, and a flat fee for volume 5. The writers participated because they wanted to write, and I am forever grateful.

I want to especially thank Karen Bovenmyer and Kri Dontje for all their help with copy editing and proofreading. They are both amazing and made these stories shine. Barbara Webb has had a lot to do with the series as well, and her help has been extremely important, especially with the print books. Justin Swapp has been awesome as well, and his concept of the Codex features prominently in the finale story. Thank you, Justin, for coming up with a great idea.

Patrick Tracy, my best friend, has been my rock throughout this process, writing many awesome stories and providing much needed support. He and I came up with the idea for "The Failed

Crusade" at World Fantasy in 2010, and we brainstormed about "Sealed with Fire" in May of 2013. I thought up the broad strokes of Cruek and the others going back to the Rusted Vale as well as a few other things, and Pat took my little flame of an idea and turned it into a salvo of planet-killing missiles. He filled in a thousand details, and we worked together to include many of the characters from other stories in the series. We wanted to add more, but packed in as many as we could manage. I'm very proud of how "Sealed with Fire" turned out. I think it's an epic and fitting ending.

Thank you all for reading about these characters and for going on this journey to so many different worlds. The Pact needed you to know about them, and now their story has been told.

Paul Genesse, July, 2013